The Legacy of the Watcher

By David Dalglish

BOOKS BY DAVID DALGLISH

THE HALF-ORC SERIES
The Weight of Blood
The Cost of Betrayal
The Death of Promises
The Shadows of Grace
A Sliver of Redemption
The Prison of Angels
The King of the Vile
The King of the Fallen

THE SHADOWDANCE SERIES
Cloak and Spider (novella)
A Dance of Cloaks
A Dance of Blades
A Dance of Mirrors
A Dance of Shadows
A Dance of Ghosts
A Dance of Chaos

THE PALADINS
Night of Wolves
Clash of Faiths
The Old Ways
The Broken Pieces

THE BREAKING WORLD
Dawn of Swords
Wrath of Lions
Blood of Gods

THE SERAPHIM
Skyborn
Fireborn
Shadowborn

David Dalglish

THE KEEPERS TRILOGY
Soulkeeper
Ravencaller
Voidbreaker

VAGRANT GODS TRILOGY
The Bladed Faith
The Sapphire Altar
The Slain Divine

Legacy of the Watcher

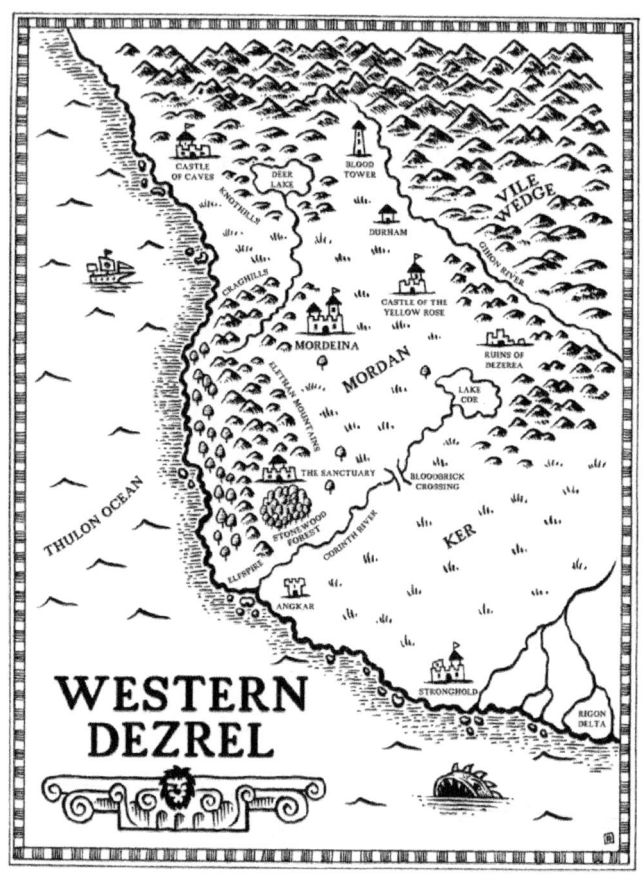

A Note from the Author:

I know you're used to finding these at the back of the book, not the front, but I'm making a special exception here. Legacy of the Watcher is explicitly continuing a storyline seeded at the very end of its sixth book, A Dance of Chaos. As such, there will be significant spoilers for events of that entire series throughout this book. I have done what I can to keep them to a minimum, just in case, but there is only so much I can do, given the nature of things. If you've started all these Dezrel books with the Half-Orcs, I highly suggest you read all of Shadowdance before continuing on with this one if you want to get everything out of this novel.

The same goes for anyone who might be stumbling onto this book having skipped the earlier Half-Orcs novels because they want the resolution to the Haern storyline from Shadowdance. I have tried to make this novel stand on its own, but being book eight in a series, some things are inevitable.

This novel is my fun, heartfelt goodbye to the world of Dezrel. There are nods to Shadowdance, to the early Half-Orcs books, even the Paladins and the Breaking World. If you've come with me on this journey through all those series, then welcome here to the end. I suspect you will enjoy the ride.

What follows now will be recaps, one for Shadowdance, one for Half-Orcs. I will try to keep the Shadowdance one as vague as possible for those who haven't read it, and hit on only the important parts relevant to this stage of the journey.

That said, enjoy, dear readers, at long last, the story of Erin Felhorn.

Legacy of the Watcher

A Reminder of Shadowdance, For Those Who Need One:

Aaron Felhorn is the son of Thren Felhorn, groomed since birth to be his father's successor, to inherit the sprawling empire of crime known as the Spider Guild. Through the influence of friends, and a chance meeting with Delysia Eschaton, he starts envisioning a life beyond the killing and subterfuge.

Alyssa Gemcroft is the heir to the Gemcroft family fortune. The Gemcrofts are one-third of what is known as the Trifect, a coalition of wealthy families who dominate trade in the nation of Neldar. That wealth, and that desire for total control, often puts them in conflict with the thief guilds. Thren Felhorn spearheads that war, spilling blood on all sides as mercenaries and assassins wage war in the city of Veldaren's streets. With the help of the mysterious Zusa, a woman belonging to the god Karak's assassin order known as the Faceless, Alyssa defends her role as leader of her household after the death of her father, taking control of the Gemcroft estate as the thief war rages on.

It is during this conflict that Aaron fakes his death and starts a life on the streets, adopting the name Haern to hide his identity. He wages his own private war against the thief guilds, putting an end to years of strife, creating an uneasy peace that is brokered with the king's assistance. Haern himself is charged with ensuring peace endures, becoming the King's Watcher, the fearsome haunt of Veldaren's night streets.

After a few years, Haern finds Delysia Eschaton once again, and joins the strange band of mercenaries her brother, Tarlak, manages. He also befriends Zusa, accompanying her and Alyssa on a trip to the southern city of Angelport. There they become embroiled in an attempt by an elf known as the Wraith to destroy the city's leadership. The Wraith's actions lead to the deaths of fellow Trifect leaders, Laurie and Madelyn Connington. Haern and Zusa defeat the Wraith, but the Connington family is ruined, with six year old

Tori Connington the only surviving heir. She is left in the care of Warrick Sun, a member of the local merchant lords. Warrick had squabbled with the Trifect, but sees becoming steward of the Connington estate a chance to establish a new era in the east...as well as a way to potentially break up the Trifect forever.

When Haern returns to Veldaren, he finds new trouble brewing. Thren's former master and teacher, the elf known as Muzien the Darkhand, has brought his Sun Guild all the way from the west to threaten Veldaren. He considers Thren a failure for being kept under the heel of the King's Watcher, and instigates a plan to burn the entire city to the ground with the aid of powerful magic. To stop him, Thren and Haern team up against the master of the Sun Guild. Together, they defeat the legendary elf.

The city, however, is not yet saved. Thren discovers Haern's true identity, and he offers his son, now in the guise of the Watcher, the chance to once more become his heir. They can rule the city together, the King's Watcher and the lord of the thieves, masters of both sides of the conflict. Haern finally reveals his face, hoping to sway his father's heart, but instead Thren denies him to the last, saying that he cannot be his son, because Aaron died in a fire. They battle. Haern is victorious, and debates killing a defeated Thren, but cannot bring himself to murder his own father. Instead he leaves Thren there on the rooftops, utterly broken.

The city is safe, but Alyssa Gemcroft grows tired of the guilds, the infighting, and the other members of the Trifect. She orders the rest of her family, Zusa and her son Nathaniel, to leave Veldaren. As they depart, Zusa reveals she is pregnant, the result of a fumbling tryst with Haern. She does not tell Haern, and come the events that follow, is never given a chance to. And so Alyssa and Zusa depart for Riverrun, their own relationship maturing as Zusa gives birth to Erin Gemcroft, where she is first raised in quiet, peaceful Riverrun...at least until the world is broken, demons flood the lands, and they are forced to flee to Angelport, to endure the Second Gods' War.

Legacy of the Watcher

A Reminder of the Half-Orcs, For Those Who Need One

It's been a long, strange life for Harruq Tun. A street urchin forced out the city of Veldaren for his orcish blood, he and his brother, Qurrah, travel to the city of Woodhaven. There, the two half-orcs are recruited by the Prophet of Karak, a long-lived necromancer named Velixar. Given power and ancient weaponry, they slaughter in Karak's name, eventually joining in an assault on the city of Woodhaven.

Velixar is not the only influence on Harruq's life, however. He has befriended Aurelia Thyne, an elven sorceress who arrived at Woodhaven to investigate crimes that would turn out to be Harruq's. They battle, with Harruq nearly killing her. Ashamed, he abandons the assault and flees with Aurelia, leaving Qurrah alone to escape the city. Velixar is seemingly killed by elven reinforcements led by Scoutmaster Dieredon. Eventually, Qurrah reconvenes with the other Harruq and Aurelia, and the trio travel north, to Veldaren.

There, the three are recruited into Tarlak Eschaton's weird little group of mercenaries, where they befriend Delysia Eschaton. Harruq is given proper training for the first time in his life under Haren, the King's Watcher himself. Joining the Eschaton, however, embroils Harruq into brand new conflicts.

A broken and miserable Thren Felhorn attempts to lure the Watcher into an ambush by poisoning Aurelia. A ruthless Haern and furious, berserking Harruq storm into the lair of the Spider Guild. Haern battles his father, eventually revealing his identity to the rest of the guild before executing Thren Felhorn, ending the life of the former master of the underworld in a most piteous manner.

Naturally, Aurelia marries Harruq for such chivalrous acts taken on her behalf. (I may be skipping over some things).

Joy and heartbreak follow in equal measure. Qurrah's romance with Tessanna Delone, one of the goddess Celestia's unimaginably powerful daughters of balance, brings tragedy to Harruq and Aurelia, indirectly ending the life of their beloved daughter, Aullienna. Battle follows, but Harruq is unable to take the life of his brother, instead demanding he and Tessanna leave Veldaren, never to return.

Neither take it well. What was a clash between brothers grows, as the brother gods Karak and Ashhur get involved and start taking sides. Eventually, Tessanna rips a hole in reality itself, opening the way for Thulos, god of war and fractured part of Karak and Ashhur, to step through, along with a host of his demons. They burn the world of Dezrel, until, through an act of faith, Harruq brings forth a host of angels to battle the demons. So begins the Second Gods' War, which results in Harruq slaying Thulos and earning himself the title of Godslayer.

In the years that follow, Qurrah and Tessanna, great betrayers of humanity for granting Thulos his demons passage into the world, try to make a new life in the land of Ker, south of Mordan, which is now known as the land of angels. Ever since Thulos's defeat, the angels have steadily grown more powerful and more involved in the daily aspects of human life, and their disgust over humanity's sin grows in equal measure. The head of their priestly order, Azariah, engineers the collapse of the floating angelic city of Avlimar as an excuse to take control over humanity directly. Ashhur punishes them for their hubris, ordering through a faithful servant that those angels who value their own power over humanity's safety shall be cursed. Their forms are perverted, and in their rage the fallen angels slaughter humanity without reason in what becomes known as the Night of Black Wings. The angels still loyal to Ashhur, led by Ahaesarus, engage the fallen in an equally bloody conflict.

It is a war with brutal casualties. Both Qurrah and Tessanna give their lives, Qurrah to save Harruq and Aurelia's second daughter, Aubrienna, and Tessanna to ruin the armies of both factions to ensure that humanity will endure no matter who emerges victorious, and resume control over itself instead of fighting at the whims of angels.

Legacy of the Watcher

Harruq leads the final assault on Mordeina, capital city of Mordan, and with the help of his wife and friends claims the lives of the fallen's leaders. Those fallen who remain flee to Devlimar, their earthbound city built in the wake of Avlimar's collapse. Even after the brutal fight to take Mordeina, Ahaesarus announces they will assault Devlimar come morning, determined to put an end to their foes once and for all.

Not all agree. Jessilynn, paladin of Ashhur, laments the coming assault. She sees yet another battle where the people whom Ashhur claims to love will give their lives only to prove Ashhur's superiority over his brother. In response, Ashhur, in the guise of the angel Ahaesarus, relents and orders Jessilynn to fire a single arrow with her broken bow. Celestia, true goddess of the lands of Dezrel, unleashes her fury upon Devlimar, adding thousands more arrows to that lone first. The fallen are broken. The war is over. The dead are many, including Scoutmaster Dieredon, who dies in Jessilynn's arms.

Ashhur's apology does not end there. He opens a portal for the angels to return to the Golden Eternity, so they might no longer be guardians of humanity, nor risk becoming their jailors. They abandon a war-torn Dezrel, with Celestia promising that the influence of both brothers, Karak and Ashhur, will be greatly diminished upon the land.

In the years that follow, Harruq does what he can to guide young prince Gregory Copernus, preparing him to take his proper seat as King of Mordan, to usher in what all hope will be an age of peace.

Prologue

THREN

The year 590 LA

Thren Felhorn stood in the center of a warehouse owned by his guild. One wall was stacked full with crates full of dyed threads from Angelport, smuggled into Veldaren to avoid import fees. On the opposite wall were barrels full of ale brewed in the fields south of Felwood Castle, hidden with Thren's aid to lessen the tax assessments of some minor lord's true worth. The wealth and power of the Spider Guild, used to help a few paltry nobles keep a bit of coin in their pockets.

How far Thren's empire had fallen.

No. Not fallen.

Broken.

"I must say, the Council of Mages rarely cares how much gold and silver is bribed their way," said a voice behind Thren. The hairs on his neck stood on end. No one could enter without his notice, not without magical aid.

"And yet here you are," he said, turning to address his visitor. He was a smaller man wearing the distinctive robes of a master of the Black Tower. His head was shaved, his black skin marred with little white scars across his face and neck. Thren wondered if they were self-inflicted, or from a cruel lifetime that came before his entrance into the towers.

"Might I have your name, wizard?"

"Aeng," the man said. Though he was smaller than Thren, he crossed his arms and managed to somehow appear he was looking down on him. "And I say so to inform you that it was not your price that brought me here, but instead, curiosity."

"It is not unusual for thief guilds to occasionally pay for services of a magical nature. Did I not already use your aid in creation of my recent pet?"

Aeng smiled. He was handsome, Thren decided, but the hungry look in his brown eyes, and the way his cheek twitched and his hands fidgeted was off-putting. But why was this surprising? The wizards of the towers were not known for their sociability.

"No, but it is odd when one requests a master in bone, blood, and death. Have you taken an interest in the darker arts, guildmaster?" Aeng's amused look turned dour. "Or do you seek information on the necromancer who assaulted your city alongside the orcs?"

Thren stayed his ground and sized the man up. He would be putting his trust in a stranger, but did he have any other choice? At least the Council's reputation was spotless. If Aeng was considered their best, he would be their best.

"I have no interest in some mad servant of Karak," Thren said, and pulled a small scrap of paper from his pocket. He offered it to Aeng. "This is my request, if you are capable of it."

Aeng lifted an eyebrow, but when Thren gave no additional explanation, he shrugged and accepted the paper. A tiny bloom of nerves tried to birth in Thren's chest, but he choked them down. His path was set. Doubt had no place in him. When Aeng was done reading, Thren extended his hand, accepting the slip of parchment back. Even now, spies from the other guilds might be watching. This request was between him and Aeng, and no one else.

"An interesting game is afoot," Aeng said, scratching at the scars on his face. "Who is this intended for?"

"Myself."

That got Aeng's full attention. "Really? Well then, how could I refuse?"

"You can do it then?"

The wizard scoffed.

"Of course I can do it. Our bodies are but meat and bone, solid matter that house the soul. They follow rules, predictable ones to those who study them." He grinned. "It will be unpleasant, though. Very unpleasant."

Thren reached into his pocket and pulled out two bags of coin. He threw the first one to Aeng.

"That is the agreed upon fee to the Council." He tossed the second. "And that is for you alone, for your secrecy."

Aeng shook them both, nodded, and pocketed them. When done, he clapped his hands. The sound was startling in the quiet warehouse.

"Well then, I need a few things from my room in the Black Tower, but that will only be a quick hop there and back with a portal. When would you like to do this?"

Everything else was already set in motion. Members of his guild were stationed throughout his territory, clueless to the real machinations at work. It would start soon with an ambush, and a well-aimed poisoned dart.

Without Thren, there could be no Spider Guild.

So long as the Watcher lived, there could be no Spider Guild.

Something had to give.

"Tonight," he said. "Weave your magic, wizard. Be it curse or blessing, I need it for when the Watcher brings his blades to bear."

Twenty of Thren's men stood between him and the Watcher, yet it was a paltry defense against his son's true skill. Another fighter was with him, a half-orc of great strength and decent aptitude, no doubt all of it owing to his son's training. They'd come to the underground lair of his guild headquarters seeking a cure to a poison one of Thren's men had inflicted upon a member of their little mercenary band.

"It is time to die, Watcher," Thren said. Pretending to not know the face hidden beneath the hood. Pretending this was all a master plan meant to finally slay Veldaren's Watcher. "The honor of thieves must be restored."

He snapped his fingers, and his guild rushed forward to die. There was no questioning it. Thren and Haern had fought after the death of Muzien the Darkhand. Thren had seen his son's true skill, and it was far beyond any person in any guild in any city. But instead of meeting the charge, the Watcher pulled back his hood.

Thren stared at the face of his son, his blond hair, slick with sweat, sticking to his forehead and neck. He was handsome, and so young. Even his smoldering rage added life to him. Pain, deep and unbearable, struck Thren's chest.

This was the second time Aaron had revealed his face to him. The first had been after slaying the Darkhand, ending his attempt to destroy the city of Veldaren. As the rain fell, and the unknown necromancer waged his war beyond the walls, Thren had

Legacy of the Watcher

spoken the only truth he was capable of bearing.

Aaron Felhorn was gone. Only Haern existed now, a man who had rejected everything Thren believed in.

I have no son, he had told the Watcher then, showing no sign that he noticed the resemblance. Acting as if Haern was the stranger he truly had become.

But now a new game was afoot, and Thren had a role to play. They were no longer alone upon the rooftops.

"Halt!" he shouted, feigning surprise. "By the gods, put down your weapons!"

Thren's men immediately halted. It was instinctive to them at this point, to never question an order. Thren had been proud of that loyalty, but no longer. Not after the humiliations he had suffered. Not after the power of his guild had been proven a lie. This thing he commanded, it was a shambling corpse pretending at life. It had to end.

Haern ran a hand through his sweat-soaked golden hair. "I have kept my face hidden for a long time," he said, his voice no longer a whisper. "I feel it right you know the truth before you die."

Several members of Thren's guild recognized Aaron from when he was a boy, and they spat or offered curses. Thren stood perfectly still, as if his blood was ice, as if his heart were not pounding a thunderous rhythm and his broken pride did not seek, even now, to best him in battle.

He had tried that already. And failed.

"You were to be our savior," Thren said, pulling back his own hood. Let all present hear and know the goal he had envisioned, and that his son had rejected. "Every man and woman would have quaked at the sound of your name."

"I am Haern, Watcher of the King. Men do quake at my name, but only those who deal in shadows and death." He bowed low. "You have hurt those I love and I will not risk their harm for my sake again. Look upon my face, all of you. Those who see my face must die. May Ashhur take pity on your souls before casting you to Karak's abyss."

Karak? Ashhur? Thren had never spoken of gods and their desires to his son. That was the doing of others, a poison dripping from the lips of the gullible and the weak. He'd put an arrow through a priestess who once tried to teach Aaron to pray. Perhaps that was one of many errors he had made that led to the path his son now walked.

Thren let his shoulders droop. There was no falseness to this pronouncement. The truth was the strongest cover for any and all lies.

"You have been dead to me for seven years," he told the man who had been Aaron. "Nothing has changed. Those loyal to my name, slay this man, and receive the highest honor I may bestow. I will call you son, and my heir, to replace he whom you slay."

And with that pronouncement, Thren executed the Spider Guild.

The Watcher could not be beaten.

"Such a shame, my son," Thren said as the bloodshed erupted. The twenty died, ripped apart by both the skill of his son and the savage fury of the half-orc brute at his side. Thren pulled out a whistle from his pocket. Everything would end this day, every shred of his guild. This legacy of his, it would coalesce into one single, glorious night. The world would be made simple.

The Spider Guild, brought to ruin by its beloved heir. The father, slain by the son. There was a purity to it that would echo, that would last.

"You are a beauty to behold, a beauty that must be broken beneath my heel," he said, and blew the whistle. Curtains fell from the sides of the rooms, revealing the last men and women loyal to his name.

"Crush them," Thren shouted, ordering them to their deaths for a promise that could never be. "Bring forth the time of the thief once more!"

The time of the thief. The time before the Watcher, when the guilds had warred against one another and stolen whatever they possessed the strength to take. The weak had been broken and the strong elevated to rule. The proper way, worth the cost, worth the infighting and wars within the underworld.

It was at the start of one such war Aaron had slain his older brother, Randith, to become Thren's next heir. The Spider Guild was now a pathetic fraction of the strength it had been back then. It could wage no such wars, but the thieves barreling into the chaos that was the Eschaton Mercenaries did not understand. The losses had been slow and steady, the work of the Watcher, masterfully bleeding dry the guilds he had devoted his life to conquering.

Blood flowed, swords clashing, the might of the half-orc more impressive than Thren first thought. The brute smashed aside his opponents as if they were children and he a rampaging bull. Into the chaos he created, Haern followed, picking apart weaknesses, punishing every errant step and every unstable footfall in the wake of the berserking warrior.

The slaughter was everything Thren expected, but then a blue portal ripped open and out stepped Tarlak Eschaton, yellow-robed wizard and leader of the strange mercenary band that had adopted his wayward son. A nearby thief flung a pair of daggers, one for the chest, one for the throat, hoping to surprise him. A wise move, but the wizard was ready. A snap of his fingers and a shield encased him. The meager steel struck the shield and bounced harmlessly to the side.

"How rude, those could have hurt." Tarlak said, glaring at the man. Energy crackled across his hands, the beginnings of a spell. "Just like you hurt my sister."

Fire and lightning blasted through the grand headquarters. Smoke mixed with the smell of blood and burning meat. Thren frowned. Too many foes. The Watcher needed this honor. The half-orc had diluted matters already, and now Tarlak was here to kill with his magic.

Thren grabbed a bow from the wall and steadily aimed. It seemed he would need to guide matters, and if he were honest with himself, there was satisfaction to be found in taking the life of one who had corrupted his son.

One smooth draw, and the bowstring locked taut. Despite the chaos of battle, the clashing of swords, and the spread of fire (gods, the wizard seemed to love his fire), he trusted his aim. He let the arrow fly. His son screamed, but he was too far, too engaged with slaughtering the guild members he should be leading. The arrow shot straight for the wizard's heart.

And then the damn half-orc stepped in the way. The arrow punched into his dark leather armor, but the overly-muscled freak did not seem to care. He roared like a savage animal and pointed with his swords. The challenge amused Thren more than anything. A bit of life flooded into his veins.

As always, he would ensure matters ran their proper course. The half-orc was a problem, and so the half-orc would die.

"Come, orc," he said, drawing his own swords. "I yearn to kill this night."

Haern tried to follow, but too many members of Thren's guild surrounded him. The half-orc crossed the space between them, his swords pulled back for a dual slash. All his might and momentum pooled into a fearsome strike that would break any man who tried to block.

Which is why Thren didn't. He kept perfectly still, the slightest smile on his face, until those swords came slamming down. He slid aside at the last moment, his own blades sweeping horizontally to parry. His foe continued onward, trying to ram him with his shoulder. Momentum was with him, but the angle was wrong, and Thren worsened it by twisting his body, all his weight carefully balanced on his toes like a dancer.

The half-orc raced past him, off balance and swords out of position. Thren spun and slashed him twice, thin cuts across the arm and neck. Certainly not enough to kill someone who could shrug off an arrow to the chest as if it were nothing. They squared off again, and this time his foe tried to fight him in test of skill, his swords weaving, striking and blocking simultaneously with their every hit.

Thren recognized each and every one. How could he not, when his son was the brute's teacher?

Indignation lit a fire in Thren's veins, hotter than the flames the maniacal wizard had set across the headquarters' curtains. An heir. His son was creating an heir. Perhaps he knew it, perhaps he did not, but it didn't matter. The skills were passed on, and to what? A wretched bastard child of some orc, more muscle than sense?

Thren blasted each and every hit aside. He made a mockery of the half-orc's defenses. The Spider Guild would die, yes, but this insult would die with it. Blood flowed across dark leather as Thren dissected the half-orc's every move, every counter. No feint worked. No block was fast enough. The injuries rapidly grew more numerous, a thin gash across the cheek, multiple cuts along the arms, a vicious line along the stomach. None lethal. Just enough to bleed, to weaken. Softening him up for the killing blow.

At last the half-orc's confidence was broken. He

abandoned any attack to instead defend, and Thren went on the offensive. He lashed twice with his right hand sword, pulled back, and then feinted with his other. His foe fell for the feint, left hand sweeping to block a hit that was not coming. Thren shot forward, vaulting into the air. His heel led, striking the half-orc's face and crushing the cartilage of his nose. Blood splattered, and the half-orc gasped. His legs wobbled, the pain of the fight finally registering.

"Miserable," Thren muttered as he landed. No more games. His sword pulled back, hesitated the slightest moment to ensure the half-orc mistimed the parry, and then thrust straight for the bastard's eye.

Haern parried away the fatal thrust.

Careless, Thren thought as his son's foot smacked the left side of his neck. He rolled with it to soften the blow, came up to one knee, and slashed. Again, a misjudgment. His son was too fast, too prepared. He was already in the air, leaping over the blade. His knees struck Thren's shoulders, slamming him to the ground. Thren gasped as two sabers pressed against his throat.

The leader of the dying Spider Guild met the eyes of his son, and he saw turmoil in them, but nothing like when they last crossed swords. They had already waged their battle. They had already given each other everything in the shadow of the Darkhand's carnage.

"You abandoned us, now you come to murder us, murder your own father," Thren said. One final lie, so that doubt would live on within his son. Their rain-swept duel upon the rooftops, forever shrouded in mystery. "I would not have tried killing the Watcher if I had known it was you."

Haern flinched, but then something cold and hard entered those blue eyes of his. No, there was no doubt, no confusion. Thren gave his son too little credit, for he refused to believe the lie. Yet there was something else, something he did not expect. Something akin to hate, or abandonment.

"You were a wretched father," Haern whispered into Thren's ear. "And I was not your son. I was your assassin, nothing more. Now, I am your better."

He yanked both blades viciously to either side. Thren felt the pain, felt the warmth of his blood flow, but he did not look away. Those words haunted him.

I was your assassin, nothing more.

Aaron Felhorn was meant to be so much more than assassin. An heir to a legacy. The culmination of a lifetime of blood, sweat, and tears. The lessons of the Darkhand, the brutality of Veldaren's streets, the wisdom of tutors, the pride of kings, all for him, just him.

Whatever doubt Thren had felt, he let it die. This, this was the fate he deserved, if his son believed so little in him. His hatred, he could bear. His fury, let it burn. But such contempt? Such horrid understanding of those gifts? No, Thren had failed the Spider Guild, failed where it mattered most.

Let it die.

Blood trickled, and he gasped for breath, but no air would come. His head went light. The fire burned so hot around him. The world darkened, but he could not close his eyes. His body turned cold, his limbs stiff and unresponsive. The blood turned brittle against his flesh. But he could not close his eyes. He could not close his eyes.

A blue portal opened above Thren, swirling with strange stars and light. Aeng stepped out, and he immediately muttered a curse.

"You said you'd be killed, not the whole building set to flame."

He leaned closer and pressed his hand against Thren's throat. The sensation entered Thren's brain from a far distance, as if his every limb were asleep.

"Got you good, didn't he? Two cuts across the throat. Be glad for the fire, I suppose. If he stuck around, he'd have noticed you hadn't bled near enough."

Aeng grabbed Thren's heel, turned, and dragged him into the portal.

"Let's get you somewhere more pleasant, shall we?"

Thren could not argue. He could not move. He felt nothing, not even the pain. His mind was a fly, buzzing around a glass jar. If only he could look around. If only he could shift his view, or his body would respond

The panic will be the worst, Aeng had warned him, and Thren focused on that as they passed through the portal. His mind was his strongest weapon. It would not break, not here, not now.

They reappeared in the same warehouse in which they had first met, Aeng dragging Thren across chalk lines he'd carefully drawn hours prior. The wizard had a bag of supplies waiting, and Thren heard him rummage through it. Thren's gaze remained locked on the ceiling. His eyes, they were so dry, even the numbness of his mind could not fully prevent their aching, cracking pain.

Aeng's face reappeared in view. He held a needle and thread in his hands.

"Most in my trade tend to be awful with their hands," Aeng said. "But luckily for you, sewing is a skill I have honed rather well, given my…preferred specializations. They'll scar, that is unavoidable, but you'll at least have a neck." He whistled as he dug the needle into the stiff flesh. "The Watcher really wanted you dead. I'd take that as a compliment, if I were you. It takes a lot of skill to get someone to hate you that much."

And I was not your son…

Time crawled along as Aeng sealed the first of the wounds. At the second, he studied and poked at the cut for an interminable amount of time.

"He cut your windpipe," Aeng said eventually. "Deep, too, real deep. I'm going to have to sew it back together. It's going to hurt like the Abyss for months, I'd wager, until your skin finally heals and gets rid of the thread. No getting around this, though, unless you want to choke on your own blood."

Get on with it, Thren wished he could tell him, but his lips would not move, nor could he draw breath to say the words, given the shape of his body.

The needle pierced into his throat, deeper, stranger. The sensation of every tug and pull was a nightmare. His mind rebelled, manifesting agony, the idea of nails scraping on glass becoming something close to physical sensation.

Yet it wasn't true pain. Pain would have been preferable. Damn it all, if only he could close his eyes, or ask the wizard to cover them with a cloth. He could see the needle after every pull, see it slick with blood, see the thread tightening, tightening…

And then it was over. Aeng snipped the thread and started one anew.

"All right," he said. "Second cut, same as the first."

This stitching was far easier to bear. Thren endured, now finding it almost comforting. He'd been stitched and bandaged many times before. He knew intimately the interplay of needle, thread, and flesh. His current predicament was simply...odder.

Once that was done, Aeng vanished from Thren's view. More rummaging in his bag, then back again, this time holding strips of pale gray cloth. He looped the cloth around and around Thren's neck, covering the freshly stitched wounds. Once done, he settled onto his knees and put his hands atop Thren's chest.

"I will not lie," he said. "My spell put a halt to your every motor and biological function the moment you suffered your fatal wound. In more layman's terms, think of it like freezing your body in ice. However, it is time for you to thaw. If you've ever warmed up a limb after frostbite, you have an idea as to what you should expect. If you have not, well..."

Aeng laughed.

"It won't be something you're likely to forget anytime soon."

Warmth spread throughout Thren's body, radiating out from the wizard's hand.

"Oh, and given the shape of your throat...don't scream."

Thren pulsed and thrashed on the floor, but as requested kept his teeth clenched tightly shut. He bit his tongue at one point, adding blood to an already blood-soaked mouth and throat, but he did not scream. The pain, he could bear. All new lives upon Dezrel were born in blood and pain.

After several minutes, he felt the worst of it ease, and he was able to breathe at a steady pace.

"Not bad," Aeng said, stepping away. "Of the three others I've done this for, two died during the reawakening."

A fact you did not share beforehand, Thren thought, but dared not speak. His throat felt aflame. Even the trickle of air from his light inhalations brought torturous sensations. He sat up, gingerly stretched his frighteningly tight muscles, and then struggled to his feet. Aeng helped him with that, holding his arm as he swayed in the center of the dark warehouse.

Once it was clear Thren could stand on his own, the wizard stepped aside and observed him.

"Alive and well," he said. His grin spread ear to ear. "Just

Legacy of the Watcher

like I knew you would be. This is so exciting. The implications of biological functions, of stasis...I mean, the fact your soul remained within your body alone is a fascinating idea. I might need to find a priest of Karak, Ashhur, or even an elf of Celestia, to—"

Thren hit Aeng square in the mouth, ending the ramble. Aeng staggered backwards until hitting the wall of crates. He touched his lips, glanced at his fingers, saw blood on them.

"All right," he said. "I probably deserve that."

Thren lumbered over to the other side, where he'd stored a rucksack full of supplies, multiple changes of clothes, and enough coin to live comfortably for the rest of his life. The first thing, though, was his cloak. It had to go. He removed it and held it aloft, staring at the gray fabric.

The Spider Guild was gone. Truly gone. Its legacy ended in death at the hands of the Watcher. Thinking on it, knowing it done, he expected to feel sorrow or fury, but instead he felt...nothing. Emptiness.

He dropped the cloak to the floor, along with the rest of his bloodstained and smoke-stained clothes, and dressed in an outfit from the rucksack—a plain white shirt and brown trousers. Once dressed, he hoisted the pack over his shoulder and turned, shocked by how tired he already felt. Aeng was right. This would take so much longer to heal from than he expected.

The idea of speaking caused him pain, so he gestured with his other hand to show he was ready. Aeng nodded, still dabbing at his gradually swelling lip.

"Why do this?" the wizard asked. "Sorry, I know you can't really answer, but I have to ask, because I suspect it will drive me to madness over the coming years. Why would you go to such lengths to ensure your death when you could just...leave?"

Thren shook his head. He could not speak, not given the condition of his throat. But to leave? To abandon all he'd done? His pride would not allow it. Stories would linger. The great Thren Felhorn, fleeing the city he'd once lorded over. Fleeing the Watcher. Those he left behind would elevate a new leader for the guild, one who would be weak, foolish, and turn the Spider Guild into a joke.

Thren's legacy, broken in an instant. His guild, a sham ruled by another. No matter where he went, rumors would follow. People would tell stories of where he'd fled, or the comical ways in which he may have died. The fear of him would ebb away, replaced with mockery. Thren could never have accepted such a fate. Even a true death was preferable.

Thren closed his eyes and smiled. The last of his doubt washed away. His time ruling Veldaren was over. Perhaps he could have won when he was a younger man, but the years moved only in one direction.

Haern the Watcher was now the slayer of Thren Felhorn and destroyer of the Spider Guild. Thren's legacy, passed on to his son. Not in the way Thren envisioned when he first put a pair of training swords in his young hands…but perhaps more appropriate. Aaron had become heir by slaying his own brother. Why shouldn't his final ascension follow the slaying of his father?

"That's fine, keep your secrets," Aeng said. "I have my coin, and truly, your revival is the culmination of multiple theorems my colleagues have long denounced as unproven. I dare say, you even did me a favor." The wizard clapped his hands and smiled. "And so I shall do *you* a favor. Speak a location, and I'll send you there. You can begin your new life, wherever that is, this very night."

Thren had debated the location for the past several weeks, and at last settled on a destination. He needed to be far, far away from the kingdom of Neldar, that was obvious. But living in Mordan in the far west carried its own dangers, for there were still those who remembered the Darkhand.

It hurt, oh how it hurt when Thren spoke, but it was one word, he could manage one word. Blood dripped down his throat as he pushed each syllable out through cracked, dry lips and a swollen tongue.

"Ang…kar," he said.

"My, such a distance. Give me a moment, then."

Aeng brushed aside the chalk circles he'd used for his prior ritual and carved new ones on the floor. When done, he stepped back, did a few quick loops with his hands, and a new portal burst open, swirling blue and beautiful.

"To the distant port jewel of the west," Aeng said. "Good luck, Thren Felhorn…or whomever it is you'll become to live out your remaining years."

Thren ignored him and approached the portal. Deep within

he saw the faintest hint of stars, the wood boards of a dock, and lanterns hanging from the roofs of short, squat buildings. A new life. He reached for it.

No more legacies. His was done. Head lifted, he stepped through, to discover what life even meant when living, not for fate, not for heirs and legacies, but for yourself, and yourself alone.

Second Prologue

ZUSA

The year 600 LA

Zusa Gemcroft knelt by her wife's bedside, clutching Alyssa's feverish hands. They were alone in their room. Outside, the city of Angelport waited deathly silent for the battle to come.

"Tonight, it ends," Zusa told the once powerful paragon of the Trifect. "For good or ill, it all ends."

Alyssa Gemcroft lay underneath blankets, her face horridly pale. She'd removed the red blindfold she'd worn the past few years, and she vacantly stared to the ceiling, seeing nothing. The sickness had come two months prior, a blight that steadily sapped her beloved's strength and spirit. After the first month, she'd barely been able to walk. Near the end of the second, even eating and speaking were tiring.

The angels could heal her, Zusa knew. But the angels would not come. They ruled over Mordan, their new Paradise, and all suffering beyond its borders meant nothing to them.

"Keep...you'll keep Nathaniel...safe, won't you?" Alyssa asked, needing to take rasping breaths between every few words. Zusa kept her face perfectly serene, hiding the pain she felt at hearing her wife's exhaustion. There was a time when Alyssa had commanded the Trifect fearlessly, even after Veldaren's collapse and the chaos that followed. When war demons conquered the east, they had sailed the Queln River to take refuge in Angelport. When Warrick opened up the city to Thulos, Alyssa had seethed, and she had plotted.

When the war ended, Alyssa took control of the city. She executed the cowards who had allowed the war demons to have their way by refusing to fight back. With a crowd cheering her on, Alyssa had hung the leader of the Merchant Lords, Warrick Sun. War was coming, and Alyssa promised to fight it. She'd been strong, so strong, and Zusa fought at her side every step of the way.

"The moment we break the siege, we'll have you on a boat

headed west," Zusa said. She kissed Alyssa's hand and then began to brush her hair. It had once been a lively red, but now was faded. Or perhaps Zusa only imagined things, and it seemed it had lost its color due to the dark hour and faint candle light.

"I won't…"

Zusa did not let her finish.

"You will," she said, a lump swelling in her throat. "You're going to live. You're going to see Angelport made free, and then you're going to accompany me to Ker. And if no physician in Ker can cure your illness, we'll march our way all the way to the boy king's throne and demand Ahaesarus himself lay his hands upon you. Do you hear me, Alyssa?"

Alyssa closed her eyes and leaned away. A thin sheen of sweat coated her neck. Zusa kissed her face. Her skin was clammy to the touch.

"Wait here," she said, as if her wife had a choice. "I'll make sure Nathaniel keeps you company."

Their bedroom was in the old Keenan mansion, though its halls were long stripped of valuables. Instead of wealthy guests, soldiers bunked in the many bedrooms. Angelport had been a city of war ever since the east fell, and though the city had maintained freedom after Thulos's death, the lands of the Ramere were not made free.

Instead came the orcs. At first they had seemed an endless tide, more numerous than the people could hope to resist, but it had been an illusion, cultivated carefully by the war demon who led them. His name, gleefully given by the orcs as they waged their war, was Nahorash, the last survivor of Thulos's invading army.

That first siege had been relentless, but Angelport held. As the weeks passed, cracks appeared in the facade of supposed total conquest of the east. Reports slipped in from beyond the Crestwall Mountains of how Veldaren was a ghost city, as was much of Neldar. The orcs' numbers were highly concentrated into a single army, with no real cities built or occupied beyond the many tents scattered around Angelport. Nahorash wanted to build a wall protecting the crossing of the delta and then steadily cultivate his loyal forces.

Angelport was a thorn in the war demon's side, a potential weakness that could be exploited if the people of either Ker or

Mordan sought to launch another invasion. And so Nahorash assailed the walls. He had his best swimmers sabotage ships, but it was never enough. The boats risked the dangers, bringing back supplies, keeping the dwindling survivors of Angelport alive.

But sickness came. Disease. Hunger. And now the reaper's touch came for Zusa's wife.

Just outside their bedroom door waited Nathaniel. He sat in a chair, a book opened on his lap, reading quietly by the light of the candle beside him.

"Where's Erin?" she asked him. Nathaniel looked up. He was becoming a handsome young man, having just turned twenty, but in the flickering candlelight he looked so young and afraid.

"I don't know," he said.

Zusa glanced at the book he held. It was a favorite of Erin's, which Zusa had managed to barter from a crewman off one of the few boats from Angkar that made its way to Angelport's docks. Many new books had been written—and grown popular—in the wake of Thulos's defeat. Attempts to understand the reasons for the war god's invasion, and paint vivid portraits of those who fought back. Most of those stories retold the histories of the Tun brothers, exaggerating higher and higher both their crimes and their heroics.

This book, however, focused on one of the fallen heroes of the second Gods' War. Zusa had read it carefully before giving it to her daughter. It was a fairly accurate retelling of Haern the Watcher's life, at least, that which was known by those friends of his who'd survived. The author had spent hours chatting with Tarlak Eschaton, and the Godslayer himself, Harruq Tun.

Zusa wished she could have added more than a few details, and when she gave Erin the tome, she'd made it clear she was willing to talk about what was and was not true. Erin cherished it more than any possession she owned, reading and re-reading the heroics of her father as the long years in Angelport crawled along.

Zusa closed the book, her fingers brushing the title.

The Legacy of the Watcher.

"I don't want your mother to be alone tonight," she said. "Go be with her."

Nathaniel nodded, and stood from his chair.

"Stay safe," he said, wrapping his arm around her in a hug.

Gods, he was getting so tall. She remembered when he was a squealing babe in a wetcloth. How the years flew by.

"Tonight is not the night I die," she said, and pushed away from him. "Hold faith in me, all right, Nathaniel?"

"You know I trust you more than anyone else," her adopted son said. "Do what you do best, Zusa. Do it for us all."

He walked past her to join his mother's bedside. Zusa did not look back. She had to steel her heart against the night, for the sake of all who depended upon her. The time for weakness and tears would come later.

Her daughter, Erin, was waiting for her outside the door. She was dressed as she did for their sparring sessions, in dark clothes and a long cloak, daggers sheathed at her hips. The hood of her cloak hung low over her face, hiding her dirty blond hair but still revealing the fierce determination of her deep brown eyes.

"I want to join you."

Zusa crossed her arms. "There is no time to argue this, Erin."

"Then don't argue. Let me fight. You've trained me for this, exactly this, haven't you?"

There was truth to those words, but Zusa would hear none of it.

"Our plan relies on so much luck," she said. "You're only eleven, Erin. You're not ready for battle against orcs ten times your weight, or to face off against their leader, a demon of a hundred battles."

"And you are?"

Zusa pushed past her. "I don't have a choice. Now stay with your mother and brother. If you are so determined to use your blades, then consider yourself their final bodyguard should the battle turn ill."

Erin seethed with anger, but Zusa shut it out of her mind. Too much was at stake, and her attention was already splintered by her fears over Alyssa's rapidly deteriorating health.

Zusa exited the mansion, which had been built a quarter mile from docks that currently teemed with people. She could hear them as she approached northward toward the walls. Part contingency plan, part bait, she could only pray they served their purpose. She walked the dark streets, eager for battle. She wore no wrappings, no cloak, just her weapons and her tightly buckled vest, trousers, and high boots. No veil would hide the hate in her eyes when she killed the brutal invaders.

Ahead, at one of dozens of chosen gathering spots, Zusa climbed a ladder laid alongside a tall but thin home with a slanted roof. The height gave her a vantage point to view much of the city, as well as the sprawling red dots that were the orc campfires beyond the walls.

"I see you, you bastard," Zusa said, watching the pair of crimson wings hovering in the far distance. Nahorash, carrying on a war for a dead master. It seemed conquest was forever in his blood; he needed to be put down like a rabid dog. Zusa drummed the hilts of her long daggers. Tonight, she prayed she was the one given the privilege.

A stocky man, clean shaven and wearing finely polished chainmail overlaid with a faded green tunic, joined Zusa atop the roof, having taken the stairs within the home instead of climbing the outside ladder. His name was Vick, and he was the captain in charge of the city's defense.

"Everything is ready," he said, looking out across the city with her. "We await only your signal."

Zusa nodded. Her stomach twisted with nerves.

"This is it," she said. "There's no recovering from this if we fail. All or nothing. Victory, or death."

"It is not too late to reconsider," Vick said, arching an eyebrow her direction. "Do you doubt the potential of your plan?"

Zusa shook her head. "No," she said, thinking of Alyssa burning with fever. "We've all endured enough. It's time to force a deciding battle out of these orcs and their demon master. Are the boats ready?"

"I have been told they are."

"Then let us not delay further. Give the signal."

Vick kept a horn buckled to his waist, and he lifted it to his lips and blew it once, long and loud. It was repeated again by a waiting soldier at the docks, beginning Zusa's plan. A strange relief filled her, the release of anxiety that came when a plan turned into action.

Every single ship in Angelport's harbor took sail at once. It was organized chaos, the ship captains having discussed extensively who would leave and when, to give the illusion of a panicked departure. Zusa watched with the help of a spyglass Vick offered her. She squinted, wishing she could see better in the dark. A momentary annoyance.

It wouldn't be long before the entire city was lit with flame.

"A convincing display," she said as the various-sized ships took to the waves. Women and children unable to fight both filled the ships' holds and were crammed atop their decks. Zusa felt relieved. Even if everything went wrong, at least several hundred people would escape the ensuing slaughter to find sanctuary in the west.

The purpose of the boats, though, was to give the illusion of a city abandoned. The outer walls were almost entirely empty, as were the homes built along its edges. Seeing the boats departing would grab Nahorash's attention, and once he inspected the walls…

Zusa grinned as she heard the sudden thunder of distant drums. The war demon had taken the bait.

"They're coming," Vick said needlessly. The orcs needed no torches to see in the dark, so it was only by the light of the stars Zusa watched the vague shape of their force gather for an assault.

"Give the second order," Zusa said, and a heavy weight settled upon her. This was it. No going back now. Vick lifted his trumpet and blew it twice. A scout closer to the walls repeated it in the distance, and then those few soldiers still stationed on the outer line of defense quickly fled down the steps.

Zusa crossed her arms and waited. Their perch allowed them to see over many of the homes between them and the outer wall, but as the army drew nearer, they were shielded from view. But she didn't need to see them to know what they would do. They would shatter the gates. They would climb up to find unguarded ramparts. They would think the city theirs, and they would charge toward the docks overwhelmed with bloodlust.

The wait was agonizing, but the invaders arrived as she predicted. They did not even bother with a battering ram, relying solely on their siege ladders. Zusa watched the movements along the walls, and then a moment later, the main gate opened from the inside. Zusa grimaced at the numbers. Several thousand. This would be brutal.

"Everyone is in place," Vick said. "Hold faith in our

people, my lady."

Vick was speaking more to himself than her, and she understood his need for courage. This was it. Life or death, the survival of thousands, and perhaps the future of the entire east, would be settled here and now.

"My faith is in myself, my family, and my people," she said as the orcs flooded into the city.

Certainly not in Karak who tormented me, and Ashhur who abandoned us all.

About one third of the way into the city, the orcs reached the barricades. They were haphazard things, torn boards, broken walls, and stacked furniture piled up to hamper their progress. These barricades were unmanned and proved but a momentary deterrent as the orcs shoved and pushed through their center to continue onward to the docks.

But those first barricades weren't meant to stop them. They were there to burn.

"Enough are through," she said. "Give the next signal."

The city was much too large for the orcs to search thoroughly, and they themselves were far too eager seeking out a fight. The rows upon rows of empty houses meant nothing to them, and only furthered the belief the people were clustering around the docks to flee. Perhaps Nahorash would sense something amiss in time, but even the cruel war demon would struggle to rein in his forces given their hurried, scattered state.

And so the hundred or so volunteers hidden within the homes went unnoticed when the orcs rushed past. They emerged all throughout the outer third of the city, carrying torches and oil. Every drop of oil in all of Angelport's possession, splashed across the barricades and the walls of the nearby homes. What began as a faint flicker soon became a roaring blaze as enormous swathes of the city began to burn. No home was spared. Every barricade was rebuilt and then set to light. The volunteers would go until the smoke overwhelmed them, and then they would flee to assigned cellars to hide underground while the battle raged above.

With chaos and confusion overcoming the attacking army, Zusa drew her daggers. She saw their progress stall, and could almost imagine the arguments. She scanned the sky, but still saw no sign of the war demon.

Legacy of the Watcher

What order will you give? she wondered. *Will you flee, or will you still seek your conquest?*

The answer appeared to be a mixture of both. The orcs were surrounded by fires on all sides. Some fled for the city entrance, only to find rebuilt barricades burning in their way. Others collapsed choking from the billowing smoke that overran them. Most, though, rushed the docks, pushing past the fires to the clean air beyond.

"Come," Zusa said, sliding down the ladder to the street below. She turned a corner to join several dozen Angelport soldiers gathered before a similar barricade built of stacked boards, tables, chairs, and whatever else could be scavenged from the abandoned homes along the outer third. Over the past several weeks, they had built a wall fully encircling the interior third of the city beside the docks, creating the true line of defense once the fires were lit. All else would burn, if it must.

Zusa pushed to the front as men and women bowed their heads in respect. She saw fear in their eyes, but also resolve. They knew the stakes. They would not break.

"The first few moments will be the worst," she told them as, far down the street, the first of the orcs came sprinting into view. "They will hurl everything against us to break through and escape the flames. Give them nothing. Two options await them, fire or the blade. Tonight, Angelport takes her due."

Zusa retreated a step, knowing she would be at her most dangerous when attacking from reserve, with the battle at its most chaotic. The roar of fire, battle cries of orcs, and pounding of drums washed over her. She closed her eyes, and all sound faded away. In her mind's eye she saw Nathaniel, fearful and with a book in hand. She saw her daughter, fierce and strong, enduring every bruise and cut of her training.

Saw her wife, sick and in desperate need of care.

Zusa opened her eyes, and all the world was silent. The night narrowed in her mind as the orcs slammed into the barricade in a clash of steel and explosion of blood.

Her enemies would die. Nahorash would die.

Zusa waited, waited, watching soldiers thrust their weapons over the barricade, their shields raised to endure the chops of the orcs' axes and swords. Blood flowed, spilled on both sides. The tight lines thinned, bodies collapsed, the barricade crumpling as orcs smashed and flung their hulking bodies against it in an attempt to break through.

Now.

Zusa dove into the heart of the fray, her focus narrowed to the point of a pin. She buried both daggers into the chest of an orc before he even realized she was near, then ripped the blades free while spinning. She almost wished she still had her cloak, for it would have twirled about her, disguising her movements. But that cloak had surged with life from Karak's gifts, and she would never accept his presence in her life again. Instead she ducked underneath a frantic chop, spun behind a nearby soldier screaming from a broken arm, and came back in with a second thrust. Her arms extended to their maximum, enabling reach so the dagger points could each slice into the side of an orc's neck.

With a violent flourish, she planted her feet on the orc's chest and used his dying form to vault herself over the falling barricade. For the briefest moment she was upside down as her momentum carried her, and she smiled amid the bloodshed of the night.

I bet even you would be proud, Watcher.

She landed amid the dozens of orcs, and their bafflement was quickly replaced with rage. Her daggers ripped into flesh, their sharp edges enhanced with magic so that her foes' leather armor meant nothing. They tried to overwhelm her, but the battlefield was chaotic, strewn with corpses, orcs swinging and thrusting at awkward angles to not strike down their fellows. Zusa ricocheted about, parrying thrusts, slashing arms, and then leaping again, a cartwheel that had her heel striking the chin of her foe.

When she landed, soldiers of Angelport rushed past the barricade, swarming the invaders. Her feet had barely touched ground before she lunged to join them, the sharpened point to their spear, plunging forward with lethal force. Zusa's heart pounded in her chest, the world glassy, the distant fires too bright. She was all instinct, hard-earned from a lifetime of training. Her every movement opened flesh. Her daggers drowned in blood. Kill after kill, her speed too great, her ferocity beyond match.

And then there were no enemies to kill. Soldiers rushed forward, crying out orders as they swept both east and west to join the other battles. Vick hurried with them, wrangling their enthusiasm into something usable, to reinforce other portions of the barricades surrounding the docks. Zusa stood among the dead, the corpses of humans and orcs alike draped over one another in stinking piles of flesh, bone, blood, and entrails.

"What a fucking waste," she said as the fires continued to burn.

Only instinct saved her. Her mind cried out warning, a threat of something behind, and she trusted it without hesitation and dove into a roll. She felt a swish of air above her, and then she was on her feet, spinning to face her attacker.

Nahorash loomed before her, his red wings spread wide and fluttering in the moonlight. His scarred face was twisted into a hateful glare. His long black hair, sickly and unkempt, bunched around his neck as he lifted his spear.

"Tricks and cowardice," he said, his voice an aching rumble. He thrust for Zusa's abdomen, and she slid aside to avoid being impaled. "And you lead them, don't you, human?"

"Cowardice?" she said, pretending not to be so out of breath as she was. Another thrust, and when she dodged he was there, his elbow leading. It struck her chest, and she gasped as she fell, stumbling over the corpse of an orc. The fall had her twisting awkwardly, and she had to fling herself all the way to the ground to avoid being impaled. Zusa slid along the smooth stones of the cobbled road, her body slick with blood.

"I have held the walls against your every assault," she said, digging in a heel to halt her momentum. She glared while on one knee, blood trickling down her face and hair. "Where were you, demon?"

"A commander leads," Nahorash said, gripping his spear in two hands. His crimson armor rattled with his every movement. His wings fluttered, readying for another thrust.

"And now you have no army left to lead," Zusa said, teeth bared. "I made sure of that."

Rage overwhelmed the war demon, and he hurled toward her, his wings beating to give him speed. Zusa flung herself right back at him. Her youth was much too far in the past to endure a lengthy battle against a demon blessed for war. She had to end this quick, and so she gambled. No lengthy back and forth, especially not with him holding greater reach over her daggers with his spear. It was in this one moment, with his rage in full control, that she would find the opening to kill.

The space between them vanished. His spear raced for her breast. The world slowed. Her body turned. Twisted. The spear passed underneath her, for she was in the air, leaping, turning. Its tip shredded the front of her vest, ripping off two of the buttons and tearing the fabric of the blouse underneath. Her arms extended. Her momentum carried.

Their bodies collided, and she screamed when his metal breastplate struck the top of her head. Then came another burst of pain as her shoulder collided, and the two rolled, his wings folding underneath him. That pain, though, she could endure, even as the warring pair struck the ground and rolled. The dizziness that overcame her as she struggled to stand would pass.

The two deep holes her daggers had punched into Nahorash's neck would not.

The war demon gagged and clutched at his throat, but nothing stopped the blood leaking between his pale fingers. Zusa closed her eyes, waited for the world to stop spinning beneath her feet, and then opened them.

"Thulos is dead," she said, kneeling over the dying war demon. "There is no god to mourn you. Know torment, you foul thing, and be gone from us."

Zusa slammed a dagger into Nahorash's eye, burying it until the hilt clacked against the skull and stuck. She twisted it once, then ripped it free. The explosion of gore was sick but satisfying. She shook her weapon, then wiped it clean on her trouser leg.

Softly, slowly, she exhaled.

"It's over," she whispered.

Zusa limped back to the mansion. The stars were hidden beneath clouds of smoke, the midnight sky painted red from the many fires. Every part of her body ached. She wanted nothing more than to collapse into her bed, wrap her arms around Alyssa, and sleep until the dawn.

Erin waited at the door, her spine curled and her head low. At Zusa's approach, she looked up. Tears were in her eyes. She need not say a word. The heartache on her face was explanation enough. Zusa slowed to a stop, all the world turning gray. Air would not enter her lungs. She tried to speak, to find words, but none came to her leaden tongue.

"Mom," Erin said, the first to break the silence. "She…she…"

When her words failed, her feet took over. Erin sprinted across the distance, slamming into Zusa to bury her face into her stomach. Her arms wrapped about her, and then came the sobs, deep and heavy, wracking her entire body.

Zusa slowly returned the embrace with shaking arms. Try as she might, she could not stop the tears that fell from her own eyes. She had been strong for so very long, and now, when they might finally live the peaceful life they had both sought, there was nothing left within her but aching muscles and broken dreams.

"But we're free now," she whispered to the damned night. "Alyssa…we…we're free."

There was naught to offer comfort, only a sky full of ash. No celebrations would mark Nathaniel Gemcroft's rise as the last of the Trifect. No feasts. No parades. Just a city full of the dead.

The fires burned, and the smoke billowed.

Zusa wept.

Erin wept beside her.

Together, and yet alone.

1

JESSILYNN

The year 601 LA

Jessilynn patted Sonowin's side to gain the horse's attention.

"Slowly now," she whispered. "There's no reason to hurry when we're finally here."

The white-winged horse nodded her head up and down, as always understanding more than Jessilynn expected. A welcome surprise, every time. It made her feel less alone as they trod the roads south. Rode, not flew, for behind them rattled a small cart carrying the corpse of the slain Scoutmaster, Dieredon Sinistel. Sonowin had bucked at the heavy additions to her saddle at first, until she saw its purpose. Then she had accepted quietly, her wings folded and her head lowered.

They had not flown this path, no. Slowly, grieving, they had ridden the lands. Jessilynn brushed the winged horse's mane and whispered soothing words.

"You've been a fine companion. Thank you, for this."

Though she hardly considered herself an equestrian master, it did not take much to sense the nervousness overcoming Sonowin. If Jessilynn were honest with herself, she felt it, too.

Up ahead loomed the Stonewood Forest, newfound home of both Quellan and Dezren elves. They had come together after their homes in the east were ruined by Thulos's war demons. Once the wars ended, she'd heard rumors of supposed attempts to return to Quellassar and rebuild it from the ruins, but so far as she knew, they remained only words and dreams.

The elves, they were so few, and now they were one fewer.

Just go to the forest's edge, Aurelia had told her before she departed. *Their scouts will find you in time, so do not be impatient. Let them bring you within, and do not be intimidated. In this, you are both Ashhur's and humanity's representative. Your grief is valid. It belongs with them among the trees.*

Jessilynn clung to those words as she and Sonowin skirted

the edge of the forest, the little cart rattling behind them. They were long past any road or path, not since she continued on past Ashhur's Sanctuary. She had stopped and spent a single night there, listening to the few remaining priests tell the story of their former leader, Bernard. Of his dreams. Of his warnings. Of his sacrifice at the Bloodbrick.

Jessilynn had listened to it all, tired and emotionally drained. In a different time, hearing how the priest had struck down Queen Loreina might have filled her with a sense of fear-tinged awe, and reinforce her belief that the righteous would always win out over the cowardly and selfish. Now, she knew only that Bernard was dead, along with soldiers, retainers, advisers, and the Queen herself. Slain lives, all for the two brother gods' game.

You put an end to it, she told herself then. *His love remains, but it is for us as his children, not his warriors.*

A hard thought to keep when the world referred to her as the Arrow of Ashhur, but she clung to it nonetheless.

"Halt."

The voice wrenched Jessilynn from her thoughts. She leaned back in her saddle and looked to the trees. A young elf, or at least one who looked young to her human eyes, leaned against one of the dark trunks. Dressed for war, his silver chainmail sparkling in the light of the setting sun. A bow was strapped to his back, and at his hip, a long sword. His auburn hair was long and flowing, his smile handsome but uninviting. Or perhaps that was just her reading into the harsh tone of his voice.

"You ride a horse that should never be ridden by humans," the elf said. He tilted his head to one side. "I pray you explain yourself quickly, lest I think you enslaved that majestic creature."

"Sonowin would let no one ride her that was not welcome," Jessilynn said, keeping Aurelia's words in mind. If she backed down to their arrogance or challenges, she might not be granted the audience she desired.

The elf looked to the cart, and all life faded from his emerald eyes.

"Then pray tell me, woman, whose body do you bring wrapped in corpse linens?"

She stood tall. "Dieredon Sinistel, Scoutmaster for the Quellan elves," she announced, and braced for his reaction.

Though she had anticipated some sort of anger or denial, she was shocked by the speed in which the young elf readied his bow. Before she could even blink, an arrow was nocked and aimed at her forehead.

"The greatest among us," he said, his words trembling with rage. "Tell me how he died, woman."

She refused to cower before the arrow. "He was slain by a spear in combat, thrown in the final assault upon Mordeina by one of the fallen."

The drawstring tightened further. The elf's green eyes shimmered with hate.

"He died fighting for humanity, then," he said. "He died fighting for *you*."

Jessilynn had her armor, but it would do no good with her head exposed. She knew the lethal aim of an elven bow. There would be no stopping this. If he released that string, she would be dead. With no other recourse, she glared back at him, meeting his challenge.

"I am Jessilynn, loyal Paladin of Ashhur and ambassador of Mordan. I have brought Dieredon to be mourned and buried. I did not come to be insulted, nor blamed for the death of a dear friend."

"Friend?" the elf asked. "You would dare call him *friend?*"

This was it. That hate. That rage. There would be no defusing it, even if it meant sparking conflict with Mordan. Whoever this elf was, looking into those eyes...it reminded her of the fallen, and the comparison frightened and sickened her in equal measure.

"Cyth!" a voice thundered from the forest. A wrinkled elf emerged, robed in green silks, his long hair braided and his eyes shining a vibrant gold. Jessilynn was shocked to see an elf so visibly marked by age. Just how old was he?

Two more elves exited the forest with him, and they seemed nervous as they watched the exchange, their hands resting on the hilts of their swords.

"Elder," the young elf said, refusing to lower his bow. "Have you come to deny me my revenge?"

"And would you feign ignorance to justify actions born of hurt and pain?" the elder snapped right back. "This woman did not kill Dieredon. How then could you take revenge upon her?"

Cyth slowly lowered his bow. He said something in elvish, then sneered at Jessilynn.

"Humanity's guilt runs deep," he said, switching back to the human tongue. "And you are far too willing to ignore those depths, mentor."

The old elf hardly looked impressed. He pointed and said something in elvish to those with him. They nodded and made for the cart, unhooking it from Sonowin so they might pull it instead. As for Cyth, he vanished back into the woods, and Jessilynn was glad to see him gone.

Far more welcoming was the old elf, who approached Jessilynn while offering his hands.

"My name is Elydien Marosi," he said. "Come with me, paladin, and visit the quaint beginnings of a city we have built within the Stonewood."

The new elven city was certainly quaint, but there was no doubting the care they had taken in building their homes. The trees were not sturdy enough to form towering canopies, and so they built around them—thin, elongated structures rising multiple floors that curled and shifted so they need not cut down the trunks. Their rooftops were sharp and slanted, their doorways decorated with all manner of carvings, though most were of either animals, or the goddess Celestia's four-pointed star.

Elydien guided her to one of the smaller homes, cozy and well-furnished within. A fire burned in a hearth to one side. Paintings of beautiful landscapes covered the walls, and she was strangely delighted to recognize one of them, the Kinel River that she and Dieredon had flown over while traveling across eastern Dezrel atop Sonowin.

That memory brought along a fresh wave of sorrow, realizing that such a journey would never happen again.

"Please, make yourself comfortable," Elydien said, still at the door. "I must speak with my brethren, for there is much to do before nightfall."

He left her alone in the den, and so she took a seat beside the hearth. The chair was padded and surprisingly comfortable. Letting out a soft groan, she let her body settle, all too happy to rest her road-weary muscles and let the warmth of the fire wash over her. Her eyes closed, and the minutes passed in silence. It was so still and peaceful that Jessilynn dozed off.

When the door opened she jerked awake, feeling out of sorts as she got back to her feet. It was Elydien again, looking tired but pleased.

"The arrangements are made," he said. "Given the state of the body, we could not afford patience."

"I'm sorry," Jessilynn said. "We could have arrived sooner if we flew, but I'd have had to carry...him, and I didn't...I wasn't..."

"Hush now," he said. "We hold you no ill will, nor cast you any blame. If Sonowin wished to arrive here sooner, then you would have. I suspect she also needed her time to grieve."

There was no doubting the love the horse had felt for her master, but before Jessilynn could remark on it, the door burst open and a furious Cyth stormed inside. He made straight for Elydien, and shouted as if Jessilynn were not even there.

"I can scarcely believe what I have heard," he exclaimed. "I know your heart is soft, elder, but your mind cannot be so brittle as to think this...this *insult* acceptable." He gestured toward Jessilynn. "She does not belong at his pyre, and by the goddess, she most certainly does not deserve the right to *speak*."

The kindly elder crossed his arms, and there was something about his tone that was simultaneously condescending and sympathetic.

"Would you argue Jessilynn's grief false? Or would you claim that a student does not deserve to say goodbye to her former master?"

"Student?" Cyth said. "For the Quellan Scoutmaster to take a human as a student is—"

"Is what?" Elydien interrupted. "Out with it, young one. Let me hear you speak from one side of your mouth of your respect for Dieredon, and then from the other, mock his decisions and insult those he cared for."

Cyth retreated a step, and when he next spoke it was with a far calmer tone.

"These starlight mournings are one of our most deeply held traditions," he said. "Dieredon spent years protecting humanity, and now he has given his life, all for their wretched war that has torn Dezrel asunder. Can we not at least let his soul return to the stars free of their presence?"

Elydien put his hand on Cyth's shoulder.

"In his own way, Dieredon cared for humanity, and for the fate they would carve for themselves. Let one be there to represent their kind as the pyre's flames rise."

Cyth glared once more at Jessilynn, then shook his head.

"This is a mistake," he said. "But I see there is no hope in opening your eyes to it."

He stormed out of the home and slammed the door shut behind him.

Elydien let out a long, burdened sigh.

"The youthful so often confuse passion with righteousness," he said. "To surrender to every emotion, if only to feel it blaze hotter within you, is a reckless folly." He shook his head. "But think not on him. This night belongs to Dieredon. If you would allow me a moment, I must go change into more regal garments for the funeral rites."

"And when will that be?" she asked.

He smiled at her. "Tonight, beneath the stars."

The rite was performed in a clearing deep in the heart of the Stonewood Forest. Several dozen elves were in attendance, a paltry number compared to what a hero like Dieredon deserved. The ground had been smoothed out, all trees cut and their stumps removed. Painted stones formed circular patterns throughout the clearing, forming windows into their past.

In the center waited a pyre nearly as tall as Jessilynn. A torch burned in a silver holder attached to the pyre, its threads twisted to look like a curling tree branch. Dieredon's body lay in the heart of the stacked wood, his previous wrappings replaced with green cloth edged with gold.

Chairs formed a semicircle facing the pyre. Jessilynn took her seat beside Elydien near the front, and she felt a pang of guilt. Half these chairs were old, the others clearly of newer construction. How many of those original chairs had been lost when they fled the ruins of Dezerea? How many more of the elves' possessions had been destroyed by the fires of the war demons in the east? The

Quellan and the Dezren were one now, united out of necessity, for it seemed the world of Dezrel was determined to crush their numbers into nothing.

The funeral began, strangely quiet and peaceful. Elves walked up to the pyre, put a hand on Dieredon's body, and spoke. Some told of encounters with the slain Scoutmaster, moments they had shared. Others told stories of the elf's legendary deeds, from destroying Velixar after the battle of Woodhaven to helming Dezrel's defense against the war god, Thulos. They were familiar stories, but Jessilynn felt it joyous to hear them from the lips of those who knew him.

The night deepened, and the stars shone all the brighter. When it seemed there was no one left to speak, Elydien patted Jessilynn's knee and then stood. At first he spoke elvish as he took his place before the pyre, but then switched to the human tongue.

"Though the sharing and celebration of Dieredon's life should be ceaseless, the hour draws late, and the moment of grieving must come to an end. Jessilynn, Paladin of Ashhur, come share your remembrance."

Elydien stepped away while gesturing for her to take his place. If only she could. It felt like her stomach was filled with lead and her feet nailed to the stone.

Help me out, Ashhur, she prayed, and found the strength to stand up. The eyes of the crowd looked upon her, so very many not kind or loving. She was unwanted. Unwelcome. Just like Dieredon had been unwanted in so many places, and yet he went anyway. It made her crack a smile.

"I knew Dieredon for but a fleeting time," she said, putting her hand upon the pyre as the others had done. "For me, it was a year. For you, the blink of an eye. But even in such a time, he forever changed me. When I was uncertain, he was there to teach me. When I was lost, he was there to guide me. When I lacked confidence, he lent me his own. When my order summoned him, they wished for him to teach me the bow, but at his side, and I learned so much more than how to pull a drawstring."

Though she had grieved his loss for many lonely nights on her travels here, she felt herself struck anew, and shocked by the power. The memories of his final words, carved into her soul. Her fingers tightened about the kindling, bits of twig biting into her

Legacy of the Watcher

hand.

"'A perfect student', he called me," she said. "A perfect student, as he lay bleeding on the steps of Mordeina's castle. As if that could be true. As if a perfect student would be helpless to stop his bleeding. As if a perfect student would…would…"

They didn't know. None of them. She was terrified to tell them, but here before this solemn power, she would reveal the truth.

"He died because of me," she said. "He died saving me. I fell, and he caught me, but his attention, it was distracted. He didn't see the spear. It…it knocked him from Sonowin's saddle. Even then, he might have lived, but Ashhur, my prayers, I couldn't heal him. I'm sorry, all of you, I could not heal him. I could not save him. I could only hold him, hold him as he died, as he called me is 'perfect student'…"

She was crying. She was rambling. She barely realized where she was anymore, overcome by so many memories of flying over the beautiful landscape of Dezrel, her arms wrapped around Dieredon's waist as he guided Sonowin to their next destination. Blinking away tears, she looked to these guarded faces, these stars, and felt alone, so alone.

And then she wasn't. Elydien was with her beside the pyre, his arms wrapping around her. Her face buried into the soft fabric of his robe, wetting it with her tears.

"Grieve, my child," he said, his deep voice carrying across the clearing. "Grieve, as we all grieve, and know that your guilt, blame, and doubts shall be cleansed by the pyre."

The sound of wood scraping upon stone caused Elydien to withdraw. Free of him, she saw Cyth near the back of the crowd. He stood from his chair, his hands shaking at his sides. He said nothing, only glared at the pair with a look most vile for such a solemn occasion. Wordlessly, he turned and exited the clearing. Several other elves followed him, silent in their protest. Others muttered, and for once the glares and disapproving remarks were not reserved for Jessilynn alone.

Elydien gently separated himself from Jessilynn and moved to the pyre. When he lifted the burning torch from its ornate perch, those who remained in audience stood and lifted their hands toward the heavens. Likewise, Elydien raised the torch. Words flowed from his lips in the elvish tongue, few of which Jessilynn understood beyond the name of the goddess. When Elydien finished, he paused, and then clearly for her benefit, repeated himself once more.

"Look upon us, mother goddess. Look upon us, on our sorrow, and lend us your grace. We mourn what was lost, even as you rejoice. What was love to us is now dust. In your arms, he goes. Cherish him, and forgive us our tears as we light the pyre."

Elydien lowered the torch. The pyre caught fire with ease, first the kindling, then the thicker logs near the bottom. It strangely burned with a lavender smoke, and when the faintest wind blew it her way, she smelled only flowers and honey.

The smoke lifted to the stars, as did the voices of several elves, a low, humming song that surely would have sent her back into tears had she known the words. Jessilynn stood before the pyre, awkward and tired. She dreaded the ride back to Mordeina, and that was assuming Sonowin remained with her. In no way did she wish to walk all that way.

Elydien dropped the torch into the center of the blaze consuming Dieredon's body, and his gaze lifted to the stars.

"Celestia knows, we have suffered much by the hands of others," he said softly. "Is it over at last, paladin? Have the brother gods ceased their war?"

A single memory flashed through Jessilynn's mind, of the great barrage of arrows leveling the city of Devlimar. The words of Celestia came to her, spoken through her two daughters, Tessanna and Mira, as they unleashed their fury.

"No more false balance," Jessilynn repeated. "No more wars. Peace, if humanity may keep it." She turned to Elydien. "That was the promise the goddess made to us, at the hour of Devlimar's destruction. I hold to it, Elydien, and I will do all in my power to ensure others hold to it, too. Dezrel has seen enough of war. For once, let us know peace."

"Peace," Elydien said, and he breathed in the smoke of Dieredon's pyre. "We have seen it so little, paladin, I fear I would not recognize its face. This world's cruelty seems to loathe its presence. It is the hope of dreamers and fools, but tonight, let us be fools. Let us all dream."

More elves joined in the song as the pyre burned to embers, all that was Dieredon now reduced to fire and ash. Jessilynn closed her eyes and let the heat of it seep into her.

"Peace," she whispered, wanting to believe it, to cherish it. If only she could unsee the hatred in Cyth's eyes.

2
TARLAK

The year 605 LA

If there was anything Tarlak Eschaton was certain about, it was that he could not stand any more whining from a certain full grown half-orc father during their travels upon the main road from Mordan to Ker.

"Why don't you just make a portal?" Tarlak said, echoing Harruq Tun's whining right back to his face. "Why not snap your fingers and make me some food? Would you like me to give you a massage too, buddy? Some ethereal hands to rub the callouses on your feet?"

They were gathered around a campfire, settling down for the night. Harruq sat on the other side of the fire, his wife snuggled against him. Not far away, Aubrienna and Gregory chased after the glow of fireflies.

"Could you?" Harruq asked, arcing an eyebrow. "That sounds pretty neat, actually."

Tarlak pulled his pointy hat off his head and set it beside him on the grass. The yellow was a stark contrast to the healthy spring green.

"No," he said. "I cannot. You want a foot rub, there's an elf you should be asking instead."

"This elf has sores on her own feet, thank you very much," Aurelia said. Tarlak somehow found that hard to believe. Travel did not affect the elf like it did others. She wore a blue dress sewn in Mordeina, with a sharp low cut along the front, as was currently in fashion. The garb was decidedly unfit for long travel, and yet she looked immaculate, her auburn hair hardly out of place and not a thread unwoven. Her boots were sturdier than one would expect in a court though, the thick leather dyed a darker blue. Perhaps there was a bit of hidden practicality there after all. Or maybe she was cheating and using magic. Tarlak wouldn't put it past the sneaky elf.

Harruq poked her side.

"I get that Tarlak loves to complain," he told her. "But you've opened portals for us to farther locations than Angkar. All this travel seems…unnecessary."

Tarlak groaned. "May I remind you we were fleeing an army of war demons at the time?"

"Exactly," Harruq countered. "You'd have a lot more time now. No rush. No threat of death. I don't get the refusal."

Tarlak wondered why, if the half-orc was so bent on teleporting about instead of walking, he didn't bring this measure up *before* they had traveled some hundred miles from Mordeina and crossed the Corinth River into Ker on their way to its capital city of Angkar. Perhaps he hadn't thought the journey would bother him so much as it did, now that the days stretched long and the tedium settled in. It was a feeling Tarlak shared, not that he'd dare let Harruq know.

"The point of this entire trip is to forge a connection between our two nations," Tarlak said, lecturing as if he were addressing a toddler. "That means our whole caravan lumbers along, stopping at every tiny village so they can gawk at Gregory, mumble about how big the child prince has gotten, and give everyone in Ker weeks of warning before we show up in Angkar to sign Aurelia's precious peace treaty."

"It's not *my* peace treaty," the elf protested.

Tarlak laughed at her protest. "Try telling that to, oh, the rest of the world."

Aurelia pushed away from her husband and leaned closer to the fire. Its warm light washed over her fair and delicate features so that she was all the more beautiful in the fading light. Tarlak had to admit, for the thousandth time, that Harruq was a lucky bastard for her to have ever given him the time of day.

"I've spent most of my time by Gregory's side," she said, her jovial tone hardening into seriousness. "Tarlak, you've been more free to go about during our visits and meetings. What do you believe? Will this work? Or is this treaty a fool's hope?"

Tarlak sighed. Mordan had been devastated by the Night of Black Wings and the ensuing war against the fallen. The southern nation of Ker had endured far, far better due to abstaining from the conflict. Yes, there were the raids from orcs across the rivers from the east, but those had lessened the past few years with the war demons' defeat. Their only true loss had been the death of their queen, Loreina, at the hands of Ashhur's priest, Bernard Ulath. It had taken two years for the power vacuum to be settled, and a fair amount of blood shed between rivals vying for power.

When the dust settled, Queen Brynn Sloane emerged the victor, establishing rule over Angkar first and then spreading outward. In the years that followed, Aurelia had been insistent they sign an official peace treaty with the new queen. Mordan was weak, her army broken, and many of her people now refugees making new lives for themselves in Ker. If Queen Brynn looked north with a lust for power in her heart, Dezrel would face yet another war.

After years of letters, Aurelia's hard work paid off. The nobles of Mordan, many of them newly appointed by Harruq himself, agreed to honor all existing borders for two decades, and the new queen consented to make no attempts to force back the refugees who did not wish to return to Mordan. In repayment, Mordan would forsake all claims on the east. Given the flourishing trade between Angelport and Angkar, and reports of Ker sending out numerous expeditions to form tentative settlements across the Corinth, it seemed like the queen was all too happy to be allowed to fully expand without any real competition.

There was, however, one other condition, made to appease the elves rebuilding their civilization deep within the Stonewood Forest. Something Harruq still fumed about when the subject was broached, and agreed only at Aurelia's insistence…

"I'm not sure if what I've seen will make you feel better or worse," Tarlak said. "For many, we're the people who were enslaved to angels, and the name of Ashhur carries a strange weight now."

"We weren't enslaved," Harruq muttered.

"A point hard to argue after the Night of Black Wings," Tarlak said. "But in general, people seem happy to see us. I think overcoming opposition in Mordan was the far harder trick than anything here in Ker. Everyone is convinced a golden age is upon them, and there's already talk of re-establishing the nation of Omn as a vassal state. If you want my two copper bits, the real danger isn't now, but two decades from now when an even wealthier Ker owns three-fourths of Dezrel and starts looking to round up. And if that happens, I'll be way too old to make much of a—"

Legacy of the Watcher

Gregory and Aubrienna came barreling into him with full blown tackles, cutting off his words. He wrapped his arms around them both and laughed.

"What is this for?" he asked, surprised.

"Nothing," Aubrienna said, peering up at him with features as fair and beautiful as her mother's, only hiding far more mischief.

"Absolutely nothing," Gregory confirmed. "But...we were hoping you might make us another fire stick."

The parents on the other side of the fire shot Tarlak a look.

"They make it sound way scarier than it is!" he insisted, and then returned his attention to the kids. "Did you bring me what I need?"

The pair stepped back, and in answer, Gregory held out a stick he'd been hiding behind his back. Tarlak accept it, ignored another glare from Harruq, and waved his hands over the top. Words of magic flowed from his lips, and all at once one end of the stick burst into flame. Sparks showered from the tip, flashing all sorts of colors. He handed the stick to Gregory, who slashed it twice at Aubrienna as if wielding a sword. She shrieked, and then together the pair raced back off into the field.

"It won't be long until she's able to cast that spell herself," Tarlak said, watching the kids go.

"I pray she need not learn more than that," Aurelia said. She snuggled against Harruq. Tarlak kept his mouth shut. He knew her worries, confided to him over the years as Aubby grew older. The young girl would be expected to carry on the Thyne legacy, some of the most powerful magic casters in all of elven history. It was a legacy that had been thrust upon Aurelia against her wishes when her parents died upon the Bloodbrick, and one she held no desire to force upon her own daughter.

"Give her time," Harruq said, watching them play. "Let her make her choice. She'll be casting spells long before any of us are ready. I don't want to imagine what I'll do five years from now when she's angry at me *and* able to throw a fireball from her fingertips."

"Ah, the perils of being a parent," Tarlak said, and he laughed. "Thank Ashhur I'll be forever spared that trauma. I just get to be the uncle in yellow. It's a much safer role."

Harruq waved dismissively at him and rose to his feet. "I'm going to bed. Got a long march ahead of me tomorrow, after all, since someone thinks we should keep stopping and saying hello to every little village we meet."

"Ignore him, he enjoys the attention being the Godslayer earns," Aurelia said, standing with him. "It's his role as steward that leaves him so miserable."

"Good night to the both of you then," Tarlak said. "I'll keep an eye on Gregory and Aubby, and make sure they don't stay up too late."

"Like it matters for them," Harruq grumbled as they left the fire. "*They* get to ride in the fancy wagon, unlike *me*, who has to walk..."

Tarlak laughed in the ensuing silence after their departure. Sometimes it seemed the half-orc was getting less mature over time, not more. An influence of the children, perhaps? Or maybe, with the angels gone and peace settling over Dezrel, he was finally allowed a chance to relax and be his dumb immature self?

Tarlak settled closer to the fire for its comforting warmth, shifted a bit, and propped his chin on his hands to watch the two children play. Aubrienna had taken over the fire stick once it was halfway burned, and she waved it all about as if a conductor...or a spellcaster. The sparks lit up her face, illuminating her laugh.

You've both been through enough, Tarlak thought. *Have a laugh. That's the real reason we're coming south. To give you two a chance at peace.*

The pair were inseparable lately, and more than just the immediate family had begun to notice. Harruq shot down every rumor he heard, but there was no stopping it. It was good, though, thought Tarlak as he watched the sparks fly. It would make the announcement easier on them, and maybe, just maybe, not ruin the friendship they'd developed over the years.

The other condition of the agreement was an arranged betrothal between Aubrienna and Gregory. A uniting bond between elf and man, meant to begin the healing process for the destruction caused by King Baedan so many years ago.

Aubrienna held the fire stick directly above her head, and as the two stared up at it, sparks showered down on them, landing on their faces and hair. They howled, half with delight, half with panic, as they brushed at their hair, fearful it would catch flame.

"To our future king and queen," Tarlak said, and toasted the emptiness about him. "May Ashhur save us all."

3
THREN

Thren walked the early morning streets of Angkar with a spring in his step and a scarf around his neck to hide his scars. Not even the smell of fish wafting in from the harbor could dampen his mood. As much as he hated to admit it, his favorite day of the year had come back around: Angkar's tournament of pride.

It was still a few hours from starting, but already several dozen men and women gathered at the entrance to the stadium. For most of the year, it was a wide dirt clearing along the northern outskirts of the city, filled with tents and tables where merchants could hawk their wares. But for the tournament, the tents were cleared, the tables removed, and rows of benches set up for a crowd of hundreds.

Registration was managed by the same man every year, a likable fellow, his hair fluffy and white where it wasn't balding, which was everywhere above his ears. His clothes were plain but for his hat, at one point its leather brilliantly painted with a mix of reds, yellows, and blues, but now faded. Four feathers drooped from the top. His name was Boris, and some two decades back he had won the tournament of pride, and that prized hat had been his reward.

"Hey there, Gray," Boris said, waving him over once a trio of young men in armor finished. 'Gray' was the named Thren had taken as his alias upon fleeing Veldaren. No last name. Just Gray.

Boris sat at a table, inkwell on one side, a few pieces of parchment on the other. Beside him was a wood post. Nailed to it was the tournament bracket, upon which a young man barely able to grow fuzz on his chin would dutifully write the names Boris told him, steadily filling it out.

"How goes the signings?" Thren asked.

"Even more than last year. I feared you might lose your spot, assuming you even wanted one."

Thren grinned at him and reached for the quill.

"You know I can't miss my chance to live out my glory days."

Those glory days, so far as Boris knew, were when 'Gray' had been a soldier of Neldar. It was a convenient enough explanation as to why Thren was skilled in the use of the two swords he kept forever strapped to his waist.

Boris dipped the quill in ink and gave it to Thren, along with a sheet of paper already bearing dozens of signatures. It was a vow to fight fairly, fight honorably, and make no attempt to harm your opponent beyond what was necessary to achieve victory. The tournament was not to the death, after all.

Thren signed his alias below the others. Every year he entered the tournament not with hopes of winning, but for a bit of entertainment. He also bet on himself, scoring an easy bag of coin to take home after winning a few rounds before throwing a fight. He didn't want to get noticed, after all, and the crowd was usually happy to cheer for an old dog surprising a few upstarts.

"I can't say I blame you," Boris said, taking back the quill. "Every year I see these young men strapping on their armor and wish I could be among them. Alas, these old bones aren't good for much more than sitting and eating."

"At least you excel at both, do you not?" Thren asked, earning a laugh. He handed over his two swords so the man could inspect them and ensure they were properly blunted for safety.

"Boy, add Gray to the bracket," Boris shouted when satisfied, and the assistant quickly obliged. Thren accepted his swords back, then wandered toward the bracket, passing through fighters eager to prove the worth of their training. They were the youngest, their formative years after the Gods' Wars were over and Queen Loreina's invasion had failed miserably. They knew only peace, or had fought a few bandits their wealthy families had sent them after while accompanied by house guards at worst. Fancy armor, poorly tested in battle.

The older men and women were the true competitors, and they gave Thren either wary looks or respectful nods when they saw him. Thren had fought many of them in the prior tournaments, and learned a few of their names and faces. There were soldiers who fought in the Gods' War and mercenaries who faced the occasional raiding party of orcs that crossed the rivers into the west. These challengers had lived through the Night of Black Wings. They knew what it meant to fight for survival.

"Good luck today," one of them said, a large man named Misha whose smile and eyes painfully reminded Thren of his childhood friend, Grayson. "It's always a treat watching you beat the arrogance out of some young noble with more money than sense."

Thren answered with a curt nod, not wishing to talk, only scan the bracket for names. He recognized multiple nobles, as expected, and a few mercenaries and soldiers from the year prior. One specific name caught his eye and he froze, every muscle in his body tightening. One name. One entry.

Erin Felhorn.

"Erin?" he whispered. His hands curled into fists. Was this a joke? A mockery? Thren had given himself the Felhorn name when he was little more than a homeless and hungry mongrel pretending at having a real future. His wife was dead, murdered by the leader of the Scorpion Guild. His first child, Randith, died the night his war against the Trifect began, killed by his only other child, Aaron. The man who became Haern the King's Watcher, savior of Veldaren and conqueror of the Darkhand.

Aaron Felhorn, who died saving the life of some elf as Karak's fanatics conquered Mordeina. There were no more Felhorns. Thren was the last. He glared at the name, whatever simple pleasure he'd anticipated no longer on his mind. He found his own name, then compared it to Erin's.

Three rounds. He'd need to win three rounds to face her. If she was truly good enough to make it that far. Given her chosen name, she damn well better be.

His hand itched for his swords. "So be it," he whispered.

⚜

The tournament of pride was hardly the grandest Thren had witnessed. The Trifect used to hold larger when they held their Kensgold, and the far larger capital of Mordeina hosted yearly feasts that lasted a full week, and was full of jousting and archery competitions along with the swordplay. The tournament here in Angkar had started out decades ago funded by merchants, who would then hire the various winners to protect their cargo as they sailed east or took the roads north. A smaller affair, and focused on swordplay, even as Queen Sloane took over and made it a matter of civic pride.

About a thousand spectators could watch the proceedings if crammed together uncomfortably, which appeared to be the case. As usual, a segment was cleared of benches for the entrants to gather and watch the fights. Thren mingled among them, scanning faces and seeing remarkably few new from the year prior. More maddening, not a one went by the name 'Erin', at least not that he overheard.

Where are you? he wondered.

Thren tapped his foot, his arms crossed and his hands resting atop the hilts of his swords. His first match was scheduled after Erin's, but the both of them would be near the last to go in this first round. The pomp and circumstance didn't normally bother him, but now he hated every delay as some noble paced about the center of the arena rambling about the tournament's history and the supposed great deeds of prior winners.

Thren's eyes narrowed when he gazed upon the far side, where the wealthy and noble were seated. Not cramped elbow to elbow like the unwashed masses, though they were still forced to endure the humiliation of sitting on benches. One woman among them stole Thren's attention.

She was striking as always, her tanned skin looking almost golden in the morning sunlight. Her dark hair was cut short, and unlike the dresses of the other noble ladies, she wore a fine pair of black trousers and a lavender blouse. She was Zusa, long rumored to be Alyssa Gemcroft's lover, rumors confirmed once the two women were wed some years after they'd fled Veldaren to start a life in Angelport. A life free of the influence of people like Thren.

And then the world ended, and they were left trapped against the sea as demons and orcs ravaged the east. Yet they somehow survived, and some five years ago, Zusa and her adopted son Nathaniel arrived at the docks of Angkar to proudly announce Angelport's freedom and the defeat of the war demon that led the orc forces.

It'd been cause of much celebration, and over the years since, the beaten and battered people of the Ramere had slowly spread out from Angelport to the lands beyond as the orcs retreated northward. Yet Zusa kept her family in Angkar. Perhaps there was still more wealth to be made in the shadow of the angels' departure than in rebuilding the broken kingdoms of the east.

Thren had avoided Zusa easily enough. He lived a secluded life, his small home and meager spendings hiding the significant amount of gold he still possessed. Not once since her arrival had the woman attended a tournament of pride, yet now she was here. He frowned and scratched at the scarf around his neck. Should he don a disguise? He tried to do the math in his mind. It had been...fifteen years since he last saw her, perhaps longer. Would she recognize him, a man long believed to be dead?

Would it even matter if she did? he wondered. Veldaren was rubble. The entire east was still in shambles. The guilds in Mordan had crumbled beneath the ire of the angels. If people learned he'd survived, would anything change? Would anyone even *remember?*

That bitter thought swirled around his belly as the first duel began. Boris hurried out to a cheer of the crowd, for he would be the judge. Blunted swords were offered to the first two contestants, who did not yet possess weapons of their own. A man and a woman, both in their early twenties. They dueled to the crowd's delight. Their moves had too many flourishes, their attacks intermittent with pauses that would get them killed in true battle.

Thren barely watched. He couldn't shake that nagging thought. His entire legacy, left in his son's care...all his accomplishments...what did it even matter, when the gods broke the world?

The next match started, just as dull as the first. He watched Zusa more than he did the fight. She looked as bored as he was. Perhaps forced to attend? Her adopted son was at her right, dressed smartly and befitting his wealth. A handsome lad, and constantly awash in rumors of how he was going to marry into this or that noble family. At Zusa's left was some waif of a girl Thren did not recognize, constantly chatting away with Zusa. He suspected her a handmaiden, one who had been with the family for a long time given her relaxed familiarity.

He could approach Zusa, Thren realized. Once revealed as himself, she would eagerly grant him a seat, if only out of curiosity. The temptation was far stronger than he'd anticipated. They could talk of the past, of the guilds, and of his son. Aaron had been friends with her, he knew. They'd worked together when the Darkhand brought his Sun Guild to the east with aims to conquer Veldaren.

Thren shook his head and abandoned the idea.

"Is this how lonely you've become?" he muttered quietly to himself.

Another match, equally dull. Boris marched out to announce the next, and Thren's excitement heightened. Finally, he would see this Felhorn impostor in action.

"Geoff Portwright!" Boris shouted, throwing all his energy into the call. He had been a showman as a fighter, and still a showman in his twilight years. The man standing beside Thren, a burly sort wearing chainmail, clapped his hands and stepped out. He was in charge of the house guard for a noble family. Well-trained, and often a legitimate competitor for the win.

"Erin Felhorn!"

Thren's entire world came to a halt the moment the girl he had thought was a handmaiden stood up, waved to Zusa, and then bounded down the benches two at a time to enter the arena.

"What?" he asked, and was not alone. Dozens in the crowd expressed similar confusion. Though there were no age limits to the tournament of pride, the unofficial tradition was that no one could enter until their seventeenth year. If this girl had reached it, it was only just. Geoff towered over her, and he shrugged at the crowd as if he were equally perplexed.

But Thren's confusion was not the same as the crowd's. He cared not for her age. It was her dress, and her weapons. Dark gray cloth from head to toe. Her cloak had a hood attached, and she pulled it up and over her head. That cloak…it was split in three at the sides, allowing easy movement of her hands when wielding her pair of sabers.

Thren looked back from her to Zusa and saw the similarity instantly. Not a handmaiden. Shared blood. A child. One dressed exactly as the Watcher had, wielding the same weapons. A girl who had assumed the Felhorn name.

Erin.

Aaron.

"You didn't," he whispered. He had believed her and his son to be friends. Perhaps they were far more than that.

"Don't dismiss our little challenger just yet," Boris shouted to the crowd as he paced between the pair. "I put her through her paces myself, and she's a quick little tart. Give her an extra cheer, would you? We love seeing new blood in the arena at the tournament of pride!"

Erin drew her sabers. They were dulled for the tournament. No loaned weaponry for her. Her gaze was fierce, her attention locked on her foe without a care to the smattering of claps and cheers.

Boris turned to Geoff, and he said something the crowd could not hear, but Thren read the words on his lips.

Go easy on her.

Thren glanced toward Zusa. Some noble fool was chatting away in the seat behind her, and though she pretended to listen and nodded along, her eyes never left Erin...never left her daughter.

Thren's jaw locked tight.

He looked back to the arena. Geoff wielded his sword in both hands, and between his weapon and his taller stature, his reach was beyond hers by almost two feet. A brutal disadvantage, and it would spell doom for any equally-skilled combatant.

Thren studied the way Erin bounced on her toes, the sharpness of her attention, and the lack of nerves at having so many watching her for the first time. His throat tightened.

"Prove it," he whispered. "Show me you're worthy of that name."

The rules were simple. If you struck your foe with either the tip or the flat edge of a blade, you scored a point. If you knocked your opponent on their ass, you scored two points. The first to three won. Boris would be the judge, and settle any disputes over who struck first.

The older man lifted his hand, glanced at both contestants, and then dropped it low.

"Begin!"

Geoff sauntered closer, his sword up and at the ready. Even though he seemed unimpressed, he did not let his guard down for an easy hit. Thren had battled him two years prior and purposefully thrown the fight. The man was strong, and he knew how to use his advantage of reach. It hadn't been hard to pretend to be overwhelmed.

Erin remained in place, bouncing lightly on her feet. Geoff seemed almost confused, and he shrugged to the crowd to show it. Up came his sword.

"I don't know who you bribed for a spot in our

tournament," he said, seemingly to her but projecting his voice so all the arena heard. "But they were a fool. I'll try not to break anything, girl."

Down came the sword. Erin hopped left, her cloak rippling from both her movement and the wind of his weapon's passage. Upon landing she continued bouncing on her toes. Her placid expression never changed.

"A quick one," Geoff said. "Is that your plan, run about until I tire?"

Another swing. Another hop to the side.

"You'll tire before me, girl. It takes far less to swing this sword than for you to scamper."

A third swing, this time deceptively angled. His weapon started high but sliced sideways so it would catch her waist and not her shoulder. He was hoping to intercept her dodge, and there was no hesitance to his swing. If it connected, it would certainly break ribs. Thren held his breath.

Erin dropped into a roll the same direction the swing came from, the larger weapon slicing harmlessly above her. He kicked at her as she ended the roll, for his sword, swung with such strength, had far too much momentum to halt in time to block. Erin bounded out of the roll, over his kick, and into the air. Her feet were not even on the ground when her twin dulled sabers thrusted into the larger man's gut.

"One point for the newcomer!" Boris shouted, and there was no hiding the surprise in his voice.

Erin landed, paced out a distance between her foe, and turned around. Her calm expression remained, but there was a crack in the facade, one Thren wondered if anyone else had seen. The faintest hint of a grin as Erin turned around and heard the point call.

You have speed, he thought. *You can read basic patterns. But he will be ready now. See you as an equal.*

Geoff pulled his arms back, elbows cocked and sword ready for a thrust. All traces of good humor were gone from him. His pride was wounded. He'd be dangerous now, blunted weapon or otherwise.

Boris lifted his arm, then dropped it low.

Geoff barreled toward the girl, determined to show she was

not the only one capable of speed. His sword thrust in and out, quick hits like vipers despite his weapon's size. Erin batted them aside each time, but the superior reach forced her to retreat. Geoff pressed the advantage, getting closer, closer, denying her a chance to retaliate.

At last, Erin stopped retreating, parried another thrust aside, and attempted to score a hit with her own thrust. The problem was, they were much too close, and Geoff was ready. He slammed his hip against her, finally able to use his size to his advantage. Erin tumbled, and she dropped one of her sabers so she might use the hand to balance herself instead. Dirt flew as she skidded to a halt, her lone sword up and ready. Geoff was already thrusting, and she had to arch her back to avoid it, her sword barely parrying it high.

When he pulled the sword back, she followed in its shadow. Despite having lost a weapon, she took the offensive. Her first slash at his chest missed by a hair's width, and when he retreated a step and swung his sword wide, Thren saw nowhere for her to flee.

And so she blocked it instead. She flung her sword in the way, pressed her other arm against the flat edge to help brace it, and took the hit. Her feet left trails in the dirt, but she held.

She's strong, thought Thren. *Much stronger than she looks. Her cloaks hide muscle.*

From the corner of his eye, he saw Zusa lean forward, her chin resting on her hands as Erin withstood the blow.

What training have you given her? he wondered. *What Abyss have you put her through in the forsaken east?*

Erin might have held through the blow, but the toll was too much. Geoff closed the distance between them, feinting a withdrawal of his sword only to swing yet again. He caught Erin retreating, the flat edge smacking across her right arm.

"One!" Boris shouted, pointing to Geoff. Erin retrieved her lost saber and twirled both in her hands. Her look was iron. There was no hiding her disappointment.

"Have you nothing to say?" Geoff asked. When silence was his only reply, he shrugged. "If you insist. No disrespect meant, girl, but I got my pride."

He closed the space between them, just as he had before,

with quick in and out strikes...or at least, he tried to close the space. This time Erin weaved sideways at all times, keeping him slowly revolving around the arena. Her swords parried away the hits, and though his range kept her from attacking, she seemed in no hurry.

No, this time she looked like she was settling down and developing a feel for her opponent. Her parries grew more confident. Her feet danced faster, and Thren felt a strange sense of pride blooming in him as he watched Erin accurately predict more and more of Geoff's attacks.

Again she attempted the same maneuver, a sudden lunge inward after a parry to close the space. She needed within his reach, and doing so put her at risk. Geoff countered as he did before, flinging his body forward to overwhelm her with his superior strength and size. Thren clenched his hands into fists. She had been foolish to try to block a strike by her stronger foe. Would she replicate her earlier error?

And then he saw it, a half-second before Geoff did. As their weapons locked together, and his hip bashed into her, she lifted her left foot an inch off the ground.

Erin pirouetted with the hit, spinning with the grace of a dancer. Geoff, expecting some resistance, staggered past her on uneven footing. Her twirl continued, her weapons not so interlocked with his larger sword as it first seemed. Down they both came, one after the other, onto the man's back.

"Two!" Boris exclaimed as he gestured toward Erin.

Again the pair positioned opposite one another. The first hints of panic showed in the way Geoff kept unsteady on his feet and twitched when positioning his blade. He was unsure of the proper defenses now, or of how to use his superior strength to his advantage when his opponent was so fast. Thren's heart quickened, and again he saw that faint hint a grin.

"Strike fast," he whispered. "Your foe is weak. Go for the kill."

The moment Boris dropped his hand, Erin lunged. No more dodging, no more letting the larger combatant guide the fight. She leaped off her feet, her weapons already slashing. They bounced off his raised sword, but her momentum hardly slowed. The moment she landed she dug in her heels and reversed direction, her swords striking for his legs. Again Geoff blocked, a low sweep that should have easily batted her aside.

Instead she spun with the hit, dancing with perfect balance on one heel…and then she cartwheeled backward. Her foot struck his chin, and blood sprayed as he bit his tongue. Her feet barely touched ground before she was already lunging, both swords extending.

Her entire body shook with the exertion, her shoulders heaving with every deep breath, but those swords remained perfectly still as their tips pressed into the man's neck. Shocked silence filled the arena.

"Three," Erin said, the first time she'd spoken since leaving Zusa's side.

The crowd lost its mind. Cheers and claps greeted her, as did jeers to mock Geoff's loss. All throughout the crowd, coin changed hands from the gamblers, and by the looks on their faces, many had just lost sizable sums.

Thren fled the arena as fast as his legs could carry him. A bustling market was just beyond, every merchant there eager to sell to those on their way to watch the bloodsport. Thren dashed through the stalls, searching, searching…there, a clothier.

"Here," Thren said, dropping a handful of coins onto the merchant's counter without bothering to count them. He yanked a gray cloak off its hook and wrapped it about his neck. The merchant's eyes widened, but he was wise enough not to say a word, only pocket the money.

"A hood," Thren asked as the cloak wrapped about him. "Have you a hood?"

The clothier reached behind him into a bin and pulled out three.

"None match," he said. Thren grabbed a blue hood, pulled it over his head, and then sprinted back to the arena just in time for his name to be called.

"The old soldier, Gray."

Thren strode out to the center and sized up his foe, some whelp nearly a third his age, no doubt trained by the finest tutors in Ker. Thren barely saw his face, for his mind was locked on the future.

Three matches. Three victories until he could face his granddaughter in the center of the arena.

"Begin!"

Thren blocked the initial swing, closed the space between them in a step, and then slammed the boy across the forehead with the blunted edge of his other sword. His opponent's eyes crossed, his legs buckled, and he dropped instantly.

Thren sheathed his swords and strode back to the other contestants as, behind him, the young man's family raced out from the stands to check his health.

Two matches left.

4
ERIN

Erin bounded back up the stairs to Zusa's side, glad for the protection of her hood. It hid the burning red of her cheeks at the sudden cheers and shouts that erupted when she won her match. She took it off only when plopping back down in her seat, and then ran her fingers through her short hair to pull errant strands away from her face.

To her annoyance, her mother was busy talking with some ugly merchant seated behind her, rambling about transport rights. If Erin remembered correctly, he wanted his company to be the only one allowed to bring textiles in and out of Angelport, and had been trying at this for over a year.

"An excellent win," Nathaniel said, leaning forward so she could see him on the opposite side of her mother. He grinned at her. "And I think you'll have far more betting on you for your next match."

"I don't care about their bets," she said, a half-lie. There was a definite pleasure in knowing those who had doubted her now suffered the consequences. They likely thought her entrance had come about by her mother's fortune and not her own skill.

Now if only the stupid textile merchant would stop blabbering.

Erin crossed her arms, rested her elbows on her knees, and watched the next match. She knew she should pay attention, for the winner would be her next opponent, but she kept waiting for her mother to finally acknowledge her win.

In the arena, the two challengers both wielded swords and shields, but one of them was clearly of fine birth, his clothes and armor shinier and his shield brand new for the tournament. Shiny man got his ass beat down by his well-worn opponent. A mercenary, Erin suspected, or a veteran of the third Gods' War.

Finally, Zusa turned away from the merchant and gave Erin a pleasant smile.

"I see you took down one of the favorites," she said.

"Amazing you could see it, since you weren't watching."

That pleasant smile turned to stone. Ah yes, that expression, the one she was more familiar with. The look her mother wore during their training. Hard, blunt, and expecting unobtainable perfection.

"You tried to block one of your foe's swings straight on," Zusa said. "It's a wonder your bones are all intact."

"I thought I was strong enough," she argued.

"You're not."

"Then what is the point of all those drills every morning? Why the weights and the lifts and the runs if none of it will make me stronger?"

Zusa crossed her arms. "It does make you stronger, but only so that you may wield your weapons with grace and not tire during a prolonged fight. It does not mean you can go toe to toe with a man twice your weight."

There was merit to her mother's argument, but Erin's ire was raised and she didn't want to surrender so easily.

"I'd lost my other sword, and if I missed my dodge, he'd have absolutely broken something," she said. "I thought it better to endure the hit than suffer the risk."

Her mother leaned closer, her voice dropping in volume. Her brown eyes drilled into Erin's.

"No choice is without risk. In true battle, *every* missed dodge is a potential death. Lacking one of your swords, and on the defensive, meant retreating was your better option. You chose a worse one out of fear and doubt. That will kill you quicker than any blade."

Despite the berating, hearing all this made Erin feel better. At least her mother had watched the fight after all…

"You're right," she admitted, and slumped in her seat. "I'll do better next time."

Zusa's soft smile returned, and she patted Erin's knee.

"You won your first ever match, and against a skilled, experienced opponent. I'm proud of you, Erin, even if you fail to do better than that."

Erin stared at the arena below. A new match had started, with names she had not caught due to her argument. It was quick and boring, the old man in the blue hood knocking out his foe in a single blow. A few people even jeered, for they'd been denied their entertainment, though an equal numbered shouted in joy. No doubt they'd bet on the winner.

When it was over, she shifted in her seat and glanced at her mother.

"It did hurt my arms really, really bad when I blocked his swing," she confessed.

Zusa laughed. "I teach so you may avoid my errors, Erin, and if I am a good teacher, it is only because I have made so very many errors." She wrapped an arm around her daughter in a quick embrace, then pulled away. "But do not ever think my eye is not upon you. You are vastly more interesting than any deal to be made with the Gemcroft estate."

The sudden emotion made Erin feel embarrassed for reasons she could not explain, and she hunkered down in her seat even further. Her fingers tapped the top of the hilts to her sabers. Nearby, Nathaniel had turned away to chat with the same merchant. The both of them were laughing. She felt a pang of jealousy at how easily Nathaniel held conversation. She'd long viewed him as her older brother, and he had grown fully into himself over the last few years living in Angkar.

Some were calling for Zusa to fully hand over the reins of the estate to Nathaniel. He was the blood of Alyssa Gemcroft, after all, while Zusa was not. Though Zusa never admitted as much, Erin could see the way it enraged her mother. As if their union by marriage was not as strong as blood.

Still, her mother's ability to refuse was almost certainly at an end. Nathaniel was more than old enough, and he'd already taken over many aspects of daily management.

"Erin Felhorn!" the tournament master called, stirring her from her thoughts. She took in a deep breath. *All right. Time to go again, and this time with very, very little blocking.*

She bounded down the steps, weirdly feeling more nervous than in her first match. The people knew her now, knew her name, knew she was dangerous. Already there was a feeling of expectation upon her. Her foe, the grizzled mercenary in patchwork armor, had an idea of her skills, and the way she would fight.

"Give a welcome to the biggest surprise of the tournament so far," Boris called out, the big man keen to the feelings of the audience. As the cheers came in, Erin realized she had developed, for perhaps the first time in her life, a reputation. A small one, spread only among those in attendance. She felt the onset of unease.

If it made her so nervous, and her opponents so much more aware of her, how then had her father endured as the Watcher of Veldaren? And how could she believe herself capable of living up to that legacy?

What are you afraid of, Erin?

She bounced on her toes, her nervousness gradually replaced with excited energy. She stared at her foe, who lifted his shield and readied his sword, and wanted to laugh.

Every day, she fought against Zusa Gemcroft, one of the finest killers in all the land. Every day, her mother beat her, bloodied her, and pushed her to her very limits. This man, this stranger with a shield, was *nothing* when compared to the former faceless.

"Are you ready?" she asked aloud.

"That is my question, not yours," Boris said with a wink. He lifted his arm. "Begin!"

Zusa had taught Erin how to battle against every conceivable weapon arrangement, and while she had focused more heavily on short swords and daggers (the weapons of a thief, as Zusa described them), there had been plenty of work against a shield as well.

The shield would protect her foe, but it would also slow him down. He could swing it as a weapon, but it would be cumbersome. While she had not the weapons to break the shield, she possessed the speed and skill to bypass it, if she could confound her foe and force him out of position.

And confound her foe she did. Perhaps he was a veteran of the Gods' War, but he had not faced an opponent quite like her. She weaved side to side, constantly turning him so he could never settle his feet nor be confident in the position of his shield. Keeping him uncomfortable. Keeping him uncertain. Her swords battered his shield, and whenever he tried to counter she danced away.

Speed. More than anything that was her advantage, at least until she grew older and put on even more muscle. Her swords battered his shield, mocking it, almost daring him to strike back. Meanwhile the crowd grew louder, jeers and cheers coming together into a meaningless roar in the back of her mind.

Legacy of the Watcher

After a minute her foe's patience faltered, and he thrust for her midsection. She parried his weapon upward, and then struck him hard on the elbow with her other sword.

One.

When Boris began the fight again, her foe charged at her full speed. Like Geoff, he wanted to use his superior strength against her, and to close the space between them and limit her movements. Erin's eyes widened. It felt like time itself slowed as she did not retreat, but instead leap straight into him.

A thousand lessons from her mother rattled through her mind, guiding her, making her every reaction instinctual. She could almost hear her mother's voice giving her instruction.

Punish his arrogance.

Her body swayed left, avoiding a thrust.

Turn his momentum against him.

Her legs twirled, spinning to rob the hit from his shield of all its power. Around, around, to her opponent's rear.

When your foe is vulnerable, hold nothing back.

She came out whipping her twin swords about with all her might, cracking into the man's knees from behind. He buckled and fell.

"And that's two and three!" Boris shouted. "Little Erin has done it again!"

As the cheers rained down, she pulled back her hood, flashed her teeth to the crowd, and waved.

If she was to build a legacy, she might as well start here and now. Unlike her father, she would never need to hide who she was.

5
THREN

Thren needed actual effort against his second opponent. Not much, but enough to leave him winded. He returned to the dwindling number of contestants gathered to one side while his foe lay unconscious, though this time it had not been Thren's intention. With impatience he'd grown careless, and the young man, some fop with blond hair down to his waist, paid the price.

"You're a true bastard, Gray," one of the remaining fighters said. She was a rugged sort, most definitely a former mercenary. A wicked scar cleaved her face in half from forehead to chin, and it left portions of her scalp unable to grow hair. What remained had been tied back in an uneven blond ponytail. A similar scar marred her left ear so its upper half was a mutilated nub, whereas her right was gone entirely. Her name was Brit, and she had come in second twice before.

"Am I to put on a better show to the crowd?" he asked, holding no desire to debate the issue but suspecting he would not be given a choice in the matter.

"That crowd is why we have a tournament in the first place," a lanky man said, glancing their direction. A long polearm was strapped to his back, its end heavily blunted. A newcomer, one Thren did not recognize. He wore less armor than most, just padded leather that would not hinder his movements.

"I wasn't talking about the crowd," Brit snapped. "Two opponents, and two men passed out in the dirt. Are you trying to win, or commit murder before hundreds of witnesses?"

Thren grinned at her. "I learned to fight where there were no rules, and no mercy given. It is a hard habit to break at my age."

"Bullshit," polearm man said. There was something almost amusing about how casually he said it, without any real animosity. "You've certainly trained for thousands of hours, and I doubt you killed your every training partner. You're too skilled otherwise. Only fools and incompetents are incapable of controlling their weapons, and I see you as neither, Gray."

A strong argument, Thren had to admit. He would have berated both his sons if they had tried to offer a similar excuse to the one he used.

"Then what am I, if not a fool or an incompetent?" he asked. Let others define him through their guesses, instead of revealing his own truths.

Boris interrupted them with a great holler from the center of the ring.

"And now our next match, one I think we all are eagerly awaiting, is up! Erin Felhorn, facing off against the spear from Mordan, Rao Swift!"

The polearm wielder pulled the weapon off his back and spun it over his head.

"What you are is someone who wants to win more than anyone else here," he told Thren before departing. "I just wonder why."

Brit stood beside him as they watched Erin and Rao meet. The young Felhorn bounced down the steps to a great many cheers. Her two wins had upset many a bettor's predictions, to the joy of some and the agony of others. Her youth, and her energy, won over the rest.

"I've seen you fight before," Brit said casually. "Even beat you three years ago, if you remember. You're different today. Were you playing games, Gray? Throwing fights for coin, perhaps?"

Erin drew her swords and twirled them in her fingers as Rao spun his own spear about with exaggerated sweeps and swirls, all to the crowd's delight.

"Perhaps I have something to fight for," he said as he watched.

Brit grunted. "Rao is right. For the first time in this tournament, you actually want to win. I look forward to finding out just how much, Gray. I'm your next match."

He risked taking his attention off the start of the battle to glance her way.

"Do you miss the excitement of real war, Brit?"

A faint smile cracked the side of her face. "The past years of peace have grown dull. Give me a real fight, old man, and I won't mind if I bow out early."

A shout from Boris began the fight. Thren narrowed his

eyes as he watched his granddaughter (his *granddaughter*, how surreal that seemed) steadily bob left to right on her toes. He wondered if she were trained to deal with polearms. The reach was far greater than any sword could match, and the shaft could still be used to block and deflect attacks. Getting in close, and staying close, would be key.

At least, that is how Thren would have fought. Erin appeared to have other ideas. She let Rao make the first attack, a quick thrust for her abdomen, and then spun sideways. Her swords slapped the weapon away so it could not attempt to follow. Coming out of her spin, her feet planted, her balance recovered, and she resumed bouncing on her toes.

Rao pressed the attack once it was clear Erin had no desire to maintain an offensive. Again and again he stabbed at her, his strong, lithe form lunging in and out as if he were a scorpion, and the spear his tail. Erin dodged and weaved each time, rarely even using her swords. The smile on her face had vanished, replaced with extreme concentration.

She's learning your moves, Thren thought. *Learning your speed. Such patience for one so young.*

This was a riskier tactic to take, for granting Rao complete freedom to attack meant she could not get in close and take away the advantage of his preferred weapon. But this was a fight to three points, not one, and he knew, as she likely did, that she could afford a hit or two if it led to an eventual victory. He hated the idea of giving compliments to the faceless woman, but he must admit that Zusa's training had been exemplary. Even when Rao closed the space between them and assaulted her with quicker, shorter stabs, she did not falter.

At least, not immediately. Rao feinted, not once but twice, and on the second her left arm reacted a bit too much. This time he was the one to fully close the space between them, and with both her weapons to her right he was able to position the shaft of his spear to block her attempted swing the opposite direction. Weapons pinned, he swept his left leg behind her.

Erin predicted the attack, and she hopped up while curling her knees to her stomach. The kick failed to trip her, but when she landed she was unsteady, and Rao pressed all his weight against her. She stumbled, and he twirled his spear once over his head and then brought it down. The blunted edge struck her arm hard enough to illicit a cry of pain.

"One!" Boris cried, to far more boos than cheers.

Thren crossed his arms and studied Erin's reaction. She'd avoided the trip, and the two points it would have cost her. She'd also fallen for a double feint. Which would affect her concentration more?

Then he saw the look on her face, and he struggled not to laugh. By the gods, the young woman was *furious* at herself for the error. This was a girl who, if struck by lightning, would stand up and scream at the storm to try again, and try harder. That drive, that motivation…it could lead to great things if properly harnessed.

If she had the right teacher, as he had Muzien the Darkhand.

The fight began anew, and Thren fully expected Erin to leap into the assault, guided by her anger and frustration. Again he was proven wrong. Her concentration was only tighter as she watched Rao move. It was her foe who went into a sudden offensive, correctly realizing Erin was trying to study and learn from him, and so he attempted to punish that with speed and aggression.

Erin's dodges became less frequent, for doing so was increasingly risky with the distance closed between them. Parrying became her main form of defense, though given Rao's strength, she often had to use both her sabers to push a thrust aside, whereas Thren could have done so with one. Despite several openings those parries gave her, she did not attempt to counter. Thren trusted that she was choosing not to strike. Her training was too good for her to not see them.

She was learning from this fight, and not just to beat her current foe.

You're starved of true battle, aren't you? he thought. At last she countered with a wickedly quick stab after shoving a spear thrust high and then ducking below. Her saber struck Rao's gut, earning her a point.

Training isn't enough. This is the first time you battle with stakes. You test your skill. You wager your pride.

This was something his own son learned across the years of his absence. As Veldaren's Watcher, his every fight was life or death. It honed him in ways even Muzien's training could not do for Thren. What had started as the occasional bloody eye left by Aaron to mark the death of some lowlife grunt working for the Spider Guild steadily became a symbol that terrorized Veldaren's entire underworld. And Aaron had done it corpse by bloody corpse.

Suddenly, all of this girl's concentration and focus felt like an absolute waste to Thren. She craved both a test of her limits as well as proof of the skill she had learned. Training would grant neither. She needed real battle, real blood, and he doubted Zusa would ever give it to her. He suspected she viewed this as a form of self-defense against a cruel world.

Thren knew he was reading much from very little, but his gut said he was correct. The skill, the desire, the drive, it was all there. It just needed to be given purpose.

The next exchange was a bit more back and forth, Erin and Rao taking turns on the offensive. Sabers smacked into the spear shaft, occasionally at first, then faster and faster as she launched into a series of attacks that Rao struggled to predict. At last he stumbled, and she was there, a saber smacking his elbow.

Even before the third point was scored, Thren knew the fight was won. Rao was graceful in his moves, but he weaved through about nine different stances, and Erin had seen them all. Her familiarity with them grew with each passing second. He'd thrust, she'd bat it aside, and then before he could even transition to his next move she was already positioning herself to appropriately counter.

Her blades lashed out ever earlier due to her growing confidence, some hitting the shaft before the thrusts could even fully extend. The gap between the two closed, slowly and steadily. Rao's movements turned frantic, and as previous opponents had before, he tried to use his superior strength against her. His spear slammed straight down at her, as if he wielded a club instead.

Her sabers lifted up in an 'X' to block, and Thren's stomach sank for a split second at such foolishness. That disappointment turned to elation as she expertly faded to the left at the last possible moment, her hips sliding, her swords together pushing the spear aside so it struck only the air where she'd stood. Her movement continued, feet twirling, body spinning, so the downward parry of her swords became an upward slash ending with both sabers pressed against Rao's exposed neck.

"And that's three!" cried Boris. "The little girl is magic!"

Erin withdrew her sabers, and when Rao bowed to her, she imitated him. He whispered something to her, but Thren could not make it out, nor have hope of hearing it amid the chorus of cheers and groans. They then departed, Erin for the stands with Zusa, Rao for the remaining entrants.

"What did you tell her?" Thren asked as Rao returned.

"To beware of you," the man said as he trudging past, headed for the arena exit.

Thren grinned at him but said nothing.

"Our next bout, you're well familiar with both names by now," Boris continued, drawing his attention back to the center. "The old soldier, Gray, and the vicious blade of fallen Neldar, Brit Caram!"

The pair walked to the center, barely an arm's length of space between them. Thren's hands rested on the hilts of his swords, while Brit pulled the enormous two-handed blade off her back and then casually leaned the flat side upon her shoulder.

"You remember what I asked for?" she said. "Give me everything, and I won't care if I lose. Show me the real you, Gray, the beast you've been hiding."

Thren drew his swords. The faint smile on his lips was as much a threat as it was a sign of amusement.

"These swords may be blunted, but they will hurt nonetheless," he said. "Are you sure you're willing to endure the risk?"

"I've cut down orcs, war demons, and the undead," Brit said. "Do you think you can rival them?"

Thren lowered into a stance, his swords up and ready before him. "I fought the Darkhand," he said. "And he was more fearsome than them all."

Boris signaled for the fight to begin, and Thren gave the woman her wish. He dashed straight at her, challenging the speed of her much larger and heavier sword. The muscles in her arms were up to the task, and she swung her blade horizontally with impressive speed.

Blocking should have been foolish, but she did not yet understand her foe. He leaped into the swing, his swords striking with the combination of his natural strength and momentum. The weapons slammed together, and at the moment of contact Thren pushed off with his feet again, adding even more to the block.

Brit's sword, and all her might, flung backward out of position. Thren kicked off with his right foot, shifting his angle. His left elbow shot out, striking Brit in the face, while he flipped his grip on the sword in his right hand. Blood splattered from her nose as the cartilage broke. Their weight collided, but he was far better prepared. With his reverse grip on his right hand, it was all too easy to punch her in the throat.

When she doubled over, hacking blood, the edges of his swords pressed to her neck.

He said nothing as Boris cried out, "One!"

Brit met his gaze with her bluish-green eyes sparkling and blood dribbling down across her lips and chin. She flashed a grin that was all teeth.

"*There* it is," she said. The crowd went wild at the sight of blood.

Thren retreated two steps, settled back into his opening stance, and waited for Boris. Brit readied as well, this time with her sword high and angled forward for a thrust.

"A bit of blood's fine, but try not to maim," Boris said, his deep voice low and for them alone. "Especially *you*, Gray. Now...begin!"

Brit immediately took the offensive, as she should have at the start of their duel. Such a heavy, long blade needed aggression to find victory, and with momentum on her side her swings were more powerful than ever. Thren retreated step after step, drifting left or right each time so she could never fully anticipate his moves. Her sword slashed air, but she showed little sign of tiring.

"Quick for an old man," she shouted.

Instead of simply dodging, Thren started smacking her sword with one of his own, a mocking reminder she could not catch him. His movements grew more exaggerated, his stride lengthening, his dodges becoming farther and farther hops to the side. He was challenging her, forcing her every swing to retreat in time to prevent a strike from the side. It would exhaust her far more than his own deft movements, especially given he was unarmored, and she burdened with heavy leather armaments atop a chainmail shirt.

Brit sensed the game and refused to play it. Her sword

pulled back, once more ready for a thrust. Her rushed steps became a steady approach. She was giving up an advantage, but it was the wiser move against an opponent she could not overwhelm.

Thren planted his feet and lifted his own swords. If she wanted to dance instead of chase, well then, he would show her how well he danced.

She thrusted for his chest, attempting surprise, but he sensed it coming nonetheless. The flexing of muscle in her arms, the tensing of her legs, the way her eyes narrowed the tiniest bit, they all gave her away. He dashed toward her and to the side, allowing his off hand to connect with the steel and guide it harmlessly over his left shoulder. His right struck her shoulder and bounced off the leather pauldron protecting it.

"Two!"

Brit thrust her sword into the dirt of the arena and stretched the struck arm as they prepared for Boris to start the next point.

"Who trained you?" she asked as she worked the arm in a circle. Even with the pauldron protecting it, he'd struck her hard, and it would most certainly bruise. "You don't fight like a soldier, so that's a lie. Then who? And for what?"

Thren knew he should protect his identity, but he found himself suddenly tired of all the lies and deception.

"The Darkhand," he said, expecting no comprehension, or perhaps the vaguest of recollections. Muzien had been dead for years…as had Thren Felhorn.

"Is that so?" Brit asked. She wiped her face with the back of her hand, smearing a bit of blood dribbling from her injured nose. "You fought the Darkhand and lived? There's more to you than you let on, Gray."

She ripped her sword free and readied it.

"No more playing. Let's dance."

Neither waited for Boris to call the start. They lunged at one another, and it was Thren's turn to realize his foe had been hiding things. The movement of her sword was even faster now, and her gauntleted left hand held the blade halfway up with every other movement, granting quicker, and better, positioning for the much longer weapon in the close quarters fight. Thren's swords rang out with steel on steel as they collided with Brit's.

He couldn't break through, not immediately. He weaved his slashes in and out, testing her skill. She was definitely faster than before, but why then had she been playing with him? Thrusts he thought would slip through were instead blocked and batted aside. He increased his intensity, striking at her with unrelenting fury. Let her block. Let her play games hiding her skills.

Instead of frustration, he felt elation. His heart raced with each hit. He felt alive again, in a way he had not since leaving Veldaren in disgrace. His every swing shed years. He was a smoldering fireplace suddenly doused in oil. He was a lake bursting through a broken dam. His swords pounded against Brit's, forcing her to exactly the position he desired. Twice she tried to counter, but he was ready, never motionless, never letting his opponent believe for the slightest instant that she could hold her ground against him. Strike. Overwhelm. He was better, faster. The flow of battle was *his* to command, *his* to master.

Two hits on the lower portion of the blade, then one higher, forced Brit's defenses to crumble. Thren feinted, and amid the gap left by her attempt to block, he thrust his right hand straight forward. His sword struck her square in the chest, quick and brutal. She let out a cry of pain and staggered backward. He suspected he'd broken one of her ribs. If the tip were sharpened, and her chain shirt poorly made, it would have pierced her heart.

Boris declared victory, and the crowd responded far more negatively than it had for Erin. Brit rested her sword across her shoulders and spat blood. True to her word, she was not upset in the slightest, and offered him her other hand. When he shook it, she pulled him close so she could speak only to him.

"What is it?" she asked. "What awakens you now?"

He glanced over his shoulder, toward the little shaded section the Gemcroft family was seated in. Brit saw and immediately recognized Erin in the stands.

"I see," she said. "But what is she to you?"

"My business is my own," Thren said, and pulled away from her. "I pray you enjoyed our fight."

"Indeed I did," she said, and offered one last wave to the crowd. "I look forward to our rematch."

"I may not enter next year," he said.

Brit winked at him before leaving the arena. "When did I

ever say it would be in a tournament?"

6
ERIN

The crowd was on her side, Erin knew that for sure. They clapped and cheered at her name, and when Boris called for her opponent, the hooded soldier Gray, they jeered with matching enthusiasm.

"You're not too beloved around here," Erin said as she bounced on her toes.

Gray grinned back at her. "I am used to it."

Her hops grew a bit wider, her weight shifting back and forth from foot to foot to warm up her muscles and get her blood pumping. She'd watched enough of Gray's fights to know the man was ruthless. Rao's warning would not leave her mind.

Beware the man whose name is a lie, he had whispered to her. *He is here, not for victory, but for you.*

That the man whose sole name was 'Gray' used an alias was no surprise. The implications of Rao's warning, however, left her uncertain and confused. Though his face was hooded, she could see more than enough of him to know she had never encountered the man before. He was a stranger to her, so why then did he pose such a threat to her specifically?

Erin clanged her swords together, appreciating the ringing metal in her ears. Perhaps he was an enemy of the Gemcroft family. Accidents did happen in tournaments, and killing Erin in full view of the city would be a particularly cruel way to hurt her mother. The unconscious state in which he'd left his first two opponents was enough to warrant caution.

Boris stepped between them, and with his pre-fight theatrics finished, he lifted his arm high up.

"Give them a show, would you?" he asked, his attention focused on Gray.

"He won't knock me out in the opening moments, if that's what you're worried about," Erin said. "At the least, I'll make him work for it."

"I was worried *you'd* knock the old man unconscious,

actually," Boris said, and he winked her way. Erin laughed, and her nerves eased the tiniest bit. Perhaps Rao was leaping at ghosts, or merely hoping to unnerve her to his own advantage. She settled into her stance, elbows and knees bent, muscles tensed and ready to spring into action at a moment's notice.

Gray shifted only a little, and at first she thought him disrespecting her, but then she studied him further. His arms were relaxed to his sides, but his grip on his swords was tight, and the angles of his wrists bent slightly so he could thrust or slash, depending on the movements of his arms. His right leg was back behind his left by a step, the heel turned slightly inward. Braced against an attack, yet also ready to lunge.

The man looked calm and bored, and yet he could explode into violence within the blink of an eye. She imagined him standing similarly, not in an arena where a duel was expected, but in some secluded street or darkened building. How might he be misread? How unprepared would his foes be?

Beware the man whose name is a lie, indeed.

"Begin!"

Erin decided to test her theory with a quick hop forward, her body bending at the waist and her arms thrusting to add the most possible distance to her dual thrusts. He didn't move. Her swords would not reach, and he knew it. Erin pulled back, her face flushing. She'd thought he'd parry them, or meet her thrust. Instead he stood there, watching, as a few people in the crowd snickered.

"Do better," Gray said.

She thrust again, this time with proper reach so that if he did not block she would strike his chest. He batted it aside and countered with his off hand. Erin blocked, and so began their dance. Their weapons bounced off one another, filling the arena with the sound of steel on steel. Erin's nerves settled. She knew he was a skilled opponent, and a ruthless one. His first two bouts proved as much. Yet this was the interplay she understood, and she started to gain confidence in how she correctly read each and every one of his reactions.

Sweat trickled down her face and neck as she heightened her intensity, her swords battering Gray with four quick slashes in a row, testing his defenses. No opening was found, but she did force her foe to retreat a step.

"Interesting," he said.

He went fully on the defensive, and Erin was all too happy to keep him reeling. She weaved side to side, thrusting for his stomach, and when that was blocked, slashing high for his neck. That, too, he blocked, and with almost maddening ease. Was he trying to exhaust her, perhaps? It made her grin. Good luck with that. She was young, and her mother had put her through grueling trials to build up her stamina. So many late nights racing the setting sun, pausing only to vomit as the miles passed in sweat and agony. Strike after strike, each one meant to guide an opponent's hands and, over time, force them out of position so that her killing strike could not be stopped. Every feint, every swing, worked to that end, and she knew from experience how overwhelming such an assault could be. When her mother cut and weaved with her daggers during her training, Erin could feel the way she was being manipulated, while simultaneously struggling to break the masterful control.

Gray appeared to wilt under that same pressure. His hands went where she steered them, and at last she found the opening she sought. Her saber lunged forward to tap against his chest, earning her a point. The crowd cheered, but Erin's joy was measured. Something about the small victory felt too easy, and there was a look in her foe's eye she disliked. When they separated, he shook his head at her.

"I've seen enough."

When the next bout began, it felt like she faced a brand new opponent. He did not surrender the offensive, nor did he seem content to let her control the pace of the battle. What had been a smooth flow of swords, a rhythm between them, turned into a panicked retreat as her every swing was countered. She parried as best she could, hesitant to block against such newfound aggression. He was bigger than her, stronger. She needed speed, she needed surprise.

Erin slashed at an angle, attempting to force his hands out of position, yet he never even tried to block. Instead he tilted his head an inch to the side, easily avoiding the hit. When he countered, she retreated, her swords lashing out in a futile attempt to hold him at bay.

"What happens if I do not fear your swings?" he asked her, yet again ignoring the swipe that passed in front of his chest, hitting nothing. "What use then are your feints? What hope have you of intimidation?"

Nothing about her foe made sense. None of his moves matched what Zusa had taught her to face, and she had faced so many varied tactics and weaponry. It was maddening. It felt like he could read her as easily as one read a book, and whatever reaction she chose, it was one he had already predicted. She thrusted, he parried. She swung, he blocked, so casually, so dismissively. It stung her pride.

Why do you care about your damn pride? she thought. Was it the crowd? Was it knowing Zusa and Nathaniel were watching? Or was it how Gray kept getting under her skin with his every spoken word? She closed the space between them, her feet a blur beneath her. She had to take advantage of the curve of her sabers and her smaller stature. She twisted, avoiding his counter that nearly impaled her, and then came out swinging in return with his other blade.

Hers struck first, her saber clipping the interior of his arm, and then his own hit her collarbone hard enough she cried out in pain.

"Unbelievable," Boris hollered, clapping with his hands high above his head. "That's two for the little surprise of the day!"

Thren did not pull away his sword. His icy blue eyes held her in place.

"A cut to the elbow," he said, glancing at where her own saber rest against him. "Whereas I have split you in half. You may have hit first, but I would have hit last." He withdrew his sword and stepped back two paces. "You keep fighting to win sanctioned duels, Felhorn girl. It is not good enough."

Ignore him, Erin told herself. She had faced the very best by training with her mother. Zusa had been a silent blade of Karak, and she fought the most fearsome foes of Veldaren's underworld and survived. None were faster. None were more skilled. Erin relied on that training, on the instincts her mother had instilled within her, and pressed forward.

Her swords weaved in a specific pattern, two hits with her right saber, a thrust with her left, and then a sudden lunge forward, her weight shifting, her body turning to avoid a potential counter while extending her reach. It was quick, and sudden. Few foes would expect it, her mother had told her, and fewer still would react quickly enough to avoid being impaled.

Gray's swords were improperly positioned to block, and so he didn't. He hopped forward, meeting her thrust while lifting his arm and turning his own body sideways akin to hers. Her sword passed just underneath his armpit, the tip harmlessly cutting a tiny hole in the fabric of Gray's shirt.

Erin tried to turn her sword and swing inward in a panic, but Gray was faster. His upraised arm dropped, and at the last moment twisted at the wrist so the flat edge of his sword struck her square in the forehead. She let out a cry as the pain rocked through her, momentarily blurring her vision.

"At last, the soldier scores his first!" Boris shouted.

Erin glared at Gray as she rubbed her forehead. Something about the look in his eye twisted her insides. The way he carried himself as he separated from her. The little shake of his head. The dismissive look in his eye. It was as though he found her unworthy of facing off against him, and the insult hardened her concentration. Whoever this old soldier was, she could beat him. She *would* beat him. She only needed one more hit.

When Boris called for them to begin anew, she weaved back and forth, occasionally lashing out with her swords. She was trying to get Gray to react, to fall into a sort of rhythm she could learn and anticipate, yet he barely even moved. His legs remained firm, one sword held back, his other slapping and parrying each and every probing strike. If his look was dismissive, the defense was doubly so, and it only heightened her frustration.

"You forget the purpose of your blades," Gray said, carefully watching her. "You wish to dance. You want our swords to play at combat, to strike and parry in rhythm and rule so all your training makes sense." He clanged his swords together. "You swing in hope I block or parry so you can continue the game you've built in your head."

She charged at him, aware her self-control was compromised but unable to do anything about it. The man was infuriating in a way her mother could never be. Zusa cared for her, and no matter how much they bickered or how brutal their training became, she knew her mother would not dare seriously hurt her. This man, though? With every word, she felt herself that much smaller, like an ant beneath the boot of a giant.

Legacy of the Watcher

"Then how should I fight?" she asked as she swung, her body moving through stances meant to guide the weapons of her opponent. Each time, Gray countered them in a way she did not expect. He sidestepped when it made sense to block, or parried when doing so would nearly leave him impaled if he had been the tiniest bit slower. It made her transitions awkward, weakened her strikes.

"There is only one way," Gray said, and it seemed he became a totally new man. His retreat became an attack. Her thrusts were batted away like nothing. Her swords felt clumsy in her grip. *To kill.*"

She stumbled back a step, then panicked as his swords chopped for her face. Her sabers crossed before her, a jarring, painful block that made her arms ache. He slammed against her twice more, mocking her, making her defenses crumble. All the while, he berated her failings.

"Every movement." He batted aside a frantic counter. "Every block. Every thrust. Not to win. Not to play." His heel struck her knee, and when she buckled he bodied her with his shoulder. She stumbled, only her excellent balance kept her on her feet.

"To kill," he said, and though the volume of his voice had not raised since the fight begin, the intensity of it, the overwhelming certainty, left her shook. "To survive. Break your opponent, little Erin. Shatter their will. End their life. Anything else is playing games with death."

Why was he so intent on lecturing her so? Why did he care? This man was a stranger, yet he seemed determined to worm his way into her mind. Was it meant only to undermine her confidence? No, that didn't feel right. The way he focused on her, the way he spoke…there was something here she was missing, some connection invisible to her.

She charged back at him, hoping to surprise him while he spoke. A vain hope. He crossed his swords, then looped them outward in opposite directions, parting her swords and leaving her vulnerable. Both their weapons continued their circling, but his were faster. By the time she skidded to a halt to end her momentum, his swords pressed to her chest.

"And that's two for Gray!" Boris shouted.

Erin clenched her jaw to hold back a curse. There it was again, that look in her opponent's eye. She understood it this time, though it did nothing to ease her confusion. He wasn't dismissive of her, nor attempting to insult her with such a glare.

He was disappointed in her, in allowing him so easy a hit.

"Fine," she muttered. "You want everything, I'll give everything."

Though the score was even, she felt she were losing badly. That meant holding nothing back. If this was to be her last bout, then she would go out attempting her very best.

Erin had practiced it a thousand times, but never used it against an opponent, only the imaginary recreations of history. It was the epitome of her father's abilities, the fighting style he had developed across his brutal lifetime to survive battle against any number of foes. The stuff one could only read about in stories…unless your mother had lived through it, and could offer a first-hand retelling.

Her fingers tightened around the hilts of her sabers. She slid her arms back, allowing her cloak to fall forward, split in three for exactly this purpose. Each portion could be guided independent of the others. With her every twist and step, she could flip and shift them in a flourish.

Haern's gift. The cloak dance of the Watcher.

Vigor flowed through her nerves, electric and strong. She always practiced this in secret, hiding it even from her mother, but now she would reveal it to an entire crowd. Would she make a fool of herself? Or would she find victory, as her father always had?

"Begin!" shouted Boris.

Her feet spun beneath her.

Dance, she told herself. *Let yourself dance.*

Her arms lifted and dropped as her hips twisted. Her cloaks billowed about her, whipping through the air. She coupled each rotation with a lash of her swords, ensuring with every rotation she was a deadly tornado of gray cloth. The first of her swings hit Gray's swords, and the ringing of metal was comforting. It was battle resumed, and each subsequent hit proved her foe remained defensive against the display.

Faster, she urged herself. Make the cloak dance bewildering. Turn her entire body into a blur. The collisions of their blades grew louder, and her steps wilder, vaulting her back and forth as she turned so nothing about her remained in place. Her excitement grew. Gray still only blocked, his feet planted firm, and then one of his swords flew from his hand at the next collision.

Even faster. Her lungs burned in her chest, and her stomach protested the constant motion, but victory was so close, her opponent bewildered by the maneuver. One more rotation, and her swords were swinging aim, aiming for his chest.

His lone sword blocked them both, and suddenly Gray was so close he filled her vision. His block jarred her arms, her foe so strong, his sword angled so perfectly it put a complete halt to her rotation. Her feet pushed anyway, trying to dance, trying to turn, but his free hand shot forward faster than an arrow. His fingers closed about her throat, shockingly tight so she could not draw a breath.

His hand may have been what held her, but his eyes kept her prisoner. The intensity in them terrified her more than the lack of breath.

"The purpose of such a dance is not to overwhelm, or impress with your speed," he said. "It is to confuse, and to disguise the motions of your hands and feet. You might have been a blur, Erin, but you were still predictable, and that is why you would be dead if we battled true."

He let go, and she dropped to her knees, gagging.

"How?" she asked, her throat raw. "How would you know?"

Points and duels no longer mattered. Whoever this stranger was, he knew too much. He crouched before her, his sword casually resting across his knees. The ice in his eyes was warm compared to the tone in his voice.

"I have faced the one whom you imitate," he said. "I have seen the dance of a master, and compared to him, you are a child at play."

Fury pushed her into motion. Its fire drowned out her questions, and her wounded pride demanded she act. Though all she could hear was the blood pounding in her ears, she imagined the hundreds in the crowd watching her, and laughing. Laughing at her failures. Laughing as the old soldier proved that she never actually belonged in this tournament.

Her feet kicked, and her swords slashed, one after the other, straight for his neck.

Gray never moved. The swords struck him and sank deep into the muscle, reddening his skin and immediately starting to bruise. The man didn't even flinch, nor did he break the contact of his stare. For the briefest moment, the entire arena faded away, and Erin felt only the deep desire for her swords to be sharpened instead of blunted, and for blood to be drawn instead of blossoming bruises.

"And that's three!" shouted Boris to an accompanying roar. The darkness of her vision broke, and she was suddenly overwhelmed with noise and cheers and the sight of men and women standing and clapping in the stands from all directions. She'd attacked without thought to the game.

Victory, perhaps, but not even a stolen victory. Gray had no intention of winning. She'd seen his speed. He could have blocked her swings if he wished.

"Why are you playing with me?" she asked as she jammed her swords into their sheaths.

"I am not the one playing games," he said. "And if you wish to stop playing yours, come find me at the broken fountain near the docks. I will be waiting there, just after dawn, to see if you possess the necessary courage."

He sheathed his swords and turned for the arena exit.

"Wait!" she shouted. "The Watcher? Did you actually fight him?"

Gray hesitated. With his back to her, she could not see his reactions, nor attempt to read them, which made it all the more frustrating when she heard his answer.

"I did."

Was he telling the truth? Or was he lying? And just who was he? A refugee of the broken thief guilds, perhaps?

"Then how did you survive?" she asked. Every story said her father was ruthless. Veldaren's underworld had been terrified of his arrival, his every attack shattering guilds. No one who challenged Haern's cloak dance faced it and lived.

Gray turned. She caught the faintest hint of his face through the shadows of his hood. His cheek twitched, a brief smile of grim amusement.

"I didn't."

He departed the arena, seemingly no longer interested in watching any other match. Erin stood awkwardly where she was until she caught Boris staring at her. The old man smiled, but his head tilted toward the stands, where her mother sat. It was time for the next duel.

"Of course," she said and rushed off.

"Are you all right?" Zusa asked when Erin took her seat.

"I'm fine."

She watched the next few duels in a daze, seeing little of them. Her fight against Gray replayed itself again and again in her mind. Every twist, every turn, and most importantly, her every failure. When she scored hits, they felt like gifts. When he struck her in turn, it felt like complete humiliation and disregard to all her talent and training.

I am not the one playing games.

But wasn't it just a game? This tournament? These duels? And why did Gray act like she even had a choice?

She didn't even realize Boris was calling her name until Zusa nudged her with an elbow. Her mind was so taken, her focus so broken, that she fought her opponent fully distracted. She could not shake Gray's words.

When the first point was scored, she already knew she had lost.

7
ERIN

Erin hadn't the heart to watch the victor's match, and so instead of returning to her seat beside her family, she slunk off past the benches to the streets beyond. She didn't go far, just past the arena entrance toward the backs of the stands, where she plopped down with her back against one of the tall wooden support beams. The rumble of the crowd was still near, hundreds of people just on the other side, but she had a measure of privacy now.

Privacy that did not last long.

"I suspected I'd find you hiding somewhere in the shadows," Nathaniel said.

"I'm not hiding," she muttered. Why did Nathaniel always know where she'd be?

He sat beside her, nudged her with his elbow. "You finished in third place in your first ever tournament. That should be worth celebrating, not sulking."

"Third is not first. I still lost."

"Third place is a good start."

"In a real battle, I'd be dead. Dead is where you finish, not where you start."

The argument felt flawless to her, but her older step-brother would hear none of it. Always the cheerful one, to the amusement of even his mother. Zusa swore there was a time he was quiet and studious. There was no doubting he had a sharp mind, and he did still like to read, but it seemed adulthood had brought him out to shine, made him clever and charismatic in a way that Erin wondered if she could ever be.

"Yes, but real battles aren't fought in grand arenas with crowds watching and strict rules of what is and is not allowed," he said. "You can bite and scratch and fight dirty when lives are actually on the line. Knowing you, I bet you'd do better in a real fight. The true, vicious, and evil Erin Gemcroft would come out to play."

She punched her step-brother in the chest.

"You would assault a helpless one-armed man?" he said

with a whimper, feigning a great wound. "See, you are truly, truly evil."

Erin rolled her eyes. She just wanted to go somewhere quiet and replay the battle in her mind. It wasn't even her elimination that bothered her, but the match beforehand. The one she *should* have lost. The way Gray had so easily broken her cloak dance, familiar with it in a way no one should be, not unless he spoke the truth and had faced her father in battle. He seemed old enough, but it easily could be a lie.

"Hey." Nathaniel nudged her again. "I came out here for a reason, and we need to hurry if we don't want to miss it."

"I'm not interested in the final match," she said, feeling childish even as she said it. Watching two skilled fighters could prove useful, but damn it all, couldn't she at least be a little upset about her failure, if only for a while?

"I'm not talking about the final match," he said. "I'm talking about something better. A show match."

Erin buried her face in her arms. Gods, her step-brother could be so very persistent.

"I said I'm not interesting."

"Really now?" Nathaniel pushed back up to a stand. "Surprising. I thought for sure you'd want to watch the Godslayer swing his swords about."

Erin shot to her feet, her mouth dropping open.

"Harruq?" she asked, her eyes widening. "Harruq Tun is *here?*"

8
HARRUQ

It had been a long journey, with a lot of nights spent sleeping on heavy blankets that did little to soften the hard ground, but at last their royal procession arrived at the capital city of Angkar. A large part of Harruq was happy to find whatever inn or tavern or fancy mansion they'd be staying in and collapse on a real bed for three days of sleep.

But then a much larger part of him heard of a swordplay tournament happening within the city, and after the tedium and boredom of travel, he could think of nothing better.

"Have fun, and don't get in too much trouble," Aurelia had said, giving him a goodbye kiss on the cheek after he informed her of his plans. "You're a diplomat now. That means you have to behave."

"I'm going to watch, not to cause a ruckus," he'd insisted before hurrying down the street. There was something familiar about Angkar's layout that felt comforting as he made his way through the city. Perhaps it reminded him of growing up in Veldaren, the way the roads seemed to wind instead of flow in straight lines, like in Mordeina. Or how the whole city felt like it had grown far larger than anyone imagined when first founded. It meant tall buildings clearly expanded multiple times, narrow streets, and even narrower alleys where one could vanish in an instant.

Of course, unlike Veldaren, there was the ocean along the southern border, and the bustling docks. With how the city sloped gently downward toward the sea, Harruq was gifted a grand sight of it as he trudged along. The sparkling blue entranced and frightened him in equal measure. It just seemed to…go, and go, forever on.

Nothing should be that big, he thought.

Finding the hastily constructed arena wasn't too difficult given how it stood out like a sore thumb among the rest of the city. Not to mention it had blocked off multiple roads. Harruq cracked his knuckles and suppressed a grin. If Ashhur was kind, he hadn't missed most of the matches. He wondered what the rules would be.

Surely not to the death; that seemed a bit extreme. A scoring system? A duel to exhaustion and an inability to stand, like knuckle-brawlers did in Mordan?

The closer to the arena he got, the more people milled about, and he felt their eyes upon him. He'd dressed up for their caravan's arrival to the capital, and the initial meeting still droning on between the various nobles, lords, Prince Gregory, and Queen Sloane. He wore his fine black leather armor and his flowing crimson cloak. As ever, sister swords Salvation and Condemnation hung comfortably from his hips.

Harruq had felt bad for abandoning Aurelia to the pomp and circumstance, but she insisted she'd be fine, and there was no reason for him to be miserable with her. Permission given, he'd wasted no more time in fleeing.

More whispered conversations among those he passed, and even some finger-pointing. He pretended not to notice. After the second Gods' War, he'd become used to the attention, but matters had grown worse after the war against the fallen angels. Stories spread of the cause, which heightened interest in the previous war, too. New opinions and understandings of the angels' role within it sprung forth.

Which meant, even before setting a single foot within Angkar, he suspected far too many people knew who he was, and what he looked like.

"At least the stories have softened up your role within it, Qurrah," Harruq muttered. He had made damn sure everyone knew that his brother had sacrificed himself to ensure both Aubrienna's and Gregory's safety. A life given, to repay a life taken. It was how Qurrah viewed it, and so Harruq honored it with stories of his own, of the violence inflicted upon them both by the prophet Velixar.

It had been five years since he lost his brother, and yet he still felt the sharp pang in his chest. It was one thing to go years without seeing him, as he had several times before, particularly during Qurrah's and Tessanna's self-imposed exile into the northern reaches of Ker. It was another to know that, no matter where he went and what he did, he would not see his smaller brother's pale smile or hear a clever remark from his biting tongue.

The memories dampened his enthusiasm, but the noise of the crowd put a bounce back into his step. The entrance was blocked off by an armed guard, a sizable young fellow with arms that were thicker than Harruq's. His voice was calm, but the language of his body screamed nervousness.

"Sorry," he said, refusing to move. "Only the fighters can bring in weapons. Leave 'em home."

Harruq glanced down at Salvation and Condemnation. He had no home to leave them at, and under no circumstances would he abandon them here at the entrance, among a scattered little pile of knives and daggers. The temptation to steal and sell one of the fabled weapons used to slay the war god Thulos would be too much.

"I'm not taking them off," he said.

"Then you're not getting inside."

Harruq tilted his head to one side. "Are you sure about that?"

The entrance guard tensed. Harruq could practically hear Aurelia screaming in his ear.

You have to behave, remember?

"Whoa, whoa, hold on there," an older man said, arriving at a run from inside the arena. His balding head was covered with a ludicrous hat, multi-colored and donned with four long feathers. He pushed aside the guard and offered Harruq his hand. "My name's Boris, and I'm in charge of this tournament. You, you're the half-orc, aren't you?"

Harruq shook the burly old man's hand.

"Aye, Harruq Tun, here to watch some fights."

"There's only the one left, and it's about to start," Boris said. "It's the victor's bout, though, so it should be a skillful match. Mayhap not something to impress the Godslayer, mind you, but good for we folk down here in Ker."

Harruq winced. He just wanted to watch a fight. Must everything somehow be compared to his fight against Thulos?

"Fine with me," he said. "Just find me a seat, and I'll cheer along like all the rest, yeah?"

"Of course, of course." Boris dipped his head. "Come with me. You deserve a proper seat, of course. No nosebleed bench for a hero like you."

Harruq followed Boris into the arena, fully convinced the older man had a trick or three up his sleeve. No one laid on the compliments that thick unless they wanted something. And since he didn't look the sort to pick a man's pocket, Harruq feared ulterior motives...and hoped for them in equal measure.

Two fighters stood in the center of the arena, impatiently waiting for the duel to start. Their gazes turned first to Boris, then to Harruq. He could tell they realized who he was by the sudden stiffening of their limbs and straightening of their backs. Murmurs quickly spread through the crowd as Boris led Harruq to a section covered with tents and umbrellas for a bit of shade. The clothes were much fancier here, along with scattered servants carrying trays of sweets.

"We are so excited to have Prince Gregory here with us," Boris rambled. "And for such a great purpose, too. Peace? Now that's something we've had precious little of on Dezrel. A nice long peace, and may it last forever."

"I hope so," Harruq said.

"Here, here we go, empty seats are rare but I think this will have to do," Boris said. He leaned toward a tanned woman in black trousers and an exquisitely tailored lavender blouse. "Do you mind if my friend here takes this seat, Lady Gemcroft?"

"Not at all!" the one-armed young man sitting beside her answered.

Harruq took the offered seat, even if he wished he could sit a bit closer to the action among the poorer folk. They were certainly the rowdier, more enthusiastic portion of the crowd, and the alcohol was flowing readily among them. Half the people here seemed to ignore the arena altogether, their conversation on trade and the implications of the treaty Prince Gregory had come to sign.

"Excuse me," the young man beside Lady Gemcroft said, standing and sliding past Harruq's knees. "I have someone I need to find."

A servant came to offer Harruq something to drink. He could only guess as to which fancy family the man worked for.

"Whatever you have, give me the strongest of it," he requested.

This meant a vibrant red drink, surprisingly tart on his tongue. If it was alcoholic, it was deeply hidden, and with a slight sigh Harruq settled in to watch the victor's duel. Boris rushed back to the center of the stage and began a bit selling up the fighters. The first was a man in chainmail wielding a sword and shield. His name was Omar, and Boris hailed him as the captain of Queen Sloane's royal guard. His opponent was some mercenary captain named Gilgoth, wielding a longsword in a two-handed grip.

Harruq watched the two pace one another, and he decided if he had any money, he'd put it down on Omar. A man responsible for protecting a king or queen was not one to be chosen lightly. Harruq would know. That's why he watched over Gregory. No one else was good enough to do the job.

Well, maybe Aurelia.

"Begin!" Boris shouted, and the battle started in earnest. The crowd cheered on the fighters, and Harruq joined in, pumping his fist when Omar scored the first hit. That he was the only one nearby giving even a modicum energy only amused him more. So he could watch a fight *and* make a few stuffed up nobles annoyed or uncomfortable? He drained his drink. All the better!

The fight was entertaining, if a bit one-sided. Omar used his shield to perfection, expertly positioning it to intercept Gilgoth's swings at their midpoint, robbing them of power and keeping the mercenary's arms constantly at awkward angles. Omar's only error came when Gilgoth rushed him, throwing his weight into Omar's shield and knocking him to the ground. It was a trick that did not work a second time, and the match ended with Omar's dulled sword pressed to his foe's throat. The crowd cheered, but it was relatively unenthusiastic as Boris rushed to the center stage. Harruq suspected the people had hoped for a fiercer competition, not one where the winner had been evident from the very first point.

"Before I present Omar his reward," Boris shouted, "I would first proudly announce a special guest among our number!"

Harruq winced. *No. Please, Karak and Ashhur both, no.*

"The Godslayer, Harruq Tun!"

Boris gestured wildly toward him. Reluctantly, Harruq rose to his feet and waved to the people. Many gaped, others stared in stony silence. Harruq wasn't entirely sure how he was viewed by the people of Ker who, by and large, had escaped the worst of the violence inflicted by the fallen, but he now had a clue. If Qurrah were considered responsible for Dezrel's destruction, it seemed he bore a bit of equal blame. Which, while fair, also annoyed him. Hadn't he *killed* the damn war god? Surely that counted for something.

Legacy of the Watcher

"Now I'm sure we've all heard the tales," Boris continued. The cold reception of the crowd bothered him not the least. "But tales are just that, tales. They can stir the heart, but they pale before the proof of the eye."

Suddenly Harruq realized what it was Boris had been hoping for, and he grinned from ear to ear. Oh, now this, this was just fine with him.

"I think we all here would love a demonstration!" the master of the tournament boomed. "A show match, against our victorious Omar Wrye"

The first of many excited cheers rose up as people realized what they might have the privilege of witnessing. Harruq stood, more than happy to play along.

"I just got here!" he shouted, ensuring his deep voice thundered over the din. "Can't a man rest?"

"Are you tired, Godslayer?" Boris countered. "Then that is for the best, for surely Omar deserves a handicap against such a famed opponent!" He winked at the half-orc. "And don't worry. Should you lose, you'll have your excuse at the ready."

Harruq crossed his arms and made a show at looking around with feigned insult. He could tell Boris meant no actual attack on his pride. It was all a game, meant to goad him into a battle he was more than happy to participate in.

"Fine," he shouted, to a chorus of cheers. "I'll show you how well a half-orc fights."

He climbed down the benches to the arena below. Boris was quick to intercept so he might talk quietly, without the crowd overhearing.

"Just a show match, for a bit of fun and a lot of memories," he said. "Omar knew nothing of the plan, so don't take anything out on him."

"You got nothing to worry about," Harruq reassured him. "If we'd arrived sooner, and I knew this was happening, I'd have entered as a contestant."

A flash of eagerness was quickly replaced by disappointment—Boris probably imagined just how many more people would have attended had he been able to advertise that spectacle.

"The rules are simple," Boris said after shaking his head.

"Score a hit on your opponent before they hit you, that's one. Knock your opponent to their rear, you score two. All else doesn't matter."

"Fair enough."

Harruq walked past him to the center of the arena, his hands resting casually on the hilts of Salvation and Condemnation.

"Blunted blades only," Omar said. "Is that not the rule?"

"I'm not blunting Salvation and Condemnation's edges," Harruq said. "Not that I'm sure I *could* even if I tried. Besides, the crowd here, you know what they want to see, and it isn't me wielding some dull, drab pieces of metal."

Omar glanced at Boris, who shrugged.

"Grab a real sword, if you'd like," Boris said. "You're no stranger to combat, and neither is the Godslayer."

"And what sword may I wield that will compare?" Omar asked.

Harruq drew his sister swords and twirled them in his grasp. A faint red glow shimmered across the black steel. The murmur of the crowd grew.

"He's right," he said. "Let's make this fair."

He turned Salvation about and offered it hilt-first to Omar. The royal guard hesitated a moment, and then sheathed his own blade. The moment he touched Salvation's hilt he flinched, as if expecting it to shock him. When it did not, he closed his gloved fingers about it and then swung it a few times to test its speed and weight.

"Incredible," he muttered. "The vile prophet gifted you these weapons?"

"Not a gift," Harruq said, shaking his head. "Payment, for the sins I would commit in his name."

Omar stood tall, his shield tucked to his side, and saluted with the shimmering blade. "Sins you have made amends for across a lifetime," he said. "I am honored, for both this duel, and for the privilege of wielding such a storied weapon."

It seemed his opponent was no stranger to the many tales told about him. Harruq grinned. So not everything was dour and negative about the Tun brothers down here in Ker. Nice to know.

"The people will have to suffice watching me wield only a single blade," he said, turning to address the crowd with his shout.

"But I suppose it is only fair I give myself another handicap, is it not?"

A few of those on Omar's side jeered him, but most the others cheered or clapped. Harruq clapped with them, then turned back to his opponent.

"Careful with its edge," he said. "And hold nothing back. Let me see everything you have, captain. It's been a boring trip, and my muscles need broken out of their stupor."

"Are we ready?" Boris asked, and lifted his arm. His question was for the crowd as much as it was for Harruq and Omar.

"Let's go," Harruq said, stretching his arms and neck. "Before Aurelia drags me to the castle to attend some awful meeting, yeah?"

Down dropped Boris's hand.

"Begin!"

Harruq was immediately impressed by Omar's skill. He approached calmly, his sword held at ready and his shield up and blocking the bulk of his body. When he thrusted it was quick and strong, without any hesitation or uncertainty. If he was intimidated by facing off against the Godslayer, he did not let it show.

Harruq rewarded him with a casual parry. Salvation and Condemnation struck each other and released a shower of sparks. Strange, experiencing it from the other side. It felt as if Salvation had aided in the retaliation, making it feel like he struck a stone wall and not a sword. Omar would experience the same, but Harruq trusted his strength over his opponent's to overcome the magical aid.

"Come on now," he said, batting away two more hits. "Are you going to attack me, or are you going to hide behind that shield forever?"

Pride warred against tactics in his opponent's eyes. His shield was his greatest advantage, but he was also the tournament champion. To act cowardly now, or afraid to engage in a real fight…

There it is, Harruq thought as Omar rushed him, his sword chopping and slicing with quick, expert movements. Harruq blocked each and every one, focusing only on defense instead of attacking while he took measure of his opponent. Well-trained, yet still mostly in traditional warfare, not duels. The way he kept his shield forward hinted at him expecting shield brothers to his left and right. His attacks were meant to test his reactions, not guide his sword about and out of position over the course of a dance.

Harruq, meanwhile, had been trained by Haern the Watcher. Even if he were a bit more cumbersome in the dance, he had the muscles and sheer rage to make up for it. He blocked two more hits and then exploded in retaliation, Condemnation slamming aside Omar's shield with a single blow. A quick step forward, and he had the glowing blade hovering a few inches away from the man's throat.

"I'd say that's a point, wouldn't you, folks?" Boris hollered from the side.

Omar stepped back, reset his shield, and narrowed his eyes.

"You're faster than I expected," he said.

"You're hardly the first to be surprised," Harruq said. "I'm smarter, too. More handsome. Some even say I'm a bit of a charmer."

"Do they compliment your humor, too?"

He laughed, deciding that underneath Omar's professional demeanor was a man he might get along with.

"No, only insults in that regard," he said.

Omar smirked ever so slightly. "In that, I am *not* surprised."

Boris dropped his arm, calling out to begin anew, and Harruq lunged at Omar. Condemnation bashed into his shield from every which angle, denying his foe even the opportunity to retaliate.

"You would insult me so?" he asked. "And here I thought we were becoming friends." Metal struck metal, and with each blow, the shield dented and crumpled inward. "Stop holding back, Omar. Tell me how you really feel."

With a fully defensive tactic clearly doomed, Omar attempted to hold his ground. Harruq shifted the angle of his hits, baiting out counters he knew would not be fast enough. Twice more Salvation and Condemnation clashed, and after the second, Harruq shoved his weapon upward, guiding his foe's blade up and out of position. Omar retreated immediately, correctly realizing his weakness, but Harruq was faster, his sword already looping up and about to smack the flat edge against his opponent's side.

"Two for the Godslayer of Mordan!" cried Boris.

Harruq and Omar separated again. Now that he was warming up, and the crowd clearly enjoying themselves, Harruq did a bit of mugging for their benefit. He waved his sword at them, a shit-eating grin plastered on his face.

"Here I was hoping this would be interesting!" he shouted to them, earning as many cheers as good-natured boos.

He turned back to Omar, and was surprised to see how serious his foe had become. Though he smiled, it felt like a mask.

"You belittle me for holding back, but what of you?" Omar asked. "You are good, but hardly enough to boast the title of Godslayer. Where is the strength to break nations, half-orc? Where is the might of the hero that fills our tales?"

Harruq grinned at the man. "You don't know what you're asking for."

"No," Omar agreed. "I do not. Enlighten me. Show me what it takes to kill a god."

Harruq stabbed Condemnation into the dirt and cracked his knuckles. A bit of chill swirled into his veins, and he bared his teeth in a savage grin to make his orcish ancestors proud.

"You want to see everything?" he asked, and braced his legs with his arms raised. "Then have it. No swords. No magic. Just my bare fists."

Omar's brow furrowed, and while not willing to engage hand to hand, he did thrust Salvation to the dirt and prepare his blunted blade instead. His shield raised, and he braced for the final point.

Harruq's heart pounded in his chest. The amusement of the duel turned to true excitement. He bounced twice on his feet, building up motion, awakening his blood. He looked to Omar, and he forced himself to see, not a dueling partner, but a true threat to his family.

"Begin!"

Harruq launched himself at Omar. The man anticipated the aggression, but he was woefully unprepared for the sheer speed and brutality unleashed upon him. Harruq easily pitched to the right so the counter thrust missed. His shoulder slammed into the shield, and he dug his heels in and pushed. Omar fell back two steps, off-kilter, but slashed a wide arc in an attempt to drive Harruq away. Harruq caught the wrist with his left hand. With his right, he blasted Omar in the face with a punch and then shifted sideways so he could deliver an elbow to the man's chest.

Omar's shield pulled in, trying to protect against another assault while he fought to free his wrist. Instead of fighting against it, or even holding back the sword, Harruq released his wrist, tucked his shoulder, and barreled straight into that shield. A scream bellowed out his throat as his muscles flexed and his legs pushed, and pushed, driving the shield up and into Omar. Harruq's arms reached around it, grabbing knees, and then he was lifting Omar fully off the ground and into the air. With one final cry, he slammed his opponent straight to the dirt flat on his back, kicked the blunted sword free, and then placed a heel directly atop the man's chest.

"How many points is that?" he asked. The crowd, restless and already overly drunk, roared their approval. Harruq closed his eyes and for the briefest moment let himself bask in the praise. There was never applause and cheer in real battles. Just blood and death.

The match clearly finished, Harruq stepped away and offered his hand to Omar. After a moment's hesitation, Omar accepted, and Harruq pulled the man back up to his feet. The crowd's cheer continued, and he felt a bit of pride at giving them the spectacle they'd hoped for. Some chanted his name, others his title of Godslayer. In the center, Boris shouted and clapped to egg them on. His attention split Harruq's way for but a moment, and he winked to show his appreciation.

"Not bad," Harruq told Omar, hoping to assuage any wounded pride.

"But not good enough to win in battle," Omar said, slinging his shield over his back. He dipped his head in respect. "Which I pray never comes to pass. Welcome to Angkar, Godslayer. May your stay find you well."

Harruq grinned at him, and to make sure the crowd itself knew no hard feelings existed, he grabbed Omar's wrist and held it up high.

"Give some applause for your champion," he bellowed, reminding them that their own duel was but a show match. "A fine opponent, and a blade for all of Ker to be proud of!"

That got a cheer from the crowd, and once more Harruq heard his name chanted. A tiny part of him ached that he arrived too late to join the tournament at the start, and enjoyed the cheer and challenge of multiple opponents. Still, his arrival had already been far more entertaining than he'd anticipated.

You know, Harruq, he thought to himself. *Maybe your stay in Angkar won't be so bad after all.*

9
CYTH

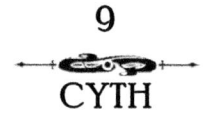

Deep below the elven palace, Cyth Ordoth walked clandestine hallways carved into the granite. Once, it had been forgotten to most living within the elven capital, as had the shrine to Celestia at its end. Now it was remembered, but for different reasons.

Now, it was remembered for a murder.

Cyth came here for exactly that reason. Within this shrine, Muzien the Darkhand had murdered the high elven priest in cold blood. It had taken years before the body was discovered, but by then tales of the event had been spread by Muzien himself.

Torches burned from hanging sconces, producing no smoke, so their faint light cast across the emerald walls. Cyth paused before the statuette, the naked goddess lifting her arms up to the heavens while her head arched. An act of pleasure, or perhaps one of pain, supposedly based on the mood and faith of the viewer. Cyth saw pain, only pain, for what else could his goddess endure after the brother gods devastated her world with their war?

His twin, Vala, waited for him at the foot of the altar, kneeling before the statuette. She wore finely crafted elven chainmail, but unlike his, which gleamed of silver and had decorative plates across the shoulders and waist, hers was even thinner so it could be hidden underneath her brown shirt and trousers. Twins they may be, but Cyth was often considered the more ostentatious of the two, Vala the more practical.

Even more importantly, Vala was as deadly with the twin swords sheathed to her waist as any elf alive.

"A dire place for a meeting," she said, not turning to face him. That she had heard his footsteps did not surprise him. Silent as he may be, she could hear the passage of a mouse through an overgrown field.

"Did you think it chosen by happenstance or convenience?" he asked. "We come for a reason, sister. A sign, one might argue, or perhaps a test."

"A test for who?"

Cyth walked past her to the statuette. Such a little thing, with a four-pointed star hovering over her head, painted gold. He hovered his fingers before the star and recalled the years of training he'd received to become the next high priest of Celestia, a status he finally rejected upon witnessing Dieredon's funeral pyre. That his uncle, Muzien, had slain a high priest in this very room was not lost on him.

"Us," he said softly. "And her."

He glanced over his shoulder. His sister watched him closely, her green eyes sparkling like the emerald walls. Like him, she had long auburn hair, but while he kept his flowing about his neck and shoulders, she tied hers in a tight ponytail that hung down to her waist. Ever ready, his sister. Tutors had tried to turn her into a priestess, but though her faith was strong, she never took to the books and the prayers. The blade was ever her true companion. And so the priests turned their hopes to Cyth...only for him to reject them all the same.

Not for a lack of faith, though, nor a love of his people. But the priesthood had obligations and rules to follow. Instead, he took up training with Vala, hours and hours each day, to make up the gap between them so he might wield the sword strapped to his thigh with skill equal to hers.

"Every night I pray for Celestia to grant us guidance," Vala said. "And every night I am given silence. If you seek to test our goddess, then you waste our time. She is not here to test."

Cyth brushed his fingertips against the star above the goddess. It was in that form she had visited the human gods and taken Ashhur as her lover. There was much debate about what exactly that meant, and if the stars were merely a disguise to a more elven form mirroring their own.

"Do you think she regrets it?" he wondered aloud. "Falling in love with Ashhur? Letting the humans populate and spread across the paradise she created?"

"She loves them, both god and human, and she does not regret what she loves." Vala stood and crossed her arms. Her patience with him was starting to wear thin. "We know this. Despite their crimes, despite their bloodshed, she has always protected them. Only love can explain it."

She was right, of course. Even upon imprisoning the

brother gods after their first war, she had shown Ashhur preference. And when the war god Thulos marched upon the human capital of Mordeina, she had pierced the walls of her prison to allow Ashhur's angels to fly forth and fight on humanity's behalf. So began the second Gods' War, and untold destruction across all of Dezrel.

"Dezerea is in ruins," he whispered. "Much of the Quellan forest burned at the hands of demons. The rivers are choked with the dead, and the daughters of balance, slain. So much devastation...and yet, before us now, a chance for growth. A chance to rebuild."

He grabbed the statuette with his left hand so hard the pointed star pierced his flesh. Blood dribbled down his palm and wrist as he clutched it tightly. More dripped along the star, a crimson trickle making its way toward the arching body of the goddess.

"For once, their gods are absent," he said. "Their paladins no longer hear their words. Their priests no longer receive their blessing. The war between the brother gods is over, Vala. This should be our time to flourish, our time to remake Dezrel into the paradise it once was. But what is it we are granted?"

He lifted the statuette and watched the blood flow.

"*Silence.*"

Vala put a hand on his arm.

"Our plans are just, and our aims for the betterment of all," she said. "If you carry doubts, shed them here."

Cyth shook his head. He knew the stories. He knew the punishment his uncle had suffered. While details were murky, and oft retold from what stories Muzien had let slip before his death, all agreed he had come here to meet with the high priest Valen. War with the humans was on the horizon, and Muzien wished to challenge it somehow.

The priest had rejected him, and been slain with the statuette in return, a vicious blow that caved in his head. In punishment, Celestia had burned the hand that held the statuette, granting Muzien his moniker as the Darkhand. But it went past that murder. It was a rejection of his desire for war, and to rule over a feckless and wretched humanity who so easily succumbed to fear and hatred. Celestia had condemned his desires, and so Muzien had abandoned Celestia, cutting off the tips of his ears and glorifying himself in the riches and excess of humanity.

Muzien's greatest accomplishment...and also his greatest failure.

Cyth would not cut his ears. He and his sister would not abandon their homeland, nor leave them to suffer misery and destruction at the hands of the humans. In Muzien's absence, Dezerea had burned to the ground. Vala and Cyth would not allow the same to happen to the Stonewood.

"Doubt did not bring us here," he told his sister. "A need for truth did."

Vala stepped away, her eyes narrowing, but she kept silent. The gods adored ceremonies and majesty, as did their little children, the elves and humans. They cherished grandiose statements. They clutched greedily to life pledges, held them deeply in their chests. Paladins and priests, were they not lifelong commitments?

And so as the blood dripped across the statuette, Cyth knew his goddess would be listening.

If she *could* listen.

"I vow upon my life, this era of coddled humanity is at an end," he began. He had practiced this speech a thousand times in his mind, yet still his tongue burned with each and every word. "What our uncle created out of pain and rejection, we will recreate out of need and defiance. Not a guild, but a Kingdom of the Sun, to rule the lands beyond our sacred forests. Humanity shall kneel before their betters. They shall appoint themselves no kings. They shall declare themselves no laws. They shall command no armies. Enough blood has been shed in their name. I will *end* it, Celestia, do you hear me?"

He slammed the statuette down upon the altar and stared at his hand. His bare flesh. His pale skin.

"Everything my uncle proposed, and that you rejected, I shall perform. Their blood will paint the landscape. Their deaths will atone for the ruin of Dezerea and the burning of Quellassar and Nellassar. The names of Ashhur and Karak will become curses they are forbidden to speak. I will cleanse Dezrel of their stain, and in their absence the little children you love will come to know the peace of a lamb safely secured in its pen."

So much blood upon the gold, but no fire. No pain. Cyth stared at his hand and waited, waited, perhaps even *wanted* to see it burn. An edge of desperation entered his breast. His voice cracked.

"Do you *hear* me, Celestia? Do you hear the words I speak? Do you know the blasphemy I shall perform? Are you listening? Are you watching?"

The curse of the Darkhand did not come to him. There was only silence in the forgotten shrine.

Cyth broke that silence by smashing the statuette upon the altar. The four-pointed star separated into pieces and bounced across the stone. The statue's legs remained in his hand, the upper half twisted and coated in his blood upon the altar. He seethed even as his chest hitched. Even as tears came to his eyes.

Silence. Why must it always be silence?

Vala wrapped her arms around his waist from behind and pulled him close. "You were a fool to bring us here," she told him. "But you've always been a soft-hearted fool. Your answer will always be silence. The goddess has abandoned this world, as have all the gods. It is just us now. Us to live. Us to make our future."

"Forgive me," Cyth said. He closed his eyes and tilted his head back. "But I had to know. The lengths to which we will go, the destruction that must follow…I will not build the Kingdom of the Sun in defiance of our goddess. Only in her absence."

Vala rested her face against his shoulder.

"We Ordoths have long been forgotten by the goddess we love. This is no different. Hold faith, Cyth. In time, her gaze will return to us, to her true children. In time, she will see the works of our hands and grant us her blessing, even if only in the realms beyond that lay waiting at the end of all life."

Cyth pulled away from her and lifted his left hand. Blood completely coated his fingers and palm. A sign granted by Celestia, but in a way opposite to the one given the Darkhand. He smiled. A name he could adopt nonetheless.

"To the resurrection of the Sun," he told his sister. "To the birth of the Bloodhand."

In return, Vala gave him an exaggerated elven bow.

"And to the death of kings, queens, and the great cities of man."

10
ZUSA

The Gemcroft family arrived home from the tournament. A tall iron fence surrounded the property, its tips pointed and sharp. Petty thieves were a problem in Angkar. Nothing like the guilds of Veldaren, thankfully, which meant a guard posted at the door every night and a fairly tall fence was enough to keep their valuables safe and their sleep undisturbed. The home itself was also a pale imitation of the grand Gemcroft mansion. Small, two stories, its windows thin rectangles and its walls painted a faded crimson. When asked, Zusa always said they would begin construction soon on a proper mansion.

A safe enough lie, but one whose believability was running low after the past three years.

"Welcome back," said one of their two house guards, a pleasant if simple man named Dags. He'd been a soldier for Queen Loreina, and survived the destruction at the Bloodbrick with minor burns across his face and hands. In the years after, he abandoned the royal service for more profitable work. Zusa trusted him fully. He lacked the ambition for any true malice beyond occasionally swiping a bottle of alcohol from their cellar and hoping she would not notice. She did, but said nothing.

"How goes the tournament of pride, and our champion?" he asked.

"Third place!" Nathaniel said before the other two could answer. "I wish you could have been there, Dags. The way the crowd was cheering for our Erin? Louder than the other contestants combined."

Erin's face and neck flushed a deep red. "I should have gotten second," she insisted. "And I would have, if I hadn't messed up my parry."

"Aye, we all could do better if we always did better," Dags said, opening the gate using keys chained to his belt. "Don't let it wear on you, Erin. You have years and years to try again. You'll take the champion crown in no time, I believe it."

Erin smiled at him despite the obvious disappointment she'd carried since the tournament ended. It was one of the reasons Zusa overlooked his minor indiscretions. When her daughter entered one of her more dour moods, the scarred man always seemed capable of dragging a smile out of her.

Once inside their home, Nathaniel immediately made for the kitchen.

"Do you think Blanche has prepared us something for our return?" he asked, referring to the lone servant tasked with preparing meals. "I bet she has."

"You ate like a pig the whole tournament," Erin said as he hurried through the hall.

"And it wasn't enough. Not all of us eat like squirrels like you."

Erin let out an exasperated sigh and turned for her room. Zusa reached out to touch her shoulder. She tried to let the two be as they were, without her interference. The bond between them was unbreakable, and she knew their little squabbles and jests would only strengthen it further.

But she also knew her daughter. Erin craved encouragement and confirmation, yet was also deeply embarrassed when receiving it front of others.

"Despite your errors, and despite not living up to your best, I am proud of you," she said now that Nathaniel was gone. "So much of what you know is training. Safe. Controlled. Routine. You performed excellently when thrust into such different circumstances, and that will only improve as your experience grows."

Erin hesitated a moment and then nodded. "I was flustered, and distracted. I hate feeling either. I should be in control at all times."

"No one is in control at all times."

"Not even the Watcher?"

"No," Zusa said, crossing her arms and staring at the younger mirror image of herself. "Not even him."

Erin hardly looked convinced, but neither did she argue the point.

"Thank you," she said, and then departed for her room. If there was anything Erin craved more than confirmation, it was

Legacy of the Watcher

solitude.

Zusa let her go. Instead of joining Nathaniel in the kitchen, she retreated to her own bedroom. Her clothes were hardly the most constrictive, but they were still more extravagant than what she preferred to wear at home. The finery expected of the Gemcroft line was still foreign to her. During the lengthy siege of Angelport, she spent far more time as a murderer of orcs than the fancy-garbed wife of Alyssa. It was only when coming to Angkar that she forced herself to don the occasional dress and drape a bit of jewelry around her neck and wrists.

I suppose it is easier if you grow up with it all, she thought as she stepped into her room. *A far cry from my own faceless upbringing, though.*

The comparison forced a bitter chuckle out of her. She'd grown up vilified, her face and the face of her sisters hidden behind veils and their bodies wrapped in cloth. They were given no indulgences, only taught to kill.

Alyssa had rescued her from that life. And now, so many years later, Zusa did what she could to pay her back by protecting what little remained of her Gemcroft legacy.

The moment Zusa shut the door to her room, she froze in place. Her every instinct cried alarm, and she trusted them fully. Her hands dropped to her daggers, forever belted to her hips no matter her attire. Her eyes swept the room. To her left were a pair of dressers. Against the far wall, a wardrobe. Her bed filled the middle of the room, wrapped with curtains so thin they could hide no intruders.

The closet, though. The door was open, and from within its darkness she saw the faint silhouette of a man.

"I pray your intentions were merely robbery," she said, drawing her daggers. "I can forgive the poor and desperate, but if you seek my flesh you will leave bleeding, if I let you leave at all."

The man exited the closet. Her brow furrowed. It was the blue-hooded man from the tournament. Gray, the announcer had named him, just Gray. Her curtains were drawn, and his hood low, so she saw only a shadow where his face should be.

"I seek neither robbery nor rape," he said. "Only words."

The admission calmed her not at all. His voice...something about his voice frightened her. It felt like a phantom wrapping its fingers around her heart.

"Words?" she asked, her weapons not lowering an inch. "If you wished a conversation, there are better ways to hold one than sneaking into a woman's bedroom."

"Perhaps," Gray said. "But none so clandestine. I would avoid rumors, if I could, as well as the attention of your hapless door guard."

Zusa took a step back and bent her knees slightly. The man's confidence was unnerving. He approached her slowly, with easy movements that showed not the slightest fear of her daggers. And again, that voice. Deep. Commanding. Most strangely, familiar...

"No closer," she said. "Name your purpose, Gray."

As an answer, the man brought his hands to his blue hood, pulled it back, and then shook out his neck-length umber hair. His blue eyes pierced into hers. The faintest smile appeared and then disappeared from his lips. Zusa stared at him in dawning horror and disbelief.

"No," she said. "You're dead."

"I assure you, I am anything but."

Her grip on her daggers tightened. For fifteen years she had thought the world free of the monster that had led the Spider Guild. With the help of the Eschaton Mercenaries, Haern had crushed what was left of their guild and cut the throat of their brutal leader. Word of it had reached all the way to Riverrun. Zusa herself had read the letter bearing the joyous news to Alyssa.

Thren, slain? she'd said, and allowed herself a smile. *Then perhaps there is still some justice left in this world.*

It seemed not.

"What do you want?" she asked. "To start again? Build up your Spider Guild? Maybe claim a bit of bribes and security payments from the Gemcroft estate, just as we paid all those years ago?"

He took a lone step toward her.

"I want answers, Zusa, about the girl who bears my name."

Fuck. Fuck. Fuck.

A dozen attempted lies spun out and died in her mind. Erin had entered the contest, not as Erin Gemcroft, but Erin Felhorn. Her daughter insisted it'd been done on a whim, to avoid the appearance of preferential treatment. Zusa suspected there was more to it than that, but it now meant Thren had heard the announcement. For Gods' sake, he'd even fought against her.

Fought, and thrown the fight, she knew in an instant. It'd been apparent to her when she'd watched, and was doubly so now. Thrown, but why? What games had the old bastard already begun to play?

She looked into Thren's eyes and knew he would accept no lie. The truth must suffice.

"Your son and I...we did not spend much time together, but it was enough. When we abandoned Veldaren, I was with child. *His* child."

Thren stood perfectly still. Even statues showed more life.

"A granddaughter," he whispered. "I have a granddaughter."

It felt foul to hear those words spoken by a ghost who should have died over a decade ago. She shivered as if someone had walked over her grave. This situation...she'd never conceived of such a meeting. Thren was dead. Haern was dead. Zusa, and the Gemcrofts, were the only family Erin would know.

Not anymore.

"Did he know?" Thren asked. "Before he died, did he ever know? Did you ever tell him?"

Zusa swallowed down the rock in her throat. Her fingers ached from the pressure with which she held her daggers, but she refused to lower them.

"No. I wished to protect Erin from the life her father led. From the life you forced upon him."

And suddenly all her dread came to a stark realization. She did not fear Thren Felhorn's swords. If it came down to a fight between them, she trusted her skill to handle the old man. It was his presence she feared. His words. His mind. Erin was enraptured by the story of her father. She'd devoured the few books written about the Watcher in the years that followed the Gods' War. To her, Thren was a monster slain, but a monster who had shaped her father, molding him into the hero she adored.

How would she react to Thren's presence? And how would Thren react to her?

"You stay away from her," she snapped, vicious, sudden. "You deserve no part in her life."

"She is my blood as much as she is yours," Thren said. Though no hood covered his face, it seemed a shadow stretched to cover it anew. "You, who hid her presence from her own father, would deny me, too?"

Zusa dropped completely into a crouch, eyes narrowing, blood pumping in preparation for battle.

"Haern spent his whole life trying to recover from the scars you inflicted upon him," she growled. "I will not let you do the same to my daughter, do you understand? She is beyond you. Leave, and do not return."

Thren ignored her protestations. Instead he walked about the bed to one of her windows and shoved it open. When he spoke, he kept his back to her, almost daring her to strike.

"She may be your daughter, but I have fought against her, Zusa. I have glimpsed the truth of her. She is not so coddled and innocent as you would believe."

He glanced over his shoulder. His icy blue eyes plunged into her, sharper than any blade.

"I need not set a foot upon your mansion grounds again. It is *she* who will come to *me*."

"Never," Zusa insisted as he leaped out the window. "She will never know. You hear me? Never!"

She sprinted to the window, but all she could see of him was the faintest ripple of a gray cloak on the other side of the fence. She beat her fists against the wall, her heart pounding against her ribcage.

She can't know, she thought. *She can never know. He broke Haern. I won't let him break Erin. I won't let him ruin her.*

Frost settled over her heart and mind. She might be years past her prime, but she was still far younger than the elder Felhorn. Years as a Gemcroft had not dulled her ability to kill.

"I don't know what trickery you used, but it does not matter," she whispered. "If I hear one rumor, one *hint* of your existence, I will hunt you down and murder you, Thren. I will succeed where your son somehow failed. You are a ghost, nothing more, and I will burn this whole damn city to the ground before I let you haunt us with your memory."

11
TARLAK

"Why did I tell Harruq it was all right for him to leave?" Tarlak whispered to Aurelia. They stood in the grand hall of Angkar's grotesquely opulent four-story royal mansion, which Queen Brynn had chosen as her seat of power in lieu of reigning from a castle. Ker, and Angkar in particular, thrived on trade, and one could see the wealth such trade generated in the fine carpets, dozens of portraits, silken curtains, and furniture polished to a sheen and decorated with silver and gold bits and bobs that served no real purpose other than to showcase said silver and gold.

"Because he's no good at this," Aurelia murmured in reply. "Now shush."

Tarlak held back a groan. While not a castle, the royal mansion did possess a throne set inside an enormous entry hall that rivaled even Veldaren's conquered castle in size. The new ruler of Ker, Queen Brynn Sloane, sat surrounded by a dozen minor lords and advisers. She had a severe look to her, the angles of her face sharp and the color of her skin carrying an ashen hue despite its dark color.

Gregory knelt before her, the young lad doing a remarkable job imitating the greeting they had drilled into him during their travels. As Steward, Harruq should have been with him, but the oaf was off fighting in some tournament. Lucky bastard.

"Well met, young prince of Mordan," said Queen Brynn, rising from her throne. She was an imposing sight, tall and lean with muscle. What stories of her that had reached Mordeina insisted she had taken to the battlefield after her husband's death in the opening months of civil war that followed Queen Loreina's demise at the Bloodbrick. Even with her body half-buried in an elaborate red dress overdecorated with ribbons and lace, Tarlak sensed a warrior's resolve, and very much believed the stories.

"I am honored by your visit," the queen continued. "And I pray that this is the start of a lasting and beneficial friendship."

The words were for the audience, of course, not for

Gregory. The young lad looked dashing enough in his little suit, and when he looked up at the queen he gave his best practiced smile.

"So do I," he said.

Brynn clapped, signal enough that the introductions were at their end, and she was quick to approach Gregory while gesturing for him to stand. With those introductions finished the celebration could begin, which Tarlak was far more excited about. Servants flooded into the hall from two side doors, carrying trays of wine glasses. After them came more servants with little tables they set down, covered with white cloth, and then quickly filled with little slices of cheese, honey-slathered bread, and cubes of fish doused in a dark oil that smelled deliciously salty.

"Shall I mingle?" Tarlak asked Aurelia, who was busy pointing her daughter toward the table of snacks.

"Go ahead," she said. "I'll keep an eye on Gregory and Aubby."

"Ever the responsible parent and guardian, you are," Tarlak said, and tipped his hat. "I, however, am going to eat some cheese and get tipsy on free wine."

Tarlak did exactly that. He munched on various cheeses as he wandered through the crowded hall, feeling extremely out of place, and not because of the garish yellow of his robes and hat. Everyone was too prim and proper around here. Barely anyone even looked like they were enjoying their food, which was a shame, because the pale-white cheese in particular was delicious, as was the bread, baked from the rye fields they had passed through just outside the city.

Finally Tarlak found a spot of wall to park himself at, leaned against it, and finished his snack. He was still wiping crumbs from his beard when a woman approached, striking up a conversation as she slid beside him against the wall.

"The young king is mature for his age," she said, gesturing toward where Gregory was smiling and holding conversation with Queen Brynn. "I expected worse. Is that your doing, wizard? Surely the half-orc has not been the one teaching him his manners."

Tarlak raised an eyebrow at the finely dressed woman. She was younger than most in attendance and seemed unsure of herself. Her brown hair hung low over her face with heavy bangs, the rest draped completely over her neck and shoulders. It was as if she sought to hide, even as she dressed in a lovely crimson dress that shimmered with silver across the hem.

"And who might you be, my lady?" he asked. "I would have a name to give when I share such glowing compliments later with Gregory."

The woman's pleasant demeanor was as practiced as it was false.

"Tori Connington," she said.

Tarlak waved over a servant. Oh, he was going to need a drink for this.

"Connington?" he said, accepting a tall glass filled with a shockingly sweet white wine. He sipped at it, his curiosity awakening for the first time in this whole dull political ordeal. "As in, the family of the Trifect?"

Tori accepted a glass as well, her brown eyes studying Tarlak carefully.

"There is no Trifect," she said. "Not anymore. The Gemcrofts are a shadow of themselves, stripped of their lands and mines after fleeing west with but a scrap of coin to their name. As for the Keenans, well..." She sipped at her own drink. "We fared no better when the east fell. I am the last of their line. My guardian sent me west before the orcs arrived and lay siege to the city, to be married to Gilbert, the last eligible bachelor of the Conningtons."

Tarlak glanced at Aurelia, caught her chatting happily with Ker's new queen. The elf glowed in the light, and there was no doubting how taken Brynn was with her. A good sign. Perhaps Tarlak could make a few more allies of his own so this whole peace treaty might go off without a hitch.

"And where is your husband now?" he asked, returning his attention to Tori.

The woman smiled so sweetly at him. "When Queen Loreina was killed, we threw our support behind Queen Brynn in the civil war that followed." That smile wavered briefly. "My husband was murdered by those who sought a different ruler."

Bumbled right into that one, didn't you Tarlak? he thought, and hid his hesitation behind a lengthy drink.

"Forgive me," he said when finished. "I am ignorant to much of Ker's people, and what little I know of the Trifect comes from living in Veldaren."

"And being friends with the Watcher," Tori said.

"Oh." Another quick sip of wine. "So you know about that, eh?"

There was something almost patronizing about the Connington woman's smile.

"Yes, Tarlak Eschaton, the stories of your extended family's exploits have reached us even in Angkar. Given the Watcher's history, one might think me reasonable to consider you an enemy."

"Now hold on," Tarlak insisted. "May I remind you of all we did to help Alyssa Gemcroft maintain power when the Darkhand arrived in Veldaren?"

"Only the Gemcrofts," Tori said, and sipped her own drink. "Enjoy your visit, wizard. May your stay in Angkar be pleasant."

Tarlak bowed low to her, downed his drink, and decided he needed another to survive this meeting.

"How's it going?" he asked Aurelia an hour later, sliding in beside her as she chatted with a little congregation of noble ladies in dazzling dresses, all of whom still paled in comparison to Aurelia's beauty in her simpler garb.

"As well as one could hope for," Aurelia said after politely dismissing herself from the gaggle. "Are you surviving?"

"Barely," Tarlak said. "Mind if I depart? I'm afraid my fingers will slip and I'll strike someone with a lightning bolt if they ask me one more question about what it's like to be 'friends with the Godslayer'."

"You poor dear." Aurelia winked. "The queen's departed for the day, which means you're free. Get out of here, wizard, before you cause a diplomatic incident."

That sounded great to him. Tarlak fled for the exit, but it seemed freedom would yet be denied. One of the soldiers recognized him, an admittedly easy task given his outfit, and stopped him at the door.

"Tarlak Eschaton?" the man asked, as if that were necessary.

"I am," Tarlak said with a sigh. "Something amiss? Or is this when I learn I must pay for all the food and drink I devoured?"

The soldier looked decidedly unamused. "Her majesty

would like to speak with you. If you would follow me to her chambers."

Tarlak blinked. "Well now. I most certainly will."

The room was on the second floor, and so they climbed a spiraling set of carpeted stairs, then hooked a left at the hall. A second armed man stood guard before the door, and upon seeing Tarlak he knocked twice. The door opened, and he caught a glimpse of a handmaiden whispering something before the guard pushed the door open further.

"You're expected," the guard said, and stepped out of the way for Tarlak to enter.

Queen Brynn sat before an ornate oval mirror decorated with silver molded into waves that washed across the mirror's sides. She'd shed her bulky gown for a simpler dress, this a deep blue with black ribbons tied about the waist and wrists to help shape it. A handmaiden stood behind her, steadily undoing Brynn's intricate braids and then brushing through her hair with a comb. The handmaiden's skin was shockingly pale, her hair a red somehow even livelier than Tarlak's.

"I must admit, I had high hopes when I was invited to meet with the queen in her private chambers," Tarlak said, leaning against the door after the soldier shut it behind him. "But I'm a bit old and travel-weary to entertain two women at once."

Queen Brynn remained seated, taking her measure of him through the mirror.

"You're a crude one, aren't you?"

"I like to think of myself as humorous, not crude."

"We all have our delusions, wizard." She patted her handmaiden's hand, halting her brushing. "Leave us, Lumi. I must speak with this...humorous man in private."

The handmaiden tucked the comb into a pocket of her dress and then swiftly bowed.

"As you wish," she said, and then gave Tarlak a most impressive glare. "Please, call for me if he does anything...uncouth."

"Uncouth," he said, feigning heartbreak as the handmaiden departed. "I have ever been a gentleman."

When the door shut and they were alone, Brynn stood to face him. Her arms crossed, and her dark brown eyes surveyed him with caution.

"You're not here because I need a gentleman," she said. "You're here because I need a mercenary."

Tarlak didn't bother hiding his smile. Oh, this was already much more interesting than he'd hoped.

"I haven't been much of a mercenary since the Gods' War," he said. "The pay was terrible. I had to settle with saving the world for free. I did make some powerful friends, though, so I suppose that itself counts as payment."

Queen Brynn smiled. Just a small smile, the tiniest hint at her amusement.

"My father told me that once a man sells himself for a coin, he will forever have a price. I suspect you have one as well, and I am in need of someone with your magical talents. With the treaty ceremony approaching, I cannot afford distractions, nor threats to my rule. You, an eccentric outsider, could investigate without anyone else being the wiser."

Tarlak removed his pointy hat and bowed low. It'd taken time, but he decided he very much liked this new queen of Ker.

"Your father was wise, though it is my curiosity that currently wins me over, not the promise of coin. What is it you need of me, your highness?"

Brynn hesitated, perhaps feeling one last moment of uncertainty, and then she spun the chair before her dresser about and sat down. Her hands folded in her lap. Her gaze was iron, that indecision over and done with. Replacing it was a resolve that had helped her unite a divided Ker.

"I need answers. My people are under attack by a phantom group known only as the Bloodhand."

12
HARRUQ

A knock on the door stirred Harruq from his nap in the room given to them to use within the royal mansion.

"Eh?" he asked. The finery surrounding him gave him pause in his sleepiness. He lurched off the bed wearing only a loose pair of trousers and padded barefoot to the door. He found a finely dressed servant standing out in the hall when he yanked the door open. Despite the man's excellent composure, he still took a step back and widened his eyes slightly.

"My lord," the man said, and dipped his head.

"I'm not a lord," Harruq corrected. He crossed his arms. The servant blanched, and Harruq caught the man's eyes flicking to the many scars across his chest.

"I meant no offense," the servant said, his bow deepening. "Forgive me for any interruption, but you have received a summons to the Gemcroft family estate."

He lifted an eyebrow.

"The who?"

Thankfully, Aurelia was able to fill in the gaps in his knowledge as he dressed. She'd been with Gregory in the garden, enjoying a chat with some of Queen Brynn's extended family, when a servant had fetched her for him.

"The Gemcroft family was once extremely powerful in Veldaren," she said, watching him strap on his armor. "One-third of the Trifect, which you surely heard of. You did grow up there."

"Probably," Harruq said while tightening his belt. "It's been a few years, and those rich families were all the same to me. How'd they survive the east's ruining?"

She helped him with a buckle he'd been struggling with. "Poorly. They retreated to Angelport and kept their heads low during its occupation until Thulos's defeat. Their matriarch, Alyssa Gemcroft, took over both the port city's trade and defenses. They managed to endure a siege by the orcs and their war demon leader, and a couple years ago they arrived here in Angkar to lots of fanfare and promises of renewed trade and resettlement of the east."

Harruq finished strapping on his sword belt, turned about, and kissed her.

"Thank Ashhur you studied up before we arrived," he said. "I'd be helpless without you."

She poked him in the side, through a tiny gap in his armor, so that he flinched. "You're helpless even with me. Should I accompany you to the estate? Their family leader is a woman named Zusa, and I've heard she is particularly cold and ruthless when it comes to any family dealings. At the very least I could have Tarlak go with you. He's even more knowledgeable about the matters here in Ker than I am."

He waved her off. "Nah. They probably want to meet the fabled Godslayer, see if they can use my relationship with Gregory to secure some special trade arrangement with Mordan."

"And what will you do if that is the case?"

Harruq laughed. "Tell them they're talking to the wrong Tun. This head's empty, and unless they want something wrecked with my swords, they're getting nothing useful out of my visit."

◈

After receiving directions from one of Brynn's servants, Harruq headed back out onto the streets of Angkar. As expected, he received many stares and murmured comments as he walked. Perhaps he would be less noticeable if he wasn't wearing his armor and carrying his swords, but then again, people would still see his gray skin and the curved ears of his orcish heritage. Hiding was never something he'd been good at. Better to stand out, and do it well.

Harruq had expected something a little fancier than the nice-but-not-extravagant manor house he arrived at. He'd panhandled in front of larger while growing up in Veldaren. A lone guard stood in front of the gate leading through the iron fence surrounding the place, confident in his pose. His face bore the faint echo of burns.

"Harruq Tun, yeah?" the man asked before Harruq might introduce himself.

"That obvious?" he replied, grinning.

"Not sure who else you'd be, and I was told to expect your

arrival sometime today." He looked him up and down. "You really killed a god with those swords?"

Harruq tilted his head to one side. "That's what the stories say."

The man shook his head and removed a key from his pocket. "I fought in the defense of Ker when Thulos was still trouncing about. Orcs alone are terrifying, but those war demons? Shit. Just one of them was enough to overwhelm five of us, and when I blocked a thrust from its spear, I thought my arm was gonna break." He finished unlocking the gate and pushed it open. "I can't imagine what it'd have been like to fight, not just those demons, but their damned god. Whatever you're made of, it's of better stuff than I."

Harruq slapped the older guard in the chest with the back of his hand. "Not better, just way more stubborn. So are you my guide to whoever I'm supposed to meet?"

The pair entered through the gate, which the guard then locked behind them.

"The name's Dags," he said. "Follow me. I was told you're to meet with the lady of the house."

"Zusa, right?" Harruq asked. They crossed the stone pathway to the front door. He decided he liked this Dags fellow. He was remarkably straightforward, and probably talked much more than the Gemcroft family would prefer. That was just fine with Harruq, though. "What's she like? I've heard she can be a bit...intimidating."

"What could possibly intimidate the Godslayer?" Dags asked with a laugh. "Zusa's ruthless when it comes to coin, but she ain't cruel. She'll treat you fair, so long as you don't try to pull a fast one on her."

"No intentions of that here."

"Good. Be disappointing to meet the famed Godslayer only to discover him a cheat on the same day."

Harruq laughed. "If I have any concerns today, disappointing *you* is far from the top of the list, Dags."

The guard shrugged. "Fair's fair I suppose. It ain't me you should worry about disappointing. It's the little lady."

Upon entering the manor, Harruq found himself surprised by how sparse it was. Few paintings on the walls, and none were of family members. He walked single file behind Dags along a narrow hallway, heading toward a den kept pleasantly warm by a burning fireplace. Two bookshelves well-stocked with leather-bound tomes lined one wall. Near the windows were paintings of mountains and forests—lands nearby, Harruq assumed.

Waiting for him within was a woman he recognized, the dark-haired lady from the tournament he'd been seated beside. She was a smaller woman, the top of her head barely reaching his chin. She looked stunning in her deep lavender dress, which wrapped tightly about her body in a way that made him feel a little bit guilty for noticing.

"Lady Gemcroft, I present the Godslayer Harruq Tun," Dags said. He quickly bowed and then exited the room, leaving the pair alone together.

She said nothing at first, only stared at him with her dark brown eyes. Harruq crossed his arms and let her stare. He was used to being judged.

"I thank you for coming at my request," she said, breaking the silence. "Before we discuss matters further, I must ask for a vow of secrecy. Your reputation is legendary, and I trust you will not stain it with a bit of paltry gossip."

"Doesn't tend to be my thing," Harruq said. "I'll swear secrecy, but with one condition. My wife, Aurelia. I hold no secrets from her. Whatever you tell me, assume she also hears."

"And will she also honor your vow to tell no one else of what we discuss?"

Harruq shrugged. "She will, if she thinks it wise. No one tells that elf what to do, and if what you reveal to me is a danger to others, she'll act accordingly. That's the way it is, Zusa. If you don't like it, I'm happy to head back home and resume my nap."

Zusa slowly approached, and he realized that a dagger hung from the thin belt cinching her dress to her waist. A dagger whose hilt her fingers were curling tightly about.

"There are many stories about you," she said. "No doubt most are exaggerations, or outright lies. I would hear it from your own lips. Aaron Felhorn, the man known as Haern the Watcher…was he truly your mentor?"

Harruq shifted his own stance so that his sword hilts were just within reach. The hairs on his neck stood on end. Something was wrong here, but he couldn't quite piece it together. Aurelia's words ran through his mind. If the Gemcrofts were from Veldaren, perhaps they bore a grudge against the Watcher? But there was such a thin connection between Haern and him…

"I was a brute who barely knew how to swing a sword when I joined Tarlak's mercenaries," he said. "Haern took me in under his wing. He taught me how to fight, and how to overwhelm with speed as much as strength. All the battles I've won? He deserves the credit for them as much as I do. So yes. It is true." He stepped closer to Zusa. "The question is, why do you care?"

The dagger was suddenly in her hand.

"Because this world is full of liars."

She lunged at him, that dagger aimed straight for his throat. For some rich noble lady, her speed was incredible, her passage across the room done in the blink of an eye. Harruq instinctively dashed, not away from her, but into her charge. He had size and weight over her, and there would be no way to draw his swords in time to deflect that initial hit.

The steel plunged, and his hands punched, just as quick. His left hand caught her wrist, his right formed a fist and blasted her in the stomach…or at least that's what he'd been aiming for. She twisted so it missed, and his arm ended up wrapping about her instead. Their momentum continued, and they slammed into one another as if engaged in a brutal yet intimate dance. The dagger hovered an inch from his throat, his hand on her wrist holding it in place. The fingers of his free hand wrapped around her neck, closing about her slender throat so he could strangle her if he must.

She peered up at him, not moving, not attacking. The excitement in her eyes left him baffled.

"You're quick," she said. "I thought you'd be slower, all muscle and no speed."

"You're not the first to make that mistake. Now can I let you go, or will you try to kill me again?"

The faintest smile curled the edges of her lips. "Yes, Harruq, that brief dance was enough."

He released her, and she sauntered away, her dagger twirling between her dexterous fingers. Harruq shook his head, his bafflement growing. Such speed…he'd fought skilled assassins who couldn't move that fast. Was she an impostor, perhaps? Not the real

Zusa, but a bodyguard? He'd heard tales of royalty doing such things if they believed they could be in danger, and it wasn't like he knew what the real Zusa looked like.

"Care to explain?" he asked, all semblance of diplomacy leaving him. "Good hosts don't try to murder their guests just for a bit of fun."

Zusa sheathed her dagger and spun about. Her other hand brushed a few errant strands of her short hair away from her face.

"I want you to understand this was not my idea," she said. "But my daughter is insistent, and so I have relented. She would like you to become her tutor while you are here in Angkar."

Harruq held back a groan. He'd had many wealthy and noble families try to get him to give sparring lessons to their brats. It didn't even matter if they learned anything, since they'd be able to brag about 'learning from the Godslayer' or however they planned to spin it. Harruq rejected them, each and every one. He had better uses for his time.

"I'm not interested," he said.

"If it is a matter of price, I assure you, we can pay it."

Harruq's stare hardened. "I said, I am not interested. Find someone else to teach your kid. I'm leaving."

He was halfway to the door when she called out to him: "You will teach her, because you owe Haern that much for what he has done for you."

Harruq froze in the middle of the den and slowly turned to glare at Zusa.

"How dare you invoke his name like that?" he asked. "I gave everything for him, and he, everything for me. I have never trusted another person in battle like I did him. When Veldaren fell, we fought side by side against a legion of the dead. He saved my life a thousand times, and yes, Zusa, I owe him greatly, and if he had lived, I would be spending the rest of my life trying to repay him."

His ire grew with every word. He wanted to draw his swords. He wanted to shake the stubborn pride out of this stupid woman.

"My life, my victories, they are his to claim, not that he'd ever wanted the glory," Harruq said, taking two steps toward her. "And you would take that kinship, that trust, of my friend who died a hero, and tell me that this somehow means I should train *your* little snot-nosed brat? Why? Fucking *why?*"

Zusa did not back down. She tilted her head up at him and delivered the words that sent his mind reeling.

"Because Erin is his daughter."

Harruq required several seconds before he could form speech.

"How?"

"You have children. I dare say you know how."

"That's...not..." He flung his hands in the air. "Haern never once mentioned he had a child."

"That is because I never told him," Zusa said. "I was with child when Alyssa had us depart Veldaren for Riverrun. I had plans to one day bring her to meet him, once she was older, but then, well..." She shrugged. "The brother gods ruined the world. I suspect you're intimately familiar with that aspect of the story."

A mystery child. Harruq could hardly believe it. And for Haern not to know...

"Convenient, that you supposedly never told Haern," he said. "How do I know you're not lying? Haern never talked about much of his early life."

"I suppose you don't," Zusa said, placing a hand on her hip and giving him a look that could wither lesser men. "But I believe the wizard, Tarlak, accompanied you here? Ask him about me. Ask about my trip with Haern and Alyssa to Angelport. He'll remember. I was no stranger to your mercenaries in the days leading up to the necromancer's assault on Veldaren's walls."

Harruq shifted in place. He wanted to pace about, to mutter and grumble and think aloud, but he could not do so before this enigmatic woman.

Haern's daughter. Zusa wanted him to train Haern's daughter, just as Haern had trained him. If it were true, if she was his blood, then how could he refuse? Zusa was right. He did owe Haern that much, especially if Haern had never known of her. The shame of it hit him, the lost potential. He thought of never knowing of Aullienna or Aubrienna, and it killed him.

"Fine. I'll do it."

This time, Zusa did not hide her smile. "Very well. Thankfully, you already have your swords, and surely you can spare a little bit more time today for an initial spar. Follow me, Godslayer.

It's time you meet my daughter, Erin."

13

HARRUQ

The Gemcroft manor had a quaint little garden in the rear courtyard, guarded with a much more impressive stone wall than the fence out front. Ivy grew across thick portions of it, and two giant elm trees gave shade from the east and west sides. There were few bushes or flower gardens, with much of the space's soft grass carefully trimmed. It'd be a fine training area, albeit a little cramped.

Waiting within, her arms crossed and her head down and hidden beneath a hood, was Erin Gemcroft.

"Hey there," Harruq said, grinning. "Sounds like I'll be your mentor for a bit."

She looked up at him, granting his first good view of her face. Erin had her mother's tanned skin and deep brown eyes, but there was no disguising Haern's influence on her dirty blond hair as well as her nose and chin, both broader and wider than Zusa's. Seeing her wearing a gray hood only added to the effect, so that it almost felt like, if he let his imagination carry, the ghost of Haern stared back at him.

The image faded, replaced with a very nervous looking young woman. She wore a passive expression, but it clearly took effort to keep it that way. He could tell by the way she fidgeted, how her fingers kept drumming her saber hilts, that she was bursting with excitement.

"So you're Harruq?" she asked, and looked him up and down.

"In the flesh."

"The stories say no one alive is stronger than you. That true?"

His grin widened. "Oh, there's plenty stronger. I'm just more stubborn than all of them put together."

"A stubbornness you'll need when dealing with Erin," Zusa interjected. "I'll leave you two be. Harruq, when you're ready to leave knock on the door. Dags will be there to escort you out."

Harruq nodded at the wealthy woman and then turned his attention back to his new student. She was studying him closely. He wondered what she wanted from him, what she expected. Seeing the cloak, hood, and sabers, it wasn't hard to put an idea together. She was trying to walk in her father's footsteps. A father that, if Zusa told the truth, she had never met, and who had never known she existed.

His heart ached for her. She was trying for something she could never have. She likely didn't even know she was doing it when she donned that hood and learned the use of those sabers.

"Let's start with some basics, shall we?" he said. He had little experience training others, and pondered how exactly to even start. He drew Salvation from its sheath. "How much training have you had already?"

Erin drew her sabers. "My mother's trained me well. I came in third in today's tournament."

Given how quickly Zusa had moved when attacking him, Harruq imagined her training would be useful.

"Third place, eh?" he said. "I fought the first place winner. Wasn't impressed. Not a good sign for you, I'd say."

Her eyes widened, and he choked down a laugh. The girl was absolutely convinced he'd meant to insult her.

"Kidding," he said, twirling his sword once and then holding it before him at the ready. "I'm just kidding, Erin. I try not to be too serious. It don't fit me well."

"What does fit you well?" she asked, eyeing his glowing sword.

"Armor and a battlefield."

He batted at her with the sword, a simple hit meant to judge her reactions. In return, she slammed into it with both her sabers, stepped close, and thrust for his abdomen. He kept perfectly still, and stared at her as the tip halted just shy of his leather armor.

"Eager, aren't we?" he asked.

Her face flushed, and she pulled back her weapon. "Aren't we sparring?"

"It seems more like you were ready to kill me. I thought we were training?"

"You don't know what it's like to train with my mother."

Harruq laughed. "Correct, I do not. But I see you're used

to things being a little more...intense."

He withdrew Condemnation and readied both his blades. Erin crouched opposite him, her sabers up and her eyes narrowed. Harruq knew it'd be wiser to use wooden swords, but he suspected Zusa would not take kindly to the idea. Real weapons, to prepare for real battle. Hopefully it did not cost anyone a finger.

"Try to hit me," he said. "Let's see just how good you are."

Erin bounced up and down on her toes, just the tiniest little movements to limber up, and then lunged with her right arm extended into a thrust. Harruq batted it aside without moving an inch.

"Your elbow gave that one away," he said.

She retreated two steps and settled back into the same stance. The glower on her face could melt glass. Directed inward, not at him. She charged again, her hips twisting to add strength to a dual slash, her swords coming at slightly different angles. Harruq stepped into the twist, swatted aside one of the hits, and parried the other low and to his right. A shift of his wrist, and he locked the blade out of position. His elbow halted just shy of her face.

"You're not anticipating my reactions," he said.

"I don't know you, how could I anticipate what you'd do?"

He stepped back and twirled his swords once, relaxing his grip as she prepared for a third attempt.

"You judge the position of my hands," he said. "You watch the movements of my feet. When you strike, you remain aware of your weaknesses, and how they could be exploited."

She leaped at him, her sabers chopping overhead with commendable speed. Harruq crossed his swords, blocking the hit so viciously she staggered backward. Again that miserable glare. The young woman's focus was fierce. Useful, but only to a degree.

"You judge yourself harshly," he said. "I can see it eating you alive. Let your desire to be better fuel you, Erin, but not consume you. That desire will turn into self-loathing if left unchecked."

Erin nodded, but it felt more like a reflex than true understanding. She wanted to showcase her skills to him, and that he rebuffed her so easily was tormenting her. The pride of youth, he supposed. He'd certainly been no better during his first training session with Haern.

"Stop trying to impress me," he said. "Go again."

She bounced twice on her toes, feinted a thrust, and then lashed out with the other hand. When Harruq blocked, she countered immediately, forcing him to retreat a step lest it strike his armor. Erin maintained her aggression, and their swords rang out with a rapid series of exchanges. It felt good, a rhythm finally established between them. Harruq let it play out for a bit, refusing to strike at any openings even when they were there.

It seemed Erin, however, sensed it immediately. After a few seconds she retreated, and this time her glare was real.

"You're going easy," she said.

"We're sparring, remember? I'm not trying to kill you."

Her frustration grew, and something about it felt pointed in a way he did not quite understand.

"But you should be," she said. "I want to fight you, Harruq. I'm tired of everyone playing games."

Harruq highly doubted her training sessions with her mother were anything resembling games. Her frustration was at herself, and at others, not him. Still, it wasn't up to him to figure that out. If he was to train her, he needed her to be willing to listen, and cooperate. Having her silently fuming at his every instruction, thinking he was going easy on her, or playing some sort of game, would only delay progress, if not prevent it entirely.

"No more games then," he said, lifting his glowing blades. "I am your foe. Cut me down, Erin. Show me the limits of your skill."

She closed the distance between them slowly, almost casually, and then spun into a slash. He blocked, and she continued her momentum, trying to circle around him. Her sabers were a blur of steel, her feet dancing to keep her balance. Harruq twisted his own hips, following her, putting his swords in the way of her every strike. He let her fully complete the routine, and could almost visualize the individual stances she rotated through.

And then, when she finished, he unleashed his full strength upon her. When he parried her slash, Condemnation nearly smacked the sword out of her grasp. His legs flexed, catapulting him toward her with speed she never expected. Her defense was panicked, the placement of her swords suddenly clumsy and unprepared. Harruq batted them out of position with ease, still

Legacy of the Watcher

charging her, still overwhelming her with strike after strike that rang out a new tale of steel in the garden.

Her backwards retreat finally cost her, a misstep ruining her balance so that when she tried to block, she faltered completely. The blocking saber slipped from her grasp, and instead of retreating further, she reached for it. In return, he blasted her in the face with his elbow, punishing such incredible foolishness. She cried out, swung with her other saber, and gasped when Salvation struck it so hard the steel sparked. The toe of her left foot struck the heel of her right and she tripped, landing on her rear in the grass.

Blood trickled down her neck, her lip split by his elbow. Her entire body appeared to be locked down, the only motion the rise and fall of her shoulders as she gasped for air. Harruq fought back an impulse to show mercy or compassion. The girl was humiliated, but she wanted neither.

"You must do far better if you are to beat me," he said, deciding the obvious truth would suffice.

"How could I ever beat you?" she asked, exasperated. "You're bigger than me, you're stronger than me, and look at your swords! They're blessed with magic, unlike mine. You have every advantage."

Harruq knelt before her in the grass. A memory came to him, so clear it was as if it had been only yesterday. It was of himself collapsed on his knees during his very first training session with Haern behind the Eschaton Tower.

You possess greater strength than most alive, and ancient blades from a time long past, and you act as if these alone will grant you victory. It is arrogance, Harruq Tun, nothing more.

"Haern had none of those advantages, either," he said softly to Erin. "When we first met, I had these same swords, and these same muscles. He beat the ever-loving shit out of me without even trying. When I complained, he broke my nose with his heel."

"So he was weaker than you, like me? And because of that, it's supposed to make me feel better? Convince me I could still be like him one day?"

"No," Harruq said. "No one could ever be like him. Perhaps no one ever will again. But I could never train him, and I don't want to. I want to train *you,* Erin. Not someone pretending to be a man long dead. I want to get to know you, who you are, and see just how quickly you'll learn when pushed to your limits. I think that's what would have made Haern happiest, too."

He brushed a bit of Erin's hair from her face, exposing her bleeding lip.

"Haern claimed his teacher broke his nose on his first day, as he did mine," he said, and grinned at her. "I feared I'd passed on the tradition."

She glanced up, and after a moment matched his grin. "I did, too. And I guess it's fine if you want to go easy on me. I'm far from fighting you at your best. That's...that's pretty obvious, isn't it?"

"Give it time, Erin, and be happy you have so much yet to learn." Harruq stood and offered her his hand. "Get up. We go again."

※

Zusa intercepted him at the front gates an hour later, before he could depart the grounds.

"Well?" she asked. The wind played with the hem of her tight violet dress. Her beauty rivaled her deadliness, and he almost wished he could have sparred with her as well.

"A bright girl," Harruq said. "Skilled, of which I'm told you deserve the credit for."

"I've made sure she can survive this ugly world of ours." Zusa tilted her head slightly. "So will you train her? At least during your stay in Angkar?"

Harruq peeked past her, to one of the front windows, where Erin was spying on him leaving. He pretended not to see her.

"If I tried to say no, she'd hunt me down wherever I'm staying and force me to change my mind. But yes, I'd be happy to train her...if you help me in return."

"Oh?"

This was not the game he was best at, but he figured he should try to get something out of all of this.

"You're wealthy, and you're influential," he said, stepping closer to the diminutive woman. "And I'm sure there's ears you can whisper in. Tell them this treaty between Ker, Mordan, and Stonewall is a good idea. Dissuade anyone from causing scenes or making our lives miserable while we're here. It's for the benefit of everyone, right?"

Zusa crossed her arms and smirked. "You ask for a lot, while claiming to ask for little."

Harruq shrugged. "I dare say you did the same with training that burning piece of the Abyss you call your daughter."

That earned him a laugh, and her posture immediately relaxed.

"It is a deal, Harruq Tun. Shall I send an escort whenever Erin requires more training?"

He waved her off as he stepped through the front gate.

"Nah. See you tomorrow, Zusa. We're doing this daily, until I feel confident I've made an old friend proud."

14
CYTH

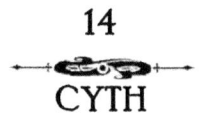

Cyth lay on his stomach in the tall grass watching the wagons roll by. His sister held the identical pose beside him, her sharp eyes observing every detail.

"Are they the right ones?" he whispered.

"They are," she said, nodding. "They ship to the Conningtons. It's painted on their lead wagon."

"Perfect. Give the signal."

Vala cupped her hand to her mouth, her fingers twisting, creating the proper form to whistle a specific bird call. It was a sparrow native to the Quellan, and only Quellan, forest. Cyth doubted any human would note the difference. Their study of Celestia's creatures was often rote and incomplete. They cared only what they could kill for their coin purses and their bellies.

A matching bird call sounded from the opposite side of the road. The other half of their ambush group was ready, and together they would emerge from the tall grass when the caravan was directly between them. As it neared, Cyth counted their opponents.

"Eight guards," he whispered. "More than usual. We need to be careful. Our numbers grow thinner with each passing day. We cannot afford a single casualty."

"I'm not scared of a few caravan guards," Vala said. "If they pose us a threat, then our hopes of conquering kingdoms are all but foolish dreams."

"They may still be foolish dreams," Cyth said. "But let us fight for them nonetheless."

Four wagons, the first three covered, the last in line stacked with crates to an almost comical level so that they swayed and pulled against the ropes binding them, rumbled along the road. Cyth imagined the goods within, trade meant to enrich the humans of Angkar, and his stomach soured. They and their gods had burned half the world, and while elvenkind struggled to rebuild what few cities they once possessed, humanity prospered with the ease of cockroaches.

He drew his swords in the tall grass. With such thoughts in his heart, it was easy to give the order to kill. The extermination was necessary. Justified.

"Give the signal," he said.

One last bird call, and then Cyth rushed the road, moving with his back crouched and his swords held low at his sides, in harmonious movement with the swaying grass. The humans would not see them coming. Cyth picked the closest guard and lunged at him, his sword sliding underneath the man's breastplate before he knew he was under attack. The man gargled blood as the sword pushed upward into his lungs. Cyth saw the pain in his eyes, and it lit a fire in him that felt divine. It was the rage Celestia should feel, were she not beholden to her love of the wretched Ashhur.

Vala was with him in a heartbeat, striking like a falcon at the driver of the nearby wagon, her twin swords reaching hungrily. They collided in an explosion of blood, the driver flung off the wagon. Vala landed atop him, her swords piercing deep.

Guards shouted in fear and confusion as twenty more elves emerged from the grass. Arrows flew with precise aim, thudding into chests. It didn't matter who the victims were. Guards, drivers, haulers: they all died screaming. What few could ready their swords in time were easily cut down, for what human training could match the decades of mastery of Cyth's brethren?

"Let none escape," Cyth shouted as five men abandoned their wagons and fled north as fast their legs could carry them. Two of his elves took chase, readying their bows to shoot them down once within range. Meanwhile, Cyth approached the first covered wagon, rounding to the back to check its contents.

His confidence nearly cost him his life. A spear shot out from seemingly nowhere, and if he were a single footstep closer it would have found purchase. Instead the thrust of the soldier hiding in the back came within a whisker of piercing his neck. Cyth scuttled backward, swords at the ready. His attacker's eyes were wide, spittle sticking to his beard, as he hollered nonsense. A dozen other armed men were in the covered wagon with him, and they surged out the back to a chorus of bloodthirsty yawps.

Cyth turned tail and fled, shouting, "A trap! All of you, to me!"

More soldiers appeared from within the second wagon,

decked out in shining chainmail and wielding weapons sharp and gleaming. They were no strangers to battle either, for despite the eagerness of their ambush, they remained close to one another as they approached. Cyth reached the edge of the grass before spinning. Vala slid to a halt by his side, blood dripping from her swords.

"How many?" she asked. Steel rang out from the other side of the caravan as Cyth's fellow elves battled the soldiers from the second wagon.

"At least twenty," he said. Two more of his people joined he and his sister, their swords at ready. "Bring them down."

Four against the ten heading their way. Cyth narrowed his eyes, his every muscle growing taut. Four was more than enough.

Vala led the assault, all too eager to see blood flow. The ten soldiers moved in lockstep, shoulder to shoulder. Several wielded shields, and they held them high, protecting themselves and their neighbor. Fine armor. Solid tactics.

And Vala made a mockery of it all, diving straight into the reach of their swords and spears. Her lithe body twisted, arms lashing, swords lifting and parrying away every attack. She created an opening, her spine twisted, bending backward, and as a spear passed underneath her she stabbed a man in the throat. When he fell she dropped to a roll, ducking underneath a beheading chop, and then came up standing on the corpse of the man she'd killed. Both her swords found flesh as she thrust behind her without even looking, yet still exploiting the weak spots of their armor.

Cyth charged headlong into that chaos, assaulting one of the men screaming from Vala's stab. A swipe, and he easily shoved aside the man's shield. A thrust, and he ended his life. A sickly joy filled him as he ripped his weapon free. The sight of spilled human blood was a beautiful thing.

Vala danced around the back of their line, slicing out heels and stabbing spines. Cyth thrashed another shield bearer, and then the two elves with him pushed harder against their flanks. Suddenly the ten were five, and surrounded on all sides. Three heartbeats later, they were all corpses on the road.

"Where are the rest?" Cyth asked, sheathing his swords. The sounds of battle had faded. In the distance, he saw the fleeing humans were dead, their bodies being dragged along the road by the elves who had given chase.

"Dead," Vala said, gesturing for him to follow. At the opposite side of the road, they discovered a similar scene, ten armed humans bled out on the dirt. The stink of it was already seeping into the air.

Cyth grimaced. The ten humans were not alone; an elf corpse lay beside them, her lovely eyes frozen in death.

"Celetha," Cyth said, dropping to his knees beside her.

"Bastard caught her with her back turned," a nearby elf said.

Cyth gently cupped her face in his hand. Her blond hair ruffled through his fingers. He knew her, as he knew all of those with the bravery to join him in his pursuit of a better Dezrel. Celetha possessed a kind heart with a wicked sense of humor. She preferred knives over swords, and could make them dance between her fingers. It hadn't been enough. A sword had opened her from the back, and now she was dead and gone. How many years had she lived? Two hundred? Three? How many hundreds more was she now denied in death?

Cyth closed her eyes with his thumb and shook his head.

"Carry her back to our camp," he said. "We will mourn her when the stars rise, and burn her pyre where Celestia may watch and shed her tears."

He pressed his hand to her back, drenching his fingers with her blood. The warmth, already fading. Cyth sighed, remembering his purpose, remembering the need for his crusade. Resolve hardened, he approached the nearest wagon and pressed his wet hand against its side.

There would be no confusion as to who was responsible. Yet one more victim of the Bloodhand. As he looked upon his handiwork, his sister joined his side.

"Did Tori Connington prepare an ambush against us?" she asked, her voice low as to not be overheard. Her face darkened. "Because if she did…"

"No," Cyth told her. "These wagons are destined for the Conningtons, but the shipments are from wealthy traders in Mordan. I strongly suspect this was their doing instead."

"We're earning a reputation," Vala said with a shrug. "I suppose that is something."

Even though the wagons had carried soldiers, there were still some crates piled up within them. Vala moved through the nearest, giving a cursory look at the contents of the crates, using her sword to pry open any that were nailed shut.

"Mostly clothes, linens, and fabrics," she said when finished.

"Useless then," Cyth said. He looked to the wagons, and his soldiers dragging out the bodies to dump to the dirt.

"We need the space. Burn it all."

15
ERIN

"Where are you headed, little lady?" Dags asked when Erin came trudging toward the front gate. "You're up earlier than normal."

"Felt like doing a long run," she said, which wasn't much of a lie. Part of her mother's training involved running several miles every other morning, and it would take a bit of a jog to reach her destination.

"Expecting trouble?" he asked as he opened the gate and stepped aside. He gestured toward the sabers strapped to her hips.

"Better safe than dead, right?" she said, pretending it were no big deal. Pretending her heart wasn't ready to leap out of her chest.

"I'd think a knife would suffice for that," the old soldier said with a shrug. Erin lowered her head and prayed her hood would protect her from her own incriminating expressions.

The sun had barely crawled above the horizon, yet already Angkar bustled with life. Such was expected for a port town reliant on fishing and trade. Heavy fog lifted off the sea, adding a gray haze to the homes on either side of her. So similar to Angelport in many ways, though here the buildings had a bit more flair to them, built taller and with their roofs sharper. The wood was darker too, which combined to make Erin feel like the city were more ominous.

Not that Angelport had been all that kind in those few agonizing years they'd been besieged. That final year, every night she went to bed expecting warning bells to signal another attack from the war demon's army.

Focus, Erin thought, pushing away the memories. Her nerves made her run faster than she should. A steady, consistent jog that she could do for hours had become a near-sprint that left her breathless. She slowed her pace, waited for her heart to settle, and then resumed once more.

As promised, Gray waited for her at the broken fountain splitting the main road, a quarter mile from the docks. He stood with his arms crossed over his chest and his hip braced against the side. Water trickled down the fountain, and she wondered if it were natural trickery or magic that maintained the flow. Atop the fountain was a broken statue of an angel, the upper half chopped away completely—a symbol of the rejection the people of Ker had delivered to Ashhur's rule. Erin was glad for it. Those angels had never come to Angelport when her family was in need. They had not brought their healing magic to her mother as she lay dying in a city besieged by a war demon and his army of orcs.

Gray said nothing, only stood observing her. The feeling of his eyes upon her made her skin crawl.

What are you doing here? she asked herself, and not for the first time. She already had Harruq Tun training her, the famed Godslayer and savior of Mordan. Her lip was still swollen from his elbow. His skill was clearly superior to hers, and it would likely take years before she might hold her own against him. What could Gray possibly offer her that Harruq couldn't…and why did she so desperately want to cross swords with him again?

"I'm here," she said, standing awkwardly before him.

"You are."

He obviously didn't care that it was awkward. The realization surprised Erin somehow. What was it like, to simply not care how one was perceived? Or to know you were fully in control of a situation?

"Well," she said, hating the silence and how impotent she felt. "You said you'd train me if I came here, and so I did. You're not going to go back on your word, are you?"

His blue eyes pierced through her. "My word, when given, is iron. And I offered to help you stop playing games. Never did I say I would train you. You voice only your assumption."

Erin clenched her jaw to prevent a scream. Heavens help her, the old man was maddening.

"Was my assumption wrong?" she pressed.

"If you take everyone's words for their implied meaning, you will soon be fooled out of house and home," gray said, his hands drifting to the hilts of his swords, sheathed and buckled at his hips. "The lawyer and scribe will bleed you dry through the letter of the law, not the spirit, and the crook and thief will have you walking blind into a thousand traps. Ignore what I offered. Focus on the purpose. Think on the reasons."

"I didn't come here for tutoring lessons," she said.

"No, you came to learn how to stop playing games. Did you think that involved weapons alone?"

Yes. The damned answer was yes, but she didn't want to admit that. Her silence betrayed her though, and she saw the faintest glimmer of amusement flicker in those ocean blue eyes of his.

"As I thought," he said. "Follow me, Erin Gemcroft."

"It's Felhorn," she said as he led her toward the coast.

"So you told the people at the tournament," Gray said. "Yet your mother is Zusa Gemcroft. Why do you claim a name that is not yours? Are you ashamed of the wealth you were born into?"

Erin hesitated, waiting for a trio of fishermen to pass by with their stinking buckets and heavy nets. She refused to let anyone else overhear this confession.

"I'm not ashamed of it," she said, watching Gray's reaction as best she could. His back was to her, and though he'd not raised the hood of his cloak, she could see only the tiniest bits of his expression. "My father is Haern the Watcher. Aaron Felhorn. Am I wrong to take my father's name as my own?"

Nothing. The old man gave her nothing. She might as well be following a statue.

"It is if seen as a rejection of the mother," he said.

"It's not a rejection," she insisted. "I know who I want to be, and it isn't her."

Damn it all, why was she confessing all this in the middle of the street? She didn't know this man. She had zero reason to care for his opinions, and yet here she was, vomiting out her innermost secrets.

"That sounds like a rejection to me."

Erin didn't bother arguing. It may sound like a rejection, but it wasn't and she knew it in her core. She didn't want to one day be shackled by the Gemcroft legacy, and all the baggage of being a member of a crumbling Trifect. That didn't mean she hated her mother, or thought her unworthy. She wanted to be like her father. She wanted to be someone who made a difference.

They veered left, tracing the twisting paths toward the many warehouses storing goods for shipping, either out to port, or through carts and wagons farther inland. Gray led her to the door to what appeared to be a shipwright, based on the sign hanging above the door. Without a word he stepped inside, and did not hold the door open for her. Erin caught it halfway shut with her elbow, pushed it open, and followed.

The moment she was inside, a sword was pressed to her throat. Her entire body went rigid, and her breathing ceased. Gray loomed before her, swallowing her entire vision. His cloak wrapped about his body, and it seemed to add weight to his presence. This man was not the one she faced in the tournament. He was crueler. He was deadly.

"You know not who I am, where my allegiances lie, or even my true name," he said. His voice was colder than a winter evening. "Yet you followed me alone, to a building you have not scouted, under vague promises of things you desire. Worst of all, when my betrayal is revealed, you did not act, but instead locked in place. You are foolish, child, and if I wished ill upon you, you would be dead."

Erin kept perfectly still. She had no argument. Her sabers were still sheathed, the door behind her closed. The shipwright warehouse was mostly empty, containing only half-assembled beams and stacked piles of cut lumber. If Gray wished it, she would be a dead woman.

"Do you?" she asked, and stared into his icy blue eyes. "Wish ill upon me?"

For the first time ever, she saw him flinch.

"No. I wish for you to survive." He withdrew the blade. "Are you naive, or merely stupid, to trust a stranger so?"

Erin had never felt more like a child in her life. *Playing games*, Gray had said during their duel, and she had thought he meant the way she battled. Now she knew differently. Everything about meeting him was stupid. Damn it, she hadn't even been truthful about where she was going when she left home. If she went missing, no one would know where to start looking for her.

"Fine," she said. "I'm a fool. I should be dead. I should be asking questions, so let's start right now. Why *do* you care so damn much about me?"

Gray beckoned for her to follow him deeper into the warehouse. She hesitated, wondering if this would be just another trap or trick, but gave in and followed anyway. It didn't seem like the strange man would pull the exact same lesson twice. That would be beneath him.

"I care because I see potential," he said, walking between the stacks of cut sycamore planks. "And I would see that potential realized."

He stopped in the center of the building, which was conveniently empty. She wondered if Gray had connections that allowed him to use the place, or if perhaps he even owned it. She knew nothing about this man. Even his reputation at the tournament had been of an old soldier living out his glory days. After having faced him, she knew that was completely false. He was more, so much more. But in what way? And how was he connected to her?

"That's not an answer," she said, refusing to let him off the hook so easily, not after humiliating her so. "I asked why you cared, not what your goals were. You're avoiding the question."

Gray pulled the hood of his cloak up and over his face, and it seemed his entire body relaxed with its presence. He looked more at home with his face hidden, more like his true self as he crossed his swords before him in an 'X'.

"I shall make you a deal," he said. "When you score a single true hit against me, I shall give you the answer you wish for. I make no promises as to whether or not you will like what you hear."

"That's all? Just one hit?" Erin asked, drawing her sabers from their sheathes.

"That is all."

She twirled her weapons in her fingers. "Are you sure we don't need blunted weapons?"

He smirked at her. "I am safe from your weapons, Erin, and I assure you, my control over mine is absolute. If you bleed, it is because I want you to bleed."

Again that maddening level of confidence. Harruq Tun had killed gods, and even he didn't seem so sure of himself. Who *was* this old bastard?

She braced for a charge. Well, there was one clear way to find that out. A single hit? She could do that. Zusa's training was not to be scoffed at.

"Any rules?" she asked.

"Are there rules in—"

She leaped at him before he finished his sentence, her saber thrusting for his chest. Just before she could tap its edge against his shirt, he twisted sideways and batted it with his off hand. It harmlessly cut air. When she pulled back, he retreated two steps and grinned at her.

"Better," he said. "Perhaps there is hope for you after all."

He assaulted her in turn, his swords crashing in from either side. She sidestepped one and attempted a block on the other. It wasn't as foolish as trying to block a hit from Harruq, but it was close. She winced at the pain as her sword clanged out of the way, and Gray's sword halted an inch from her head.

"Blocking me is foolish," he said. "Did you not learn that from our duel at the tournament?"

"You weren't trying for most of it. I had to see what you could do for real."

He pulled back the sword. "Fair enough. Again."

Her turn. She weaved her weapons back and forth, all of her mother's various stances fluid in her memory. She tried to push through them even faster, to let them come naturally to her to address the complaints Gray had levied against her during their duel. The urgency only caused her to stumble, and what should have been a killing thrust was easily parried away. His elbow struck her cheek hard enough to leave a bruise.

"You're too focused on yourself," he said, stepping back to give her space. "Stop obsessing on your moves, and start watching mine."

But she was, she swore she was. He thrust for her chest, and when she tried to parry, she realized she'd misjudged the angle. He was so quick, his movements so deceptive. Only one of his short swords was redirected, while the other halted just shy of her shirt.

"Why did you fail?" he asked, gently tapping her with the edge.

"I read the angle of the thrust wrong," she said.

"Good," he said, and settled low. "How do you prevent it from happening again?"

"I watch closer?"

"Wrong."

He performed the exact same thrust, just as quick. She attempted the same parry, only faster, and half-succeeded. The thrust pushed wide, but not wide enough. The tip pushed against her left shoulder, just deep enough to draw a trickle of blood.

"You failed again," he said. "How do you prevent it?"

The failures were starting to fluster her, and she hated trying to guess what answers would appease the older man.

"By being better."

He withdrew his sword and prepared yet again.

"Meaningless," he said. In came the swords, and she reacted on instinct, this time ensuring she swung hard enough to sufficiently parry both hits aside. The moment they were past, she slid closer, the steel of their blades scraping along each other, and then tried to break them off for a dual swipe at his arm.

He read it immediately, and before she could close the distance he kicked her knee. The pain of the twisting joint collapsed her to the ground, and she choked down a scream of pain.

Gray, meanwhile, calmly paced before her.

"That time you succeeded," he said. "What did you do differently?"

"You did the same move three times in a row," she said. "Of course I finally parried it correctly."

The toe of his boot struck her face, splitting the already swollen lip Harruq had created. She cried out and collapsed onto her back, a spray of blood flying to stain the floor. Gray's swords were at her throat in an instant.

"Either you are here to learn, or you are not here at all," he said, breaking the eerie silence. "I don't give a single shit about your pride, Erin. You've had years of training, excellent training, I will freely admit, but you are a member of the Trifect. You will have many, many enemies, and they will send men and women after you who have spent *decades* learning how to kill. Against that, your five or six years tutoring under an aging woman like Zusa will be nothing. *Nothing.* Do you understand me?"

Erin stared up at this man, this stranger, and her bafflement grew. He cared for her life. Had her mother hired him? A clever way to train her without Erin knowing? But amid all the hardness in his voice, she could hear it so clearly. A hint of fear. Of seeing this future, of her death, come to pass.

"Who *are* you?" she asked softly.

"You know how to hear that answer," he hissed. "Now I will ask again, Erin, and this time I expect a true answer. No bluster, no sarcasm, and no ego. Why did your third attempt succeed when the first two failed?"

She licked her swollen lips, tasted blood. "After the first two, I knew what I needed to do, and with the third, I finally did it right," she said, the closest she could think of to the plain truth.

"Exactly," Gray said, withdrawing his swords. "Nothing worthwhile in this life is easy. You learned through pain. You learned through hardship. This means you must see your every failure exactly as it is. No excuses. No justifications. Is that clear?"

Erin pushed herself back to her feet.

You can leave right now, she thought. *Zusa and Harruq can teach you anything and more that this man can.*

Except that wasn't true. She couldn't shake those words, that feeling, of playing games. Harruq wanted her to learn. Gray wanted her to survive. If she wanted to live up to everything her father had done, she needed to be pushed to her absolute limits, and there was something about Gray's ruthlessness that convinced her which of the two would accomplish that.

"Learn through doing," she said. "But does that mean you will judge me for my every failure? Even when you expect me to fail?"

Gray clanged his swords together. "I will judge ignorance. I will judge laziness. I won't judge failure in act, only failure in judgment itself. You walking blindly into this building with a stranger, for instance. You were a fucking idiot, Erin. Be glad I am who I am."

"And who is that?"

"You know the game."

He dashed at her, and she thought he might use the same parry for a fourth time, but the positioning of his hands was wrong. She caught it just in time, her sabers properly deflecting a chop and then parrying the accompanying thrust. She countered, he blocked, and then they danced, swords clanging back and forth, the very first hint of the song that developed when she practiced with her mother.

It lasted three seconds. Her growing confidence had her try to react quicker than he might anticipate, countering one of his high thrusts by ducking low and thrusting right back. He rewarded her with a hit to her forehead with the hilt of his sword. When she staggered, she swung wildly at him anyway, refusing to relent. This was no game after all, no points, no judges to call an end. Her hit was easily blocked, and this time it was his heel that greeted her face.

She tumbled to the ground in a rattle of wood, steel, and sawdust. One of her sabers slipped from her hand.

Gray paced between her and her weapon, his face hidden in the shadow of his hood but for his deep scowl.

"You learn through failure," he repeated. "But in true combat, failure is death. That is why I must push you the closest I can to that breaking point. Your mind knows I will let you live, but I need your body to disbelieve. I need you panicked, and exhausted, and reacting on instinct. I need you to be broken and still fight on, because you will not be given such chances when facing true foes."

He grabbed her saber, flipped it, and offered her the hilt. She did not yet accept.

"Your opponents will see a young girl," he continued, "and believe they are stronger than you. More skilled. Better trained. They will have taken lives with their own hands, and seen death so many times they will not blink at its arrival. You must be greater than them all. Every weakness within you, shattered. Every doubt, broken. Your will must be iron. Your confidence, earned and true. Only then will you achieve your fate."

"Achieve my fate?" she asked. "And what is that? And who are you to even know?"

He crouched lower. His extended hand remained firm.

"Because you chose the name Felhorn. Because you wish to become like your father, the Watcher of Veldaren."

Erin felt like she was losing her mind. She stared at the face beneath the hood and tried to see, to imagine, to know.

"Who *are* you?" she whispered once more.

His own voice lowered in answer. "One blow, Erin. Stand equal with me, and you shall have the name you seek."

Erin took the saber and stood. She turned and spat blood. Her knuckles turned white with the strength of her grip.

"And I'll have it," she said. Harruq's words came to her, and they felt appropriate. "We go again."

Their swords crossed, and he showed her no compassion, no mercy. By the time she left, her lip was swollen, her wrists aching, and her body covered with bruises. She left with all of those, but no

name.
 Not yet.

16
CYTH

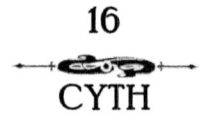

Cyth knelt before the shrine of the four-pointed star. It was small and simple, just carved and stained wood no taller than his knee. That simplicity hid its significance. It had been crafted using a branch from the first tree grown in the Dezren Forest, in an age before the creation of man.

And yet he had found it in a forgotten room in Stonewood, stashed among aged trophies and belongings carried about during their exodus. He'd cut it from its base and brought it with him, to plunge the long, sharp bottom point of the star into the dirt when he prayed.

The stars in the night sky were bright, shining through the faint canopy of trees Cyth and his followers camped within. Celestia was among those stars, Cyth believed. But was she listening? Was she watching?

"Ever are we meant to be the peacekeepers," he breathed, closing his eyes. Wind blew through the leaves, and he pretended it was an acknowledgment from his goddess. "Ever are we to watch, and aid, and endure, all while the world suffers. Do you regret it, goddess? Revoking the fields and hills from us, and granting them to humanity? Do you weep for the world that was lost, when you elevated the Brothers above your own children?"

There would be no answers to those questions, not in this life, yet he repeated them nonetheless. He burned them into his soul, so when he joined Celestia among the Weave nothing would hold him silent.

Cyth put his hands upon the old wooden star and pressed his forehead to the sharp top point. He let the pressure build, the wood digging in deep, until the first trickle of blood flowed down his forehead.

"We are here," he whispered, and clutched the wooden shrine. "Bleeding for you. Dying for you. Despite your abandonment. Despite your failures. Precious mother, never doubt our love, even as we turn from the path you would have us walk."

He looked up to the stars, and despite the sting of blood dripping into his eyes, he did not look away. Somewhere up there, she watched. She must watch.

"This world was ours once," he said. "And it will be ours again."

Soft footsteps alerted him to the arrival of another. Cyth stood, pulling a cloth from his pocket to wipe away the blood.

"Am I entitled no privacy amid my prayers?" he asked.

"Celestia never desired solitude for her worshipers," said a woman's voice, but not Vala's as he had expected. "Only gathered souls come to offer celebration."

He turned about and frowned.

"It is dangerous coming here," he said. "Especially with our plans already in motion."

"Plans that have yet to include me," said Brit'tari Caram. She wore the armor of humans, chain and plate meant to turn away their thick, brutish blades. Her face was split down the middle with a scar earned years ago when the Dezren elves battled King Baedan's soldiers. Before the fires claimed their homes, and their most powerful gave their lives at the Bloodbrick to ensure their people could escape.

"You speak as if you are uninvolved with the city's conquest," Cyth said. "Your information has been invaluable. No amount of coin I offer would ever have me trust a spy within Angkar as I would one of my own kin."

Brit'tari smirked at him. She was a dear friend, one of the first to encourage him when he spoke his dissenting voice to the elven councils. She was also one of very few who could make him feel like the reckless child others claimed him still to be.

"I am capable of more than information. I pray you do not forget me when the time comes to lay the foundation of the Sun Kingdom. I more than most am deserving of retribution."

The ruins of her ears were proof of that. She lost one ear in battle against the king's forces. The other, she had mutilated upon hearing of Cyth's need for a spy to infiltrate the human city. The sight of the scarred flesh made Cyth's chest ache. That they must give up their beauty and uniqueness to live among the squalor the humans called their cities was yet another sin to stain their souls.

"Matters are not yet finalized, but I assure you, you will

have your place," Cyth insisted. "I pray you had a better reason than that to risk forfeiting your secrecy to come to my camp?"

Brit'tari drew the enormous sword of hers off her back, spun it once, and slammed it into the soft earth. She then crossed her arms over the hilt and leaned her weight upon it. Mischief sparked in her eyes, lighting curiosity within Cyth's heart.

"No," she said. "I come because of what you desire most of me. Information."

Brit'tari was much too pleased for this to be some random tidbit. There were multiple ways for her to pass messages without leaving Angkar and potentially attracting attention.

"And what is that?" he asked.

"I found a student of the Darkhand."

Cyth stood perfectly still. The words refused to make meaning in his mind.

"That's impossible. They're all dead."

Brit'tari shrugged. Her smile never wavered.

"I assure you, it's true. Bastard confessed it with his own mouth, but even without, I'd have sensed it. I sparred with your uncle, back before he left in exile. The styles are the same. The question is, who is he?"

The excitement flooding through Cyth made it difficult to concentrate. Could it be possible? After all this time? But who could it be? Muzien had two well-known pupils. One was Grayson Lightborn, the other Thren Felhorn. Grayson had managed much of the Sun Guild in the west, while Thren eventually broke away to found his own Spider Guild in Veldaren. As far as everyone knew, both had been slain by the King's Watcher, and he told Brit'tari as such.

"Stories are fanciful lies dressed as the truth," she said, and pulled her sword free. "I trust my instincts. The old man is a student of the Darkhand. My question is, what do we do about it?"

That was no question at all. Cyth had never met his uncle, whose exile had begun long before he had been born. He had been a mere rumor at first, whose name was muttered like a curse. His achievements were mocked, his betrayal to the goddess, absolute. His prowess was never questioned, and instead used to exemplify wasted potential. But then King Baedan chased them across the rivers. The second Gods' War ravaged the land. Angels reigned, fields burned, and the golden city fell from the sky. Cyth had been born into a world ruined by humanity, and very few of his fifty years of life had known peace.

To Cyth, Muzien was the first to truly see the light. His uncle knew the wretched animals created by Karak and Ashhur from the mud would destroy all of Dezrel if left to their own devices. Power and wealth were their only rulers, and so elvenkind must hold wealth and power. If only Cyth could have met him, learned from him! What knowledge had he gained during his many years of exile that was never shared with his elven brethren? What understanding of humankind had died with him on the rooftops of Veldaren, lost to the rain?

"Perhaps Muzien had a secret disciple," Cyth told Brit'tari. "Or perhaps Thren or Grayson survived, and told lies of their deaths. It doesn't matter. Bring them here, my dear friend. They served the Sun Guild once. Let them pledge their allegiance, not to the guild, but the kingdom."

Brit'tari kissed her fist and then held it to her forehead, the same spot where Cyth still faintly bled.

"I'm not sure he will come willingly," she said. Her grin widened. "But then again, I did promise him a rematch."

17
TARLAK

"Here we are," Tarlak's escort said. "A shame you couldn't have been here beforehand."

Tarlak looked about the scattered mess that remained of what was apparently the ninth trade caravan attacked just that month. Three wagons lay broken on one side, the bodies of their oxen stinking up the air. Torn sacks were piled up behind them. Blood smeared the grass and dirt. No bodies, though, which Tarlak found intriguing.

"Where's the dead?" he asked his guide, a younger man named Oliver. He was an apprentice for one of the Gemcroft merchants, sent with Tarlak to lead him to the location of the latest assault on the traders making their way to Angkar. Oliver's blond hair was tied back in a bun, and his sleeves rolled up to alleviate the sudden heat that had come with the morning breeze.

"Buried over there," Oliver said, gesturing to the opposite side of the road. "We're a bit too far from the city to bring them to their families, so we had to make do."

"How many in total?"

"Ten. Eight managing the carts, plus two guards."

Tarlak wandered off the road, taking stock of his surroundings. The lands surrounding Angkar slowly flattened the closer one came to the ocean. They were about thirty miles distant, the road rolling up and down across hills so gentle their rise and fall was almost imperceptible when traversing them. Tall grass speckled with pink-flowered weeds grew all the way to the road's edge.

"The grass is tall enough to hide an ambush," Tarlak said. "You could hide a hundred people without anyone noticing."

"A couple guilds once banded together to pay the local farmers to hack it down," Oliver replied, trailing behind him. "The first Gods' War put an end to that. Everyone was far tighter with their coin, and the people, more frightened to travel beyond their homes."

"I don't blame them." Tarlak glanced at the broken crates.

"Did the attackers take everything?"

"Hard to say. It's been a day since the attack. Anything left behind would be picked clean by opportunists."

Tarlak frowned. From what he could tell, the wagons were carrying milled wheat for the coming celebrations. Not the easiest of goods to barter with black market dealers, nor the most profitable. He inspected sack after sack, all of it left to dry, most unopened.

"Strange," he muttered, and continued looking. He tried not to notice the amount of blood that stained the grass, nor the smears within the wagon. These wagons were uncovered, the interiors bleached mercilessly by the sun. A thick patch of blood marked the front of the first. The driver, no doubt killed the moment the ambush started. But by what? He'd assume an arrow or crossbow bolt, but yet he saw not a single one in the area. If the attackers used bows, they also cleaned up every arrow and removed them from the bodies after killing them.

"No survivors, right?" Tarlak asked, scratching at his chin.

Oliver stood awkwardly by the middle wagon. "None we're aware of. It was just a clean hit, real professional, by what we can tell."

"I don't like the sound of professional bandits, Oliver."

"I doubt those escorting the wagons liked it, either."

Tarlak moved from wagon to wagon, searching for any sign of the attackers. On the lead wagon, he found a clue—at least, he suspected it might be. A single, bloody, perfect handprint pressed to one of the baseboards running lengthwise.

"That bloody hand," Tarlak said, pointing. "Has anyone seen something like it when inspecting the scenes of the other attacks?"

Oliver's discomfort grew. "Yes. At least twice I know of. We hoped it was the act of a dying man. Three times, however, puts it beyond coincidence and into certainty."

"A bloody hand," Tarlak said. He scratched at his beard with his thumb as he thought. "That fit any mercenary bands you know? Perhaps some bandits trying to make a name for themselves? Blood hand, red hand, anything even close?"

His escort shook his head. "Sorry, Tarlak, if there are, I don't know of them. Perhaps they're new?"

A new group of bandits, striking just as Prince Gregory had come south to build a new peace accord with both Ker and the elves of Stonewood? Tarlak's frown deepened.

"I don't like it. Don't like any of this, to be honest."

As much as he hated to agree with Oliver's early point, the whole attack had the look of extreme professionalism. Which then begged the question...

"Why this wagon train?" he asked. "People have been coming and going every day in anticipation of Prince Gregory's arrival. Of all the targets, why a trio of wagons carrying nothing more than milled flour? It doesn't make any sense."

In the third wagon, he found what he hoped was another clue. A mark was carved into the base, just above the wheel. He snapped his fingers to call Oliver over and pointed it out to him.

"Recognize that?" he asked. The symbol was a bisected triangle with a circle half-hidden at the left corner.

"That's a family crest," Oliver said after inspecting it. He tapped the circle portion. "Well, family and business together, I suppose. The wagon company is the Brentfellows, and this circle here means they've pledged exclusivity to the Gemcrofts."

"The Gemcrofts?" Tarlak grunted. "Interesting. Are they expanding out here in Ker?"

Oliver shrugged. "Have been since they arrived, though I can't say how much. I know my master was muttering quite a bit about it. Zusa Gemcroft has been making a lot of promises, and taking on a lot of debts to do it. Relying on their name, my master insists, and not their actual wealth."

"Their name, and the assumption they'll benefit tremendously once reclamation efforts begin in the east," Tarlak said. "But that's not here nor there. So the wagon was carrying goods for the Gemcroft family. What about the other attacks? Are they targeting the Gemcrofts specifically?"

"I can't say," Oliver said. "Sorry. We work mostly with Brynn contracts. I know ours have been attacked, as well, so it's not the Gemcrofts exclusively."

Tarlak bit down a curse. As much as he wished it were that simple, it still annoyed him how little he had to go on. Queen Brynn wanted him to get to the bottom of these attacks, but the only thing he was learning was how well executed these ambushes were. When he paced the area, he found only a few footprints, and he suspected them belonging to those driving the wagons, not the ambushers. Goods were stolen or left to rot. What was the purpose?

Desperation had him searching everywhere, including underneath each wagon. At last, he spotted something that drew his suspicion. It wasn't much, just a single arrow wedged into the grass from an errant shot. Tarlak grabbed it and crawled out from underneath the wagon to get a better look. Oliver joined him, curious at what he'd found.

"An arrow of theirs?" he asked.

Tarlak stared at it, his stomach sinking. "It is," he said, inspecting the razor sharp tip and expertly laced fletching. Well. At least he knew why the ambushers had scoured the area to remove any errant shots.

"Well?" Oliver asked, confused by Tarlak's reaction. "Does it have a mark on it?"

"It's not the mark, it's the make. *Elven* make."

"Elves?" Oliver's face paled. "Why would elves be attacking our shipments?"

Tarlak twirled the arrow between his fingers, chewing on the inside of his cheek as he thought.

"Celestia knows, perhaps, but I don't," he said. "Keep this quiet, Oliver, and pretend I said nothing. The last thing I want is rumors of war."

The apprentice's eyes widened. "Surely you jest."

Tarlak looked to the scene, and its perfectly executed ambush.

"There's nothing to jest about here," he said, convinced of his theory. He started swirling his hands, summoning a portal straight back to Angkar's outer gates. "Come. I've seen enough. It's time to ask a few more questions of those who might have answers."

18
THREN

Thren woke early as always and slipped out of his house. The cool morning air did wonders for his groggy mind. Sleep was harder and harder in coming, an annoying aspect of getting older no one had warned him about. He wrapped his cloak tightly about himself and hunched as he walked, eager to buy some early morning catch from the sea, filleted and mixed with freshly baked cornmeal.

It was strange, wearing a cloak again. He'd refused to do so once he traveled to Angkar. Cloaks had been used to identify various guilds in Veldaren, and the deep gray cloak belonged to his Spider Guild. To wear any cloak, of any color, felt wrong amid his exile. It was a part of him he'd cast aside to be forgotten. A past that training with Erin had awakened. Some memories, kind and warm. Others, painful and better left buried.

A cart blocked his path, and Thren was so wrapped up in his thoughts that he nearly walked right into it.

"Pardon," he said, stepping aside. The woman pulling it looked over at him, her brown hood shifting. A familiar scar cut across her face, forehead to chin.

"It's no bother," Brit said. "I was hoping we'd run into one another. I meant to give you this since our last meeting."

"And that is?" Thren asked, curt and quick in hopes he could resume his walk. He was much too tired and hungry for whatever nonsense she wanted.

In answer, she offered him her fist, turned it upright, and then opened her fingers. Smoke blasted out of it, tinted red from some sort of powder. Thren instinctively gulped in a breath to hold, but the explosion of powder was too strong and sudden, and it burned down his throat.

Immediately, he felt lightheaded. His legs wobbled, and the sounds around him went weird. He opened his mouth to protest, but his jaw hung open, his tongue refusing to produce but the most sluggish of sounds. The world slanted. He was falling.

"I have you," Brit said, catching him. With how strong she

was, it was no trouble for her to guide his limp body onto the bed of the cart. He tried to protest, or at least call her a bitch for her betrayal, but doing so took far too much effort.

Once he was in the cart, she flung a blanket atop him, bathing him in darkness. Her voice floated over him, seeming to come from so far away.

"Sleep tight, Gray. It's time we go for a ride."

※

Thren awoke with a hood over his head. A fire crackled nearby. He kept still, hoping his kidnapper had not noticed any movement. The slightest flex of his wrists confirmed them bound behind his back. Similar to his ankles. Good knots, by the feel. Escape would be difficult.

"I know you are awake," Brit said from somewhere to his right. "I pray you are not thinking of anything foolish like an escape."

Thren counted to three before responding. Even like this, he must present himself as unflustered and in control.

"Why would I escape, when you will soon grow wise and release me yourself?"

The hood was yanked off his head. He squinted against the daylight, though it wasn't too bright. Sunset was an hour away, perhaps two at most. Brit had already set up a camp somewhere off-trail. A fire crackled nearby, a little kettle pot hanging over it. The smell of food cooking within sickened his stomach, and it seemed the pain in his head arrived all at once. He clenched his teeth and fought against vertigo.

"It's cute you're still so confident even when held captive," she said, and sat back down on a blanket she'd placed beside the fire.

His planned retort died on his tongue as the vertigo intensified. It took all his willpower to keep the few contents of his stomach down. Eleven long, deep breaths later, the sensations eased. Sadly the same could not be said about the pounding in his forehead.

"What did you drug me with?" he asked. He was no stranger to the chemicals and poisons of the assassin trade, but he did not recognize whatever he'd been forced to inhale when she ambushed him.

"A protected secret of the elves called Ochle," she said. "It's a powder extracted from the stems of crimleaf, which I suspect you are intimately familiar with."

"I never touched that shit."

"Oh, but I'm sure you sold it, if you are who I believe you to be."

Thren gave no outward reaction, but his mind raced at the tell. Brit believed she knew his real identity? How? He'd never met her before coming to Angkar, and from what he knew of her, she'd never even lived east of the Rigon.

"It sounds like you're confused," he lied. "I'm a soldier, not a crimleaf dealer. Now release me, before I decide to take this attack personally."

"I will indeed release you, in time," Brit said. "But first, I've a friend you must meet."

"If a meeting is all you required, you could have asked. My days are not so full. I could spare a few words with a stranger."

Brit picked up a small stack of paper loosely bound with string along one edge and flipped through its pages. Thren recognized them as the pauper tales one of the local presses spat out. Cheap stories meant to entertain the masses. Quite a few detailed the supposedly lurid and depraved acts by the great betrayers, Qurrah and Tessanna Tun. The woman browsed their printed words even as she talked.

"I did not ask, because if you knew your identity was discovered, you would slither away to some new hole to hide in. That, I cannot allow." She lowered the book slightly to smirk at him. "You told me you were a student of the Darkhand. A false boast, some might believe, but I have sparred against Muzien. One does not forget his skill with a blade, and your movements, and your swordplay, are remarkably similar. Muzien had only two apprentices, though, and both are dead. So you are either a dead man, or a hidden third."

Thren squirmed against the knots. Damn it, if only they had the slightest bit more give. He shifted his weight a bit, testing his hip. No luck there, either. The dagger he kept hidden within the interior pocket of his trousers, a pocket he sewed himself into every pair, was also missing. Brit was maddeningly thorough with her work.

"You would call me an heir of the Darkhand, and then claim I would flee," he said. "Muzien did not teach cowards. He executed them."

"And yet here you are, a nameless nobody, *Gray*," she said. "Spare me your arguments. Whatever Muzien expected of you, you failed long ago. I only pray Cyth drags some use out of you. If it brings a bit of happiness to him, then it will be worth it."

Thren heard and marked the name in his mind. Cyth? An elven name, and the person he was to meet, he assumed. The question was, why? Less confusing was why Brit might be working for the elves. They hoarded more than enough wealth in their forests to buy the loyalty of a scrappy mercenary. Then again, she claimed she had sparred with Muzien. How? When? A duel against the Darkhand meant death…

"Once I meet with Cyth, will I be executed, or free to leave?" he asked. He had no intention of believing Brit's words, but it'd be nice to have a response to judge.

"That will be up to Cyth to decide," she said, grinning at him. "But if it will make you behave, know that I believe the memories you possess, and the training you've received, make you worth more alive than dead."

Thren relaxed and did his best to put his bound arms into a comfortable position. Should he need to escape, he couldn't have cramps and numb limbs hampering him.

"Wonderful," he said. He eyed her book. "Care to read that aloud? I see no reason for both of us to be bored."

Brit lowered the book momentarily. "I see you're going to be a fun prisoner."

He laughed at her. "You have no idea, Brit."

This was not his first time being held captive. He knew all the reactions, the way his heart would beat faster in a mild panic, the deep instinct to struggle and fight to free oneself, and the need to speak to the one who took you captive, even if speaking was the most foolish path to take.

What he did not expect, and found surprisingly strong, was his irritation that, because of Brit, he was going to miss his next few training sessions with Erin.

Thren rode in the back of the cart Brit pulled herself. He

lay there, hands bound behind his back and his ankles firmly tied. As the hours passed, he slowly rubbed both wrists and ankles together, up and down motions that left his skin raw. Even if the knots seemed solid, he wanted to test them over time, to wear on them and strain them. He didn't know where they traveled, or how far they had to go. If Brit didn't check them, she might not notice one of the knots loosening…

The sun baked down on him, and the road was far from smooth, doing Thren's already sick stomach no favors. That she only gave him water to drink was no help.

Near the end of the first day, he'd had enough. His stomach heaved, and he turned onto his side and vomited into the otherwise empty cart. The bile burned, and his empty stomach clenched in pain with every heave.

"Finally got sick, did you?" Brit asked. She set the two hand poles down. "Ochle isn't the kindest on the senses, I know."

Thren lay there, his cheek pressed to the wood, the smell of his vomit overwhelming his nostrils. It was enough to cause another surge, and he did not even turn. There wasn't much left in his stomach, after all. The burn in his throat worsened, and he greatly exaggerated his pain with loud, choking noises.

"Celestia help me," Brit said. "If you die on your own vomit…"

She leaned over the side of the cart and grabbed his shoulder to roll him onto his back. The second he felt the pull, he rolled with it, adding to the momentum while flinging his legs out. His heels caught her in the chin and snapped her head back hard. She staggered, blood spewing from her mouth from where she bit her tongue.

Thren's legs hit the cart side, and it would surely leave a bruise, but he ignored the pain and twisted to continue his momentum. His legs draped over the side, and he wrenched his back, every muscle in his abdomen screaming in agony. It worked, though. His weight lifting high enough so that when he rotated his body he slid over the cart's side feet first and dropped to the ground.

The moment his feet touched, he pushed off again, lunging with his head and shoulders as if they were a battering ram. His forehead smashed Brit's stomach, and she doubled over as he careened to the ground. He spun his head to the side to avoid smashing his face. Upon landing, he twisted like a worm to attempt to sweep Brit off her feet. If he could get her to the ground, his hands might grasp something, or her throat and veins could be within reach of his teeth.

A kick to the chest halted his struggles. He gasped, his lungs empty and fighting to properly inhale. Tears swelled in his eyes when another kick followed, this one directly to his crotch. He clenched his teeth and fought through the pain. Damn it. If only his feet hadn't been bound so tightly. That kick to her chin should have broken her neck.

Strong hands grabbed him underneath his armpits and lifted him up. A half-second later he was tossed through the air and smashed down upon his back in the center of the cart, his own vomit smearing across his clothes and hair. Thren inched to the side, and when he looked up, the blade of Brit's enormous sword was positioned just shy of his chest.

"There," she said. A mixture of rage and amusement sparkled in her eyes as she spat blood. "Right there's the resolve I would expect of Muzien's heir. Who are you, Gray? What failures led you to such a small, forgettable life in Angkar?"

Thren spat onto the blade tip. "Fuck off."

She pulled the sword back for a thrust, then slapped him with the flat edge. He grunted his disapproval.

"Perhaps one day," she said, and sheathed the weapon on her back. "But I promised Cyth I'd deliver you relatively unharmed, and I do not break my promises. Keep that spirit up, though. It will make executing you that much more pleasurable."

"Will Cyth not do his own dirty work?"

"Oh, he's more than willing," Brit said as she grabbed the poles. "But if it comes to killing you, trust me, I will *beg* for the privilege."

Thren shifted as far away from the filth as he could. Not much he could do about the vomit drying on his shirt and in his hair, but he could at least try.

"You'd beg?" he asked as the cart resumed its journey across the dirt roads running across southern Ker. "Have some pride, Brit. No one is worth debasing yourself for."

"Says the man covered in his own vomit."

He closed his eyes, resumed testing his bonds, and smirked.

Legacy of the Watcher

"Only yourself," he whispered. "Sacrifice the world for yourself, and nothing for all others."

His ankles twisted, found the knots loose for the first time in hours.

※

Brit denied him even water when night fell.

"You're staying in the cart," she told him, dropping the poles several hundred feet off the road. No fire either, nothing to give them away other than the light of the stars. As for herself, Thren could not see her depart, but he heard her faint footsteps, and by direction and sound, he suspected she had positioned herself a good distance away.

Thren risked the additional noise as he swiveled and kicked with his ankles. The give wasn't much, but enough so he could start to add a bit of momentum to each kick. His ankles ached, and besides the burn from the friction he felt a bit of blood trickle along his skin from rubbing it so raw.

The hours passed. He did not care about the pain. He could afford to lose the blood. He kicked, and twisted, and rotated his feet every which way, until finally, finally, his right foot slipped out. Thren grinned, his entire body awakening with elation. His feet were free. The question now was what to do about it? He had two options. He could flee, and pray Brit did not track him. Or he could ambush her where she slept.

Thren shifted onto his knees and peered over the side of the cart. He saw Brit asleep in her bedroll a few hundred feet away. Not far. He could cross the distance without making a sound. No knife, no weapon but his bound hands. It would be enough. He patiently slipped out of the cart, careful not to make a single board groan.

Fleeing was not his style. Besides, his head was light and his muscles weakened from lack of food and water. Brit would outrun him without question. Losing her would be the better tactic, but her familiarity with both Muzien and the elves worried him. She might know how to track his footsteps, and if she did, she would catch him with ease.

Once out of the cart, Thren tested the strength of the binds holding his hands behind his back. The rope was still taut, but slightly loosened now so that he could twist his wrists, at least a little. That was good—the knots must have slackened during his struggles to free his ankles.

Leaning forward, he looped his arms over his rump until they came to a stop behind his knees. While in that rather compromised position, he lowered himself to the grass as silently as he could, Thren then rocked, and rocked, inching his arms ever toward his feet. He held his breath the whole while, and it took a few attempts, but finally he slid one foot between his bound wrists, then the other. He gave an inward sigh of satisfaction as he stretched his body out on the ground, his hands now resting comfortably on his stomach.

He might be old, but still capable. He'd been bound like this before. And those who had done the binding had paid dearly.

Thren got back to his feet and lifted his wrists to check the knot. Though the rope was loosened, this was still an expertly tied manacle. He grimaced. Cutting it without a blade would be impossible. He could maybe undo it with his teeth, but that would take time and patience. Neither were in good supply, not after how long it had taken to get his hands out from behind his back.

It wouldn't be the first woman you've strangled, Thren thought, and crept across the grass. He tested every step, ensuring his silence. The wilds were never his home, but Muzien had ensured his students learned how to pass unnoticed in both city streets and wilderness passages.

Thren hovered over the sleeping Brit like a shadow. Her sword lay beside her, but one of her arms was over it. If she had a knife, the blanket atop her hid it from him. Thren took in a deep breath, held it, and lowered until he was crouched over her. When his hands were just shy of her throat, he dropped.

His knees struck her stomach, pinning her there. His hands wrapped about her throat, thumbs hooked together to form as much strength and pressure as possible despite the burden of the ropes. Brit awoke gasping, her eyes bulging as air refused to enter her lungs. Thren leaned harder onto his knees, needing to keep her pinned. He had no way to lock her arms out. This had to be quick. It had to be fatal.

Brit bashed him with her fists. The first broke his nose. The second loosened a tooth. He squeezed harder.

Just die. Just die. Just die.

When pain would not work, she tried a new tactic. Her hands closed about his wrists and pulled. Thren clenched his fingers, willing more strength into them. It wasn't enough. Brit was younger, and stronger. Decades ago, she might have died before ever waking. Now? His grip slipped, and she sucked in a harsh breath.

"You...bastard," she gasped.

Thren flung all his weight forward to slam his forehead into hers. The sound of bone hitting bone rocked through his mind, and all the world swam about him. Damn it, the angle, he got the angle wrong, and now darkness was coming...

When Thren awoke again, his hands and ankles were again bound, lashed together this time as if he were a captured boar. The wheels of the cart groaned with their movements along the dirt road.

"Damn it," he muttered, and thudded his head against the wood.

The cart halted, and Brit appeared at the back. Her forehead was red and swollen, and along her neck were deep purple bruises in the vague shape of his fingers.

"Am I still a fun prisoner?" he asked.

Upon seeing the rage swelling in her eyes, Thren was convinced his life would end. She even reached for the hilt of her sword before stopping herself.

"One more incident like that, and I will execute you, regardless of what Cyth wants," she said.

Thren closed his eyes against the waves of vertigo and the growing delirium from his empty stomach.

"One more incident like that," he said. "And Cyth will have to come find me himself, because you will be dead, and I, long gone."

19
CYTH

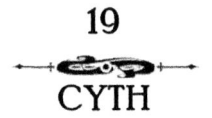

Cyth paced the interior of his tent, his fingers twitching at his sides. He could not contain his excitement.

Muzien's heir, he thought. *He's here. Right here.*

The mystery burned at his insides. Muzien's two heirs had died at the hands of the Watcher. One led to the utter collapse of the Sun Guild that had dominated the entire west, while the other, the pitiful end of the Spider Guild that had been a shadow of its former glory. Who, then, was this person Brit'tari was absolutely convinced had trained with the Darkhand?

The tent flap opened, and Vala ducked her head inside.

"He's arrived."

Cyth clapped, and he grinned like a child on his birthday. "Bring him to me."

Vala vanished. Cyth's heart raced.

At last, we shall learn your true name, and perhaps the story of your survival.

Whatever Cyth had expected, the old man dropped to the floor of his tent was not it. Brit'tari stood over him, her neck bruised a deep purple and her face swollen. She looked utterly miserable.

"Here's the sorry sack of shit," she said, and then left without waiting for a dismissal.

Cyth crossed his arms and peered down at the man. He was human, and well past the prime of his life. His arms and legs were bound together behind him, his face equally bruised and swollen as Brit'tari's. Cyth took in his brown hair, his pale skin, and his blue eyes, and compared them to what he knew of the chosen heirs.

Not Grayson, he thought, that much was clear. Then that meant...

"Thren Felhorn," he said, and the man immediately tensed. "It must be you, but surely it cannot be. Not unless the Watcher spread lies that Veldaren's underworld was all too eager to swallow."

"The Watcher did not lie," the man said. "So far as he

knew, I indeed died to his blades."

"So you are Thren Felhorn, Heir to the Sun?"

The prisoner struggled to prop himself up, but being tied up the best he could do was sit on his hip at an angle. He grinned at Cyth, and there was something unnerving about the confidence he exuded despite his predicament.

"Heir to what?" the man who would be Thren Felhorn said. "That empire died in Veldaren, slain by the same Watcher's hand."

Cyth bit his tongue to halt his retort. He should not be surprised that any handpicked student of the Darkhand would be arrogant. Instead he placed his hands behind him and paced, using Vala's arrival as an excuse to wait for his temper to quell.

"So who is it?" Vala asked, hopping up onto the small table in the center of the tent and resting her heels on the head of a chair. She gestured toward their prisoner. "Thren, Grayson, or a liar?"

Cyth stopped pacing, already feeling more in control. He smiled down at the older human.

"Would you care to introduce yourself, or shall we make assumptions?"

"I will if you remove my binds."

Vala shot him a look, and when Cyth shrugged she hopped down and drew a knife from her belt.

"I do not share the same fascination with the Darkhand as my brother," she said as she cut the ropes. "Do something foolish, such as attempting an escape, and I will eagerly make you suffer for it, heirs and tutelage be damned."

Their prisoner stood once freed, and he stretched his arms and kicked his legs to restore their proper blood flow. All the while, those icy blue eyes lingered on Cyth.

"I have taken a new name here in Angkar," he said at last. "But for a time, I was Thren Felhorn, master of Veldaren's Spider Guild and student to the Darkhand. Who are you, to seek me out and speak of a past that should remain buried?"

Cyth took a deep breath to hide his excitement. The man spoke no lie. That confidence, it could not be faked.

"I am Cyth Ordoth, and beside me is my sister, Vala Ordoth."

Thren's careful expression never changed. "Muzien sired

no children, so if you are blood relatives, it is distant. Why then this fascination?"

"It is not a 'fascination' to know one's history and revere the history and accomplishments of one's family," Vala said, hopping back up onto the table, her heels balancing the chair before her on its back two legs. "But you, well, you're an oddity, aren't you, Thren?"

Cyth stepped closer to the man and forced himself to abandon any and all preconceptions. Forget this was a human and not an elf. Forget the man's age. Study him. Check his movements. Watch his eyes.

The more he studied, the more Cyth saw the hidden influences of the Darkhand. The way Thren looked relaxed and yet ready to move in an instant. The way his eyes pierced into Cyth's, and yet still cheated glances at Vala to ensure she remained where she sat. The way their prisoner had kept a piece of rope from his bindings clutched in one hand, hidden and ready to be used as a weapon if necessary.

This man was exceedingly dangerous, and despite his dire predicament he appeared *eager* for a chance to battle his way out of it. It didn't matter that he was beaten and bloodied, his face a bruised mess. It didn't matter that he was outnumbered. Thren trusted himself to succeed. There was no breaking a man like that with intimidation. He would not be coerced with bribes. Cyth smiled. Yes. Yes, this man was everything he expected Muzien's Heir to be...if only with a bit more gray hair.

"For once, I shall try a tact I rarely use with humans," Cyth said. "I shall give you my full honesty. I admired my uncle greatly, but I was not privileged to meet with the Darkhand before his passing. However, his legacy is one that I cherish. His ideals I would take as my own. I have done all I can to learn of him, of his beliefs, his accomplishments, and his vision for the future. All of it, though, is from those who knew him before his exile. The few who knew him after are dead, lost in the wars your human gods ravaged upon Dezrel, or merely passed away due to old age."

Cyth stepped closer, amused by how Thren tightened his grip on the rope. Did he think to strangle him? Vala still had her dagger ready, and he trusted his sister to keep him safe.

"But then there is you," he said. "Muzien's chosen heir.

Legacy of the Watcher

You knew him, truly *knew* him, in a way no one else did. That makes you special, Thren. It makes you irreplaceable."

Thren's relaxed posture seemed to remain the same, but Cyth caught a subtle shift in the angle of his feet. He was preparing for an attack.

"Does it now?" Thren asked. "And was is it you want from me?"

Ah, but the man knew the answer to that already. This question, it was meant to keep Cyth talking. To distract him. Cyth played along, and he stepped even closer, within arm's reach.

"I want to learn who my uncle became once freed of the traditions and laws of my people. How he taught. How he fought. What drove him. I cannot fulfill a legacy I do not understand."

Thren grinned. "There is no fulfilling that legacy, Cyth. There is only a gaping pit, and at the bottom, a quagmire of blood."

He lashed out, his fist aimed for Cyth's throat. Cyth dodged sideways, having predicted the movement by the faintest flex of the old man's muscles. The punch missed, but Thren continued his momentum, the two of them colliding. It seemed perhaps even Thren had known the attack would miss because he was ready with his offhand already slamming two quick blows into Cyth's stomach.

Cyth rocked backward, one of his legs locking tight behind him to brace himself. He moved to catch the third punch, but realized too late that Thren had grabbed the end of the rope with his other hand, and now holding it in both, he flung it like a garrote across Cyth's throat. Thren pushed forward, his legs pumping, and Cyth's bracing leg gave out so they both collapsed.

The impact knocked the wind from Cyth's lungs, and it was air he could not afford to lose as Thren pressed all his weight down upon him, jamming the rough rope harder against his throat. Cyth punched the man thrice in the stomach and then reached up for the man's wrists, fighting to free his limbs from the awkward tussle.

He never had the chance. Vala's heel struck Thren across the forehead, and then her second kick clipped him across the temple. When Thren staggered, his eyes losing focus, Cyth seized the opportunity to shove him off and then hop to his feet. Thren tried to chase, but Vala kicked out the backs of his knees. When he crumpled, her dagger slipped around his neck and pressed against his throat. Only then did the older man freeze in place.

"Goddess burn it all," Cyth said, rubbing at his neck. "I seek knowledge, and yet you respond with violence? Why, damn you? Why not share with me your history with Muzien?"

"You want to know who the Darkhand was?" Thren asked, and then spat a bloody glob to the dirt. "You're a damned fool to think you need me to answer. That you need *anyone* close to him to learn the truth."

Vala's dagger pressed tighter to his throat, but Cyth waved her off. He wanted to hear this. Vala let him go, and Thren pushed to a stand. The calm facade was gone, the ice in his eyes turned to fire.

"Muzien was victory at all costs," Thren said, his voice raw. "He cared for no one. He loved nothing. Imagine a bloated beast, fat with power and yet still unsatisfied. He was hate. He was loathing. I was not an apprentice. I was not an heir. I was a thing he owned, built by his hands, no different than a carpenter hammering together a table."

Thren neared, but there was no threat of an attack this time, just a rage that had been swallowed down for years suddenly burst free like a ruptured pustule.

"When I was but a child, he had Grayson and I murder strangers in a wicked game to prove our worth. 'Never forget that the door was always open,' he told me. 'In your time of suffering, you chose not to step through it.' That was his only lesson. We could have been broken, we could have fled, but instead we stayed, we fought, and we killed. You want to fulfill his legacy, Cyth? Then seek power above all else. Seek to rule from the shadows, or a throne, it doesn't matter, so long as men and women fear the very mention of your name. And then, when your ruthlessness and cruelty have left you barren of love, starved of joy, and hated by all, you can die at the hands of someone stronger, and have all you ever built crumble away into dust." Thren grinned like a madman. "Only then will you have truly fulfilled the Darkhand's pathetic legacy."

Cyth smashed his fist straight into that grin. His heart seized in his chest, his mind so overwhelmed with fury he could barely think straight.

"And what legacy did you leave behind?" Cyth screamed at him as the human rocked on his heels. "What grand accomplishments remain in your name, that you would insult the

Legacy of the Watcher

Darkhand so?"

Blood stained his teeth and lips, but still he smiled, mad, insane, terrifying. "None. But I am not blind as to why."

Cyth pointed a finger at him.

"Out," he shouted. "Get him out of here. I never want to see his face again."

"With pleasure," Vala said, though there was a hesitance to her movements when she grabbed Thren's wrist. The older man did not resist. His gaze lingered on Cyth as he left the tent, and Cyth shivered against a sudden chill.

Damned humans, he thought. *I never should have held hope. I never should have believed them capable of greatness.*

But at one point, Muzien had, which meant Cyth had to extend that same hope. Thren had been chosen for a reason. Beneath the hate, wisdom remained. If only he could reach it. If only he could...

No. Cyth smashed his fist against the table just as Vala returned alone to the tent. He beat against the wood, striking it until his hand was bruised and aching.

"Why did you let him live?" Vala asked when he finally calmed.

Cyth stared at the splinters in his flesh, at the little beads of blood starting to swell up.

"I don't know. I shouldn't. I know I shouldn't. But he..." He shook his head. "He's our final link to Muzien. The final creation of our beloved uncle. To extinguish it now? No. I want him to bear witness to our rise. I want him to watch as the Sun returns to prominence. And then maybe, once time has passed and he sees I am worthy of the name, he will speak with me stripped of his pride and arrogance. He will tell me of Muzien, and all the things he whispered in those dark days separated from our people." He sighed. "Again and again, I extend hope to where there is none."

Vala slipped beside him, and she settled her fingers over his. Her gentle touch stopped his hands from shaking and stirred him from his loathing. He sought comfort in her green eyes.

"You do it because you believe in Muzien," she said. "But he was not infallible. Desperation led him down roads he might never have walked. To leave his legacy in the hands of humanity? Perhaps he thought himself capable of molding their children from so young an age. But that was a task beyond even him. Their failures are deeply rooted and cannot be undone." She leaned her head against his shoulder. "It cost him his life, in the end. I pray you do not pay the same price."

Cyth pushed the older man's wicked grin out of mind and instead focused on his sister's beloved face.

"Victory at all costs, Thren claimed, and I think he may be right, Vala. There are those of our brethren who will hate us, or call us traitors. We must not listen. The truth of our path will be made clear when we sit upon twin thrones of the Kingdom of the Sun."

"And Thren?" she asked, kissing him softly on the cheek.

Cyth shook his head. "He told me what I needed to hear. I focus too much on the Darkhand's legacy, and none upon my own. That ends now. It is not Muzien that shall wear a crown. It is not Muzien that will shape the future of Dezrel."

Vala smiled, her emerald eyes lighting up with life.

"No," she said, her excitement palpable. "It shall be *us*."

20

ZUSA

This wasn't the way Zusa preferred to spend an evening, but it was rare in her life to get what she wanted without drawing her daggers. She sat at the long table, casually resting her hands in the lap of her tight violet dress and waiting for the meeting to start. That it was inside the Connington estate only annoyed her further.

You could have picked a more neutral place, wizard, she thought, glancing at the yellow-garbed buffoon pacing at the far end of the room. She'd not been told of any reason, either, only that it was important, and that Tarlak had the backing of the queen. Why he'd chosen Tori's estate and not Zusa's, she could only guess. Maybe he had an ulterior motive. Maybe he simply didn't like her from their time spent butting heads back in Veldaren.

Nathaniel sat beside her, his happiness the opposite of her obvious annoyance. She brought him with her for every official venture. Though she ostensibly still ruled the Gemcroft fortune, or what little was left of it, Nathaniel would eventually inherent it. To many he was already the one in charge given the steadily increasing responsibilities she had given him. The fact he now joked and laughed with Tarlak as if they were good friends from childhood only served to irk her all the more.

"I can't believe you nearly killed yourself with one of Muzien's tiles," Nathaniel was saying as Tarlak sipped wine from a glass. "Surely you could tell it was magical?"

"Of course I knew it was magical," Tarlak said. "But that's like saying a bug and a bear are the same because they are both alive. Sure, you're right, but you're going to find some differences between the two when you poke them, and I sure as the Abyss didn't know I was poking the bear."

Zusa could hardly believe they spoke so jovially of a time when all of Veldaren, and the thousands upon thousands of lives within, had been at risk of death at the hands of the ruthless Darkhand and his Sun Guild. Granted, Nathaniel had been so young at the time, and the leader of the Eschaton was hardly known for being serious even in the most dire of circumstances..."

"Listening to this story makes me feel I should trust your wisdom less, not more," Tori said, sitting opposite Zusa at the table. The woman had been quiet most of the evening as they waited for Queen Brynn to arrive, speaking only when necessary to play the kind host. There was a strange standoffishness to her, which was why Zusa was convinced Tarlak had chosen this as the location. It was as if she were uncomfortable with it being in her estate. As to why, Zusa could only guess.

"He held something he did not understand, and his solution amid his ignorance was to destroy it," Zusa added. "Should anyone be surprised it nearly ended disastrously?"

"Surprised, no," Tarlak said, unbothered by her interruption. "But was it amusing? Yes! One gigantic eruption of fire and smoke and debris that nearly singed the beard off Brug's face, Ashhur rest his soul."

"And burned off the tip of your pointy yellow hat, too," Nathaniel said. "Hey, can I ask why you always wear yellow? Is it your signature, perhaps a way to stand out, or are you just in love with the color?"

"Why, I'd be more than happy to explain," Tarlak said, setting down his drink and then rubbing his hands together eagerly. "You see—"

"Forgive me for being late," a young woman said, barging in through the door all hurried and panicked. Her hair was redder than Tarlak's, and her skin rivaled marble in its paleness. "Her highness the queen regrettably cannot make this meeting as first promised, and so I have come in her place."

Zusa frowned. The young woman was familiar, but she could not place her. "And you are...?"

"Lumi," she said. "Handmaiden to Queen Brynn."

"Handmaiden," Tori said, the word spoken like a curse. "It is good to see that her highness is taking the matter of banditry seriously."

"I assure you, she is taking it most seriously," Lumi said She paused next to Tori and gestured to an empty chair. "May I sit?"

"But of course," Tori said, and waved at a servant. The fine-suited man came over with a bottle, and when Lumi nodded in the affirmative he poured the handmaiden a glass.

Lumi took a sip and smiled. "A welcome treat, thank you. Please, do not wait any longer on my account. Mr. Eschaton called us all for good reason, and I'm eager to hear it."

The wizard crossed his arms, one eye squinting as he stared at Lumi.

"May I assume you will relay everything I say to Brynn?" he asked.

"Of course," Lumi said, and tapped her forehead. "I am taking many notes, and will remember everything. Everything that is important, at least."

"That won't be much," Zusa muttered quietly enough so only Nathaniel overheard. The young man choked down a laugh that sounded more like a cough.

Tarlak shrugged. "All right. Well, I don't exactly have a lot to offer. I more dragged you all here because I have questions, and I want answers. Let's start with the biggest. At the last attack, I discovered a symbol left to mark the identity of the attackers." The wizard hesitated. "Have any of you heard of the Bloodhand, or perhaps Bloody Hand?"

Zusa's spine prickled at the name. "I have," she said. "Once. A rumor of a new group seeking to make its name in the southwest."

"I have heard not even rumors," Tori said. "Are you certain they are responsible?"

"It's their symbol that's been left on at least three attacks, and even more, I suspect, if people knew what to look for." Tarlak scratched at his beard. "But if you two don't know of them, then I assume this Bloodhand group has given you no messages, no ransom notes, or the like?"

Tori and Zusa exchanged glances.

"Nothing," Zusa answered for the both of them.

"Hrm," Tarlak grunted. "Strange. Because from what I can tell, this group is targeted you two specifically."

Now that was news to Zusa. She knew she'd taken heavy losses, but reports reaching her made it seem like traders of all sorts were being robbed. If it were only Tori and her, then that left only one real possibility.

"Might the Bloodhands carry a grudge against the Trifect?"

Nathaniel asked. "If so, why? Our influence was vastly stronger in the east. Why would bandits in the west care?"

Zusa felt a tiny spark of pride that the young man had reached the same conclusion as her.

"Both Ker and Mordan are overwhelmed with refugees from the second Gods' War," she said, thinking aloud. "Alyssa made her fair share of enemies, as did the Conningtons. It is possible this Bloodhand group, or gang, or whatever they are, were once major players around Veldaren."

Tarlak made a face she could not interpret. "I suppose. But they sure did wait a long time to exact their apparent revenge. I'm not sure I buy it, Zusa, but I confess I have no other theory to put forth. Which leads me to my next request! I'd like manifest lists of every caravan group that was attacked from each of you. Can your families do so within a reasonable amount of time?"

"Of course," Zusa said, even though she chafed at the thought. Better to play along than argue and risk a more thorough gaze at her finances, perilous as they were. "We have nothing to hide."

"I will, but only on one condition," Tori said. "You will keep the information confidential to your investigation. I hold no desire for the intricacies of my trade to become public gossip."

"You will have my utmost care and confidence," Tarlak said with an exaggerated bow. "Well, that's all I really have to say. Sorry. I was hoping perhaps you two might have more information to share. Perhaps I'll decipher a bit more of this riddle once I have your manifests."

"Perhaps," Zusa said, struggling, and failing, to keep the exhaustion from her voice. She stood from the table and shot a glance at the queen's handmaiden. "I assume you have little to share?"

"Oh, me? No, only the queen's insistence she is treating this matter very seriously and holds the highest confidence in Mister Eschaton's ability to hunt down and capture those responsible."

Zusa's eyebrow arched at 'Mister Eschaton'. Something about it struck her as painfully false, which made her question the handmaiden's entire bumbling demeanor. Perhaps the woman was more shrewd than she let on...

"Very well," Zusa said. She abruptly stood, and Nathaniel

rushed to join her. Tori also stood.

"Shall I escort you out?" Tori asked.

"Of course," Zusa said, and dipped her head in respect to her host. The other woman stepped in beside Zusa, and together they walked the halls of the Connington mansion. Nathaniel fell in step behind them.

"While we speak of rumors, I have heard interesting ones concerning your own spendings," Zusa said as they walked. "You have hired many soldiers and mercenary groups left listless by the end of the Gods' War."

"I wish to protect my assets," Tori said.

"The numbers I'm hearing are more than enough to protect your home and what buildings you own in Angkar," Zusa went on, trying not to push too hard. Cooperation with Tori was imperative, given the Gemcroft's heavy debts and still infantile trade network. She could not afford to lose such an ally, even if Tori had always seemed resentful of their arrival in Angkar five years prior. Zusa never knew the reason, but suspected the woman had envisioned herself becoming the sole leader of trade in Ker after the war, and the arrival of the Gemcrofts put a damper on that idea, even if they were to be allies in their pursuit of wealth.

Tori held her head high as they approached the door. Her slender jaw hardened.

"I aim to protect beyond what is in Angkar. The oafish wizard can spout hot air all he wants, but I do not trust his promises. Our trade, and therefore our livelihoods, are in danger. If Queen Brynn cannot protect us, then…" She turned at the door. "Then I will do what she cannot."

Zusa bowed low, and Nathaniel did likewise.

"Thank you for hosting," she said.

"Indeed, the pastries were lovely," Nathaniel added.

Tori smiled, but it did not reach her eyes. "Farewell, Gemcrofts," she said, and left.

"Well?" Nathaniel asked as he and Zusa descended the outside steps of the mansion toward the outer gate.

"Well what?"

Nathaniel gestured behind him with his lone arm. "Well, what do you think? Is Tarlak onto something, and just hiding how much he knows while we hand over all our trade manifests? And does the queen truly know nothing of this Bloodhand that torments us?"

Zusa felt the beginnings of a migraine building behind her forehead and lamented what little wine she had consumed.

"I'm sorry, Nathaniel, I have only questions and assumptions, no answers. But this is far from the first threat to our family, nor will it be the last. We keep our eyes open, our ears alert, and our swords ready to be drawn at a moment's notice."

"I'm not much for swordplay," Nathaniel said, winking. "That's more Erin's thing."

"If only she had interest in learning other talents," Zusa sighed. "I should have brought her here, too. Even after you assume full control of the Gemcroft estate, she will still be heavily involved. She needs to learn trade, improve her mathematics, and hold her own in conversation. She will need to know how to behave like a proper lady in wealthy environs, whether she likes it or not."

Nathaniel gave her a nudge. "Such lofty goals. But if you're hoping to turn my wild little sister into a proper lady, I dare say you found the absolute worst tutor in the Godslayer."

21
HARRUQ

Harruq doubted getting drunk was the proper behavior for an instructor, but he told himself getting a tiny bit flushed was perfectly fine as he guzzled down another giant glass of wine. He was out in the Gemcroft garden, getting ready for yet another lengthy session with Erin, their tenth over as many days.

"You drink worse than a mercenary," Erin said, stretching her arms with a few specific exercises to prepare for their dueling.

"You forget, I used to be a mercenary," Harruq said. He set his glass atop a circular stone table just off the tiled path. "An odd sort of mercenary, blame Tarlak for that, but I was one! And if I'm gonna train you, Erin, I'm taking advantage of every little perk and treat I can get from the Gemcrofts." He tapped the side of the empty glass. "And that means sampling wine of rare age and quality."

"Sampling?" Erin said with a smirk.

"All right, fine, downing an entire bottle of wine my wife would never let me purchase. Does that make you happy?"

"Thrilled," she said, starting to bounce on her toes.

He drew his swords. "Arrogant little brat."

"Muscle-bound drunk."

He thrust, and the moment she moved to parry it, he closed the space between them, turned his sword sideways so their weapons harmlessly locked together, and then bodied her with his shoulder to send her stumbling back several steps.

"Muscle-bound drunk *Godslayer* to you, young one, and don't you forget it."

Harruq let the good mood push away the lingering nervousness he'd tried hard to hide from Erin. Tomorrow was the big announcement, forever altering his daughter's fate. Swinging around his swords and getting his blood pumping was a good way to pass the time and forget it all for a while.

"Always with the Godslayer title," Erin said. She dipped and weaved as she thrust at him over and over, seeking openings.

He gave her none. "Haven't you done anything else worthwhile to brag about?"

"Do I *need* to?" he asked, his swords crossing together to block a sudden chop. It was a decent break in her pattern, and almost caught him off guard. "I feel like I should be able to ride that one for the rest of my life. Bringing down Azariah and his fallen was just a bonus."

Erin's feet danced, becoming more and more of a blur as she hopped back and forth, stinging at him with her sabers like a scorpion's tail. The more she moved, the more she slashed, trying to take advantage of her gently curved blades. Harruq countered it with aggression, smashing her hits back with greater strength to interrupt her attempts at a smooth flow. Her smile vanished, turning to a frown as her concentration deepened. Her slashes grew more frantic, her frustration taking over.

When Harruq sensed she was no longer fully in control, he ended the game. His swords flung wide, easily parting her sabers, and then he closed the distance between them. His knee struck her stomach, and though he did what he could to lessen its impact, she still staggered and coughed in an attempt to regain her breath.

"I should be better than this," she fumed once recovered.

"Try not to take this so seriously, Erin. You're never going to be perfect when we practice."

"But you have to be perfect in battle, or you die."

Harruq tilted his head to one side and arched an eyebrow. "Planning on fighting lots of battles anytime soon? Maybe a war I should know about? It's been pretty boring down here. I suppose I could go for an assassination attempt or three."

"No, it's not that, it's…" She flung her arms up in surrender, cheeks reddening. "When my mother fought the orcs back in Angelport, I had to stay behind. I was too young. Too small. Not trained enough. And I *hated* it, Harruq. I hated every awful second I had to sit there and wait and wonder and watch my other mother…"

Harruq clanged his swords together so the noise would pull Erin out of her spiral. She had a bad habit of disappearing into her own mind. He forced back a grin. Quite like her father, now that he thought about it.

"Hey," he said. "We're training. You'll mess up. Accept

that, and you'll keep on getting better so that maybe, should you need to actually defend yourself, you'll know ten different ways to gut your foe." He shrugged. "Though you're almost there already. I feel bad for any fool who thinks *you* are the vulnerable one of the Gemcroft family."

"More vulnerable than my mother," Erin muttered.

"Yeah, probably, but who isn't?" Harruq smiled. "Come on. We go again."

They dueled the hour away. Harruq was pleased with her steady progress. She was getting better at maintaining her momentum during their duels. It was harder to knock her off balance, and she was learning to slide her swords off his harsh blocks so they did not interfere with the fluidity required of someone so much smaller.

At last, Harruq called it quits. Sweat covered his body and the air seemed to stick to his skin.

"What is it about this city?" he asked, plopping down. "I swear, it can be hard to breathe sometimes."

"It's the ocean," Erin said. "It was the same in Angelport. You can feel it hovering in the air."

Harruq groaned as he leaned against one of the elm trees. "Just one more reason to look forward to returning to Mordan."

Erin paced before him. She seemed nervous, and was doing a poor job hiding it. Harruq suspected she had something on her mind and decided she could broach the subject, whatever it was, on her own terms.

"No training tomorrow," he said in the meantime. "I have to look all fine and fancy for the big announcement."

"The peace treaty?" Erin asked, half paying attention.

"Nah, that's still later." He sighed. "Don't worry about it. Aurry made me promise not to tell anyone. Better to be a surprise, supposedly."

Another distracted nod. "Harruq...you knew my father well, right?"

"He trained me for years, and we fought side by side in more battles than I can remember. I'd say that makes us friends."

She bit her lower lip. "What was he like?"

"Well, that depended on who you were," Harruq said. "If

you were a friend? He was soft-spoken, even a bit shy at times. Attentive, too. Hiding things from him was pointless, for he'd see right through you. He did it because he cared, though. He wanted to know if you were happy, or upset, so he could make it better if he could. Above all, he was faithful to Ashhur, perhaps even more than Ashhur deserved."

Erin looked taken aback at that. "What do you mean, more than Ashhur deserved? Aren't you his champion? Isn't he why you're alive, and defeated Thulos?"

Harruq chuckled. "Perhaps you missed a lot of what happened in Avlimar. Let's say it's complicated and leave it at that. That's not important. What *is* important is that Haern believed in Ashhur's forgiveness, mercy, and that people can become better than who they once were. I don't know what you know about your father, but I assure you he had his fair share of blood on his hands."

The young woman slumped down next to Harruq, propped her elbows on her knees, and rested her chin on her hands. She refused to look at him. Her voice took on a thoughtful tone as she stared at the grass.

"My mother always described him as dangerous, and the books I read say he was the ultimate killer."

Harruq laughed. "That's who he was to his enemies. I wish you could have seen him, Erin. For all my speed, I am a snail compared to him. For all my intensity, it is but a fraction of the ferocity he could unleash. I can't describe it. Can't recreate it. When he tore into you—really, really tore into you—it felt like he knew what you would do long before you did it. He'd already have won the fight while you'd think it was only starting."

"That's what it's like fighting you," Erin said, then blushed a little when he glanced her way. "When you...when you went all out on our first day."

"I'll take that compliment," Harruq said, and nudged her with his elbow. "But that's what Haern taught me. I'm strong, I'm fast, and I need to use both to win. I use what I'm good at, just like you'll use what you're good at, and slowly develop your own style to match your abilities."

"Is that what it takes to become a killer?" Erin asked. "Discover what suits you best, and then perfect it?"

Harruq frowned, not liking where her focus was. He shifted

to face her, and when she would not meet his gaze, he stood and walked in front.

"Listen to me, and I want you to actually *listen,* got it? Haern was one of the most amazing people I have ever known, and it wasn't because he was good at killing people. It wasn't because he knew how to fight."

Harruq crouched before her, and he was shocked by how desperately he hoped his words would pierce through the guarded veil surrounding young Erin.

"Haern was amazing because he would see people in need, and no matter how horrid the odds, how terrible the foe, or how much it would cost him, he helped them anyway. He didn't break the thief guilds because he wanted fame or power. He did it to stop the pain they caused. He fought, and he fought, because he knew he had power to help, and so he helped."

"Until it killed him."

Harruq winced. He hadn't even been there when it happened, a regret that had haunted him for many sleepless nights amid the second Gods' War.

"Yes," he said. "It one day killed him. Just as it has killed so many of my friends, even my family. You've read the books on our lives. You might even know their names. Brug. Delysia. Lathaar. Dieredon. My brother, Qurrah. His wife, Tessanna. And yes, Haern the Watcher."

He drew Salvation from its sheath and held the glowing crimson blade before him.

"If peace isn't in our future, it will likely kill me, too," he said, his voice softening. "And I do not regret it, Erin. None of us do. If we fought for rewards, we would be no different than the thief guilds, spilling blood for coin. We help people. That's it. Haern helped people. He helped until it cost him his life, but I assure you, if he were given a thousand chances to change his mind, every single time, he'd leap down to save Dieredon's life."

Erin squirmed uncomfortably before him. "And that's enough to make it worthwhile? You've lost so many close to you, and that's what keeps you going? This idea that you're helping people? But it's so…simple."

Harruq stared into the black blade, and within it he saw the lives of innocent men and women taken by its edge.

"When I sought power, I slaughtered in Velixar's name," he said. He shook his head and looked up. "Are there people you love, Erin?"

The young woman nodded. "Yes. My family."

"And would you fight to protect them? To keep them safe? Even at the risk of your own life?"

"Of course."

"Then think of that feeling, hold onto it...and then give it to others. That need. That ferocity to aid those in peril. Apply it to a city. A nation. A world. That is the strength of the Watcher, to view a task so impossible and yet fight for it anyway, and sometimes, through skill and sheer determination, achieve miracles. That is his legacy, to my mind. And that is why I'm here with you."

He softly smiled at her.

"Simple is better. It lets you see when all else grows dark. Those smarter than me can better debate morales and creeds. I'll keep on helping people."

Erin fell silent. What he'd give to know what was running through her mind. At last, she stood, drawing her sabers.

"I want to be like him," she said.

"I can tell," he replied, grinning at her sudden eye roll.

"I don't mean just how he fights," she said. "Who he was. How he helped people. I...guess I just don't know how. I look at people like him, like you, and I feel so meager by comparison."

Harruq readied his swords, and Erin did likewise.

"Give yourself time," he said. "And have a little faith."

"In Ashhur?"

"In yourself."

Erin bounced on her toes, building up momentum for a lunge. "I'll give it a try, *Godslayer*."

22

AURELIA

Aurelia sat Aubrienna and Gregory down before her. They were in one of the finely decorated waiting chambers within the royal mansion. Murmurs of the crowd gathered outside were audible through the windows. She wished she could have told the pair their fate sooner, but she could not risk them spilling the secret before the true announcement. With Elydien Marosi's arrival that morning, that time was now.

"I need to tell you two something," she said, leaning forward in her chair. Her hands wrung together, and she watched them both carefully. Her every word was measured. "Something that may be difficult to hear."

"Is it about why so many people are waiting in the courtyard?" Aubrienna asked.

"It is." The over-stuffed padding groaned as she shifted in the chair. "And it's one of the reasons why we have traveled all this way to Angkar."

"I thought it was to ensure peace with Ker?" Gregory asked.

"That is but one part of it," Aurelia said. "But there are the elves to consider. The elves…and your own connection to the throne. Because there are some who look upon Harruq's heroics and wonder if you truly deserve the power you will inherit."

The two youngsters squirmed before her. They didn't like hearing such uncomfortable truths that challenged their understanding of the world. To them, Gregory Copernus was the future king, and Harruq just a temporary steward. Why would anyone wish for otherwise?

"In the interest of peace, and proving the prejudices of King Baedan are in Mordan's past, we have arranged a marriage between the two of you. Come Aubrienna's seventeenth birthday, she will be wed to you, Gregory, and be your queen."

The two of them froze in place. Their eyes widened. And then Aubrienna began to laugh.

"That can't be…but we…?"

Her laughter puttered out, the seriousness of it finally hitting her. Gregory, meanwhile, was pale and still as a statue.

"Is this why you made us dress up?" he asked.

Gregory wore his finest tailored suit, Aubrienna a glittering green dress. His hair was brushed, hers expertly curled and decorated with silver ribbons. Aurelia had even cast the faintest glamour upon them both, to give a sparkle to their eyes and shine to their hair.

"The crowd outside is waiting for the official announcement," Aurelia said. "After which there will be celebration and feasting. The people will adore this pairing, I promise you. Many have already assumed it in place, even without confirmation. You will be cheered and embraced, and just as importantly, talk will shift. Discussions over your worthiness to rule will turn less serious, and more vapid, as we float rumors of weddings, decorations, and celebratory feasts."

The room fell silent, and she gave them time to dwell on the sudden news. Gregory glanced at Aubrienna, his hands squirming in his lap and his cheeks blushing red.

"Well," he said. "At least I like you."

Aubrienna covered her face while giggling. "This is so stupid," she said, and giggled harder. Her face and ears turned red.

Aurelia looked upon them both, her heart aching, yet still she clung to hope. Political matching aside, they did seem to enjoy each other's company, and their union promised a potential new beginning for all of Mordan. A symbolic union, child of the Godslayer and blood of the elves, marrying the future king. And with Queen Brynn pledging two decades of guaranteed non-aggression, as well as a plethora of trade agreements, the future looked brighter than it had in decades. A peace not known since King Baedan burned Dezerea and painted the Bloodbrick red.

"What if we can't stand each other?" Aubrienna asked suddenly.

"Then I'll lock you up in a tower," a smirking Gregory said to Aubby's exaggerated shock.

"Lock me up, and I'll have my mom turn you into a beetle!"

"You won't do it yourself? I thought you were learning magic."

Legacy of the Watcher

Aurelia snapped her fingers to interrupt the both of them. "She will learn magic to defend herself, not to turn bothersome husbands into beetles. But yes, I will indeed turn you into a helpless little insect if you treat my daughter poorly. Consider that a promise."

"W...would you actually?" Gregory asked, his amusement lessening ever so slightly.

Aurelia winked at him. "Pray we never need find out. Now come with me. I wanted you two to know first so it wasn't a surprise, but now it's time the rest of the nation learns."

Harruq awaited them outside the door. Aurelia had requested he not be involved in the telling, for as good intentioned as his heart may be, she did not trust him to break the news in the most delicate fashion. He raised an eyebrow, and she nodded to let him know all had gone well.

"Hey there, my little princess," Harruq said when Aubrienna emerged. He scooped her up in his arms, then laughed as she hugged him. "I suppose that title will soon be real, won't it?"

"Not quite," Aurelia said. "I do not believe human titles work that way with a betrothal."

"She's a princess to me, either way," Harruq said, setting her down. He knelt so he was at her height, and his goofy grin settled into a calm, gentle smile. His voice softened.

"How's my girl, truly?"

Aubby crossed her arms behind her back and looked over at Gregory, lurking near the door.

"I'm good," she said. "Because this is something I need to do, isn't it? Something good, for a lot of people?"

"Aye, it is," said Harruq.

Aubrienna stood to her fullest height. Her face was so serious it broke Aurelia's heart. She looked so much older than her years, and possessing far more wisdom than any ten-year-old should. Aurelia had done so much to let her live a proper childhood, but the world was cruel. there had been nothing she could to do stop her child from watching her uncle die in the guise of her own father. Perhaps Aurelia should not be surprised by her maturity.

"You and mom have always done what you could to help people," Aubrienna said. "And I will, too. And...and it's not like it's a bad thing, right? I get to be a queen."

"*The* queen," Harruq said, and he bopped her nose with his thumb. "But don't worry. You'll always be my little elfling to me." He turned his attention to Gregory. "And I trust you will treat her well?"

The little future king stood up as tall as he could and pulled back his shoulders. "I promise," he said, every fiber of his being working to convey his seriousness. It was charming in its own way, even if he did not yet have the years on him to make it work.

Aurelia took her husband's hand, kissed his cheek, and then gestured for the children to follow.

"Queen Brynn awaits."

◁╬▷

An enormous balcony hung over the grand doors of the mansion, its entrance blocked with thick curtains meant to endure the occasional rain. Just within, Queen Brynn and a gaggle of advisers and servants stood waiting. Notable among them was the elven ambassador, Elydien Marosi, calmly holding conversation with the queen. He was finely dressed in green and silver silks, and it warmed Aurelia's heart to see him.

Conversation ceased when Aurelia led the rest into the room, and all waited for Queen Brynn to break the newfound silence.

"Are the little ones ready?" the queen asked. Her crimson dress sparkled with diamonds, and the edges of her eyes and cheeks were vibrant with red paint.

"They are," Aurelia said, and she dipped her head in respect to both the queen and ambassador. "And it is good to meet the man behind all the letters I have exchanged with the survivors in Stonewood."

Elydien placed his hands together and bowed. "And I am pleased to meet the daughter of Kindren and Aullienna Thyne. I knew them well, in days that are far too distant. Their grandness cast a long shadow, and yet you still shine brightly above them."

Aurelia smiled. "I see your tongue is as silver as your writing."

Harruq shifted uncomfortably behind her. As he often did during official announcements, he was dressed in his dark leather armor and cloak, Salvation and Condemnation sheathed on either side of his belt. His hands drummed the hilts of his swords,

Legacy of the Watcher

betraying his nervousness.

"So we ready to get this over with?" he asked. "I'm hungry for the feast that was promised."

"I suppose there is no reason to delay this further," Queen Brynn said, and gestured toward a servant. The young man bowed low and then rushed to the rope and pulley to withdraw the thick curtains that granted privacy to the interior of the balcony. The queen made for the center, while others lined up behind her, except for Elydien, who stood just to her right. Harruq gestured to Gregory, pointing to where he would stand at Brynn's left.

As everyone shuffled forward, and the noise of the crowd grew louder with anticipation, Aurelia knelt before Aubrienna. She put her hand on her daughter's shoulders and lowered her voice.

"I will not force you," she said. "Speak the word and I will halt all of this, find another way."

Aubrienna bit her lower lip, and her eyes darted to the gathered crowd of royalty and ambassadors prepared for the announcement.

"I'll get to help people as queen," she said. "Many people, of all kinds, and all places?"

"In ways even I cannot," Aurelia said, brushing an errant strand of hair away from her daughter's face.

Aubrienna shuddered as she took in a long breath, and then went still as she eased it out.

"Then I will," she said. "But...but you have to promise to be there with me, always. And teach me everything. I...I don't know how to be queen."

Aurelia kissed her daughter's forehead and offered a silent prayer of gratitude to Celestia for the gift of such a wonderful child.

"Always and forever," she said. She stood and offered her hand. Aubrienna took it as the curtains withdrew, and Queen Brynn stepped out to address the crowd. Aubrienna's fingers gripped her tightly as the people fell silent. The queen raised her arms to begin her address.

"People of Angkar," she shouted. "I come to share the most glorious news!"

In her grip, Aubrienna's fingers trembled.

23
CYTH

Cyth stared at the city of Angkar, this sprawling hive of humanity nestled against the sea, and wondered for the thousandth time how Celestia could have ever loved a god who birthed such ugliness. The night was deep, the stars shining. It should have been beautiful and calming. Instead Cyth seethed with barely controlled rage.

"He may not be coming," Vala said, lying on the grass behind him. The pair were in one of the fields just off the main road leading into the city. Their meeting place had been marked with a few pieces of grass and a twig, easily missable to human eyes but not to an elf's.

"He will," Cyth said. "Elydien may have abandoned elvenkind, but he will not abandon us."

Vala flipped one of her daggers into the air, watched it twirl, and then caught it just shy of landing.

"You hold more faith in him than I," she said.

"Perhaps I merely know him better."

Another flip of the dagger. "Or perhaps, in knowing him, you have blinded yourself to what you wish were not there."

Cyth turned away, not wanting her to see his irritation. Of course his twin would know the perfect way to undermine his confidence. It was a skill she'd honed over a lifetime.

"I promise," he said, watching a distant, shaded figure walk the far road. "My eyes are open to all that is good and ill in my mentor."

Earlier that morning, within minutes of the news of Aubrienna's and Gregory's betrothal reaching Cyth's camp, he had sent a messenger into Angkar to request a meeting with the elder who had long ago taken him under his wing. He would hear from Elydien's own lips the reasons for accepting such a union, instead of condemning it with the full voice of Stonewood as was proper.

"He's here," he told his sister. Elydien exited the road and crossed the grass between them.

"So he is," Vala said. "I suspect that will only make it

worse."

He ignored her, and when Elydien arrived, Cyth bowed low to him in proper respect to the man who had been his father in all but name since the tragedy that took the lives of their parents. The older elf eyed them warily, and he did not return the bow.

"I wish I could profess happiness in meeting you," Elydien said in the Quellan tongue. "But kindness or happenstance did not bring you here. I am not so foolish as to believe that. You come with ill intent, Cyth, and it takes little as to guess why."

Cyth lifted from his bow. "You wound me. Never have I acted with ill intent. Ever are the forests of Stonewood upon my heart."

A faint smile pulled the wrinkled corners of Elydien's mouth. "And you," he said, ignoring the comment and instead speaking to Vala, who yet remained on her back in the grass, flipping her dagger. "I have often relied on you to keep your brother out of trouble. What now leads to this lack in judgment?"

"My judgment is ever clear," Vala said. She caught her dagger by the blade and twirled it. "Save your words for someone who will take them to heart."

"Vala," Cyth snapped. To treat an elder with such disrespect was unbecoming, even if they disagreed with his choices. "Leave us be if you find conversation so tedious and unwelcome."

Vala hopped to her feet, sheathed her dagger, and then approached. Her hand settled on Cyth's shoulder.

"Careful, brother," she said softly. "Whatever you seek here will not come. You only make your heart bleed worse."

With that, she trudged toward the distant forest that hid their camp for the night. Cyth watched her go, needing the momentary silence to settle his thoughts. His anger was taking over, causing him to lash out at his family. Not good. If he were to win over his mentor, it had to be through calm, concise argument.

"Forgive me," he said, turning back to Elydien. "It has been a long few years, and we are both displeased with the recent news."

Elydien crossed his arms with a swish of his long, silken sleeves. "News you would have been aware of months ago if you had not abandoned the Stonewood." A bit of displeasure gleamed in his eyes. "You bemoaned our complacency and inaction, and condemn us now for our chosen path of action. It lends credence to my belief that neither action nor inaction were your issue, but that we refused to bend to your every desire."

Cyth stood tall before his mentor, refusing to back down as he so often did. Elydien could rip a man or woman apart without even trying. With but a few words, he would make everything Cyth had accomplished sound juvenile and rash. To overcome it meant an unbreakable ferocity of will. It meant holding faith, even when all others denied you. Muzien had understood that. If the stars were kind, so would Cyth, one day.

"Then you do not deny the stories I have heard," Cyth said. "You truly approve of this decision? To offer your blessing to a marriage of an elf and the human destined for Mordan's throne?"

Elydien stood tall. "I do. It is the path toward peace, young one. That alone makes it the right one for our feet to walk."

"Peace," Cyth said, snarling it out like a curse. His fists began to shake. He was glad Vala was not here to see it. "Every year, every conversation, I hear that word spoken like it is sacrosanct. You elders cling to it like it is a virtue. You elevate it beyond all reason and wisdom. Peace, with the butcher? Peace, with the murderer?"

"We discuss the fate of races and nations," Elydien said. "Do not simplify it down to the actions of a few and pretend they are the same. But yes, Cyth, I would still choose the path of peace, if it avoids a lifetime of bloodshed. That is what Celestia calls to us now."

"Is it?" Cyth asked. "She, who birthed the daughters of balance, is averse to bloodshed and war? Are you blind to history as well as the insult your acceptance inflicts upon us? They *murdered* us! They *hated* us! No matter the cost, no matter the death, they swarmed us with their swords and their fires and would not relent until we were gone from them!"

His temper flared, and he could no longer hold back his tongue.

"You, who watched my parents die upon the Bloodbrick, would now profess peace? You, who bore witness to the world's sundering by their brother gods, would allow the strongest of our bloodlines to mingle with the offspring of the king who slaughtered our brethren and burnt Dezerea to ash?"

Elydien reached out and put a hand on Cyth's shoulder. It was meant to be firm and comforting, but all Cyth felt was the feverish touch of the sick.

"Already Aubrienna Tun is mixed with the blood of the orcs. Do you rage against that, despite the work of Darnela in aiding them in turning away from Karak? She has shown them that Celestia's heart offers forgiveness even to those whom she cursed after the first Brothers' War. And now we witness the potential union of both elvish and orcish blood with those of the royal throne that once decreed us vile and dangerous."

His mentor stepped closer, his voice growing softer, his golden eyes, alight with life.

"You hear this and feel rage, but I beg you, young one, do not feel rage, but *hope*. The hate has receded. These people, these humans, their lives are short, and their generations pass swiftly as the seasons to us. Already we speak of returning to our ancestral home. The ink is wet for the treaties we will sign. This is a miracle, Cyth, not a curse. It is possibility blooming from the crimson fires of war. Embrace it. Let go of your own hate, lest you become as vile as those you would condemn."

Cyth shoved his mentor's hand away. Tears swelled in his eyes. This man had taken Cyth and Vala in when his parents fell upon the Bloodbrick. He had raised them and told them stories of their mother and father. On long, cold nights, he had taken charcoal and paper to draw them as best he could to ensure their memories did not fade. He had never shied away from telling the truth of their flight across Dezrel, of the crimes committed against them, or the heroic sacrifice of those ten elves, the strongest bloodlines of magic in all elvendom, to ensure the rest of their people escaped King Baedan's all-consuming war.

And now, despite everything, his mentor would walk a path Cyth could not follow.

"They hated us for what we are," he said, wishing he could be stronger. His own voice dropped to a whisper. "But I? I hate them for all they have done, and for what I know, deep in my heart, that they will do again. Your peace is a fool's lie. Humanity has ever been wretched and deceitful, and with the departure of their gods it is only a matter of time before they tear apart the treaties you would sign, rekindle their hate you think vanished, and wage another war upon us."

Elydien stepped back and sank his hands into the deep pockets of his robe. The vulnerability he had shown vanished behind the firm visage of a mentor and diplomat.

"Why are you here, child?" he asked. "What is it you plan to accomplish in these human lands?"

Cyth was tempted to tell him everything. The true numbers of his elven followers, the traitor within Angkar, and the full scope of their plan. The audacity would only harden his heart further. The necessary violence would appall him. Such change, it was no longer possible in a soul so weary of war.

It would be up to the newest generation of elves, those not yet broken like Cyth and Vala, to bring about the shining future.

"A miracle," he answered, and bowed once more to his mentor. To the father that raised him. "Leave Angkar, elder Elydien. Leave this city of humans. I beg this of you, once and only once, before the days to come."

Elydien stood tall before him. "I shall not abandon this hope of peace. Nor shall I abandon my hope in you. Fare thee well, my son. May the grace of the stars ever be warm upon your heart."

Cyth was in a daze as he watched the elf leave. His mind did not want to believe it had come to this, but he knew it inevitable. It was Elydien's strength that had earned Cyth's respect, and it was that strength that would doom him now.

His trek back to his camp was brief and solemn, and interrupted halfway by his waiting sister. She stood with her arms crossed and her auburn hair hanging low over her eyes. Cyth paused before her. No words came. None felt right. He thought she would mock him, or reaffirm how she had always known this would be the outcome. Instead she closed the space between them and gently wrapped her arms around his waist. Her head rested against his breast.

"With every step, another abandons us," she said softly. "Celestia was the first. The elven leaders second. Now the man who raised us. With every step, another blade draws blood from our hearts. With every step, the rope tightens about our throats."

"How do you do it?" he asked, his voice cracking. "You, who are always so calm and callous to the betrayals?"

She locked his gaze with her green eyes even as the rest of

her body pressed tightly against him. Her will held him captive. Even this vulnerability was calculated.

"Because we the betrayed are stronger than them all," she said. Her delicate fingers brushed a few strands of hair away from his face. "And because those who would stand against us are dead to me in my heart. I will not weep for the deceased, but fight for the living. Our time has come, brother. A time of new legends. The anointing of new crowns."

She kissed him on his lips, and he grew that much more aware of the curve of her body against his. Her breath was warm upon his neck as she whispered her promise.

"A time when *we* shall rule, free of gods, laws, and history that would bury us beneath the stone. An end to the night."

Another kiss. Her hands moved about him, undoing buttons.

"And the dawn of a new sun."

24
ERIN

Early morning, the day before she'd be forced to accompany her mother to some dreadfully dull signing ceremony, Erin crept along the outside of the shipwright building. It was the same place as always that she and Gray held their training sessions—at least those sessions he actually showed up to. He had been absent the last four days. But Erin had a feeling he would be waiting this time. And she had a plan. It wasn't a great plan, but by the gods and goddess she was going to give it a try.

All for a name, she thought as she climbed the building. Handholds were plenty, given its weathered state, the pine boards beaten by the storms that regularly swept in from the sea. Trickier was ascending without being seen through the windows by Gray, who presumably waited inside. She grabbed the edge of the roof and hauled herself up completely, then lay on her back to catch her breath. The morning sunlight felt warm on her skin, and she wished she could just lay there and bask in it.

But if she'd wanted comfort, she would have stayed home in her warm bed. Instead, Erin rolled over and crouched-walked across the shingles. Along the front of the building, where the two halves of the roof connected into a sharp 'v', there was a slender opening to allow smoke out when the open firepit was lit during winter. It wasn't large, but it didn't need to be, not for someone as small as Erin to slide through.

Erin hovered at the roof's apex, peering down at the opening beneath her. Her throat tightened. She might be making a complete fool of herself doing this…or even fall and break her neck. Wouldn't that be a fine way to live up to her father's reputation?

She dismissed such stupid thoughts. Gray demanded she score a hit if she wanted his name, but he also had made it clear there were no rules when it came to combat in the real world. This morning, once again a good half hour earlier than she was supposed to arrive, she would put that to the test. Swallowing her doubts, she grabbed the edge of the roof, twisted, and then slid over the side. She pitched her legs forward, angling them so they slipped in through the window. Her hands released, her momentum carrying her through. For the briefest moment her heart skipped, and she feared she'd pass right on through to fall to the hard ground, but then she caught the window, glad for her gloves to protect against splinters as her momentum wrenched to a halt.

Erin glanced over her shoulder as she hung from the window with burning fingers. He was actually there this time, waiting near the door. Gray looked tired, his head tilted and a hood covering his face. She didn't trust it in the slightest. The moment that door started to open, he'd be alert and ready. No ambush from there would work. She'd tried that already.

But from the ceiling? Well, it was worth a try, even as she realized how absurd her situation currently was. Hanging there, she could barely adjust her fall, and there were no rafters to navigate. She'd just have to drop and then sprint the distance. She winced in advance. This was going to hurt.

Her hands released. She dropped, all her body limp to best absorb the impact. The moment her feet touched ground she rolled, training from her mother kicking in. They'd spent a week practicing such maneuvers. Back then it'd left her spine and shoulders horribly bruised. Now she was thankful for the practice, for she barely felt the impact from the landing. Even better, she stole the momentum for herself, transferring it into a sudden sprint straight for the seemingly asleep Gray as she drew her sabers.

Three steps, that was all it took, three steps and she was upon him. Her right-hand saber swung for his chest, her wrist turning so the flat edge would strike him. Her heart leaped into her throat. This was it. This was—

Gray caught her wrist mid-swing. Her shock was so great she froze in place and just stared at the hood covering his face.

"Hrm," he said, lifting his head so his blue eyes pierced out from the shadows beneath. "We're getting ambitious." He twisted her wrist. "But the flat edge? Confident, aren't we?"

"I didn't want to hurt you." She tried to pull away, but he did not release her. She suddenly felt trapped, and panic had her wanting to thrust with her other hand. Her understanding of Gray kept her calm. Such an outburst would only disappoint him.

"How kind of you." He released her wrist. "And you must learn to be more light upon your feet. The day is young, and the streets still empty. I heard you stomping on the rooftop the entire time you were up there. There are cows better suited to stealth."

Erin retreated a step, her ego bruised. She thought she'd been quiet, but then again her mind had been focused on the drop inside. Zusa would be furious with her. They spent as much time learning to be quiet and stealthy as they did sparring with a blade.

"You exaggerate," she said, clanging her sabers together. "I may not rival a mouse, but surely I am better than a cow. A goat, perhaps? How about a chicken?"

Gray drew his swords. His head tilted, and though the hood still concealed his face in shadow, it did not hide his smile.

"Cluck, cluck, Erin. Shall I pluck your feathers?"

She swiped at him, a casual hit to indicate their sparring had begun. He deflected it with a quick turn of his wrist, so effortlessly done it barely looked like he moved.

"I don't know," Erin said, bouncing light on her feet. "Are you a fox, come to the hen house?"

The smile lost a bit of its amusement. "Not a fox. I have ever been a spider."

He assaulted her with a trio of hits, each coming from different directions but all ending with a downward chop straight at her forehead. Her forearms ached as she blocked with both of her sabers, and the sound of steel began its song. She countered, found herself on her ass in seconds as he dropped low, his leg sweeping her feet out from her under.

"Again," she said, pushing immediately back to a stand.

He paced before her, weapons low, and then he was spinning. The space between them vanished. Erin panicked, unsure where he would attack from. Knowing she should at least act, she thrust both blades forward into that confusing mess of cloaks and limbs.

Gray smashed them aside so hard she lost her grip on one, and then other went wide. The blur of movement ended with the sharp edge of a short sword on her throat. Gray peered down at her, his expression giving away nothing.

"You attacked instead of fleeing when confused," he said. "At least your instincts are being honed properly. But you're still reacting only based on familiarity and training. Watch my feet. Watch my hands. See in your mind the paths they will take based on my movements, and then judge accordingly. A spin like that limits me. Know those limits."

Erin retrieved her saber, and she repeated the wisdom in her mind, trying to burn it into memory. Hands and feet, her mother had told her repeatedly. Erin thought she did that when sparring, but Gray was giving her a solid lesson on the enormous chasm between what she thought she knew and what she actually knew.

"Again," she said, clanging her weapons together.

Five hits, and he knocked her to the floor with his elbow. She staggered back to her feet, hiding the pain in her side from the contact.

"Again."

He let her take the offensive this time, blocking and parrying her every attack until it felt like he was the one in control of her own movements. On her last thrust, she realized she was woefully out of position, her saber tip aimed the wrong direction compared to his momentum. The flat edge of a sword smacked the back of her head, and she clenched her jaw to swallow down her cry of pain.

"Again."

Every attack felt wrong, but she tried nonetheless. Every parry was anticipated, but she shoved aside Gray's swords all the same. Her concentration tightened, all the world seeming to grow in clarity. His speed was too great, his confidence unbreakable. To keep up with him, her own confidence had to grow. Her choices came quicker, often wrong, but better than delayed reactions that, even if made correctly, would still be too slow.

"Again."

Blood on her tongue, more from her split lip.

"Again."

Every part of her body ached, no doubt bruised head to toe.

"Again."

She could feel it as she assaulted Gray anew. Her mother sought to impart incredible skill with a blade, to wield it like a dancer upon the battlefield to become thoroughly untouchable. Gray sought something simpler. Something more primal. With every hit, every clash of steel, he turned thought into instinct. And he did not dance. He won with brutal savagery. He won by being better. Stronger. Faster.

The hilt of his sword struck her forehead. Her vision swam, but she would not stop, damn it, she would not be defeated. The world spun, but her body spun with it. Sheer will kept her saber thrusting. No hesitation. No turning it to the blunted side. His cloak shifted, his off-hand moving to parry, but her twisting stumble worked to her advantage.

She felt resistance, then nothing, as she went staggering past Gray. Her heart hammered in her ears as she spun. His back was to her. His swords rest low in his grip, their tips nearly touching the floorboards.

"Gray?" she said when he did not move.

The older man turned, and a faint splash of blood had soaked into his shirt from where she cut his chest. It was thin, a scratch that would never prove lethal without some sort of poison, but it was there. Erin thought she'd feel more excited at the victory, but she only felt tired and out of breath.

What she also did not expect was the sheer pride in Gray's voice when he said, "Even wounded, disoriented, and beaten, you fought on. Well done, Erin. Well done."

There it was, the elation she should feel. It came not from the hit itself, but hearing those words of praise. She fought back the impulse to smile. No, not yet. They had a deal, and she would show no pleasure in the victory until that deal was honored.

"A name," she said, standing tall.

His smile hardened. "Are you certain?"

Erin jammed her sabers into their sheaths.

"You don't seem like someone to break a promise, so why ask?"

He looked away. He…he seemed uncertain. Nervous. Why? It was so uncharacteristic of him, a sudden lacking in the confidence that exuded from his every movement. It only ignited her curiosity.

"Because I want you to be certain," he said. "I want you to understand that things must change once the knowledge is given."

Erin crossed her arms, summoning every bit of stubbornness that had allowed her to survive with a mother like

Legacy of the Watcher

Zusa Gemcroft.

"I'm not afraid of change," she said. "And I'm not afraid of you. A name, Gray. Your real name, or I leave, and do not return."

Gray sheathed his swords and pulled the hood from his head. His face was covered with purple splotches and recent scabs, making her wonder for a moment what he'd been up to since their last sparring session. That wondering disappeared when his icy eyes looked upon her. She felt like they pierced through the shadows of her soul.

"Perhaps you are strong enough," he said at last. "Then hear this, and know. My name, the name I bestowed upon myself in a distant past as a child of Mordeina's streets, is Thren Felhorn."

Erin's entire body locked in place. Her mind froze, and her heart seemingly halted. Her mouth opened, but she could not form words. The old man's gaze held her prisoner.

"Erin," he continued. "I am your grandfather."

"You..." Her mind tumbled and broke. The stories her mother had told her, and those she read in *Legacy of the Watcher*, twisted and fought against his words. "You're dead."

"I was."

"Haern killed you. The Watcher *killed* you."

This man she had known as Gray grinned at her.

"Indeed, he thought he did. I took precautions."

Every single word and deed the man had done in their time together paraded through her mind at a rapid clip. His attention. His care for her, seemingly without reason. His knowledge of her father, and his role as the Watcher.

I have ever been a spider.

Her cheeks burned. Felhorn. She had named herself Felhorn.

Erin rocked backward as if punched. Her instincts had screamed Gray was dangerous, and yet cared for her, and they were both far more correct than she ever guessed. Yet did that actually mean safety? This was a man who had attempted to kill his own son twice, and supposedly even died for it on the day his Spider Guild was shattered.

"What does...I don't know what to say." She shook her head. "What I've read. What my mother has told me of you. How much of it is the truth, and how much are lies?"

"It depends on what they told you," Thren said.

"That you were a horrible man," she said in a voice she could not stop from quivering. Her emotions overwhelmed her, making a mockery of her training. This...this old man couldn't be him, he couldn't be a ghost of her past, a face given to a specter known only in story. "That you killed without mercy. That you ruled Veldaren like a tyrant, and nearly destroyed my family when the underworld went to war."

"Then I am who you believe I am."

No guilt. No uncertainty. Erin's insides twisted and danced.

Thren Felhorn.

It couldn't be.

But it was.

"I have to go," she said, and rushed for the door.

"Wait."

His command halted her in her tracks. She shivered, afraid of him, truly afraid of him, for the very first time. She turned, looking upon the older man's face and seeing a legacy as old and broken as her father's.

"I want you to know," he said, "that until your arrival in Angkar, and your entry into the tournament using my name, I did not know of your existence. Your father's tryst with Zusa was a secret, your birth hidden from even him."

"Is that supposed to make this better?" she asked, hating the persistent shakiness of her voice.

"How you react is on you, Erin. I only wish that you understand I was ignorant of your life until recently. Had I known, I would have sought you out far sooner. I would have revealed my name, and my face, so I might be a part of your life."

"Why?" she asked. "So you could train me? Turn me into the monster you always wanted Haern to be?"

Thren stood tall, and it seemed a dozen years suddenly added to his face. "I wanted the world for Aaron. I want it for you, too, if you would accept what gifts an old man may yet impart."

Too much. It was all too much. Erin sprinted out the door of the shipwright. Her grandfather did not follow.

Her grandfather. Even the word was nonsense in her mind as she ran, and ran, weaving through the early morning traffic flowing toward the docks. She ran without thought, without purpose, just running and wishing she could leave the tumultuous monster of emotions that chased her far, far behind.

25
TARLAK

"I just want to look over the goods," Tarlak told the porter. "You don't need to make a fuss about it."

"Protecting my clients' goods ain't making a 'fuss'," the bearded man argued. "It's doing my damn job."

It took all of Tarlak's willpower not to roll his eyes. The porter was a big man, his arms full of tattoos and muscle. Behind him were two enormous warehouses with multiple entrances gated off with double doors that reminded Tarlak a little bit of a farm barn.

"And I applaud you for your dedication," Tarlak said. "But I'm also doing my job, which I must remind you, was given to me by the gods-damned *queen.*"

The porter hawked and spat. "Which you ain't proven. Sorry, but I don't got to listen to some stranger in ugly robes until I see paper with signatures that say I do."

Tarlak crossed his arms, his patience, already frayed thin, reaching its final straw.

"The entire castle is busy preparing for today's big fancy ceremony," he said. "I'm not going to bother Queen Brynn because you aren't willing to believe a word I'm saying. One last chance, my good sir. Will you let me in or not?"

The porter lowered his hand to a short sword strapped to his thigh. "And this is *your* last chance. Get out easy, or go out with a new scar. Your choice."

"My choice?" Tarlak said, beaming a smile. "Well then, I take option three."

He waved his hand, flinging ice in a wave. It wrapped around the porter's feet and ankles, locking him in place.

"The shit?" the man said, twisting and pulling.

"Now, now," Tarlak said before starting another spell. The incantation finished, he blew from his palms as if they were covered with invisible dust. "There's no need for foul language."

The magic washed over the porter. His eyelids drooped and

his body went slack. He slumped forward, and Tarlak was quick to catch him. A snap of his fingers, and the ice imprisoning him vanished into smoke.

"Easy now," Tarlak said, lowering the man to the ground. "Have a little nap while I look around, all right?"

That done, Tarlak hurried to the first of the enormous warehouses. All of its wagon entrances were locked, as was the smaller door on one side. His curiosity heightened.

Something is wrong here, he thought. The porter's rudeness, while hardly unique to the people of Angkar, still felt much harsher than made sense. *What is it you're hiding?*

No locked door was going to stop Tarlak from finding out. He cracked his knuckles, a little disturbed by how loudly they popped, and then weaved the necessary movements.

"You're getting old, Tar," he muttered as a large stone materialized from his palm and flung forward to smash against the lock. Wood splintered, and the metal within broke so that the door bowed inward. Tarlak pushed it all the way open with his shoulder and then entered the warehouse.

There were two dozen wagons inside, lined up in rows of three. Some were covered, others not. Tarlak walked through them in the dim light, coughing a little from the dust. He scanned about until finally finding a manifest written on thick, sturdy yellow paper resting atop a squat little table in the corner.

"There you are," he said, lifting it and scanning the writing. He looked for a specific symbol, the elaborate 'C' of the Connington family.

It was true that the attacks upon the wagons showed no apparent focus, with both Connington and Gemcroft family merchants assaulted, but while going over the reports, Tarlak had noticed a strange wrinkle. For those merchants that were independent, working for the queen, or loyal to the Gemcrofts, their wagons were attacked both going in and out of Angkar. The Conningtons, however, were always wagons delivering to the city, and never away.

More interesting was that while claiming to be robbed like all the others, Connington deliveries that had been attacked ended up arriving in Angkar with new crews and claims of still carrying cargo.

"Everyone else is getting robbed blind," Tarlak said, spotting a dozen listings with the 'C' symbol and tapping the ledger with his forefinger. "But you, they merely kill the escorts and then leave the goods behind? That doesn't sit right with me. Someone's playing games."

His certainty only grew when he realized what the ledger was telling him. There were ten wagons in total with goods due to be delivered to various Connington facilities, and all ten were being held in the second warehouse, separate from the others.

Tarlak set the ledger back down on the table and hurried to the exit on the opposite side. He unlocked the door, stepped out into the thin gap between the buildings, and then checked the other door. Locked, as expected. A quick spell fixed that, another stone, even larger, to knock it off its hinges.

The queen'll pay for the damages, he told himself as he kicked the broken door to the ground. Daylight spilled into the warehouse, and sure enough he spotted the wagons. All of them were enormous, topped by a pale white cover. Tarlak grinned eagerly at the sight.

"Let's see just what you're smuggling into Brynn's fair city," he said, and entered the warehouse.

He made it three steps before he felt something sharp press against the back of his neck.

"Tarlak Eschaton?" a feminine voice asked.

Tarlak lifted his hands slowly, worried at how easily he had been flanked. He'd even checked both sides before stepping in. This was Watcher levels of sneaking.

"I am," he said. "And you?"

The sharpness left his skin.

"Consider yourself lucky, wizard," the woman said, ignoring his question. "My brother will find you a fascinating prisoner."

Tarlak spun, fire on his fingertips, but his ambusher was faster. The hard metal of a sword hilt smacked him in the forehead. The world spun, and the spell vanished from his hands as his concentration broke. His stomach heaved, and with his balance ruined he dropped onto his back.

A woman in silver armor peered down at him, a faint smile on her beautiful face.

"Sleep well, Tarlak."

The last thing he saw before her boot struck was a distant blur of wagons, and the dozens of armed men and women stepping out from them with swords and bows in hand.

26

HARRUQ

"You'd think I'd be used to dolling myself up like this," Harruq grumbled as he adjusted his suit. It'd been specially tailored for him before leaving Mordeina, long dark cloth with a fine silver vest, all designed to not rip or tear when his muscles flexed.

"I never expected you to get used to it," Aurelia said, her hands a blur as she curled and looped her hair into numerous braids. The deftness of her fingers was as magical to watch as her actual spellcraft. "But at least it is quick. Shall we talk about the time it has taken to finish my hair, or the efforts to properly don this dress?"

Harruq and Aurelia were alone in the dressing room offered to them in the royal mansion. His wife stood before an enormous mirror, and while it had indeed taken time to tie the many loops and strings of her blue and crimson corset, she did look ridiculously fine within it.

"Yeah, but at least you like dresses," he said, pulling at a collar that felt much too tight despite the tailor insisting all the measurements were correct.

"I *like* looking beautiful," Aurelia said, using another ribbon to pin yet one more braid of her auburn hair up behind her head. "Dresses are how I currently prefer to accomplish that."

Harruq crossed the room and wrapped his hands around her waist while settling his lips on her exposed neck.

"You're very good at looking beautiful," he said, kissing her twice.

"I know," she said, and flicked his nose with her forefinger without even pausing the tying of the ribbon. "And don't get any ideas. It took far, far too much time putting on this human-made dress for me to take it off now." She winked. "Maybe after, though."

Harruq kissed her cheek, then released his grip. "If you insist," he said, and checked himself in the mirror beside her. His neck was a little red from constantly scratching at it, and he told himself he had to stop and just ignore the ever-present choking feeling in the name of 'fashion'. At least he wouldn't be the only one dressing up. Why couldn't traditional wear for his role as Steward be like Tarlak's comfy robes?

He frowned, a thought hitting him.

"Isn't Tarlak coming?" he asked.

"Sorry, Harruq, he's not joining us, no matter how many fantasies of his that'd fulfill."

He poked her side, taking childish pleasure in the way she flinched away from him.

"I mean for the peace treaty. I haven't seen him all day."

Aurelia sighed, the last of the ribbons seemingly done and all her braiding at an end.

"Harruq, I've spent all morning getting myself and Aubrienna ready. I've no time to worry about our wonderful but daft wizard friend. The queen's been having him chase down rumors over bandits or some such, hasn't she?"

"I think so," he said. The wizard had mentioned something of the sort at one of their recent dinners, but Harruq had been...somewhat inebriated. His way of coping with the dreadfully dull passage of time that did not include the only interesting parts of the day, which was his time spent training Erin Gemcroft.

"Then he's likely off chasing rumors," Aurelia said. "He knows how to open a portal, and this date has been set for months. He'll show up, I'm sure. Let's just pray he doesn't make a scene when he does."

Harruq chuckled. "Tarlak, making a scene? He would never."

His wife winked at him, then did one last adjustment on the front of her corset.

"I miss my own dress already. How do I look?"

He crossed his arms. "Pretty sure you should do a little twirl or something, yeah?"

Aurelia smirked but did as asked, spinning in place so the lengthy skirt flared out, the top crimson, the underneath a subtle blue. Faint golden curls wound their way down the side of the corset and grew like vines along the skirt fabric. The ribbons in her hair matched the same deep gold color, and made her tightly-wound braids sparkle.

"Perfect," Harruq said, clapping his hands once.

"Absolutely perfect. Now let's go get the kids. The little ones have a peace treaty to sign."

In the southeastern portion of Angkar, a mile from the royal mansion, a grand wooden stage had been built in the center of a large courtyard whose surface was an impressive expanse of packed dirt. From what Harruq had heard, royal events were often held there, as were feasts, plays, and whatever else groups with coin paid for the privilege of occupying for a day. Today, it would be used for the three-way peace treaty, officially locking in two decades of peace between Ker, Mordan, and the elves of Stonewood.

Harruq expected a crowd, but was still put off by the sheer size of it. City soldiers formed a walkway, shields up and armor glinting in the sunlight. Just as numerous, though, were mercenaries bearing shared blue tabards. The Connington family, Harruq knew. The mercenaries formed lines along the outer perimeter of the crowd, and it seemed like they were in charge of checking bystanders on their way to crowding about the stage.

"It's loud," Gregory said beside Harruq.

"Ignore it and smile, little prince," Harruq said, grinning down at the kid. "Make the people believe you will one day be a fantastic king."

Gregory straightened up, his arms stiff at his sides. "I'll try."

"That'll do," Harruq, patting him on the back as they continued through the gap, doing his best to ignore the occasional shout or question from those in attendance.

Together, he and Aurelia escorted Gregory and Aubrienna to the stage, the four of them arriving second. Elydien had come first, alone and bearing the scrutiny of the crowd. The elf stood waiting with his hands crossed at the front of his green and gold robes, a faint smile on his face. He looked regal and respectable, two traits Harruq knew would forever elude him.

"That robe looks so much comfier than this suit," Harruq muttered to Aurelia once the four were atop the raised platform. Aurelia subtly jabbed his side with her elbow.

"At least I let you keep your swords," she said, not needing to whisper given the constant murmur of the crowd.

Harruq patted the hilts of Salvation and Condemnation at

his hips. The leather of their sheaths was freshly oiled, the weapons sharpened and polished to a shine. After the signing, all leaders of the nations were to draw a weapon to hold while swearing. Given Gregory's age, Harruq would do so as Steward, and by Ashhur, he would ensure his beloved swords would look their best.

"I'd feel naked without them," Harruq said, and then nodded. "There's the star of the show."

Queen Brynn arrived last, looking regal while dressed in a fusion of battle chainmail and a fluttering crimson skirt. A mixture of war and beauty, and she wore it well. Six soldiers marched in formation alongside her, their tabards flying the crimson hawk of Ker, the new symbol given to the nation upon Queen Brynn's crowning. The crowd bowed their heads at her passage to the platform, and Harruq noted how easily the queen commanded their respect. She had not ruled long, but it seemed she had won the people over far more than Queen Loreina ever had.

A little table waited in the center of the enormous raised platform. On it was a lengthy scroll, half of it curled up. An inkwell and quill rested beside it, awaiting usage. Harruq stared at it nervously. He'd learned to read and write, Qurrah made sure of that, but he had never considered his handwriting anything more than blocky and childish, often joking that Aubrienna had already surpassed him in penmanship. The past years of being a Steward had helped out a bit, though he still often defaulted to a single 'H' when he thought he could get away with it.

Not here. His full name, on a document meant to secure two decades of peace, was required.

"Are you sure we can't have Gregory sign it instead?" he asked Aurelia.

"For the last time, stop worrying about your signature," she snapped, her pleasant, dignified smile never cracking in the slightest.

Queen Brynn took center stage and addressed the crowd. "I thank you all for coming to witness this celebration of peace," she said. "And so let us not linger on the act, so we may rejoice in the future. Elydien Marosi, come forth, and sign as representative of both the Dezren and Quellan elves of Stonewood."

Elydien did so, and when finished, he gave the crowd a polite bow. Scattered applause followed.

"Harruq Tun, Godslayer of Mordan," Brynn said next,

causing Harruq's heart to jump. "Come sign as Steward for Gregory Copernus."

It took all of Harruq's concentration, and a bit of courage, but he dipped the quill in the inkwell and signed his name without too much shaking or splattering of ink. When finished, he accepted the applause silently while retreating back to Aurelia's side.

"Gregory needs to grow up faster," he muttered. Aurelia winked, took his hand, and then together they watched the queen sign the last of the three lines. When finished, she lifted the treaty, holding it aloft as if it were a trophy, and pivoted so all in attendance may witness the signatures. Cheers and applause followed in waves. Harruq watched, breathing out a sigh of relief. It had taken years of letters, diplomats, and careful concessions to both Ker and the elves to reach this moment. As much as he hated it, his own daughter had become a playing piece in the game, all to achieve a lasting peace. Yet, to finally arrive at its culmination, he had to admit the hard work was worth the reward.

He heard a slight whooshing sound, and Aurelia jerked beside him. His head whipped toward her, his mild confusion turning to dawning horror. Aurelia stared down at her chest, eyes wide, mouth agape. A slender arrow protruded from just below her collarbone. Blood trickled down the corset of her dress. Their eyes met. Harruq's mind fought for words, his bafflement freezing the entire world.

"Aurry?" he asked as Elydien collapsed on the other side of him. Harruq spared a glance that way, and saw a far thicker arrow lodged directly into the old elf's throat. His wrinkled fingers clutched at the shaft, shaking as he bled out, struggling for air.

Screams followed, and the crowd erupted into absolute chaos. The Queen's soldiers rushed to form a line before the platform, struggling against men and women fleeing from the sudden attack. Aurelia's legs gave out and Harruq caught her as she fell, gently lowering her to the platform.

"I'm sorry, Aurry," he said, grabbing the arrow and then yanking it out. Not deep, he saw, and not striking anything major. The knowledge granted no relief. There, on the arrow, he saw little flecks of white.

Poison.

More screams stole his attention, and he dared look away

from his wife. The rooftops of every single home surrounding the clearing were suddenly occupied. Harruq's stomach sank at the sight. Elves. Dozens of elves, all armed with bows and quivers.

Quivers that would not stay full for long. The first barrage went out, striking with the fearful precision granted by decades of mastery. Soldiers dropped, clutching arrows embedded into their necks, faces, and abdomens. The queen's soldiers, Harruq realized with growing horror. The elves were ignoring the Connington mercenaries.

Ignoring them, as the mercenaries pushed through the crowd with weapons drawn to battle the queen's soldiers.

Ignoring them, for a good many mercenaries had thrown off their helmets to reveal the sharply pointed ears of elven blood.

"Tori betrayed us," he said, and looked to the queen. Brynn's dress was torn and her hair a tangled mess of half-ripped braids. One of her guards lay dead at her feet, the other fighting back-to-back with her as the ambushers surrounded them. From what Harruq could tell she was holding her own, impressive given the skill of their attackers, but it was only a matter of time. Elves and mercenaries swarmed through the crowd, and the rooftop archers were relentless in picking off any soldiers attempting to make their way to the stage to aid their queen.

That no arrows flew toward said queen worried Harruq deeply. Either they wanted her alive…or they wanted her death to be more dramatic than that.

"Harruq…" Aurelia said, stealing his attention back. Her skin was ashen white. The image was so starkly similar to when she'd been poisoned by an arrow over a decade ago by the Spider Guild's assassins that he felt himself momentarily lost in time. Wishing somehow to save her, he picked her up and carried her toward the rear of the platform, if only to gain that little bit of privacy.

"Get… Aubby… out," Aurelia insisted as she rocked in his arms, her eyelids drooping. Her breath, already shallow, slowed further.

Harruq kissed her forehead, his mind aflame as he set her back down. He could not fight his way out while carrying Aurelia. But if he stayed here and fought, and lost, his life may be forfeit, his daughter captured. The impossibility of it ripped at his mind. He couldn't move. He couldn't decide.

The battle raged in front of him, growing more frantic as both elves and mercenaries reached the dais. Brynn's final bodyguard was slain, and two elves in leather armor leaped upon the platform. The queen's sword weaved back and forth, holding back the combined assault, but her eyes were wide with fear and her movements grew more frantic as her situation turned dire. She managed to beat back one elf, but the second tricked her with a subtle feint, preying on her panicked state. Her sword weaved wrong, and then the elf was on her, his elbow striking her forehead. When she staggered, his fist followed, a brutal hit to the stomach that robbed her of breath and sent her reeling. His sword struck her hand, slicing open her fingers and causing her to drop her weapon.

"We were promised better," the elf said as two more joined him on the platform.

"Brynn!"

A pale woman burst out from the crowd, vaulting onto the raised platform with a single lunge. The queen's handmaiden, Harruq realized. She landed on the back of the nearest elf, a glistening dagger held in her hands. The edge jammed straight down into the elf's neck, immediately releasing a rupture of blood. The shocked elf's knees buckled, and her weight sent him tumbling as she stabbed again and again, all while screaming.

"Run, Brynn! Run!"

The queen's injured hand pressed to her stomach, smearing blood across her fine dress. Instead of listening, she dove with her other hand for her discarded weapon. A boot stomped on her fingers, and she screamed as even more ambushers piled onto the platform, grabbing her arms and pinning them behind her back.

Meanwhile, the first elf grabbed the handmaiden by the arm and yanked her away from the bleeding mess that had been his comrade. She stumbled, spun on her knees, and immediately shot back to her feet. Her eyes were wide, her mouth open in a feral scream, as her dagger stabbed straight for her attacker's throat.

The elf's sword, though, was longer. She gasped as she impaled herself on the blade, which sank all the way up to the hilt in her stomach. The blood-soaked dagger shook in her hands, then dropped.

"Lumi!" Brynn screamed while pulling against the elf

Legacy of the Watcher

restraining her.

  The bloodshed finally broke Harruq's paralysis. If he must choose between his daughter and his wife, he would not choose at all. He would let Aurelia decide, and her desire was clear.

  "I love you, Aurry," he whispered. He clutched Salvation and Condemnation tightly between his fists. Little Aubrienna stood stiff beside her mother, quietly sobbing as the battle raged around them. Gregory was with her, eyes wide, shocked silent.

  "When I run, you run after me, you understand?" Harruq told them, kneeling so he was at their height. The two children nodded. Harruq swallowed down a stone in his throat and refused the urge to look at his unconscious wife. His voice felt rough and broken.

  "We go."

  Harruq lunged off the back of the platform, toward the smallest of the exits out of the square. The Connington mercenaries were there, as they were everywhere, but fewer in number. Harruq landed amidst them, all his fear and rage adding strength to his swings. Salvation broke the wrist of a man trying to block with one hand. Condemnation shattered the bones of an arm wielding a shield. He pulled both his weapons back, then thrust, finding killing blows as they buried deep into flesh.

  Two down, a terrifying many to go. Harruq spun while stretching his arms to their limit. Another soldier fell, his head cleaved off his shoulders. The remainder retreated several steps, trying to form a corralling circle. Harruq saw the fear in their eyes, the intimidation at facing off against a foe so steeped in rumor and legend. He fed it with a bellowing roar, then bore down on the nearest mercenary. His sister swords hammered the man's raised shield, breaking the metal, breaking bones, breaking the man underneath.

  The other two scattered, and Harruq risked a glance over his shoulder. Aubrienna and Gregory lingered just behind, holding each other's hands as they watched with wide-eyed shock.

  "Do not fall behind!" he shouted to them before continuing to clear a way. Another Connington mercenary, who had just chopped down one of the queen's few remaining loyal soldiers. The fool had no idea who he faced when he swung his sword toward Harruq's abdomen. He learned the hard way when Harruq smacked the weapon aside with such strength it flew from the man's too-loose grip. Salvation shoved deep into his chest, ending his panicked shrieks for aid.

Aid did come, though. Two elves leaped down from rooftops with sharpened blades held in eager hands. Harruq shoved aside terrified bystanders, trying to clear a space. More mercenaries formed a wall blocking off the exit, and he needed to get there before the chaos subsided and those fighting near the front realized where Aubby and Gregory had gone.

The elves arrived, and Harruq took joy in watching their cocky expressions shift to fear when he tore into them. Their swords flashed and danced, wielded with undeniable skill…but Harruq simply did not care. His world was red. His blood burned like fire. He was, simply, better.

He charged directly into them, blasting aside their attempts to block. Elven steel creaked and groaned attempting to hold back the ancient magic within his sister swords. He pounded both blades into a raised block, smashing into it as if trying to tear down a wall. The steel shattered, the elf shouted as shards flew across his face and eyes. Condemnation ended his life with a single slash. His comrade swore in elvish while thrusting for Harruq's side, hoping to gut him while he was preoccupied. Salvation intercepted in a blur of red. He sidestepped a second thrust, batted aside a swipe as if it were swung by a child, and then kicked his leg out wide. The elf nimbly leaped over it, but the momentary pause in the air was what Harruq truly desired. Salvation cut him across the chest, tearing through armor and exposing ribs.

Too much time, Harruq thought as the body crumpled. He glanced back, ensuring the children followed. They did, their faces pale and eyes wide from the horror erupting around them.

"Godslayer!" an angry, feminine voice shouted, stealing his attention. An elven woman approached through the crowd, her twin swords twirling. The eagerness on her face worried him in a way the cockiness of the prior elves did not.

Harruq rushed her. No time for finesse. He thought to overwhelm her as he had his other foes, but when his swords crashed down, she did not try to match his strength. Instead the elf parried them aside, but not quite as he expected. She pulled his swords inward, toward her body, and instead rotated out of position in a blur of silver armor. Her blades lashed out as she exited the spin, a nasty slash that'd have opened his throat if Salvation had not caught it in time.

"Not bad," she said as black steel pressed against silver. He shoved her away, tried to gut her with a thrust, and then vaulted toward her when she retreated. Condemnation failed to chop off an arm, and again their weapons intertwined. Harruq marched her way, denying her a chance to find stable footing. The moment she stood her ground, his strength would overwhelm her, and they both knew it. Their swords danced, and as much as Harruq hated to admit it, this mysterious elf was capable of holding her own against him. Whatever her deficiencies, her speed more than made up for them. He had to ensure his every swing, if not avoided, was lethal, for she could easily open him up with a counter if allowed.

"You live up to your reputation," she said, finally blocking a slash with both her swords combined. Her arms braced against the impact, which shook her all the way down to her knees. "If only we could finish our duel proper."

At Harruq's confused look, she gestured behind him. Risking the potential deceit, he glanced back and immediately froze. An elf had caught up to them, and he knelt holding a hand over Aubrienna's mouth. The other pressed the flat edge of a dagger to her throat, its sharpened point aimed upward toward her chin.

"You monsters," Harruq seethed, fighting against a furious urge to lunge at the elf holding his daughter.

"Monsters, says the beast used as Ashhur's killing blade," the elf said. Her mocking smile finally faded. "Drop your weapons and surrender, or you shall see how truly monstrous I can become."

Aurelia was already surrounded. Gregory had fled but a few feet beyond Aubrienna before he, too, had been captured. The knife glinted as it adjusted its position along Aubrienna's throat, the elf sliding the sharpened edge ever closer. Seeing his daughter crying broke Harruq in a horrid, familiar way. He lowered Salvation and Condemnation to the ground, then stepped aside.

"You best keep your word," he said as two human mercenaries approached holding iron manacles. "If you lay a finger on either of them…"

The elven woman blasted him across the mouth with the hilt of her sword. He spat blood, and had to clench his teeth and close his eyes to deny the rage threatening to overwhelm him. Someone grabbed his arms, pulling his wrists behind his back to clasp the irons.

Another hand touched his face, and he opened his eyes to see the elven woman leaning close so that she might whisper and be heard above the din.

"My name is Vala Ordoth," she said, cruelty glistening in her emerald eyes. "I will be queen of the newly risen Kingdom of the Sun, and I will do whatever I wish, to whomever I wish. Your time affecting Dezrel's fate is at its end, half-orc. Let all the relics of the brother gods fade away. We will do as we must to repair the damage."

Harruq pulled at the manacles, stretching the metal, while also leaning toward Vala in a jolt. Just enough to widen her eyes. Just enough to make her take a sudden, worried step back.

"Harm not a hair on their heads," he said. "Or you will wish it were the gods you contend with, and not their beast."

Vala recovered quickly, dismissing him with an air of indifference he did not believe.

"Bring him to the platform to join his family," she told the two elves holding Harruq. "It's time the city meets their new king and queen."

27
ERIN

As Queen Brynn lifted the peace treaty accord up for the crowd to see, Erin's mother fidgeted beside her.

"Mother?" Erin asked, sensing her discomfort immediately. They and their family were at the very front of the crowd, a handful of Gemcroft soldiers forming a barricade around them to offer a semblance of separation from the rest of the common folk.

"Have you any weapons?" Zusa asked, keeping her voice low and her face calm.

Erin patted her hip.

"Just a dagger," she said. Given the public nature of the ceremony, she'd kept her sabers at home. "Why? What's wrong?"

Zusa glanced over her shoulder, rapid and quick.

"The entrances. They're filling with Connington--"

Two arrows flew over their heads. One sank deep into Elydien's throat, the other thudded into Aurelia Tun's chest. The shock of it froze everyone on stage in place, and then the screaming began. Erin spun in place, panicking at the sight of archers filling the rooftops.

"Get down!" she screamed, falling to her hands and knees.

Thankfully, Nathaniel grabbed Zusa and yanked her to the ground just as a full volley of arrows rained down upon the gathering. People fled in all directions, while her mother's mercenaries crowded closer together, lifting their shields to block. One was too slow, and Erin winced at the sight of him dropping, blood trickling down his face from the arrow lodged deep in his eye socket.

Erin came up to a squat, dagger in hand. It felt pitiful and small, and she desperately wished she had her sabers. Nathaniel crouched with her as the soldiers continued to press in. Meanwhile, Zusa grabbed both of them by the shoulder, pulling them closer.

"You two need to flee," she said. She released them so she could draw her own daggers, the glinting weapons secretly stashed in the folds of her elegant violet dress. A quick slash, and she cut the pale skirt off entirely, freeing her legs. A vicious gleam reflected in her eyes. "I will clear the way. Do not disappoint me."

"Who are we even fighting?" Nathaniel asked.

Zusa stood, a deathly look crossing her face, one Erin had not seen since the final days of the siege of Angelport.

"Whoever tries to stop us."

She cried out a command to her soldiers, and in response they started pushing toward one of the exits. The flow of the crowd was with them, but not for long. Mercenaries approached, all of them bearing Connington tabards. Erin followed in her mother's wake as the Gemcroft soldiers fanned out, preparing for battle even as arrows rained down upon them, frighteningly accurate in seeking out weak spots in armor.

Elves, Erin thought, scanning the rooftops. *But why? And how are they in the city?*

When they drew closer to the mercenaries, and she saw elves among their number, Erin had her answer, and it left her livid. She readied her dagger, the rest of the screaming, fighting, and dying fading away. She had to escape, and she would, regardless of her lack of proper weaponry and armor. Nathaniel drew his own slender sword and held it at the ready.

"I'll do what I can to protect you," he said, and winked. "Even if you should be the one protecting me."

Erin had no chance to respond, for the bloodshed had begun. The Gemcroft house soldiers, their ranks thinned by arrows, crumpled immediately against the superior numbers and skill. Fine warriors they might be, but against elven training it wasn't nearly enough.

"Forward!" Zusa shouted, ordering the remainder to surge together in a final, desperate attack. She herself took the point of that push, and finally there was someone among the assault who could match the skill of the elves. Erin saw only glimpses amid the chaos and bodies, but she felt a mixture of awe and pride at her mother's lethal dance. Every movement was an attack, every shift of her weight a way to initiate another stab.

Erin followed in her mother's wake, dagger itching in her hand. A Connington soldier, his face gashed open across the bridge of his nose, saw Erin and reached for her while shouting something unintelligible. Erin's instincts took over, finely honed across countless hours of training. A quick shift avoided his hand, and then she thrust, burying the dagger deep into his throat.

His eyes bulged. His sword swung weakly, dying strength seeking retaliation. Erin barely had the thought to avoid it. Her gaze was locked on the man, watching the light leave his eyes as his blood poured out the cavern she left when she ripped her dagger free. All the world turned silent for one brief moment as she stared at her weapon.

Her first kill. Her first time taking a life, a truth she had not even been aware of until the deed was done.

It had been so easy.

So easy.

"Move!" Nathaniel shouted, pushing her with his elbow. She stumbled over the body (*my kill*) and then found her footing. The trio battled further into the crowd, the last of the Gemcroft soldiers dropping to either Connington mercenaries or arrows from above. None of those arrows seemed aimed at the three of them, a fact that inspired far more fear than comfort. Were they to live, and why? As prisoners? Or did the orchestrator of this assault desire a more brutal and public method of execution?

Thoughts for a person not locked in battle. Erin kept to her mother's shadow, having abandoned her dagger to steal a dead soldier's short sword. It lacked the curve of her sabers, and was a bit heavier, but it would serve its purpose. She hacked and slashed at foes, most of them already wounded by her mother. Kill by kill, they marched toward the exit, and the final line of Connington mercenaries holding back the frantic crowd. So close, they were getting so close…

Nathaniel's scream stole her attention. He had collapsed to one knee, his other leg bleeding from a wicked gash along the side. Erin lunged without thinking, her new sword intercepting a thrust meant to impale her brother through the chest. Steel scraped across steel as the distance between her and the soldier shrank. He punched with his shield, and she shoved aside his sword while turning her body, absorbing the blow across her shoulder and then rolling off to the side. Her feet twirled, her movement never ceasing. Every harsh moment of training with her mother came to her. Every bruise and cut inflicted by her grandfather. Every brutal clash against a foe stronger than her when with the Godslayer.

Her sword lunged past the soldier's turning shield, straight into the man's eye. The man locked up, his mouth opening for a scream he never released as the blade punched into his brain. His entire body went rigid. She ripped the weapon free as he dropped, pretending not to see the blood and gore coating the steel.

"Nathaniel?" she asked turning.

"I can't..." he said, grimacing against the pain. He'd dropped his sword to clutch at the wound with his fingers, trying to apply pressure. "I can't stand."

Erin's heart raced, the panic she'd fought off with the excitement of battle threatening to consume her with a vengeance.

"Zusa!" she screamed, drawing her mother's attention despite the frantic battle. Zusa turned, saw Nathaniel injured, and immediately twirled away from her foe, an elf with half his head shaved and the other half tied back in a ponytail. The elf chased, and Erin dashed to meet him. Zusa, seeing her do so, immediately pivoted into an about-face, and together, mother and daughter, they assaulted the elf. He was clearly unprepared for the duo, and when forced to choose, he angled his lone sword to parry aside both of Zusa's thrusts. He thought Erin less of a threat.

Perhaps he was right, but she was still a threat, and her sword sank deep into his side. A twist, and she ripped it free, dragging a gasp of pain out of him. He kicked at her, but the connection was weak and glancing, so it only bruised her hip as she rolled away. Zusa punished him for that, her daggers slamming his sword aside, knifing him along the hand to weaken his grip on his sword, and then snap-kicking the hilt so it flew from his grasp. Both Erin and Zusa closed the distance in an instant, three blades sinking into flesh.

"What happened?" Zusa asked, yanking her weapons from the collapsing corpse and turning to Nathaniel.

"I messed up," Nathaniel said, needing to shout to be heard. Zusa knelt beside him, checking the wound. Her face paled.

"Mother!" Erin shouted, seeing several mercenaries approaching, one elf among them. Zusa saw them, then looked to Erin. Her expression froze from some sort of internal debate, and then it passed. A decision had been made. Her mother pointed the opposite direction, toward the exit they had brutally fought their way toward.

"Go!" Zusa screamed. "Leave us!"

As much as Erin hated it, as much as it went against every single instinct in her body, she obeyed. Using her smaller size to her advantage, she weaved through the crowd, pushing and shoving past men and women making their way toward the line of mercenaries in a disorganized throng. An elf shouted, demanding someone chase after her, but there was no one within earshot, and he could not chase Erin himself, not with Zusa still a threat.

Erin spared a single glance behind her. Her mother was holding her own, for now, but more elves were coming, along with mercenaries shoving their way to the platform, even hacking down innocents if necessary to clear a path. Meanwhile, Nathaniel remained beside Zusa, clutching his bleeding leg.

And then Erin could watch no more. The wall of mercenaries trapping in the remainder of the crowd was close. She abandoned her sword, and was glad for the simple attire she'd worn, against her mother's wishes, to the ceremony. Sure, her trousers and blouse were of fine make, but they were far from the elegant dress expected of a Gemcroft. With the dirt, sweat, and blood upon her, she looked no different than the rest of the people, and Erin used that to her advantage.

"Please, let me through!" she shouted, her voice one of thousands pushing against the wall of shields. She did not expect anyone to listen, only used it as part of an act. She was a frightened young girl, that's all, not armed, not dangerous. The nearest soldier in front of her glared back, not a shred of sympathy in his eyes. Erin didn't need it, though. She just needed to be closer, to hold her hands forward, to make him lift his shield in anticipation of shoving her back.

The moment he did she ducked underneath the shield, her feet spinning in a blur. She dived through his feet, skidding hard on the ground so that she scraped her elbows and forearms raw. Blood swelled along the skin, but she couldn't stop, couldn't delay. The soldier shouted something over his shoulder, but chasing her meant leaving his line, a dangerous prospect given how they were barely holding back the crowd. Erin pushed to her feet and fled out of sight. Not far. She had no intentions of going anywhere.

Once around the corner, she immediately grabbed a

windowsill to vault herself up to the nearby roof. The archers had vacated the area, their bloody work finished. With the new vantage point, she scanned the horizon and saw smoke billowing from fires burning all across the city. Other places had to be under attack. Clearing out Queen Brynn's soldiers, perhaps? One of the fires was frighteningly close to her family's mansion, and she feared the fate of their soldiers and servants.

Erin dropped to her stomach and crawled over the crest of the rooftop. The clearing spread out before her, and she scanned the crowd searching for her family. Her panic slowly increased until, at last, she found her mother.

She's alive, she thought, finally allowing herself to breathe. *Nathaniel, too.*

Her family was positioned before the platform, alongside other prisoners of note. She saw Queen Brynn in the center, along with a shackled Harruq Tun and his unconscious wife. Their daughter was with them, as was the Mordan prince. The way they were lined up made Erin's stomach clench, and she pleaded to any god willing to listen that she not witness their executions.

"You need them alive," she whispered as one of the elves took to the center of the platform. An identical looking female elf joined him. "Please, you need them alive, as ransom, as prisoners, don't…don't…"

She couldn't voice it. The horror was too close to becoming real. She could only crouch there and listen.

"Humans of Angkar," the elf loudly proclaimed. "I am Cyth Ordoth the Bloodhand, heir to the legacy of the Darkhand. Consider yourselves fortunate, for upon this day you witness the very course of history changing. You witness the rise of new legends, and the birth of a new kingdom."

He took the hand of the female elf beside him.

"*Our* kingdom," he continued. "The ruins of Dezrel prove you are unworthy of rule, and so we have taken that burden from you. Ker is gone. In its place rises the new. In its place, rises the Sun."

Erin watched, baffled. An elven kingdom, come to rule over humanity? That was preposterous. Celestia's teachings would never allow it. This splinter group sought war, even though the majority in Stonewood sought peace. Erin clutched the shingles tightly. This bold gambit would fail, surely it would fail, once the lords of Ker mustered their troops and marched to retake the capital.

Then again, walls guarded by elven archers would be nightmarish to break...

"I know you fear the future, strange and unknown as it is," Cyth continued. "You will buck against it like a horse newly saddled, but know that you will benefit, in time. Once you are broken. Once you are tamed."

He gestured to the crowd as Erin fought off a desire to vomit. For the elf to speak to humanity as if they were beasts was a terrible indignity made all the worse knowing that, for now, the people were at his mercy.

"Come join me, Tori Connington," he said.

Fury quickly replaced Erin's nausea. The traitorous woman marched through the imprisoned crowd with her head held high. Erin fantasized burying a saber right through that smug, grinning mouth. The last remaining member of the Trifect had betrayed them, and for what? An alliance with the elves? Whatever they offered her, she was about to find out.

"Know you will not go unrepresented in the Sun Kingdom," Cyth said as Tori knelt before him, head bowed. "Loyalty shall be rewarded. Obedience shall be met with grace. Behold the first among you to see the wisdom of our rule, and the woman through whom your needs and wants shall be delivered to me."

"I am honored, your grace," Tori said, her head still bowed.

I'm going to kill you, Erin thought, glaring daggers at Tori's back. *I swear, not even the gods will stop me, should they bother to pay attention.*

Cyth touched Tori's forehead, some sort of benevolent gesture, and then she stood and turned to the crowd, all regal posture and calm smiles. She gestured about her, as if welcoming all into her bosom.

"People of Angkar," she said. "Listen well, as I tell you of the future I have made for us, and the grandeur we shall create now freed from the shackles of the Sloane bloodline."

Erin dropped from the roof and fled into the conquered streets, wishing to hear no more words from the mouth of a traitor soon to die.

28
TORI

Tori was never fond of her meetings with the Ordoth siblings, but matters had only grown worse over the few past days. With crowns upon their heads, their pride and arrogance had swelled like a river after a monsoon.

"I am doing what I can, but my mercenaries are spread thin," she said, leaning back in her chair. They were inside the dining hall of the royal mansion, which Cyth and Vala had taken as their own. "We need more city guards, ones we can trust."

"I thought your coin had bought the traitors' loyalties?" Cyth asked, barely acknowledging her as he ran his fingers along the lip of his wine glass.

Tori held back a groan. She had spent most of her house's wealth on hiring mercenaries, and what remained had gone to bribing portions of the city guard to either lay down their arms or partake in the conquest of Angkar.

"Just because I bribe them does not mean they stay loyal," she said. "Many have simply taken the coin and then fled the city. Others may be plotting a revolt, or turning blind eyes to the constant fires and vandalism. Angkar's peace rests on a knife edge, Cyth, eager to topple at any moment."

Cyth pushed his glass away and leaned forward, his attention finally secured upon her.

"Then we will ensure its balance by stabbing it through that held knife," he said. "Do not fear these growing pains, Tori, nor the benefits you will reap for your participation in building the Kingdom of the Sun."

"Kingdom," she said, and wished the word did not sound so unbelievable. "We are but one city, Cyth. What of the lords all throughout Ker? Many are loyal to Brynn, and were given their positions in reward for service to her during the succession crisis. What if they unite, and lay siege to our city?"

"Then they will find themselves destroyed by an elven army upon its walls."

"What army?" she asked, unable to hide her exasperation. "Where are the promised reinforcements from Stonewood?"

Cyth slammed his hands on the table and stood. A bit of ugly hate crept into his lovely eyes.

"Do not doubt me, human," he seethed. "My people will see reason, and they will come. As for the lords, once Prince Gregory and Queen Brynn are executed, they will be faced with a choice. Wage war against us, and each other, as a furious Mordan comes seeking vengeance...or unite, and together crush the people in the north and claim their lands as our own."

"Human lords will fear elves will take their places," Tori said, repeating a warning she had given many times as they planned their uprising.

"Which is why we have you, to show that humanity will retain positions of power, so long as they bend their knee to the proper ruler." Cyth waved her away. "Enough. Keep the peace, Tori, and fill the peoples' ears with promises of wealth and conquest. They will listen, in time. Your race is all too predictable in that regard."

You think you know us so well, she thought, smiling sweetly. *I pray you are right, Cyth, because otherwise, we are all dead.*

"Of course," she said, and dipped her head. "Farewell, King Ordoth."

Tori exited the dining hall, but she did not leave the royal mansion. Her heart raced as she walked the halls toward the newly fashioned prison built within, made to keep close watch over the most important prisoners. No city jail for the former queen and her cohorts, but instead bedrooms stripped of furniture and carefully guarded by Cyth's most trusted elves. It was an entire wing of the mansion, and Tori stopped at the request of one of the elven guards.

"Did Cyth send you?" he asked, the human language clumsy on his tongue.

"I would speak with Zusa Gemcroft," she said. "It concerns matters of the Trifect."

The elf glanced over his shoulder, to one of the other guards stationed in front of a barred door. That second elf shrugged, then said something in elvish Tori could not understand.

"Fine," the first said, and stepped aside. Tori walked the carpet, her excitement and nervousness growing in equal measure.

At last, she would confront the specter of her past. At last, her vengeance would be known, and made complete. The elf at the door removed the bar and then pushed the door open.

Alone, Tori entered the prison cell.

Zusa Gemcroft sat imprisoned against the bare wall. They'd been extra careful with her, for despite her age her reputation was fierce. Her arms were manacled above her head, her feet chained together around both the ankles and knees. All chains had been looped through a ring hammered into the floor. Her mouth had no gag or binding, though, so she was free to speak. She still wore the torn violet dress from her capture, now covered with filth.

"If only I had slit your throat the moment I suspected your duplicity," Zusa said.

Tori grinned at her, but there was no joy in it. Nothing quite so innocent or pure. No, what she felt was grim satisfaction.

"That's what you do, isn't it?" she asked. "Kill those who challenge your power?"

"A Connington, questioning what must be done to hold power?" Zusa laughed. "As if any member of the Trifect is innocent."

Tori hated how easily she deflected the accusation. This moment, this triumph, had been the goal that kept Tori going for years. Nothing would steal this from her. Nothing would reduce its perfection.

"Except I *was* innocent," she said, drawing a dagger from her belt. "And you stole that from me."

Zusa tilted her head. An inquisitive look came over her face. "Why this hatred? What harm have I ever done to you?"

"Not just you," Tori said, kneeling on the carpet so they might look eye to eye. "Alyssa. Nathaniel. All three of you." She casually pressed the dagger to the woman's neck. "You never saw. You thought I was long gone from Angelport when you began your butchery."

Zusa did not lean away from the edge. She was much too strong of will to reveal even that hint of fear. Her deep brown eyes hardened.

"Speak the truth you wish to speak," she said. "Justify your hatred to me, Tori. Let the world know, and your beliefs, be judged."

Tori pulled away the blade, leaving a thin red line in its place.

"When you arrested Warrick and sentenced him to hang, he claimed I was already on my way to Angkar. But you were lied to, Zusa. I was there." She leaned closer. The knife trembled in her hand. *"I was there."*

※

Six-year-old Tori did not recognize the man leading her through the city. He was big, and he wore armor, so she thought him a house guard or maybe a soldier her godfather had hired. He was gruff, and bald but for a thin black beard hanging off his chin. When he had introduced himself, he said his name was Halgar.

"I'm hungry," she said, because she was, and because she wanted him to slow down. He pulled on her hand so hard her arm hurt, and her fingers felt squished.

"I could use a meal, too, but if you aren't on your boat, you're either swimming to Ker, or hanging like..." He paused, glared back at her. "Look, you want on that boat, all right?"

"I don't want to go on a boat," she argued. This seemed logical to her. Why should she have to do something she didn't want to do, especially because of a stranger?

"Tough luck."

He dragged her along with more force, and she had to race to keep up on bare feet. Halgar had dressed her before they left his house, or whatever building it was she had stayed in the last few days. *No shoes,* he'd told her. *Not for you. You need to look like a poor starving waif, not a little noble lady.*

Because of that, her feet hurt, and it seemed like every third step was on a rock. She'd never noticed the streets of Angelport were so uneven and cracked, at least not the nice markets godfather Warrick took her to. Her clothes itched, too, and they smelled awful. This made her remember the time Halgar cut her hair, rough and uneven using the sharp edge of his sword. The whole of it, coupled with the constant tug on her arm, crushed what was left of her patience.

"But I don't *want* to," she shouted at Halgar. She'd had enough. "Take me back home. Take me to my godfather. I don't want to go anywhere with you, you...mean person, you."

The moment the words were out of her mouth, she wanted to cry. Everything was confusing. The city frightened her. The people moved with a nervous energy that made her stomach tighten. The world was overwhelming, and there seemed no end in sight. Halgar halted them in the middle of the street, and he glared at the people hurrying to either side of them.

"I was paid to get you safely onto the *Garnet*, not listen to you whine at me for three damn days," he told her. The anger in his voice immediately silenced her. He loomed like a scary beast, all armor and muscle, but most frightening were his eyes. There was no kindness in them. She had no name for what was there in its place.

"I'm sorry," she said, regretting the outburst.

"No, no, you made a request, and the hefty coin given to me says I should obey. You want to see your godfather, Tori? Then let's go see your godfather."

Tori dared relax a little. "You promise?"

The giant man winked. "I'm ever true to my word. If we hurry, I think we'll just barely catch him."

His words should have made her feel better. She *did* want to see her godfather again. She wanted him to hold her in his lap and read her stories, or to tell her all about his day, whether it was good or bad, and whether he met nice people or bad people. She didn't understand most of what he said, only craved the attention he gave her. It made her feel safe. It made her feel tired, and it was so easy to curl up against the soft linens of his shirt, a fire crackling nearby, and sleep.

None of that comfort was in Halgar's ugly grin.

The crowd around them grew thicker as he led her in a different direction than they'd been hurrying. The road widened, the stone becoming dirt that was kinder to her bare feet. Halgar pulled her close to his side as they slowed. It was getting harder to move, and the noise of the crowd grew steadily louder.

"Too many people," Halgar said. "I'm going to have to carry you. Don't make a fuss, and don't attract any attention. No one should recognize you with what I've done to your clothes and hair, but I'd rather not risk it anyway."

She nodded and accepted his arms about her waist. The big man lifted her up, crooked his arm, and positioned her so that she sat on his forearm, most of her weight pressed against his hip. Tori did her best not to squirm. Being so close, she smelled him, and she had no names for what it was, just that it made her stomach clench.

No longer having to drag her along, Halgar resumed with speed, and he was none too kind to those blocking their way. He bullied through the crowd, elbowing several who thought to resist. At last he stopped.

"There," he said. "Just in time."

She could not see, though, not with how many people were in front of her. It was so loud, too, people shouting and chanting and screaming words she knew were bad and should never be spoken by anyone other than adults. She looked around, but all she saw were strangers, not her godfather.

"Onto my shoulder," he said, noticing her confusion. "And no matter what you do, you watch, and you stay silent."

She didn't understand why, but she could tell this was not something to argue with. She bobbed her head, and then he lifted her up onto his shoulder.

From there, Tori saw the hanging platform.

There were seven nooses stretching down from the horizontal beam. Six were already filled, and Tori recognized them from their dress and their bloated faces, even if she did not know all their names. They were the servants and helpers of their estate.

Horror overwhelmed her. Tears flooded her eyes, and she was almost grateful, for they made it hard to see the blue of their lips and the bulging of their eyes. One of them was their maidservant, Lillia. Why? Why would someone want to hurt Lillia? She was so nice, and so pretty. All she ever did was try to tell Tori stories while she tidied up their mansion, laughing and exaggerating her speech as she flitted about.

But that last rope, that was the worst. Just below it, waiting, was her godfather, Warrick. He stood on a little stool, the only thing giving slack to the rope about his neck.

Three people were up there on that platform with him. Three people in charge, and she did not understand. She knew them. They had visited her godfather often. Alyssa, Zusa, and Nathaniel Gemcroft. Members of the Trifect, Warrick had explained to her. Friends of the Keenan family, partners who worked together with her own family to the benefit of everyone.

It was Alyssa who now shouted to the crowd. She was a striking figure, her hair blood red and her eyes covered with a matching blindfold.

"There is no forgiveness for he who surrendered you to the armies of Thulos!" she cried. "No mercy for he who let your possessions be stolen, your women raped, and your men forced into the second Gods' War."

"Why?" Tori whispered. Why was Alyssa saying these things about him? "I want down," she said, squirming against Halgar's shoulder.

He did not take her down. He did not move.

"You wanted to see him," he said. "And honestly, so did I. Didn't think Alyssa had the stones to do it. Looks like I was wrong."

The shouting around her grew louder. She could barely hear Halgar beside her, yet everyone quieted when Alyssa continued.

"And when the demons were gone, did he lead the Ramere into prosperity? No! The orcs came, and your defenders bled and died. We still bleed. We still die. And yet Warrick here lives in opulence while most among you starve."

More jeers. More bad words. She squirmed harder.

"Let me down!"

Halgar finally relented.

"All right," he said. "You shouldn't watch this."

Then why did he bring her here? Why did he make her see those people, the ropes, little Lillia…and her godfather standing there, waiting, the noose before him…

She cried. She couldn't help it. Soft, quiet sobs. It was easier than talking. Easier than looking. Halgar lowered her back to his hip and then turned away. He pushed back through the crowd, which barely paid him any mind. Their attention was locked on the stage.

"Today, we mark the end of his disastrous rule," Alyssa shouted. "Today, we begin a new era for the Ramere. People of Angelport, your shining future has come!"

The cheers were so loud, the clapping so boisterous, Tori turned about to look. She had to. Given the distance, and the platform's elevation, she could just barely see the rope. Just barely see Godfather Warrick hanging there, his body softly swaying.

That image burned into her mind. She did not look away.

Warrick, hanging. Alyssa, cheering on the crowd. Zusa, her wife and bodyguard, calmly beside her with daggers in hand. And Nathaniel beside the body, the one who had kicked away the stool.

Three Gemcrofts. Three supposed friends of her family.

Tori was screaming. She didn't realize she had started. She didn't think there were any words in it. Just screaming until her breath was spent and all she could do was sob.

"Come on," Halgar said as he scooped her up so she was against his chest, and when he turned to leave, she could not see the platform. "Sorry, kid. That was a bitch of a thing to do, even for me. Not that it'll help now."

He looked down at her, and she refused to meet his gaze.

"Cry if you want, just let me carry you. Keep your face hidden against me, and I'll get you safe. That a deal?"

She nodded.

"Good. Let's go, before the *Garnet* leaves you here to die."

⋈

Tori fell silent at the end of her story. It hurt, re-opening such wounds of the past. Six years old, and she'd watched her godfather hang. Over the past thirteen years, she had fed herself with dreams of revenge, never even knowing if the Gemcroft family had survived the orcs. But then the boats came, and rumors of the city's liberation, and she knew, just *knew*, that they were responsible.

"So that is why you hate us," Zusa said softly. "Better that, I suppose. I thought you a fool, believing the elf would grant you power instead of murdering you the moment your usefulness was spent."

"I did what I did for revenge," Tori snapped, refusing to acknowledge the potential for Cyth's betrayal. "I was robbed of it when Alyssa died in Angelport, but you're here, and so is Nathaniel. It may not be everything I wanted, but it will be enough."

"Will it, though?" Zusa peered up at her. "Revenge is a ravenous beast, Tori, and its belly is never full. It is never satisfied."

Tori stood and smoothed out the folds of her skirt. "With you and Nathaniel dead, all your titles, properties, and wealth shall be mine. They shall go to the *Keenan* estate, for I will no longer abide by my deceased husband's name. With your deaths, the last of the Gemcroft line will see its end, and my own family name, restored to its proper glory."

She grinned, feral and savage.

"So when you hang before a crowd, just like Warrick did, yes, Zusa, I will be *satisfied*."

Any hope she might intimidate the older woman was immediately dashed. Zusa laughed in her face.

"Prepare your rope then," she said. "Prepare your glorious revenge. But if you want it, truly want it, you best slit my throat right here and now, because you will not have it on your chosen day."

Tori crossed her arms. "Why? Do you expect to be rescued? The Godslayer is in our custody, Zusa, as is his wife and his wizard friend. The city is isolated, and your king imprisoned and awaiting execution. No one is left to save you."

"If you insist."

Her confidence was maddening. Who had she forgotten? Who could stand against the Kingdom of the Sun when even the Godslayer could not?

"Do you mean Erin?" she wondered aloud. "I am not afraid of your daughter. One lone girl cannot stop what we have begun."

Zusa shook her head. Her macabre smile spread.

"She is her father's daughter, and I would never challenge what heights she might reach, but no. It is not her you should fear. Not Harruq, either, or the rest of the Eschaton. You should fear the beast the underworld birthed that conquered the Sun and the Trifect. He will slaughter you for this transgression."

Surely this captured woman was merely playing games, but that confidence, that grin… it was so certain. So confident.

"Who?" she asked, almost daring Zusa to give away this supposed secret. "Who will be your supposed savior?"

Her answer was cryptic nonsense, but it pulsed a shiver down her spine all the same.

"Fear the Spider, cut free of its web."

29
ERIN

Erin forced herself to walk, even when her instincts said to run. There was no reason to panic. No reason to draw attention to herself as she passed through the occupied streets of the city. There were far too few elves to form patrols, and so Tori's mercenaries were handling the job. Even they were too few, and there was no reason to believe they would know Erin existed.

And yet she still turned away when armed patrols occasionally passed, laughing and jostling with one another. Just because there seemed no need for caution did not mean caution should be cast aside. It was a truth long beaten into her by her mother.

Her mother. Erin clenched her jaw as she neared the docks. Rumors abounded of a coming public execution. Everyone assumed the boy king would be the reason, and potentially the Godslayer as well, but Erin suspected her mother and brother would be there, too. They had taken them alive for a reason, right? They wouldn't have executed two members of the Gemcroft family in some unknown dungeon. Her mother, she wouldn't die, she wouldn't leave her all alone without a chance to save her…

Enough, she thought, banishing those thoughts. They were pointless. Only one thing mattered now: saving her family and friends.

She knew only one man who could help her do it.

Thren waited for her at the empty shipwright warehouse. Thren, not Gray. It frightened her how easily the old name slid in to replace the new in her mind. His swords were in hand, though he did not address her when she arrived. She watched him slowly weave them through a few stances, each one meant to stretch out his muscles.

"You're late," he said, his back to her.

Erin swallowed down a mouthful of stones. "I'm not here to train."

Thren sheathed his weapons at his hips and turned her way.

She flinched, despite his face remaining passive.

"Then why are you here? My training is all I have to offer you."

"No, it's not." She stepped closer. Why was she so nervous? Why did she fear him so? "My mother's been arrested. I want you to help me free her."

Thren crossed his arms. "And why would I do that?"

Erin stammered, uncertain how to answer. "Because...because it's the right thing to do."

The cold glare she received told her she could not have answered that question more wrongly if she tried.

"Right?" he echoed. His hands clenched into fists. "Is it right to help the weak? Is it right to bleed and die in battles that are not your own?"

"It's how your son built his legacy!" Erin said, not meaning to shout.

"And it is how he died!" Thren roared right back. Erin's stomach clenched, and she did not hide her fear. The older man towered over her, his blue eyes colder than ice. He bared his teeth like an animal, that naked emotion somehow even more terrifying on someone otherwise so calm and composed.

"My son fought for others," Thren continued, his deep voice shaking. "He fought in the gods' pointless wars. He slaughtered orcs while Veldaren burned. He gave, and he gave, and what was his reward? A pathetic, pointless death in a conquered city. The skills to change the world, the will to shape nations, and yet *that* is how he died? That is how his life ended, dead on the castle steps at the hand of some wretched, forgotten priest? No, Erin. I will not follow his footsteps, nor will I help you do the same."

Erin fought back tears. This was her only true hope. The task before her was so daunting, and she knew not how to start. But Thren? Thren was a legend in his own right. He'd conquered cities before. He'd know how to break the elves' hold on Angkar. He'd tell her what to do, and she'd do it, and then all would be well.

"Please," she said. "I can't do this alone."

Thren's face softened the slightest amount. It was like watching steel become stone.

"But alone is how the strong make their greatest achievements. Weakness, sentimentality, and compassion broke your father. His greatest feats, the ones the world remembers, he accomplished alone. Alone, he conquered the thief guilds and made them fear the Watcher. Alone, he broke the pride of the Trifect and slew the Wraith of Angelport. Alone, he killed the Darkhand, my greatest master who never knew defeat. You love the stories. How can you not learn their lessons?"

Tears had begun to fall from Erin's eyes, but when she spoke, her voice quivered from anger.

"But he wasn't alone," she said. "Tarlak and Delysia helped him fight the thief guilds. Deathmask allied with him against the Trifect. My mother fought alongside him in Angelport. And the Darkhand?" She stepped closer, hiding neither her rage nor her sorrow. "When he fought the Darkhand, he had *you*. His greatest accomplishment, and it was with *you*, Thren. The one moment you worked together. The one moment you let him rely on you, and demanded nothing in return."

Thren was as still and emotionless as a statue. His jaw looked to be locked tight enough to break iron between his clenched teeth. Erin pressed on, saying everything she had feared to say.

"I know you loved him," she said. "I know, no matter what you say, that you're proud of everything he became. Of how the whole world remembers what he accomplished. And they remember it *because* he did it freely. No reward. No demands. Just a desire to make things better. And at every step, he did it with the help of others. Not alone. Never alone." She wiped at her face, brushing away the last of her tears. "The strong can shape the world, but what does it matter if you do nothing with your strength? Would you hide here, Thren? Live out your life in this shed, while I run off to fight, to try to save Zusa, and Harruq, and Aurelia, and the boy king?"

She turned away from him and said, "How strong will you actually be when your granddaughter dies, and you did nothing?"

His hand settled on her shoulder. She flinched again as if expecting him to stab her. Perhaps he even would. To show him such disrespect…

"This world murders heroes," Thren said. His voice floated over her, surprisingly soft despite its depth. "It is too cruel, too uncaring. When it finds those willing to give, it will then take, and take, until there is nothing to offer but one last breath and one final heartbeat. And then it will take those, too."

Erin shivered. "Is that why you won't help me? You think it will get me killed? Or that I'm just a fool?"

"Perhaps you are a fool. Perhaps I am. Answer me this, Erin. Is this what you want? Is a war against the elves what you truly desire above all else?"

Still she would not turn to look at him. "I want to save my mother, my brother, and my friends."

"And are you willing to spill the needed blood?"

Finally, she spun around. His hand fell from her shoulder. He was looking down at her, but something was different. He was listening to her, truly listening.

"I will do whatever it takes," she said.

"And you do this for yourself? Not out of compassion, or some delusion of heroism?"

She looked him in the eyes and told him exactly what he needed to hear. "This is what I want. No one harms my family and lives."

Thren crouched before her so he was at her height, his hand casually resting on the hilts of his swords.

"You are my granddaughter," he said. "Whatever you wish to accomplish, say the word, and I will be there for you. But only for *you*, Erin. For your legacy. And for once, I will be there to help you build it, if you will not cast me aside, or fear the wisdom I offer."

"The only thing I fear is discovering my mother dead in a cell, or limp from a hangman's rope."

Strong words, and perhaps a lie. She feared Thren, too...but she knew others would fear him even more. He stood back to his full height, and another change came over him. Excitement sparked in his eyes. His fingers twitched, constantly brushing the hilts of his swords. He had a purpose now, and it filled his every word with a sense of inevitability. Yes, he was a man the elves should fear, but he was more than that, too. He was a force about to be unleashed.

"I know how to terrorize a city," Thren said. "I know how to pick and claw at a beast larger than you until it bleeds more than it even knows. Do you trust me, Erin? With your life, and the life of your family?"

"I do," she said, standing tall as she nodded. "Perhaps that makes me a fool, but I do."

To her shock, Thren grinned.

"Then let us have our fun."

30
AURELIA

Aurelia had to sit on the very edge of the padded seat, arms pinned behind her, for otherwise the contraption wrapped around her hands would slice her fingers apart. She dared not even lean back, lest she accidentally apply pressure to the interlocking razor wires and metal bolts that formed interlocking links around her each and every knuckle.

All of that was still better than the device clamped around her tongue.

"Welcome, Aurelia Thyne," Cyth said on the opposite side of the elegant table. The pair were seated in the royal mansion's dining hall. Four guards, three of them human and one an elf, watched the four entrances. She knew of Cyth by name only, for even in her makeshift prison cell, a stripped-bare bedroom on the second floor, she heard non-stop gossip from nervous servants as well as the guard stationed outside of her bedroom door.

Cyth, the Bloodhand. Cyth, the Sun King.

But to her eyes, she saw only a young, arrogant elf in a chair too big for him. He leaned forward, his fingers nervously drumming the table.

"You must forgive me for the protective measures," he said, and gestured toward his mouth. Aurelia stared, wishing she could convey just how little she cared for his apology. Two metal bars were connected to either side of her head, with the front bar jammed all the way into her mouth. Connected to it was another series of sharpened wires, two of them latching to the top and bottom of her tongue to hold it in place.

There would be no waggling of her fingers. No whispering the arcane words of magic. Just a bit of blood in her mouth and hands aching from being unable to stretch or turn.

"But I am not one who relishes cruelty or desires to see another elf suffer," Cyth continued, fingers still drumming the table.

Poor Elydien might disagree with that, she thought as the arrogant young elf continued.

"Let's get that contraption off your mouth, shall we? I'd like for us to have a talk. But first..."

He leaned back and snapped his fingers. One of the doors opened, and Aurelia's heart leaped into her throat. A red-eyed Aubrienna entered, escorted by a female elf in silver armor. The elf guided her with a hand on her shoulder and a knife held just shy of her throat.

"Over there is fine, Vala," Cyth said, pointing to the seat beside him. Vala guided Aubrienna to the chair. Aurelia's heart broke at the fear in her daughter's eyes. She desperately wished to comfort her, and ask how she had been treated, but the damned contraption on her tongue would not let her.

"Before we speak, we must have an understanding," Cyth said. "Your magic is powerful, perhaps close enough to rival Celestia's misbegotten Daughters of Balance, and you have proven time and again you will risk your life for what you believe is right. So consider this an incentive that you behave."

He pointed to Vala, who kept the dagger pressed with its flat edge against Aubrienna's pale neck, and then pointed again over Aurelia's head. Behind her, she heard the drawing of a bowstring.

"Powerful as you are, Aurelia, I suspect you cannot stop an arrow aimed at your daughter's heart at the same time you halt Vala's blade. So no magic. No whispered words. The moment I believe you attempting anything, your daughter dies. Perhaps you could still escape. You're clever, after all, a true hero of the second Gods' War...but will that escape be worth Aubrienna's life?"

Aurelia seethed with rage, but looking at her frightened daughter, she already knew the answer to that. She slowly nodded to show she understood.

"Good," Cyth said, and slumped back into his chair. "Larian, unlock her tongue prison."

A human by the nearby door hurried over, and she caught the glint of a key before he passed outside her line of sight. She felt pressure against the back bar of the tongue contraption, then heard a click. Suddenly the wires about her tongue widened, and the pressure between the bars went slack. Slowly and carefully, the soldier pulled the bulk of it from her mouth. A bit of blood and saliva dripped down her chin and onto her dress.

"Clean her up," Cyth said. "Despite the circumstances, she

is an honored guest."

"You show it strangely," Aurelia said, but begrudgingly accepted the man's efforts to wipe at her face and chin with a tablecloth. She felt like a babe, unable to take care of herself, and it bruised her pride. What she would give to unleash the full power of her magic upon these renegade brethren...

"Please, allow us to give you a proper meal," the arrogant elf king continued. A servant quickly arrived to deliver a still-bleeding hunk of meat in the center of a blue and white porcelain plate. Aurelia arched an eyebrow, and then one of the guards rushed to her side, grabbed the knife and fork, and began to cut. She watched, realizing what the guard intended.

Aurelia had had nothing to eat and little to drink barring what was occasionally offered to her in her makeshift prison, water from a cup that spilled as much across her face as it did through the little gap she could make when the tongue prison was lodged within her mouth. Her head was light, and she knew she should accept, but when the guard lifted the sliced meat dripping with blood and juice toward her lips, she could not.

"I will not be fed like a child," she said, turning away from him. "Either undo my hands, or leave me be."

"Then you will go hungry," Cyth said, dismissing the soldier. "We are not so foolish as to grant you access to both your fingers and your tongue. I seek to rule, Lady Thyne, not die in a heap of ash. You, who could be our greatest ally, are also our most dire threat."

"I don't know about that," she said, darkly grinning. "You haven't seen my husband when he is angry."

"Your husband is currently in chains awaiting his execution."

Aurelia flinched, and she grinned wider to hide her fear. Her fingers tensed against the wire imprisoning them, and she briefly wondered if the blood and torn flesh would be worth the risk casting a spell. But then there was the knife upon Aubrienna's throat, and the arrow aimed for her heart...

"Is that so?" she asked.

"Regrettably it is," Cyth continued. "There is no doubt Harruq has done tremendous good for Dezrel, in both slaying Thulos and defeating the fallen, but his role in the blasphemous

Legacy of the Watcher

peace proposals, and your daughter's engagement to the human king, cannot be ignored."

"Crimes I myself am guilty of, if you are dim-witted enough to consider them crimes," she said, sneaking a glance at Aubrienna to assess how her daughter fared. She was crying, but quietly, and her gaze was mostly locked on Aurelia, her eyes full of silent pleading. It broke Aurelia's heart that she could do nothing for her.

"Indeed, but you are not the half-orc," Cyth said. He frowned at her. "I want you to know the future awaiting you. We are all beholden to our legacies, and yours is one of our greatest. The strongest of magical bloodlines runs through you, and yet instead of sharing that blessing among our people, restoring our lost prominence, you waste it coupling with an orc."

Aurelia had thought her contempt for Cyth could not grow deeper. She was wrong.

"Sharing the blessing among our people?" she asked. "How so, o' mighty Sun King? Tell me. Say it with your own words, so you yourself may hear how ludicrous you are. Restore our prominence? Would you *breed* me, Cyth, a sow to deliver little magic-blessed soldiers for your new kingdom?"

Cyth slammed his hands upon the table.

"I would have us retain our *dignity!*" he shouted. She glared, saying nothing to acknowledge such nonsense. He did not deserve it. "By all rights, I should have you executed," he said, composing himself. "But our lives are long, and once free of foul influences, there is a chance you will amend your ways. As for your daughter…"

Her chest burned with fire when he cast a dismissive look toward frightened Aubrienna.

"Her blood may be tainted, but it is a quarter, at worst, and will dilute with time. She deserves a place in our new kingdom, and a husband who will treat her with the respect the Thyne bloodline deserves."

Aurelia stood from her seat. The guards reached for their weapons, and more arrows drew tight. Even Cyth tensed in his seat, his right hand dropping below the table for where his sword remained belted to his hip. Aurelia glared at him, relishing their fear.

"You would murder my husband, imprison me, and marry off my daughter like a prized horse to be bred," she said. "And you think I will play along with your charade? That I will one day change my mind? You damned fools. If you possess any wisdom, you will hang me with my husband, because I will *never* forgive you for what you have done."

Cyth stood as well, his hand still on the hilt of his sword. "I am aware of how powerful you are. Celestia has blessed you greatly, and such blessings must be accounted for. I would not keep you chained for the next few decades as Aubrienna grows older. So...what if I sweeten the deal?"

Aurelia maintained a passive mask, and she said nothing to acknowledge his potential offer. Cyth shrugged and continued unbothered.

"As I said, Harruq Tun has done much good for Dezrel, even if aspects of it were to counter the damage done by his own brother. Still, what if I were to let him live? Imprisoned, of course, though with better conditions, once both you and he are aware of the terms."

"And those terms?" she asked.

"If you misbehave, both Aubrienna and Harruq die," Cyth said, shrugging. "And the same would go for him, in the secret prison we place him in, far from your new home in Stonewood. His influence must be removed from you and your daughter, that is nonnegotiable. But he need not die like the others. Perhaps, once the Sun Kingdom has fully established control over Dezrel, and Aubrienna is married to a proper elven lord, he might even be allowed his freedom."

Aurelia burned at the thought of her husband suffering unknown decades of imprisonment, held hostage to keep her in line.

Cyth saw it clearly on her, too. "It's that, or he dies, and you along with him. Is it truly such a terrible choice, Aurelia? Make peace with the inevitable, or have your daughter become an orphan."

Aurelia looked to Aubrienna, who was fighting hard to keep her sobs quiet and stifled. Aurelia's insides were a squirming mess of fear, sorrow, pride, and fury. She didn't know what the right path was, but she knew if she was to one day free Aubrienna from the twisted path Cyth would lay before her, then she must survive to do it. She would not watch her husband hang. They had not survived all these years, endured countless wars and the Night of Black Wings, to die to a foolish, power-mad elf pretending at royalty.

Though the act hurt her deep in her soul, she lowered her head and let her hair fall across her face.

"No," she said. "For her sake, I will submit."

Cyth clapped, and she could hear the relief in his voice. "Excellent, most excellent. And though the hate in your voice is strong, you are but accustomed to living among these wretched humans. Your eyes are clouded, Aurelia Thyne, and your vision hazy."

"Tun," she snapped. "Aurelia Tun."

Cyth paused, then continued with the same patronizing smile, refusing to acknowledge her protest.

"Given time, decades if we must, I fully believe you will see clearly. We can still praise your heroics while recognizing the faults of your other decisions when it came to your heart."

"Perhaps," she said, the lone word bitter and dry on her cut and swollen tongue. She looked to Aubrienna, the wonderful child of her equally wonderful husband, and swore to murder Cyth and burn his flesh and bones down to the thinnest of ash.

This isn't over, she thought, desperately wishing to hold Aubrienna, kiss her, and promise that all of this would end well. It was a promise she could not be certain to keep, but she would have promised it all the same. Instead she kept silent, her mind racing for a potential way to escape this madness.

"Re-bind her tongue," Cyth ordered.

"Listen to me, Aubby," Aurelia said, now that her time was short. Her daughter looked up, the tiniest flicker of hope igniting within her eyes. "Everything's going to be fine. I'm with you. I'll always be with you."

That said, Aurelia endured the humiliation as the contraption was forced once more into her mouth, the barbed wires settling across her aching tongue. Once she was fully bound, Cyth snapped his fingers, and Vala escorted Aubrienna away. Aurelia watched her go, the fire in her breast hardening into something so powerful that 'hate' could never describe it. She turned her glare to Cyth.

Enjoy your crown, she thought as she was led back to her cell.

David Dalglish

You will not wear it long.

31
ERIN

Erin had spent the past few days living with her grandfather in his tiny abode. He purchased a cot for her to sleep on, nestled against the wall near the fireplace in case the spring nights turned chill. They did not train, though he did run through multiple stretches in the mornings with her to limber up in preparation for the day's work.

They did not train, because the time for training was in the past. With Thren's aid, Erin learned to kill.

Come on, she thought, watching the approaching trio of guards. They walked with their weapons sheathed, the lead guard holding what appeared to be a small stack of yellowed paper. *Just a little closer...*

Erin lay flat on her stomach on the rooftop of a shuttered candle maker's workshop. Thren had studied their patrol patterns and deemed her current location the proper place for an ambush. Her sabers were drawn, the comforting weight of their hilts clutched tightly in her hands. Like all her targets lately, the three men were city guards turned traitor when the elves launched their attack on the city alongside Tori Connington—or Tori Keenan, as she demanded all refer to her since.

Why not the elves? she'd asked Thren when he discussed their very first ambush. *Aren't they the most important?*

They're also the most dangerous, had been his response. *They are also fanatical in their loyalty. The Keenan mercenaries were bought with coin. The turncoat city guard? They're traitors. They're cowards. Deep in their hearts, they know they broke their vows and discarded their honor. Once blood begins to flow, they will be the easiest to break.*

They were almost below her. She pushed up onto her knees. Her heart raced, and she felt a tingle in her fingers from growing nerves. She'd killed twelve men and women over the course of the last three days. The first had been a lone man, and she'd watched him bleed out before her in a daze. Thren had kept an eye on her the whole time, and when he joined her side he put a hand on her shoulder and told her that, in time, the killing would become easier.

He was right.

Erin descended feet first, her swords angled downward like the talons of a bird of prey. Of the three guards, she struck the third trailing behind the other two, her heel striking the lowest joint of his neck. He gasped as he fell forward, unprepared for the impact. Erin's weight drove him downward, and he was unable to brace himself so his face smashed hard upon the cobblestones. That alone might have taken him out of the fight, but Erin took no chances. Her sabers slid in through the armpits of his armor, cutting into his lungs and ending his ability to breathe.

The other two spun around at the noise and drew their weapons. Erin leaped off the body at the one holding the yellow leaflets. The kill needed to be quick, the benefit of her surprise maximized. She batted both her sabers against his sword, each strike lifting it upward when he blocked. When both finished, he instinctively swung during the pause in her attack, a downward chop she easily predicted given the position she had shoved his sword into. Her entire body shifted as she spun about him, feeling the wind of his attack but losing only an errant few strands of hair to the blade. She came out of the spin swinging, her sabers opening two thick gashes across the side of his neck. Blood spurted in a torrent, his jugular opened. The yellow paper collapsed in a pile beneath him as he clutched his hands against the wounds, trying in vain to stem the flow. Erin ended his misery with another dual-stab, this time into the small of his back.

The final guard swore and charged straight at Erin while shouting the name of the man she'd killed. He swung, she dodged, and then they collided. Erin's head snapped backward from striking his shoulder, and blood filled her mouth when she bit her tongue.

Stupid, she thought as she twirled away from him. *Too slow. Do better.*

Her heels dug into the cobblestones, skidding her spin to a stop. She immediately lunged back in, right arm sweeping wide, her left pulled back for a thrust. The guard blocked while retreating, unprepared for her to suddenly be the aggressor. Her left hand slipped right past his defenses, sinking halfway up the blade into his stomach. He gasped, blood flowing, eyes widening in shock and pain. Spittle flew from his lips and landed on Erin's shoulder. She saw it and felt nothing.

Two quick slashes, and she opened his throat and ended his life. The body collapsed at her feet and lay still.

Erin cleaned the blood from her sabers, sheathed them, and then turned to the one carrying leaflets of paper. Her brow furrowed, curiosity getting the best of her. She lifted one of the yellow sheets off the ground and glanced over the blood-drenched text, her eyes widening. The long-rumored executions were finally announced. 'The Hanging Justice' it was being called. The leaflet made it sound like a celebratory event.

All are required to attend this necessary and joyous occasion, the leaflet read. *All will witness the end of the tyrants who lorded over you.*

Below that, a list of names. Queen Brynn Sloane. Prince Gregory Copernus. And in smaller writing, below theirs, Zusa and Nathaniel Gemcroft.

"What is it?" Thren asked. She glanced up to see him approaching, blood still dripping from his short swords. They'd timed their attack perfectly. On the opposite side of the street, Thren had executed the guards waiting to relieve Erin's patrol. Six traitors to Angkar, murdered in cold blood. Six less to keep order in a city wound tighter than a drawn bowstring.

"They're going to execute my mother and brother," Erin said, handing over the paper. "The queen and Mordan prince, too. We're out of time, Thren. They're planning it for tomorrow."

Her grandfather studied the paper as if committing every word of it to memory. His face, already dour, hardened further.

"They're holding it at the same ceremony platform as the peace treaty announcement," he said. "It seems the elven king has a sense of humor."

"Who cares where it is?" Erin asked, fighting off panic. "We haven't harmed them nearly enough. Their numbers are much too great for us to take them alone. How do we stop this?" She gestured to the paper. "How do we save my family?"

Thren crumpled the leaflet and tossed it to the dirt. "We alone would never be enough. I knew that from the start. Our actions have always been about preparing the way." He grinned at her, and that amusement was almost as frightening as his rage. "We alone cannot be the heroes to liberate Angkar, which means you and I need to free the actual fools willing to do the job."

32

THREN

Thren and Erin watched the self-crowned king and his sister queen travel northward. A dozen elven guards marched with him, along with a squad of the Keenan mercenaries helping to keep peace in the captured city. Among them, surrounded and bound at the wrist, were the prisoners presumably destined for execution: Zusa and Nathaniel Gemcroft, Queen Brynn, and to Thren's mild surprise, the elf woman, Aurelia Tun. The sorceress was more heavily bound than the others, and had a strange metallic contraption within her mouth.

"Can we truly fight that many?" Erin whispered. The pair were safely hidden on the rooftops across the street, and could watch without worry as the procession vanished into the distance. Thren could sense her imagining the coming battle at the execution that must be stopped. The forces arrayed against them were daunting, but she saw only themselves, and not the allies they would gain. Erin had heard the stories, but she did not yet understand the influence a single man or woman could have on a battlefield. Today, though, she would learn...if she lived.

Thren gestured to the second floor, to a window that remained open.

"There's your way inside," he said. "Once there, find Cyth's bedroom. Within you will find the swords."

"There's no guarantee they will be there," Erin said.

"You know the history of those swords," Thren said, frowning at her. "Cyth will cherish them, for their fame and their origin. Find them. Take them back. They have blood to spill this day."

"Are you sure you won't come with me?"

Again he glared. "If you must ask, then you already prove why you must go alone. I need not answer."

His granddaughter looked away, a bit of color filling her cheeks. "I can handle this fine," she said, eyes locked on the open window as if it were her enemy.

"Then prove it. I will ensure our escape path is clear."

With the prisoners and soldiers gone, the royal mansion was a shell of its former self, its curtains closed and its windows dark. Thren suspected few guards would remain, for the Bloodhand's forces were stretched painfully thin to keep the city in line. Together, Thren and Erin dropped to the ground and then crossed the street to the brick fence surrounding the estate. He offered his hands. Erin stepped into them, and with his aid, she vaulted over the top.

The moment she was gone, Thren retreated back to their hiding spot to watch and wait. If any soldiers patrolled the area, he'd take them down. But mostly, he watched for Erin, and faintly smiled when he saw her climbing up the mansion like a little spider.

"What I would give to have seen you don a gray cloak," he whispered as she slipped inside the window. He pushed those memories aside. The Spider Guild was long gone. What he needed now was to trust in Erin, and believe her capable of enduring the trials ahead. Given their plan, he could not be with her for much of it, and just as he needed to trust her, she needed to trust herself. He'd watched her killing instinct grow over the last few days, but this was something else entirely.

Today, they would forge a brand new Felhorn legacy.

"Be swift, but not careless," he whispered, trying to imagine her progress. Perhaps there'd be a guard, perhaps servants. Would she strike them down? Rush past them in a panic in search of Cyth's quarters? It was a bit of a gamble on Thren's part that the swords would be located where he said, but after his conversation with Cyth Ordoth, he felt certain he understood the elf's motivations. He was driven by delusions of the past, and of supposed honors and greatness lost to him and his people. Those swords once belonged to an elf named Aerland Shen, who had been cursed by Celestia. They would hold too great a significance, and too much history, for Cyth to abandon. One reason Thren had observed the elf's departure had been to ensure he had not adopted the swords as his own. Not yet, from what Thren saw. Perhaps Cyth wanted time to train with them, to learn their weight and feel. Perhaps he feared the touch of Karak and Ashhur upon them.

One guard neared, patrolling from Thren's right. He watched the man trundle past, looking tired and anxious in equal measure. Thren easily dropped to the ground and then slid in behind him, opening his throat with a knife. The deed done, he dragged the body back into the shadows. The blood would attract the attention of any further patrols, but, well, Thren could always silence them, too.

Minutes passed. Thren fought off his imagination, which sought only the most dire circumstances. He had heard no shouts from inside. No sounds of combat. No broken windows, no screams, no...

And then she reappeared, climbing back out the window. Thren smiled as he reached into a small satchel tied to his waist. Within was a long length of rope, and he flung it over the brick wall. A moment later, he felt the slack tighten, and he braced a foot against the brick while leaning backward. Erin climbed the other side, and when she vaulted over to land beside him, her smile was as wide as his.

"Found them," she said, and gestured to the sister swords strapped to her back. The sword belt was so large she wore it across one shoulder like a bandoleer.

"Good," Thren said. He banished his smile. "Now go to the prison and break the Godslayer out. We will need his help to even these numbers arrayed against us."

"What if I can't get to him?" she asked.

"You can, and you will." He retreated across the street, preparing to climb back to the rooftops. "And I will ensure the eyes of the city are far from the prison. Go, Erin. Do what must be done, and accept no failure. I will meet you at the chaos of the execution ceremony."

Erin paused, and she looked more uncertain than he'd ever seen her. He thought her daunted by the task still before her, but then she crossed the space between them and flung her arms about his waist. Her cheek pressed to his chest as she hugged him, her gaze to the side, as if afraid to see his reaction.

"Thank you, grandfather," she said. "For all you've done for me, and all you are yet to do. Stay safe."

Thren's entire body felt built of ice. His arms remained at his sides. He closed his eyes. Breathed out.

"Erin," he said, but no words felt justified. He allowed himself to smile. "Stand tall in the shadow of your father, and we shall make corpses of our enemies. When the blood is spilled, and silence follows, I hold faith you will have done him proud."

His granddaughter withdrew from the hug. Her eyes were red, but no tears. She was too strong for them now.

"I don't care about my father. I care about my family. That's who I'm fighting for."

"As have I, always and forever," he said. He turned and ran, the street a blur beneath him. He ran, and ran, needing the space, needing the separation, if he was to do what must be done.

◈

Angkar would never be as familiar to him as Veldaren had been, but Thren had lived here long enough to know the bend to her streets and the slant of her rooftops. He dashed across both with his hood pulled low over his face. With each step he tried to forget Erin, and how tightly she had held him when she hugged him goodbye.

These old bones are long past running on rooftops, he thought, but it felt right nonetheless as he climbed up once he was near his destination. The bulk of Cyth's forces would be overseeing the executions. What they had left to spare was spread thin throughout the city. Thren would draw their eyes west, away from the prison. Should Erin's rescue attempt be noticed, he needed reinforcements to be far away.

He paused at the edge of the roof, looking out over the market. He'd chosen somewhere public, and while it would normally be crowded, the streets were relatively barren, with many stalls shut down due to the forced attendance of the coming executions. Thren lay on his stomach and watched the patrolling guard lazily wander the street. This was one of the Connington mercenaries, though his tabard was currently flipped inside out to hide the original symbol. Tori had already ordered all her assets renamed back to the Keenan estate, and Thren suspected new tabards were in the works. He grinned as he drew his swords. As if he would allow them the time.

Do not waste this opportunity, Erin.

He dropped atop the mercenary, his sword jamming down through the neck and into his ribcage. The man's dying cry was weak, and Thren robbed him of it entirely with a savage twist of his blade. The corpse dropped. In the distance, a man and woman saw and screamed.

Thren ignored them. The second reason he'd chosen this location was the nearby firepit a street vendor used to cook their wares. The coals were smoldering, the fire unattended and the stall currently empty. Thren kicked open the wood gate blocking it off and he pulled a torch out from his belt. It caught easily within the embers. Once blazing, Thren returned to the streets at a run.

Stall by stall, he set them aflame, the rough canvases and curtains used to segregate them easily catching fire. Smoke thickened as he did his work. People shouted, but none dared engage him, not with his sword drawn in his other hand. Instead those who cared enough to do so called to the guards.

That's right, come to me, Thren thought as he started setting buildings alight as well. If it looked like it would burn, he pressed his torch against it. Eventually the fire would reach a point where the citizenry would need to band together to fight it, and that was fine with him. It would only add to the chaos, considering the order for the populace to attend the execution on the other side of the city.

At last Thren decided he had done enough, and he sprinted for the nearest market exit. His next task was to infiltrate the crowd at the hanging, ready to join when the battle began. The sheer audacity of the plan made him wince. So few of them, against so many, but what other choice did they have? There was no way he could stop Erin from trying to save her mother without imprisoning her.

He'd considered it, too, but he knew she'd never forgive him. There was a time that would not have stopped him. It did now. So the fires spread, the plan moved in motion, and Thren put his faith in a half-orc that had already accomplished miracles many times before, and would need to create another with his strength and black steel blades.

I hope you live up to your reputation, Godslayer, he thought as he crossed the road, hooking west upon seeing three Keenan soldiers rushing toward him from the opposite direction. Three against one was hardly the worst odds, but he didn't have the time to handle them carefully. He sprinted, trusting himself to be faster, to be smarter. A kick of dust at another turn, twisting a foot print to make it seem he went left instead of right. His lungs burned, but he dared not slow. He had to get out, had to meet up with Erin at the hangings.

Thren's confidence nearly got him killed when he dashed through a tight corridor between two homes. He saw a hint of movement above him moments before the glint of steel caught the light of the sun. He spun, avoiding the slash, but not the accompanying kick. It sent him staggering to the side, colliding hard against one of the walls.

The impact left Thren stunned, but he did not let hazy vision and a rolling stomach keep him still. He pushed off the wall while spinning and reaching for his swords. They drew just in time, both crossing to block a downward chop of terrifying strength. He grunted, his arms aching and his legs tensing to hold back the killing stroke.

"You," Brit snarled, and the mixture of joy and savagery lit a thousand warnings inside Thren's mind. Her muscles flexed, all her might pushing the blade of her heavy sword toward him. Thren had the better angle, though, and he stood his ground even as his arms shook.

"I was unaware you were so desperate for a rematch," he said, and he grinned to disguise his actual worry. The grin, and the cockiness it conveyed, would aggravate her further. His best hope for a quick victory involved goading her into making a mistake. Anger and frustration were potent forces in that regard.

Brit finally relented, and she took a step back to twirl her sword into an upright position, readying for another strike. Her blue-green eyes sparkled.

"Cyth letting you live was a mistake," she said. Her grip tightened. "One I am eager to rectify."

Thren bent his knees and lowered his head, all the energy in his body building for an explosion of movement. His cloak fell over his shoulders, hiding the positioning of his hands.

"Come try."

She did, her sword thrusting for his center mass. He rotated outward, both swords parrying it as he spun toward her side. The alley was tight, their movement restricted. It would normally nullify the advantage of her larger sword's reach, but he trusted her to know how to position and adjust to the limitations. This meant more thrusts, more vertical slashes. If he could keep her turning, force one of her swings to strike the wall and throw off her timing...

Upon landing, he tore into her, hacking and slashing with his swords coming in from either side. Her own sword weaved back and forth, expertly blocking. She refused to let him guide her weapon, instead keeping it tight and close to her body as she carefully watched the movements of his hands. Quick hits, her superior strength and her weapon's greater weight easily knocking about his short swords.

"I've been wondering why you outed yourself," she said as she suddenly kicked, her heel striking his hip and forcing him to retreat lest his broken balance mean his doom. "Why you cared so much about the recent tournament, but I saw you throw your final match. You let the Gemcroft girl win. At the time I could not understand why."

He tried to shut her up with a series of slashes, but his reward before he could even swing the second was a punch to the face. He spat blood, tried to keep swinging, but she held her sword with a single hand, deflecting his strike while pounding her fist into him, layering his chest and neck with bruises. Both gods help him, it felt like being hit with a hammer.

"But then I learned your true name, and the name she used when entering," she continued. "Felhorn. She claims your blood, Thren. Who is she to you? Niece? Granddaughter?"

She gripped her sword in both hands again, thrusting repeatedly with speed that bordered on unfair given the heft and reach of her blade. One was disturbingly close, cutting across his hip to spill blood upon steel. He finally managed a decent hit in retaliation, a swipe across her shoulder that only infuriated her further.

"Did you fuck a Gemcroft woman, is that it? Were you not content to humble them in your war? You had to plant your damn seed in them, too?"

She deftly shifted, pinning his back to the wall as she swung. He blocked and parried as best he could, struggling to find an opening. Twice he attempted to sneak past her, only for a heel to his stomach or hilt to his shoulder to knock him back. All the while, she mocked him.

"It doesn't matter the connection, Thren. Once I've carved your corpse, I'm going after her. Wherever she is in this city, I shall find her. She won't hang like her mother, either. She'll suffer at my hands, and I shall enjoy every bleeding second."

Thren's bruises were building, his exhaustion growing. He didn't risk dodging the next swing, instead blocking it with both short swords. The impact left him regretting it. He skidded a foot backward, his feet unable to find traction. He pushed back, only to stumble as she withdrew her sword at the exact same time, pulling it for one wide, brutal swing aiming to cleave him in half. All her strength was in the blow. In her mind he was trapped, and there would be no blocking this hit, no parrying it aside.

She was right, and so Thren did not try. He lunged, not at her, but away to the wall, climbing a single step up it before vaulting upside down. Time seemed to slow as he hung in the air. The killing blow swished just shy of his head. He saw the flash of its steel, felt the passage of air. His swords arched, already in position before his feet ever touched ground.

He landed behind Brit, both his swords stabbing down to either side of her neck so they sank into the gaps of her collarbones. The elf's body seized from the pain. His lips pressed to her mutilated ear.

"My granddaughter will live," he said, pushing the hilts deeper. "You will not."

A vicious cry, and he ripped both blades out to the side, tearing gaps in her flesh and cracking open ribs. Her body collapsed in a grotesque pile of gore. He barely had time to breathe out his relief when he heard a harsh voice speak from the entrance to the alley.

"Yet again, elven blood dies at the hands of unworthy humans."

Thren turned from the corpse, his heart plummeting into his stomach. He knew that voice. He straightened his spine, clanged his swords for a comforting ring of steel, and then turned to face Cyth Ordoth, blocking the way.

"Don't you have a hanging to attend?" he asked.

Cyth sneered at him, sword twirling in his hand. "You've been such a thorn in my side. I knew it was you killing my soldiers these past few days, and I suspected you would try something in the lead-up to the hangings. What I could never decide is...why? Why fight this hopeless war, Thren? Since when have you cared for the people of Angkar, or who ruled them?"

Thren glanced over his shoulder. Two more elves protected the opposite end of the alley. There would be no escape.

"I've ever been opposed to authority," Thren said, wishing he didn't sound so tired from his fight with Brit.

"Of course," Cyth said, slowly approaching. "The only authority you have ever accepted is your own."

"As did the uncle you worship."

Thren sprinted straight at Cyth, hoping to surprise him. Better to seize the initiative than let the elf dictate the pace of the fight. He barreled straight into his opponent, swords slashing together from the left. He wanted to test the elf's speed, to see how he'd react once the defense was made. Cyth worshiped the Darkhand, but could he match him in battle?

It seemed he could. Their weapons collided, Cyth unfazed by the sudden attack. They pressed against one another for a heartbeat, a mutual test of strength. Thren was not surprised but still dismayed by how much weaker he felt when compared to the spry elf. Other than his son, age was the only other cruel foe he could never defeat. His swords bowed inward, and then he was spinning. Raw strength would not suffice. Already he knew his speed would not match up, either. He'd have to rely on pure skill.

That meant getting the elf to dance. Thren ended the spin with a slash with his off hand and a thrust with his main, both disguised by his turning motion. Cyth easily blocked the slash, but it was meant only to distract from the thrust. The elf noticed at the last moment, and he pitched his body sideways to avoid being gutted. Thren followed up, closing the distance between them. He needed to end this fight quickly. He needed blood to flow before the two elves behind him realized their leader was in danger.

Cyth's retreat ended with his back to the wall. Thren's elbow struck him in the jaw for good measure before their swords re-intertwined. That swelling bruise gave Thren hope as he tore into the elf, hacking and slashing, his talents pushed to their limits. The ringing still drove him onward. He was the true heir to the Darkhand, not this spoiled little pup. He was the terror of Veldaren's underground, the breaker of the first Sun Guild.

His hands ached, and Cyth's blocks grew harsher. Thren felt the battle slipping, found himself responding to counters more often than he kept the assault. He missed a hit, felt steel cut across his forearm. Nothing deep, but the blood still flowed. Thren gritted his teeth, but no matter the iron will of his mind, there were limits to his body.

Whoever he had been in his past meant nothing in the present. Now he was a tired man in his sixties, worn down from battle, struggling to maintain his breath while wielding swords that felt much too heavy much too soon. Desperation gave him a final surge of energy. He deflected two hits, kicked to gain some separation, and then dove right back into Cyth. One sword thrusted for his neck, the other his abdomen. They came in at strange angles, and Thren twisted his body so it would be difficult to counter in return.

It didn't matter. Cyth parried one thrust aside and turned his own body to narrowly avoid the other. The pair collided with one another, and there was no doubt as to who was stronger. Thren gasped as Cyth's elbow struck his throat, then staggered when the hilt of a sword cracked against his forehead. A new slash, shallow across the chest that tore more fabric than skin. Thren wheezed, disgust filling him. The fight was over. The elf was playing with him.

"Surely you can do better than this," Thren said, feigning confidence. He leaned against the opposite side of the alley, hard stone pressing to his back. "It's hardly a scratch."

"Would you prefer I cut deeper?" Cyth asked, twirling his swords. His smile had returned, his confidence revived after the initial shaky start of the fight.

"I'd prefer you lay down and die, elf, but rarely does Dezrel give people what they desire unless they take it for themselves."

One last leap forward. One last swing of his swords. Thren gave it everything he had left, his bruises, exhaustion, and aching bones be damned.

It wasn't enough.

Steel struck steel. Thren's aching hands could not keep hold. A brutal hit, and both went flying from his grasp. He kicked, missed, cried out as an elbow struck his face. Another cut lashed his chest, shallow, meant only to hurt. His final punch struck Cyth in the abdomen, but it was nothing compared to the hilt bashing against his temple.

Thren collapsed onto his back, all the world spinning. An

intense need to vomit filled him, and it took all his willpower to hold it down.

That need nearly broke him when Cyth's boot smashed onto Thren's neck and pressed down hard enough to seal off his breath. Thren clutched at it as his face turned red and the world around him darkened.

"There is much I can learn from you," Cyth said, grinding his heel into Thren's throat. "But there is no potential friendship left. I will make you suffer for it, Thren. You killed my brethren. You murdered Brit'tari. Whatever wisdom Muzien gifted you, I shall bleed out of your body amid a torrent of screams."

David Dalglish

33
ERIN

Erin crept along the outer wall of the prison, mindful of guards. To the north rose a plume of smoke, a signal from her grandfather that the time was now. His distraction was at its fullest.

Thank you, she thought as she watched the nearby Keenan mercenary patrol the street outside. Just as Thren predicted, they were spread much too thin, relying on fear as much as actual numbers. With the hanging ceremony soon to begin, their strength would be gathered there, and what few remained would be the mercenaries hired by Tori and not the far deadlier elves of the Sun Kingdom.

Still, each mercenary would be more than capable of gutting her if she were not careful. Much of the city would be left unguarded, but not here. While Aurelia, Aubrienna, and Gregory were all kept within the royal mansion, the rest of the hostages were taken to the city's prison. Erin's mother was among them, and she let that discomfort and fear give her the courage she needed.

First, she needed to deal with the patrolling soldier. He looked tired, and Erin wondered if the mercenaries were being pushed hard to fulfill their duties. The city had spent the last week constantly on the verge of riot. No doubt the men and women wearing those inside-out tabards were lacking in rest. Erin sure wasn't going to complain as she crouched low and followed the guard like his shadow. She readied her sabers.

Her first thrust parted the flesh of his back, bounced off a couple ribs, and slid upwards, piercing his lungs. Her other blade she swung about to the front of his body, the sharpened edge slicing his throat. The man dropped, gasping through the new hole in his neck and unable to cry out warning as he bled out. Erin sheathed her sabers, grabbed the man by the arms, and dragged his stilled corpse toward the prison. The blood would attract attention, but less attention than an actual body.

There wasn't much to hide it behind, so she dumped the body off to the side of the building, propping it in a seated position with head bowed forward. Maybe someone would think him napping if they didn't look close enough…

Erin redrew her sabers and rolled her eyes. No, no one was going to be fooled. She needed to move fast and trust her grandfather's distraction to prevent any patrols or reinforcements from coming her way.

Back to the entrance, an enormous oak door built into the center of the squat prison sunken halfway into the earth. She carefully peered around the corner to study the guard stationed out front. The door was locked, and the key hung from a large iron ring attached to the guard's belt. There'd be no stealing it from him. It'd have to be taken the bloody way.

Quick and vicious, she told herself as she prepared for a sprint. *Give him no time to alert those inside.*

She carefully watched the guard, studying his movements. When he glanced down, scratching at an itch underneath his armor, Erin raced alongside the prison, keeping as close to the wall as possible. Her eyes widened and her heart thundered, pulse throbbing in her throat as she crossed the space. By the time the guard noticed the movement from the corner of his eye, Erin was already lunging into the air.

Her sabers jammed straight into his face, one cracking a tooth before sliding into the back of his throat, the other punching through his left eye. They both sank in deep, denying him a death cry beyond a gurgling choke. Her momentum carried her into him, and she bit down a pained yelp from the awkward position it forced her arms into. The guard dropped, and she yanked her weapons free.

No hiding this mess, she thought, watching blood pool in front of the door. She sheathed her offhand saber, then used her other to cut the key ring off the soldier's belt. Just one key on it, she assumed for the outside door alone. Another guard inside would have the keys for the individual cells.

Erin unlocked the door, leaving the key within the keyhole. She breathed in deep, relying on an exercise taught by her mother to calm her nerves. She could do this. However many guards were in there, they would be few in number, so great was Cyth's focus on the public hangings.

She pulled the door open halfway, just enough for her to

slip through, and dashed inside. Two guards awaited her, both human. No elves. Erin felt a tiny bit of relief as she rushed toward them within the cramped entry room. The pair sat at a small table, chatting with one another. Their weapons weren't drawn. The nearest, a heavier sort, shouted out a name as he stood, reaching for his sword. Erin flung herself into him, hacking with barely controlled strikes. Eagerness and nervousness mixed within her, a heady cocktail threatening to overrule her training. Regardless, blood flowed when her sharp blades slashed through the flesh of his face and neck. He dropped, flailing wildly, his weapon still not drawn.

Erin stepped onto his falling body, kicked off, and landed atop the table. Her remaining foe was of course larger and stronger than her. She had to rely on surprise and speed. Perhaps skill would win her the day, but the quarters were tight, and she had no desire to test things when she still felt so on edge. She slammed right into the guard with her knees, blasting him backward. Though he'd drawn his sword, it was not yet up and ready, and it fell from his hand as he flew backward. His head smacked hard against the stone wall with a sickening crunch, leaving behind a splatter of blood. Erin vaulted off him, landed, and then dove right back in. The man was dazed, his eyes unfocused. Easy prey to her sabers.

When he dropped she checked both bodies, finding a second large key on the first. She then crept through the narrow walkway between the cells. Given Angkar's population, the prison was of decent size, and it smelled horrendous. From what she gathered, Cyth had executed the existing prisoners when taking over the city. The bodies remained, stinking and rotting. Erin did her best to ignore them. A torch burned up ahead, and she trusted the cell beside it to be the one she sought.

Erin paused before the cell, the key shaking in her hand. There he was, Harruq Tun the Godslayer. His head was bowed and his eyes closed. She might have believed him asleep if not for how tense he still appeared. His wrists were chained to the wall above his head, his ankles bolted together with iron. Erin inserted the key, and as it turned the half-orc finally looked up, and his gaze fell upon her.

Gods help me, she thought, her entire body gone stiff. That look. Those eyes. She felt imprisoned. His kindness, his goofiness, his jokes and playfulness as they sparred: they all felt like they belonged to a different man. This was the look of the Godslayer. Seething with rage, muscles tensed, brown eyes burning with fire. For the briefest moment she thought he would tear the manacles from the wall, for iron and stone could not deny him.

"Erin," he said, his deep voice rumbling in the quiet dark. "Are you alone?"

"I was," she said, and hurried inside. She thrust the key into the lock of the manacles binding his arms to the wall. "But now I have you with me, don't I?"

The lock opened, and she knelt to undo the manacles around his ankles as well. When she finished Harruq stood and stretched his muscles. His silence was frightening. His presence overwhelmed her. He felt like a storm about to be unleashed. His every movement was rage channeled into something lethal and terrifying.

"I...I have your swords," she said, pulling the belt off her waist and shoulder. She offered the twin blades to him, and he accepted them with a hungry look that only frightened her further.

"Where is my family?" he asked as he buckled them on.

"With Cyth at the hangings," she said, then quickly added, "I don't think they're to be hung, just bear witness. We...we don't have much time."

Harruq drew Salvation, checked its edge, and then did the same to Condemnation. The crimson light washed across him in the prison cell.

"We'll have enough," he said.

"So you'll do it?" she asked as he exited the cell, brushing past her. "You'll save my family?"

He paused to look back at her. There was no doubt in his voice, only certainty.

"Yes, Erin. We will fight, and save those we love from those who must die."

He strode for the exit, but she lifted the key.

"Wait," she said. "I think Tarlak is down in here, too."

Deep into the prison, in the final cell, Tarlak Eschaton lay on the floor. Unlike Harruq, he was bound with rope, tight knots around his wrists and ankles. Additional rope wound through his fingers, locking them in place. A rag had been stuffed into his mouth and secured with an additional layer of rope.

"Wake up, friend," Harruq said, kneeling beside the wizard. Quick, careful cuts with Salvation undid the ropes. Tarlak stirred awake, and he stared groggily at the two of them. Clarity quickly followed as he realized what was happening.

"Such rude accommodation for an old man like me," Tarlak said once his gag was removed.

"You're not that old," Harruq said, helping Tarlak to his feet.

"You can say so, but I feel otherwise." He stretched and winced. "Who's the girl?"

"Erin Felhorn," she answered for him. The wizard's expression shifted to disbelief. "I'm...I'm Haern's daughter. Harruq has been training me."

Tarlak blinked. "Well. That's new." He turned to the half-orc. "Anyone else with you? Some ghosts from the past I should know about?"

"It's just us three," Harruq said.

"Wonderful. Where's everyone else?"

"Attending the hanging," Erin said. "They've gathered the whole city for attendance. All the elves will be there, as well as the Keenan mercenaries."

The wizard shook his head and cracked his knuckles.

"Those elven bastards. They don't know what they unleashed. You ready for some fun, Harruq?"

The half-orc grinned. The sight of it made Erin shiver. She had known he was the Godslayer, known he challenged the fallen angels and defeated their greatest champions. Knowing of it, though, was different than having truly witnessed it. Harruq had seemed so ridiculous at times, loud and brash, yet at other times content to goof and joke. There was no denying his skill, but Erin had fought plenty of skilled fighters better than her, including her own mother.

But that grin? Knowing how greatly the odds were stacked against them, and how badly they would be outnumbered when they attempted to stop the hangings? It was eager. It was thrilled. It was the grin of a man who knew he was the master of death, and all else was subservient to him. A man with swords in his hands and the ability to change the fate of worlds. He'd done it before. He'd do it again.

"We've faced worse," Harruq said. "I've no intention of failing now."

"That's what I like to hear," Tarlak said, clapping his hands. Another stretch to crack his knuckles, and then he began weaving his arms about. A blue portal ripped into existence before him, and through its ethereal swirl Erin saw the faint outline of rooftops, and below a gathered crowd.

"Lead on," Tarlak said, fire flickering from his fingertips as his own mood darkened. "We've a false king to kill."

34
HARRUQ

Harruq stepped out from the portal onto the roof of a home, nearly stumbling from the awkward shift in locations as well as the slight drop before his heel touched shingles. Before him was the hanging platform, as well as the enormous throng of people forced to watch. They numbered in the thousands, filling the streets in all directions. Harruq doubted those near the back could see or hear a thing, yet still mercenaries forced them to attend.

There you are, Harruq thought, kneeling as Erin and Tarlak joined him at the rooftop's edge. He saw Aurelia standing on the platform, but no noose had been readied for her. Her hands were bound behind her back, and across her face a faint glint of metal. Something to prevent her spellcasting, he assumed. Aubrienna stood next to her mother, a soldier directly beside her holding a drawn blade. It rested casually upon Aubby's shoulder, a constant threat that inspired a thousand murderous desires within Harruq's mind.

Only four people stood on tall stools underneath the nooses. In the center was Queen Brynn, stripped of her elegant armor and dress and instead half-naked in a bloodied shift. Beside her was Zusa Gemcroft, still in her faded violet dress, the fabric torn and filthy. The two women stood tall and proud, unafraid of the nooses around their necks. To their left was Nathaniel Gemcroft, stripped naked from the chest up. He looked dirty and bruised, but otherwise unharmed. On the opposite side, underneath the fourth and final noose, stood a pale and frightened Gregory Copernus. His stool was slightly taller than the others, and unlike them, his neck was not yet cinched within the noose that swayed beside him, gently tapping against his cheek as if in mockery.

Tarlak flattened himself on the roof beside Harruq. "Where's the Ordoths?" he asked. "I just see the Connington madwoman."

"She calls herself a Keenan now," Erin said, joining them on Harruq's other side. Harruq glanced at her, but she offered

Legacy of the Watcher

nothing else, only stared with poorly contained anger. Her glare was aimed straight at Tori Keenan, who was busy lecturing the crowd.

"Already we see the benefits of our newly formed alliance," the woman shouted. Her shoulders were pulled back and her chest puffed out, the young woman doing her best to appear confident and intimidating. "Trade from Stonewood arrives by caravans, and with peace between us and the elves, nothing will stop our march to the north. All of Dezrel shall be unified again, into one people, one humanity, forever free of conflict and bloodshed."

"They hang Gregory, they face war with Mordan," Tarlak wondered aloud.

"But we're not ready for war," Harruq said. "That was the whole damn point of this treaty. If Cyth and Vala can convince the remaining lords of Ker to accept their new crowns, and turn their soldiers north..."

"It won't happen, because we won't let it happen," Erin muttered. The confidence in her voice did not match her words. Her eyes flitted about the enormous gathering. "But there's so many here..."

Harruq knew what she meant. Traitor soldiers of Angkar watched over every exit. Several dozen mercenaries formed rings around the hanging platform, with a significant grouping near the front to protect Tori. And then loosely scattered throughout the entire crowd, weaving through them like murderous specters, were Cyth's elves. They wore their green and brown camouflage, which made them stand out all the more within the city environs. Harruq suspected that was the point.

"It doesn't matter," Harruq said, and he pointed. "We rescue Aurelia first. Once she's free, her and Tarlak's magic will be more than enough to even the odds."

"Even against that many?"

A dozen memories flashed through him, each forever seared into his mind. The last was of Tessanna Tun in the sky above Hemman Fields, giving her life to decimate the armies of both Azariah and Ahaesarus so the fate of Dezrel would once more belong to the mortals instead of the angels.

"Even so," he whispered, and glanced at Tarlak. "Isn't that right?"

"It'll be rough going," Tarlak said. "The platform's

crowded, and we don't have much time. We best move now, before Cyth arrives from wherever he has run off to. Question is, what's the plan? I can bombard our foes from here with my magic, but that doesn't get Aurelia free of her constraints, nor protect any of the other hostages. We need boots on the ground for that."

"That's what me and Erin are for," Harruq said. "Can you get us there?"

"Get you there how?"

He gestured. "Clear us a free path through the crowd. That's all we need."

"I can't do that without killing a lot of innocent people," Tarlak said, frowning. "And don't tell me it's worth it. Because it's not."

"What if you send us *above* the crowd?" Erin asked. "Like, with wind or something?"

Tarlak snapped his fingers, then winced at the noise he created, not that anyone could hear over the general loudness from the gathering down below.

"All right. I have an idea. It is incredibly stupid, but it will get you there. No turning back, though, so tell me when ready, and I'll get you your path."

Harruq pushed up to a crouch and drew his sister swords. Energy pulsed through their hilts, filling him with the confidence he needed.

"Do it."

Tarlak shifted so he sat cross-legged on his rear, and then he lowered his head and began muttering arcane incantations to himself. His hands twisted, fingers making the necessary symbols to bend Celestia's magical Weave to his will. After only a few seconds he halted, his eyes opening and a grin spreading across his face.

"Go get them," he said, and flung his hands forward. A tremendously thick sheet of ice sliced through the air, forming a direct path toward the nearest edge of the hanging platform. Icicles stretched along the bottom, forming pillars to support its weight. The angle wasn't too steep, given the distance needed to travel between the rooftop and the platform, so it seemed more like a gentle dip. Harruq had certainly traveled through stranger means.

Knowing standing was hopeless, Harruq hopped onto the slick surface, all his weight braced onto one hip as he slid. The speed was more than he expected, that gentle dip suddenly much more steep. He heard shouts from the crowd, shock and fear in equal measure at the sudden appearance of an enormous sheet of ice. The distance shrank in a heartbeat, the platform rapidly approaching. At the last moment, the icy path veered upward, vaulting Harruq into the air. He lifted his swords and twisted to right himself. With tremendous force, his swords cleaved through the guard standing behind Aubrienna. The man never even had time to attempt to dodge.

With blood spilled, the Abyss broke loose. Thousands amid the crowd screamed, and the masses surged toward the exits. The many soldiers pushed against them, going in the opposite direction to try and reach the platform. What had once been a tense but orderly gathering became chaos, and Harruq *thrived* in chaos.

Soldiers climbing the platform quickly met his sister blades. A trio surrounding Tori split from the group, racing toward the four condemned souls standing on their stools beneath the nooses. Harruq blasted right into the three mercenaries, denying them any progress. The first lost his shield when Condemnation slipped beneath its protective edge and flung it wide. Salvation plunged afterward, burying to the hilt in the man's chest. Harruq did not withdraw it, instead tearing right through the body to smash into the ribs of the second. The third soldier swung his sword in a panic, hoping to catch Harruq off guard, but then Erin landed from her own slide across Tarlak's ice bridge, her sabers slashing an 'x' across the soldier's neck upon landing.

"Free Aurelia," Erin shouted, twirling her sabers and glaring at Tori Keenan's formation fleeing from the ambush. "We've got this."

As if to punctuate her words, a second blast of ice from Tarlak soared overhead to shatter upon a group of soldiers racing onto the platform. The wood steps broke beneath the barrage, as did the bodies.

Trusting Erin to hold the line, Harruq made straight for his wife, impaling the nearest soldier who grabbed her arm in an attempt to escort her away. Harruq kicked the body aside, meeting Aurelia's eyes. There was no fear within them, just a fury that matched Harruq's own. If only he could free her, but the contraption binding her fingers, all metal and wire, was beyond him.

David Dalglish

"I can't open it," he told her. "Not without hurting you." Her eyes widened, and she nodded past him. Harruq spun, his swords lashing out on instinct to parry aside a spear thrust meant to pierce his spine. The wood shaft splintered against the force of his magical weapons. The soldier panicked and attempted to retreat, but Harruq's blood was up, his fury reignited. He flung himself right into the man, his right hand keeping the spear out of position. His left swiped high, knocking off his helmet but failing to score a kill. Undeterred, Harruq head-butted the man square between the eyes, and when he staggered back, dazed, it was an easy flick of his wrist to cut open his throat.

Harruq kicked the corpse off the platform and, while watching it drop, was nearly gutted by a lunging elf. Instinct saved him, his reaction speed just barely enough to sweep Salvation around to shove the long, thrusting blade aside so that it scraped a shallow cut across his forearm instead.

Another scar to join the hundreds, thought Harruq as he retreated a step and set his legs. The elf pressed the attack, thinking the advantage was his. Harruq quickly disabused him of that notion when the sword feinted a high slash and then looped around, a low hit aiming for the hamstrings. The feint was obvious, and Condemnation was in place before the low arc began. Salvation swung, and though the elf realized his danger and retreated, the tip cut a matching groove on the elf's shoulder.

Harruq's foe spun, a wide slash protecting his retreat, and then performed a sudden, vicious lunge, extending his entire body to gain reach. Against a slower foe, or one carelessly chasing, it might have worked. Harruq was neither, his own charge delayed until he saw the movement of the elf's feet and the positioning of his arms. He met the charge with one of his own, only his body shifted so the thrust passed harmlessly to the side. His own stab found purchase, however, as both his swords plunged through ribs into lungs. The elf convulsed and then dropped, yet one more body to tumble off the platform.

A platform growing increasingly surrounded as soldiers steadily made their way through a crowd that thinned as the people of Angkar fled. At the northern exit, soldiers rushed in by the dozens, and Harruq's stomach sank at the sight. The numbers were already dire, and to see so many come unanticipated…

Legacy of the Watcher

"For the true queen!" a voice thundered over the din. Harruq craned his neck, a grin spreading across his face. Those soldiers...they bore the crimson hawk sigil as they swarmed through the entrance, and leading them was a familiar face: Omar Wrye, Brynn's guard captain. It seemed they had planned their own attempt to save their queen's life, and Harruq was more than happy for their intervention.

Suddenly flanked, the Keenan mercenaries split off to engage the new threat, adding a much needed distraction. Harruq bashed and slaughtered several more soldiers, and when he could he pushed their bodies toward the remaining stairs. He'd build a barricade of the dead if he must. It would not be his first time.

A portal suddenly ripped open just below the nooses, and a bleeding Tarlak stumbled out. He landed hard on his knees atop the platform, grimacing as he clutched a cut across his arm.

"Bastards almost got me on the rooftop," he muttered. "I think we need some help."

"Then get her free," Harruq said. He kicked a man in the face trying to climb up the platform, then crossed his swords to form a meager shield against an elf drawing an arrow. "I can only do so much!"

Tarlak slammed a palm to the ground, raising a wall of ice Harruq's height up along the platform's edge. The arrow plinked harmlessly against the other side.

"If you insist," the wizard said, stumbling to his feet and then circling around behind Aurelia. He grabbed the metal contraption binding her fingers and muttered words of magic Harruq could not understand. The barbed wires broke in multiple places, freeing her.

"This part will be harder," Tarlak said as she turned about. "I see a keyhole, so I'm going to try to pretend this is like any other lock. Stay still."

Aurelia nodded faintly. Harruq forced his attention away, for the protection of the ice wall only worked against the archers in the crowd. Those rushing the platform would shatter it rather easily. Erin was fighting for her life beside her mother, and Harruq rushed to join her. Already he had waited too long to remove the immediate threat to them, and he rectified it with the magically gifted sharpness of his swords. One swing was all it took to cut through the thick ropes of each noose, freeing Nathaniel, Zusa, and Brynn. As for Gregory, Harruq lifted him off the stool, kicked it aside, and then set him down.

"Stay with Aubby," he ordered, then turned to Zusa, who already had offered him her hands.

"There's dead everywhere," Harruq said, slicing the ropes binding her wrists. "Find a weapon."

"I am in poor shape to fight," Zusa said.

"Make do," Harruq said, and nodded toward where Erin was plunging her saber through the eye of a foe. "Your daughter is."

He freed Brynn and Nathaniel next, then turned his attention back to his family. Being apart from them for any length of time made him nervous, his fear an itch in his mind he could not ignore. Tarlak stood in front of Aurelia, the strange contraption held in his hands. As Harruq watched, he slowly pulled it from her mouth. Blood and saliva dripped from the wires, making Harruq wince.

"Aurry?" Harruq asked.

His wife looked his way, and he took a step back at the light burning within her eyes.

"Is this what I awaken to?" she asked, her hands clenched into fists. Her voice was not her own. "Is this the love I am meant to return for?"

Aurelia lifted into the air, her hair swirling in a silent wind. Fire crackled around her. Light burst from her fingertips. Panicked archers fired a barrage of arrows, and Harruq's heart skipped a beat. He needn't have worried. Little jolts of lightning arced from Aurelia's chest, striking the arrows and turning them to ash before they could reach her. The light of her eyes blazed brighter, a mixture of gold and silver, light and shadow.

When she spoke, the city trembled.

"So long, you decried my silence," she said, the voice coming from his wife's mouth unrecognizable. *"I am here, my children. My eyes have opened, and I bear witness to your offering."* She clenched her fists. Storm clouds gathered across a formerly blue sky. *"If you would shed blood in my name, then let it be yours."*

Lightning shot from her hands, coupled with two more strikes from the darkening sky. They blasted into the elven archers,

Legacy of the Watcher

flinging aside their bodies. They streaked through rows of mercenaries, jolting through their metal armor with crackling brightness. Her hands clapped above her, and the ground rumbled, cracks opening to release bursts of flame that swallowed whole mercenary groups.

The crowd screamed, bystanders and soldiers alike. Thunder rumbled above Angkar, the lightning not isolated to the clearing. Thick white streaks lit the horizon, tearing chunks from the city walls. Homes burst into flame. The torrent of power, fueled by the goddess's fury, flowed into the conquered city, and the conquerors were but ash and dust before its might.

"Ashhur help us, it's like watching Tessanna," Tarlak said, his mouth hanging open.

"Told you we free her first," Harruq said, punching the wizard in the shoulder. The day was not yet done, even with the display above them. Elves rushed to safety, many still firing off arrows in a vain hope one pierced through Celestia's protection. Panicked mercenaries fled in all directions, with some rushing the gallows with a zeal bordering on mania.

"Keep us from getting swarmed," Harruq said, and Tarlak was eager to oblige. His magic was far from the display Aurelia unleashed, but the barrage of ice lances was still enough to crunch in shields and snap legs.

"Erin!" Harruq shouted. The young woman crouched near her mother, who, while still deadly, was clearly wounded and not at her best. "With me!"

Harruq charged into those rushing the platform, Salvation and Condemnation leaving crimson streaks as they sliced through the air. A strange twilight had befallen Angkar, and in its dim light the crimson glow of his sister swords was made all the more ominous. Blood sprayed from his every swing. There was fear in his opponents' hearts. He could not blame them, not when the sky erupted in fury at their deeds, but neither would he show them mercy.

Shields and swords shattered, and then Erin followed in his wake, a twisting, dancing artist still learning how to paint in blood. Her sabers more often than not found flesh, cutting the necks of those Harruq left injured and bleeding. Six men, in fine armor and wearing blue Keenan tabards. Six men, brought low in as many seconds, as Harruq unleashed his rage upon them.

He shook off the blood, his heart pounding. A rumble of thunder momentarily deafened him, and in the ensuing haze he realized Erin was shouting.

"Tori's fleeing!" she insisted while pointing. Sure enough, he saw a group of six mercenaries huddled around the smaller woman, all shoving their way toward the east exit, away from Omar's push. Harruq twirled his swords.

"Then let me clear the way," he yelled back, and then sprinted straight toward them, bodying another soldier foolish enough to try blocking his way. The man had barely landed before Erin was atop him, stabbing through the eyes in such a fluid motion it barely slowed her chase. The distance closed, Harruq bellowed out a warning, wanting the mercenaries' attention his way. A crack of lightning struck the hanging platform, as if Celestia herself agreed with his rage. Eyes turned toward him. Wide. Fearful.

The first sword raised to block shattered against the ancient magic empowering Condemnation. The blade continued forward, cleaving the man's skull in half. Harruq kicked the falling corpse into his neighbor. When he stumbled, Harruq shoved Salvation up to the hilt in his stomach, then twisted it sideways before ripping it upward, tearing apart armor and ripping the shoulder straight off his body. Blood showered across the ground.

The way clear, Erin vaulted forward, fully trusting Harruq. He repaid that trust by smashing aside a third guard moving to intercept, keeping the way cleared. Erin twisted as she flew, swirling her cloaks while her hands lashed out, sabers glinting flashes of steel amid the gray. For one brief moment Harruq felt dragged to the past, watching Haern take advantage of the chaos his half-orc pupil had created. And then the phantoms passed, and it was Erin who blasted Tori Keenan to the ground, landing feet-first atop the woman's chest.

All of Erin's weight pressed down and her sabers pressed an 'x' against her target's throat. Erin hesitated, and Tori said something Harruq could not hear. Erin's response was clear, however, shaking with rage and cold with fury.

"Let the Trifect die, then. The Gemcrofts survive."

The swords sliced, ripping open flesh. Tori's body convulsed as her blood flowed, but Erin remained atop her, holding her still. Harruq could sense the shock of the moment, and he knew how all the world would have faded from Erin's mind as she relished her kill. Instead of disturbing her, he raced past her, blocking a chop meant to open her in half. A flex of his arms, and he out-muscled the attacker and sent him stumbling backward. The two other mercenaries tried to protect their fellow with a coordinated attack, one slashing, one thrusting. Harruq's hands moved on instinct, each positioning perfectly so that he parried the thrust just aside and blocked the other with a vicious hit that knocked the weapon from the soldier's hand.

A leap forward, and Salvation chopped the man in half at the waist. A turn, and Condemnation cut the head from the man foolish enough to think his thrust would find purchase. Only the stumbling man remained, suddenly alone in the span of a heartbeat. He shouted something, incoherent in his fear, and turned to run. Harruq thought to chase, but a ball of flame slammed into him from the side, charring skin and melting portions of his armor.

"I like when they run," Tarlak shouted, clapping his hands to summon another ball of fire between his palms. "It means I don't have to worry about hitting my friends."

Tarlak's eyes widened, his fire vanishing to instead be replaced with an invisible shield of magical force. An arrow slammed into it, the shaft breaking on impact. Harruq turned to see the source, and his anger surged anew.

Cyth and Vala Ordoth, the siblings finally arriving from wherever they had been to now bear witness to the carnage begun in their absence. The sky rumbled, threatening rain, the air acrid and thick with magic.

"Yet again you and your family pervert all that is proper in this world," Cyth shouted. His sword trembled in his hand, so great was his fury. "When her eyes were to open to our realm, it was to see a kingdom shining as a beacon to her teachings. It was to see all her wisdom made manifest in a land of order and balance. She need not know the birthing pains. She need not see the blood that must be--"

Lightning tore through Cyth, interrupting his tirade. His feet lifted off the ground, and his mouth opened in a silent scream his lungs could not voice. His every muscle locked tight for the duration of the flash, and when it disappeared he collapsed. To

Harruq's shock he still lived, though the front of his vest was blackened and ripped, revealing a vicious burn mark across the elf's chest.

"Cyth!" Vala shouted. The elf batted aside her offered help and pushed up to his knees. He glared at the sky, and the elven goddess wreaking vengeance through Aurelia's hands.

"You've made a mess of everything," Vala said, turning away from her brother to glare at Harruq. Her weapons twirled in shaking fingers. "But at least now I have the privilege of murdering the supposed Godslayer."

"You're hardly the first to try," Harruq said. He slammed his sister swords together, and the blades sang. "And you'll die like all the others." He dared not look away, and so he shouted to be heard. "Tarlak? Protect Gregory and Aubby. I've got her."

"If you insist," the wizard shouted back.

Harruq immediately felt better. Normally he would trust Aurelia to keep the children's safety above all others, but she was clearly not herself. The goddess flowed through her, unleashing her rage, and Harruq trusted that entity not a wit.

"Your children are not safe," Vala said, lowering into a crouch. "And once you and the wizard are dead, I will open their throats in an offering to our stubborn, foolish goddess."

Harruq grinned despite the fury surging with fresh flame within his breast. "You should really stop threatening my daughter."

Whatever battle she expected to have, Harruq did not give it to her. His sister swords slammed into her again and again, relentless in their assault, merciless in their power. Her arms quaked, her muscles strained by every block and parry that required tremendous effort to veer aside his aim. Her speed was not enough. Harruq was just as fast. Just as vicious. His fury flowed through him like fuel upon a roaring inferno. Salvation swept aside her dual thrust, freeing up a swipe from Condemnation that gashed her side and spilled blood across her hip and leg.

"I've fought elves," he screamed at her. "I've fought demons."

Her attempted spin toward his side ended when Salvation's hilt smashed into her face, breaking her nose and splattering blood in a spray across her mouth and chin.

"I've fought angels."

No dance, no interplay. His weapons battered her, broke her, showed her how small and insignificant she was against the fullness of his rage. Harruq saw her every move before she made it. He guided her swords about as if they were his own. Nothing would stop him. With every swing he made, he felt like he could shatter the world.

"I've fought fucking *gods*."

Salvation plunged into her chest. Blood spilled across the wood, adding to the tremendous stain already underneath the cut nooses. Harruq shifted the angle so the blade hooked her ribs and then pulled her closer so she was equally impaled upon Condemnation. Her jaw dropped open, her dying words robbed by the steel puncturing her lungs.

"You should have killed me in that prison cell," he said, then ripped his weapons free and watched her body drop limp in death.

Cyth screamed. There were no words, but Harruq understood it nonetheless, for it was a scream he had both heard and made countless times throughout his life. Unchecked trauma. Fury and grief, spun together into an inseparable thread. Hate. Sorrow. The elf clutched at the wicked burn upon his chest while tears trickled down his face.

And then he fled. Harruq did not move to chase. He had not the energy left in him. Instead he looked to Aurelia, lowering from the sky. The light had left her eyes. The goddess was gone, and his beloved wife returned to him. He caught her and held her close as the battle winded down to its end. Aubrienna rushed to join them, squeezing her arms around each of them in an embrace as she wept.

"It's all right," Harruq said, glancing over his shoulder. Bodies burned and bled, many charred by lightning or crushed by ice. Omar's forces swept through the remainder of the Keenan mercenaries, who by and large flung down their weapons in surrender. What elves remained had long fled from Celestia's fury.

"It's not!" Aubrienna shouted, still overwhelmed by the horrors surrounding the platform. Her eyes squeezed tightly shut, and Harruq wished there was not so much blood on him. He sheathed his swords, knelt down, and wrapped his arms around her.

"It will be," he said softly, kissing the top of her head. The stink of corpses wafted along a sudden breeze that dissipated the dark clouds that covering the sky. Faint daylight pierced through.

"It will be, I promise."

35
ERIN

Erin followed Cyth like a shadow, every bit of her mother's training guiding her along. She moved with her back low and her cloaks disguising much of her body. At all times she was aware of the nearest place to hide should Cyth check if he were being followed. She kept to a safe distance, ensuring he was always in sight while she remained a distant figure.

Where does the rat flee? she thought as the chaos of the failed execution drifted farther and farther behind them. Cyth had pulled a hood over his head, no doubt to hide his ears, and his sprint turned to a hurried walk to stop drawing attention to himself. Erin fell even further behind, and multiple times she caught him looking over his shoulder. Erin was ready each time, her face hidden, her body flat and still. Her heart raced, but he never seemed to see her.

At last they arrived at a massive, ugly building used by porters to store wagons. Cyth unlocked the smaller side door with a key, gave one last look around, and then entered. The moment he was inside Erin broke out into a full sprint. When she reached the shut door she put her ear to it, listening for conversation while testing the handle.

Unlocked. His haste was too great, it overrode his caution.

Erin slowly pushed it open and crept inside. Within were two elves, Cyth and another she did not recognize. That unknown elf was near her, standing with his back to the door and his arms crossed over his chest. A sword hung from a belt tied loosely at his hip. The entire expanse was empty, cleared out at some point so the sizable interior was nothing but dust-covered floorboards.

In the center of that open space, tied to one of the building's support beams and with his mouth gagged, sat her father. Cyth stood over him, sword held in a trembling hand. Thren stared back with amusement sparkling in his icy blue eyes. Though the two elves spoke in their own language, it seemed Thren understood enough to know some scheme of Cyth's had gone terribly wrong.

"This changes nothing of your own fate," Cyth said,

switching to the human tongue. He pointed his sword at Thren. "I will know my uncle's thoughts and secrets, every whim, every bit of wisdom that he taught you. I have all your lifetime to spend, Thren, and no matter how great your pride, or how stubborn you believe yourself to be, even you will crack against decades of torture."

The tip of his sword pressed to Thren's neck as Erin crept toward the other elf, who watched the exchange in silence.

"Or perhaps I should cut your throat and be done with all of this? The Sun is in ruins, and my Vala…"

He hesitated, and amid that hesitation, Erin leaped onto the back of the other elf, her saber reaching around to press against his throat. One cut, and blood gushed across the floorboards. The elf dropped, Erin's weight slamming atop his back. She bounced to her feet as Cyth spun, his eyes narrowing.

"Zusa's brat?" he asked, baffled.

Erin crossed her sabers into an 'x', leaning so her hood fell low over her face. She told herself she wasn't Erin. She was something else. Someone that a skilled foe like Cyth must still fear.

"I'm here for him," she said, nodding toward her grandfather.

Cyth held his sword in both hands, his knees bending as he settled into a dueling stance. Hunger entered his eyes, one born of hurt and desperation.

"I've lost so much this day," he said. "I will enjoy this."

He leaped across the space, leading with a powerful overhead chop that Erin didn't dare try to block. Cyth was certainly no Harruq, but he was still stronger than her. Such direct clashes would never work in her favor. Instead she slid sideways, her left hand already positioned to strike her foe's sword as it attempted to continue its momentum in chase. Her other hand slashed, but he shifted as well, ensuring she struck only air.

When she pulled back from the attack he withdrew his sword, repositioned its angle, and then thrust straight for her heart. Erin dropped to one knee, both blades rising to shove the thrust overhead. Instinct took over, built by years of practicing with Zusa and then honed by the weeks spent with Harruq and Thren. She closed the space between them instead of retreating, their three weapons entangled in a dizzying flash of steel.

Back and forth Cyth's sword swept, trapped between her

two. Their movements synchronized, an exchange of skill, but she dared not believe she might succeed. On the fourth exchange she spun underneath another aggressive thrust, smacked the weapon aside, and then planted her feet. Cyth's positioning was wrong, exposing an opening to his side. At least it seemed like an opening, but his movements were so fast, so controlled, she did not trust it.

Erin spun away from him, having no intention of taking advantage of that opening, real or false. Instead she spun around the support beam, slashing twice at the ropes binding Thren's hands.

"No!" Cyth shouted, lunging with his stance recovered. Erin placed herself in the way, gritting her teeth and holding back a panicked cry. The elf assaulted her with renewed aggression, trying to break through her to get to Thren. It seemed her every block was a hair's width away from too slow, but she endured three quick chops, parried away a thrust, and then danced away from a killing slash. By then Thren had yanked the ropes from his ankles and then tumbled past the both of them. She retreated two steps and settled back into the same stance. The glower on her face could melt glass an unsteady sprint. His aim was the elf Erin had killed, and the sword still buckled to his waist.

"Much better," Thren said, holding the comforting steel in his hand as he turned about. "Care for a rematch, Bloodhand? We can make this a family affair."

"You are in no state for a true battle," Cyth said, slowly pacing between the two of them like a cornered animal.

"Perhaps not,' Thren said. "But I am not alone."

Cyth feinted an attack against him, then thrust at Erin instead. She nearly died then and there, fully expecting an attempt to bring Thren down in the opening moments. She stumbled backward, her sabers flashing, the ringing of steel a relief as she managed to barely shove the attack aside.

The relief did not last long. Cyth pressed her, his sword weaving with such fluidity it felt like the swaying of a serpent rather than a piece of metal. Thren lurked behind Cyth, clearly hampered by the punishment he had suffered during his capture. Several times he struck for an exposed back or rib, and always when Erin's defenses were about to crumble against a sudden barrage.

Despite his aid, panic scraped at the edges of Erin's mind.

Fear clutched at her chest, making it hard to breathe. Cyth was too fast, too strong. He kept reading her maneuvers, and if not for her grandfather's interference she'd already be dead. It was a losing battle, a losing...

"Listen to me," Thren said, his firm voice. He clutched his sword in both hands as they flanked the confident elf. He'd struck twice at Cyth, forcing him to defend and therefore earning Erin a reprieve. "Dance, Erin. Embrace your legacy, and dance."

Erin's throat felt too tight, and when she swallowed it was dry as sand. He wished for her to cloak dance, as she had in the tournament? He had mocked her efforts then, deriding her as a child at play. But there was no arguing with him, no debating, and so she had but on recourse. She would trust him.

"You heard him," Erin told Cyth, leaning forward so her cloaks flowed over her body to hide her arms. "Shall we dance, elf?"

Cyth smirked. "I have use for Muzien's heir, but you? I shall enjoy sending your head to the Gemcroft estate."

"You want my head, Bloodhand?" Erin bounced on her toes, building momentum, building the frailest of confidence. "Come take it."

The moment she saw him move, she spun in place, her cloaks whirling about her, their fabric light and split to perfectly follow her movements while keeping her arms free. She pirouetted on one foot, her left hand parrying Cyth's thrust up and over her head, and then she was sliding to the left. His second attack came slashing down, hitting only air. Her spin continued, every shred of her concentration on the balance of her limbs and the continued movements of her body.

Again he cut, and again she blocked. This time she retaliated, a momentary break in the spinning to offer an offhand thrust toward his waist. He was faster, though, and twisted out of the way. He attempted his own retaliation, but then Thren was there, hacking at him from the rear. Cyth sensed it, as if the elf had eyes in the back of his head, and he batted away the chop and then assaulted Thren with a sudden, savage fury of slashes. Thren retreated after each one.

"Erin!" he shouted, urging her on, and so she did, leaping at Cyth to force his attention back to her. The moment he did, his sword easily blocking her thrust, she spun again, diving back into the cloak dance. She felt her comfort growing, felt the cloaks becoming part of her as she ducked underneath a beheading chop and then came up swinging, the angle of her swords hidden by the movements of her cloaks. He blocked, but only just. The need for speed pushed her to her absolute limits. At one point she stumbled, and Thren physically forced himself between her and Cyth, bearing the brunt of his sudden assault.

Blood spotted the floorboards, little cuts across her grandfather's arms, but he endured so she might continue. Each cut was a failure on her part, and it only heightened her resolve to do better, hit stronger, and refuse to ever relent against a foe so much greater than her.

And so the battle stretched on, always in that mold. Erin danced, fluid in her movements, speed and deception her greatest weapon. She was far from perfect, but any time she faltered, or Cyth correctly anticipated an attack, Thren was there to parry aside the attack or force him to turn about to protect his flank at the last moment. Every passing second, she felt more comfortable amid the deadly exchange. Every twist, every curl, and she better understood what was happening.

It did not matter whether or not she was perfect. It did not matter that Cyth was unfamiliar with the cloak dance, for Thren *was* familiar with it. He knew it, perhaps even better than she did. He read her movements. He anticipated her reactions. Whatever her failures, he was there to protect her. Whatever strengths of the deception, he knew how to accompany with a thrust of his own. He never led the assault. He let Erin dance, and so she danced, and cut, and swung, until Cyth was hard pressed against the heightened assault between them. Faster and faster she moved, urging herself on, trusting her grandfather to be exactly where she needed him to be.

"Enough!" Cyth screamed, beyond frustrated. She could sense the harshening of his movements, their fluidity replaced with quick, choppy attacks. He kept trying to overwhelm her, but to do so meant fully devoting his attention on Erin, and Thren simply would not let him. And any time he tried to attack Thren, Erin would be there, stabbing and slashing, denying him the slightest reprieve. Together they wore him out. Together they pushed him to his breaking point.

"I am the Heir of Muzien," he continued, leaping back and forth between them, his swords a blur of steel, his assault akin to a rabid animal backed into a corner. "I am the Darkhand reborn. The Sun rises, it rises, and I shall wear its crown!"

Erin stumbled, her spin halting as one of his strikes was so strong her block broke her momentum. Her eyes widened, fearing the counter thrusting for her exposed abdomen, its speed too great for her to avoid. Her, but not Thren, who shoved her aside, positioning himself in the way. Steel clashed against steel, and for that single exchange, Erin watched, eyes wide, heart hammering. Thren and Cyth locked into their own dance, swords weaving and colliding, each wielded with a willpower strong enough to shatter mountains.

She more sensed than saw it. Thren was the tiniest bit slower. His feet slid backward, constantly needing to reposition against the savagery of his foe. Erin sprinted aside, her legs pumping and her body crouched low. Cyth's attention was completely taken. One good flank. One good assault...

Erin's feet twisted like a dancer's as she vaulted into the air. Her entire body spun, gaining momentum, gaining strength as she flew toward Cyth's flank. Their own battle reached its zenith, Cyth's sword plunging into Thren's leg just above the knee. Thren screamed. Cyth cried victory, sword ripping free and shifting the angle for a killing blow.

And then her sabers slashed across Cyth's back, tearing through cloth and opening flesh. Cyth screamed, and then they collided, her shoulder striking him with all her momentum. His killing thrust missed her grandfather. They both rolled along the ground, him rising faster. Erin bounced to her feet, her sabers eager. Cyth glared at her, his face a portrait of pain. It only fed her vicious glee.

"Our dance isn't over," she said, and clanged her sabers together.

Cyth fled.

"Hey!" she shouted, sprinting in his shadow. The floorboards clattered beneath their feet. Cyth paused at the door, pivoting on his heels to face her. She thought him changing his mind, willing to battle her without the aid of her grandfather, but the sick amusement in his eyes robbed her of that delusion. In one smooth motion, he drew a slender dagger from his belt, held it by the blade, and then lifted it overhead.

"Fool," he said, and threw the dagger. Not at her. Far past her, and to the side. Toward Thren, down on one knee, clutching at his wound.

Erin had but a split-second to decide. Thren was hobbled, his attention stolen. Cyth's path to the exit was clear. The knife sailed through the air, its path true. One choice, and she moved instantly, decision made before ever realizing.

She vaulted backward, her right arm extending to its fullest so she would have the necessary reach. There was no room to doubt, only trust herself as she swung. Her reward was the sound of steel hitting steel as her saber struck the dagger turning end over end on its path toward her grandfather. She had but a heartbeat to grin in satisfaction before she landed awkwardly on her stomach, the impact stealing away her breath and bruising her knees and the elbow of her outstretched arm.

Erin rolled over, forcing her body to draw in air against its own will. From the ground, she glanced at the door, but as expected, Cyth was gone.

Coward, she thought, but what else had she expected? He had fled when his execution ceremony was broken instead of dying with his fellow elves in battle. Erin pushed to her feet, smoothed out her cloaks, and then turned to check on her grandfather.

Thren stood in the center of the porter's warehouse, his head bowed and his back bent. Blood trickled down his arms and chest, gathering with the far greater pool on the floorboards beneath his wounded leg. His shoulders lifted and sagged with his every exhausted breath. The tip of his sword rested against the floor, as if he lacked the strength to hold it aloft. His hood hid much of him, but from what she saw of his face, he was grinning.

"The Heir of Muzien," he said, and leaned back to laugh. "Fuck your heir, Darkhand. I have mine, and she is so much greater than you ever dreamed."

Erin sheathed her sabers and she stood there, unsure. Warmth spread through her, along with relief. Her grandfather, meanwhile, finally composed himself. He yanked his hood back and beamed a smile so joyful it bordered in mania.

"You should have killed him and let me die," he said.

"But I didn't," she said, her voice raw, and then shrugged. "I'm glad I didn't."

Thren tossed his weapon to the blood-soaked floorboards. He closed his eyes and wavered on unsteady legs.

"And so you prove yourself so much more like your father than myself." He opened his eyes. They shone with sapphire light. "For that, I am glad."

36
CYTH

Cyth staggered down the street, clutching his back in a futile attempt to stop the bleeding. Worse, though, were the wounds in his mind.

You can still save this, he thought as he shoved aside an elderly woman too slow and confused to move out of his way. *You can still live up to Muzien's legacy.*

The words felt hollow, and they offered him little comfort as he saw a small group of armed men and women up ahead. Scouring the city for elves, no doubt. He cut to his right, sprinting through a slender alley that ended before a tight cluster of shops. All of them looked shuttered, and he wondered if the owners had fled the city after he captured it.

Whatever the reason, he would accept the good fortune. Cyth chose the nearest shop, checked the door with his free hand, and found it locked. A few quick hits with his sword hilt broke open the window and he tumbled inside, enduring the scrapes of broken glass on his skin.

He lay on his stomach on the creaking wood floor, his gaze unfocused and seeing nothing. A cavalcade of his failures flooded over him, each one squirming and biting inside his chest.

Thren's survival. Harruq's escape. The failed executions. Vala...

"I'm sorry," he whispered, covering his face with his arm. His sister's beloved face hovered in his mind, cruelly twisted into her final cry of pain when the half-orc brute murdered her. "I should have done better. I should have saved you. You...you should..."

He slammed the back of his head against the floorboards. Damn it all, she should be here with him! These humans, these wretched humans, would forever scrape and claw for all that should not be theirs, and the costs, goddess save him, the costs...

"I'll make them pay," he whispered. "I'll make all of them pay. Every second of my life will be dedicated to retribution. I can.

I will."

Tears slid down his face. He wished, so desperately, that Vala's face would be one of beauty in his memories.

"Alone, Muzien built his empire," he said, swearing a vow in his heart. "I will do the same if I must."

He sat up and lifted his arm to check the burn wound on his chest. It ached, but would not be fatal. As for his back, the cut did not seem as deep as he first feared, at least from what he could tell. The torn muscles would heal in time. Once they did, and he could wield his sword, he would begin anew. Allies. He would need human allies again, and a new tact to win them over. Perhaps he should start as Muzien did, in illicit trade. There were always weeds, mushrooms, and tonics the humans banned or embargoed for fear of their effects. If he could claim one, and amass wealth to wield as yet another weapon, he need only be ruthless and patient in equal measure.

Cyth pushed to his feet and pulled off his shirt so he could tie it as a lengthy bandage wrapping both his chest and back. As much as it stung his pride, he found his hope rebuilding. His long lifespan would give him perspective the humans could not match. They would think him beaten. They would believe the threat past. Never would they suspect that he lurked in waiting, to target not just their children, but their children's children.

If not for Vala's death, he might have even smiled and embraced the challenge.

"I'm sorry, sister," he said, and wiped the tears from his eyes. "But I will avenge you, I swear it. I swear..."

A blue portal ripped open in the air before him, and a familiar elf stepped through.

"Going somewhere?" Aurelia Thyne asked, ice building across her fingers.

Cyth turned to flee, but he was far too slow. Icicles slammed into his back like lances, puncturing his flesh. His run turned to a stagger, and then electricity swirled through his body, locking his each and every muscle tight. His vision flashed white, and he fought to breathe, but could not. He could only endure the long painful seconds as the elven sorceress lashed him with the power arcing from her palm.

The lightning ended and he dropped to his knees, gasping

for air. Behind him, he heard the heavy thud of Aurelia's boots.

"You never protected yourself from scrying," she said. "You never needed to, did you? Not when you were a mystery. Not when you were the unknown Bloodhand."

He drew a knife from his boot and spun on her, but she was faster. A wave of her hand, and an invisible shockwave of pure force blasted him onto his back. The knife scattered from his grip, and he screamed at the pain from his chest, his crusted burns ripping open. Fresh blood flowed out of him.

"But I know your name, now, Cyth. I know your face. You cannot hide from me."

A second blast of lightning connected with his stomach, and he writhed and twisted until it ceased. His vision momentarily blanked. As the pain subsided, he looked up from where he lay and audibly gasped.

Aurelia Thyne stood over him, fire bursting about her hands. Her hair fluttered in an unfelt wind. Her eyes blazed with magical light. It was like looking upon the visage of Celestia in all her power and wrath. An impulse to beg filled him, but he never had a chance to speak the words.

"You hurt my family," she said, her voice colder than the winds of the far north. "Be glad for the kindness of my heart, for I will spare you the suffering you deserve. Instead, accept the gift of a swift death."

The fire exploded from her palms. Its light was blinding, that which his eyes saw in the brief moment before the fire melted them away. Intense heat followed, so searing all his flesh felt aflame and his mind struggled to even comprehend the ensuing pain. His scream was pitiful, his lungs choked with the char of his own body.

As the fire washed over him, growing in intensity, he heard the elf's words pierce the din, the final moments before darkness took him away.

"Become ash, Cyth Ordoth. Become forgotten, and may Celestia show you mercy when your soul enters her hands."

37
ZUSA

The guards never let them out of sight, a fact that might have amused Zusa once, but instead she endured their presence as she spoke with Queen Brynn in the garden of her royal mansion. They walked among blooming pink hibiscus flowers and red azaleas, bathed in the pleasant warble of water flowing from a fountain into a nearby pond, its bricks carefully arranged to form a hawk.

"Has there been any word from Stonewood?" Zusa asked.

"A messenger arrived late in the night," Brynn said. "A fact I suspect you are already aware of."

Zusa shrugged. It was true. "I grew inattentive in my older years. I aim to rectify that."

The queen smiled as she led the pair toward a stone arch fully wrapped in green vines that sprouted pale yellow blooms. The woman walked with a slight limp, an injury suffered during the chaotic rescue from the hangings. Zusa masked her own injuries with her thick dress, but a careful observer would note the bulges in the fabric across her arms and back from the many bandages.

"The same sin falls upon me, Lady Gemcroft. I thought my harshest battles would be fought claiming this throne after Loreina's death. Never did I think, when celebrating a future peace, I would experience the cruelest betrayals and bloodshed."

"And yet, so very much true to the fate of Dezrel."

"Indeed," the queen said, and grimaced.

They passed underneath the archway, meandering along a path of smooth stones looping through rows of crimson irises. Zusa had requested this meeting with Brynn, yet so far the queen had patiently waited to hear the reason, instead treating the day like a relaxing social call amongst the flowers.

"There is the matter of the Keenan estate assets," Zusa said, forcing the matter.

"Assets claimed by the crown, given her traitorous actions and her lack of an heir," Brynn said. "I was unaware there was much to discuss."

"In Neldar, members of the Trifect often bequeathed their wealth to their fellows if matters of heirs were uncertain."

"We're not in Neldar, are we?" the queen said with a harsh edge entering her voice. Zusa pretended not to notice, and instead bent down to smell an iris.

"No, we are not," she said, closing her eyes. "But given the role my daughter played in saving your reign, and your life, they might have been considered a fine reward. But let us not bicker on what is already decided. If you would keep them, then I would ask you to consider a new proposal." Zusa stole a glance over her shoulder. Queen Brynn was not even trying to hide her wariness.

"Speak it," the queen said. "I am listening."

After one last brush of the flower across her nose and lips, Zusa stood, hiding a wince from the pain it caused by a bandaged cut across her thigh. "Trade between here and Angelport is only starting to flourish," she said. "And much of the land across the Ramere is currently without owners. Whispers have long insisted that Ker shall lay claim to what was once the nation of Omn. Is that true?"

Brynn crossed her arms. "It is. Between boats sailing to Angelport, and our people slowly returning east across the delta, those claims are inevitable. Omn is lost, and Angelport is best within my control."

All was as Zusa expected.

"You will need supplies to rebuild the towns, especially those first few crossings over the rivers," she said, resuming their walk through the irises. "And it would be useful for you to have a firm voice speaking in your favor to the survivors of Nahorash's cruelty. Much of Angelport still belongs to my estate, as do what lands we reclaimed after the war demon's death."

Zusa paused to lock eyes with the queen. "You need me. Let us be partners in this expansion. Your reign will grow, and with it my wealth and prosperity. Keep the Keenan trade routes, merchants, and craftsmen, if you wish. I have no desire to make an empire in Ker. My eye has always been on the abandoned east."

Queen Brynn remained silent for an overly long time. Zusa refused to back down, and as the silence stretched it only hardened her resolve.

"You're a woman used to getting what you desire, aren't you, Zusa?" Brynn asked, finally breaking the quiet.

"I merely walk in the footsteps of my wife."

At that, the queen laughed. "I am sure there will be finer details to quibble over, but know that we are in agreement in the grander picture. With Mordan still licking its wounds, we are in a prime position to expand, and you would be a most helpful ally. I shall have one of my advisers meet with you to confirm these points."

"Not I," Zusa said. Their circular path had taken them back to the entrance of the garden. Nathaniel stood waiting, prim and proper in his suit. A smile was on his face as he laughed and joked with one of the soldiers assigned to keep watch. "Nathaniel will be assuming control of most of our estate's day to day operations. When it comes to discussing these new arrangements, your advisers shall be planning them with him."

The queen crossed her arms behind her back and joined Zusa in observing Nathaniel. He was so young and lively, and so fully at ease joking with a man he just met that it was hard to remember when he had been a shy boy more content to read in Alyssa's mansion.

"Does this mean you are retiring so he may take charge?" Brynn asked.

Zusa's heart swelled pride. Between Erin and Nathaniel, she held no doubt the future of the Gemcroft family was in good hands.

"It means I will go back to doing what I do best," Zusa said, and smiled as her fingers brushed the firm weight of a dagger hidden within the folds of her dress. "Watching from the shadows."

38

THREN

Thren limped about his little abode, finding it hard to leave. "It must be done," he told the empty room. He could not stay. Staying was wrong, and so he had gathered what he needed into a single rucksack and strapped it to his back. All that mattered now was picking a destination beyond Angkar. So far, he had none. Perhaps a small village somewhere, a place where his gold would carry far while he learned anew how to make a home.

Thren exited and walked the quiet streets of the capital. The day was young, the sun barely peeking above the walls of the city. Perhaps he imagined it, but he smelled blood on the wind, and not from the fishermen already out on the waters beginning the day's catch. Yesterday's battle against the elves and Tori's mercenaries would leave their scar, just as Veldaren had endured the remnants of her own invasions and plots.

And then the city would heal, and thrive, as most cities did, for they were the strength of their people. Those here in Angkar were strong, and would remain so with a woman like Brynn to lead them.

Two guards stood bored at the north entrance of the city, giving cursory glances over anyone coming and going. They mostly just yanked down any lifted hoods to inspect ears, in case any elves remained within Angkar and sought to escape. Thren endured their scrutiny and then passed through the gate to the sprawling openness beyond. He looked upon the grass lit by the rising sun and reminded himself for the twentieth time this was proper.

"Where are you going?"

Thren flinched, a reflex born from the weakness of old age. He should be able to control himself better. Slowly he glanced over his shoulder, only half-surprised to see Erin leaning against the brick of the outside wall, dressed in clothing painfully similar to Aaron's attire as the Watcher. Her arms were crossed and her grin amused, but he sensed the nervousness within her.

"Out," he said, and began walking.

Erin pushed off the wall and jogged to catch up with him.

"I knew you'd do this," she said as they walked the road.

"Did you, now?"

"Yes I did, even if I don't understand *why*, only that you would."

Thren stared straight ahead, refusing to glance her way. The city slowly shrank behind them, granting them privacy on the well-worn road north.

"My decisions are my own, child, and I will not have them questioned."

Erin sprinted a few steps ahead and then planted herself in his path. Her hands clenched, and she set her jaw as she glared. "No. I'm not letting you get away with this so easily. You're my grandfather. Why are you leaving me? Why, when you promised to train me?"

Thren stopped, wishing his heart hadn't stung so much hearing the word 'grandfather'.

"Between the half-orc, myself, and your mother, I think you've had all the training in the world one might need," he said, and pushed on past her. To his shock she drew a saber and whirled on him. His instincts took over, his left hand drawing a dagger and blocking amid a sudden flourish of his cloak. Their weapons locked, the briefest struggle before she yanked her saber away and jammed it back into its sheath.

"That's not an answer," she said. "No one is making you leave, yet you are anyway. Why? Tell me why, so I can at least hear it from your own lips and don't have to wonder."

"I have made my decision," he said, resuming his walk. "If you must hear a reason, know that decision is the one I view best."

"But for who?" she snapped. "For once, couldn't you think of someone other than yourself? For once, couldn't you do what's right?"

Thren froze. He fought down his initial anger and instead allowed his heart to be naked. It was a vulnerability he had not shown since his days married to Marion, but he would give his granddaughter this, if only so she might understand.

"I know who I am," he said. "I know *what* I am. What stories you know are but scraps of the sins I have committed. My hands are soaked in blood, and no amount of atoning will ever wash them clean. There is no changing this. There is no redeeming this. And it is that stubbornness, that immutable nature of mine, that led to my defeat at the hands of my son."

He reached out to gently place calloused fingers upon her young cheek.

"For once, Erin, I *am* thinking of someone else. I am leaving, because it is the right thing to do. There is strength within you, and a light that blinds. But there is also darkness, and a will to be greater than you are. I will not feed it with my presence. I will not tip the scales to the values that led to my breaking, and the Watcher's reverence. I would see you walk a better path. I would see you follow in my son's footsteps…but I cannot walk that path alongside you. It is not within me."

Thren removed his hand, and he felt a tear drip upon his finger. Erin had started to cry. She held herself together well, the sorrow not reaching her voice.

"I thought you were strong," she said. "I thought you were the strongest there was, the fearless, the one man no one could break."

Thren's pride stirred. "I was, once."

"Then why are you so afraid now?" Erin's earnestness threatened his resolve as she pleaded. "If you fear nothing, then why do you fear this? Is change truly so impossible? Why do you look at yourself and see the one foe you cannot defeat?"

"And what would you have me become instead, little one?"

She shrugged. "I don't know. A different man. A better one."

"It is not that easy."

Her sorrow turned to a tired smirk. "Nothing worthwhile in this life is easy."

Thren looked away from her, his head tilting back and his gaze upon the sky. This…this wasn't possible, was it? He knew his place in the world. He knew the role he played within it, the culmination of his beliefs and deeds over a lifetime.

"Erin," he said, his voice falling to a whisper. "I cherish you above all else, and yes, I am afraid. I am afraid I will fail again. I am afraid I will lose you, as I lost Aaron. This is the safer path. The better path. What you ask of me…"

"No." She closed the distance between them, and this time

it was her hands on his face. She held him captive with her deep brown eyes. "No grand speeches. No pronouncements. Stay, Thren. Stay, and become someone new."

"Someone new," he said, folding his hands over hers.

"I don't know who," she said. "But maybe it could be someone your son would be proud of? Someone your granddaughter would be happy to still have in her life?"

Thren lowered her hands, and he held them before her. A strange chill swept through him, the fear of an unknown he had never once contemplated. For so long the brutality and ruthlessness he imparted upon Aaron had been necessary to thrive in the cruel world of Dezrel. Aaron's heroics as the Watcher had only confirmed that in Thren's mind, regardless of his son's protestations.

But what if?

What if?

"So be it," he said, and began walking alongside Erin back toward Angkar. Toward home.

"For you, I will try."

Epilogue
HARRUQ

The year 613 IA

Aurelia held Harruq's hand, clutching it tightly as the noise of the crowd grew louder and more eager outside the carriage.

"You ready for this?" she asked.

Harruq squeezed back.

"As I'll ever be."

Together, the pair exited onto a crimson carpet running through a crowd of staggering size. Thousands of people were gathered on both sides of the street, as well as crammed onto the rooftops so that barely a shingle was visible. Up ahead was a cleared platform, wreathed with flowers and atop which stood a marble statue of Ashhur. The god wore no armor, and he wielded no sword. A god of peace, as Dezrel now needed.

Harruq and Aurelia walked the carpet, each dressed in their finest. She wore a brilliant green dress set with so many tiny emeralds the fabric sparkled and shone with her every movement. Her hair was tightly wound into dozens of interlocking braids, tied behind her head, and then wrapped with silver threads. Harruq felt plain beside her, his outfit an absurdly expensive suit that his wife insisted was currently in fashion. It was all black but for a bit of green where the undershirt was visible. No swords, no armor. Like Ashhur, the Godslayer came only for celebration.

As they walked, he caught sight of a familiar paladin along the rope-lines. Jessilynn stood wearing a plain but finely sewn blue dress, flanked by a dozen young men and women. The Orphans of Ashhur, they were called, a new school of paladins she had opened in Mordeina. Their eyes met, and she winked at him. He smiled, happy to see her in attendance.

He wasn't quite as happy to see another face lurking from the rooftops above her, his dark hair and face wreathed in ash. Deathmask had fully established control of all the guilds of Mordan, though they were a far cry from what they had been in Neldar.

They exist to keep the wealthy and noble in check, Deathmask had insisted once during a rare visit to the castle. *They exist to ensure the littlest among us are not forgotten and abandoned. Leave me and Veliana to our work. If you do not forget your roots, half-orc, then you need not fear our presence.*

Harruq pushed the thoughts aside, for there was no room for them as he climbed the platform.

"What a fine couple," Jerico said, waiting for them atop the stairs. His long red hair was tied behind his head in a knot, his beard freshly combed and oiled. He wore a suit akin to Harruq's. As requested, all armor and weaponry had been left behind. "All will speak of the elven beauty tomorrow, for certain."

"Today is not for me," Aurelia said, and she winked. "But I appreciate the flattery nonetheless, Jerico."

Harruq and Aurelia took their place on the left of the platform. He took his wife's hand, a comforting presence needed to calm his shaky nerves as he stood there, visible to all the people of Mordeina.

"This is insane," he muttered, shocked by the sheer number of people in attendance. Every roof was covered, every nearby street, full. Men held their children on their shoulders so they could see over the throng. Soldiers lined the ropes stretched to form crowd-guides, stern and necessary to hold back the teeming masses.

"Everyone's excited," Aurelia whispered. "Enjoy it."

The next carriage arrived. Various lords and ladies of Mordan, come to pay their respects. Far more interesting, and earning a much more visceral, excited reaction from the crowd, was the carriage that brought Ambassador Moonfang. The wolf-man needed to bend into a low crouch to even fit into a carriage never built with someone like him in mind. He emerged and stood tall, his fur carefully brushed and cleaned with oils. He was the appointed representative of the Freedlands, the small nation of beast-men in the far north of former Mordan, given sovereign rule in the wake of Tessanna's sacrifice.

"Looking fine, Moonfang," Harruq said as the wolf-man walked past him to take his appointed spot.

"I stink of flowers," Moonfang muttered, earning a laugh from several atop the platform.

Legacy of the Watcher

    The eagerness of the crowd swelled, a continuous thrum of shifting, muttering, and whispers. The final carriage had arrived. The doors opened, and Harruq's heart swelled in his breast with a love he could hardly believe himself capable of feeling.

    His Aubrienna, his wonderful, precious Aubrienna, exited in a stunning white dress. Diamonds sparkled around the neckline. Lace swirled around her arms and waist. Her face was subtly painted, her hair done up in a similar manner to her mother's, only it also bore a veil. That veil was positioned so that it did not cover the sharp point of her ears. Her lovely eyes sparkled as she looked upon her fiancée, Prince Gregory, now a grown man in his own right. He offered her the crook of his arm, and she took it as the pair walked the carpeted aisle between a crowd that cheered and clapped with an energy that left Harruq weak in the knees.

    "I can't believe it," he said as Aurelia leaned against him. Somehow he was crying. He didn't know when he started. "That's our girl. That's our little girl."

    Aurelia kissed his cheek and gently wiped a few of his tears away. "Our little girl, now and forever. But to the people of Dezrel, she will be their queen, and I pray they love her as much as we do."

    The royal couple climbed the stairs, with Gregory purposefully bringing Aurelia to her parents. The young man vibrated with nervous energy while Aubrienna looked ready to explode from happiness.

    "Hey," Harruq said to her, at a loss for any other words.

    "Well?" Aubrienna asked as the soldiers did their best to quiet the deafening crowd so Jerico could officially begin the ceremony. "How do I look?"

    Harruq laughed, unable to believe the absurdities of fate that led to him standing there, here and now, about to give away a daughter to become queen. He stared at his precious Aubrienna, so alive, so wondrous, so deserving of all the world, and he smiled the widest he'd ever smiled.

    "You look like the world to me," he said. Fine outfits and tradition be damned, he wrapped her in his arms. "I'm so happy for you, Aubby."

    Such a simple statement. It came nowhere close to conveying the depths of it all, but what else might he say? What else mattered there at that moment? So he said it again, let it lift his spirits and break the stress and fears of the day.

"I'm so happy. I'm so unbelievably gods-damned happy."

Second Epilogue
HARRUQ

The year 616 LA

Harruq paced, his fingers twitching and his chest constricted with what felt like a thousand iron chains. Tarlak sat on a nearby padded chair, idly flipping through a leather-wrapped book he'd purchased earlier that day.

"It hasn't been too long, has it?" Harruq asked.

Tarlak turned a page. The pair were in the small servant's room connected to the royal bedroom within Mordeina's castle. The wizard shrugged without looking up.

"You're just as nervous as you always were. It's almost adorable."

Harruq swallowed down his retort. His fingers twitched, and he absurdly wished for his swords. Anything to give him comfort, or at least something to do.

"It's just hard to--"

The connecting door opened, and Aurelia paused in the middle of the doorway, radiant as ever. Pure joy sparkled in her eyes.

"I was right," she said, and stepped out of the way so Gregory could enter. The fine young man looked more tired than the Abyss, with deep circles around his eyes. Despite his exhaustion, his smile was ear to ear as he held the newborn child in his arms.

"So it's a boy?" Harruq asked as Tarlak hurried to his feet, but only after pausing to place a bookmark to keep his page. Aurelia had insisted their granddaughter would be a boy, whereas Harruq had been convinced a tradition of daughters would continue in the Tun family line.

"A healthy, chubby baby boy," Gregory said, and he laughed. "I should cover Aubby in jewelry for carrying him for nine whole months."

Relief swept through Harruq. The dangerous part was over. He grinned down at the pink face wrapped in stark white cloth. His nose was scrunched, and his eyes squeezed firmly shut. Despite sleeping, he looked grumpy, as if the entire birthing process had made him miserable. A little patch of hair grew from the center of his head, fuzzy and dark.

"Can I?" Harruq asked, offering his arms.

"Of course," Gregory said. Harruq accepted the child, struck by just how light he felt despite the wrappings. He grinned down at the kid, trying to judge likeness and resemblance despite it being far too early. Still, it looked like he'd inherit Harruq's nose, and there was the faintest hint of sharpness to the ears squished to the sides of his face.

"You're a grandfather now," Aurelia said, looping her arm around Harruq's waist and leaning against him. "How's it feel?"

"Damn weird," Harruq said, and laughed.

"A fine looking kid," Tarlak said, peering around Harruq's arm. "And I'll ask since the oaf here didn't. I assume Aubrienna is healthy and well?"

"She's resting," Gregory said, and there was no hiding the pride in his voice. "She endured the pain better than I ever could."

Harruq shifted the baby in his arms and gently brushed his thumb across that scrunched little nose, unable to help himself. Gregory watched, a smile permanently etched upon his tired face.

"We'll announce the birth of the prince soon," he said, rubbing at his eyes. "Once I feel awake enough to deal with all that hassle." He paused, suddenly uncertain. "We...Aubby and I, we've talked about names, and I pray you approve. His name, we want to name him Qurrah Copernus."

Harruq felt the tightness in his chest return, and he could not even begin to understand the sudden whirlwind of emotions that hit him.

"Qurrah?" he asked, echoing the word as if it would conjure an explanation.

Gregory cleared his throat, the young king suddenly embarrassed and uncertain. "Your brother gave his life for the both of us. This feels like the least we can give in return, by honoring his memory." He hesitated again. "But if you object, or--"

"It's a lovely tribute," Aurelia said, interrupting him. She stroked the baby's forehead, her arm around Harruq's waist tightening. "Isn't that right, Harruq?"

Harruq cradled the child, staring down at him. He suddenly

could not speak, only nod. Aurelia eyed him, then released her grip.

"Would you two mind giving us a moment?" his wife asked Gregory and Tarlak. The other two quickly accepted, Tarlak shuffling out to the hallway while Gregory hurried on through the connector door to the bedroom with Aubrienna and the midwife.

Once alone, Aurelia bent down to softly kiss the sleeping baby's forehead. Harruq watched, struck by his wife's beauty and a sense of deep inequality that he could ever be loved by someone so wondrous.

"A blessing," she whispered, and then kissed Harruq's cheek as well. "I'll let you know when Aubby is cleaned up, all right?"

"Yeah, sure," Harruq said.

She departed through the door. It shut, and in the ensuing silence Harruq stared down at the sleeping little thing in his arms. His throat felt dry and his heart thudded away at a relentless beat.

"Qurrah," he whispered, and the dam within him broke. He more collapsed than sat in Tarlak's chair, and tears cascaded down the sides of his face. He clutched the babe as a thousand memories raced through him, dulled by time but not without their sting. A full lifetime, of beauties and horrors beyond what anyone could ever believe. Fighting for scraps in the streets of Veldaren, burdened by the weight of his blood and brawling with fellow urchins to protect his weak little brother. The hate, all for the pale color of his skin and curve of his ears.

Harruq clenched his jaw. Velixar's arrival. A promise of conquest. A village slain, innocent people butchered in a drunken haze as Harruq wielded power, true power, for the first time in his life. Not just villagers. Children. Demanded by the one whose name this child now shared.

Perhaps it was age. Perhaps it was the stress and exhaustion of waiting and fearing for his daughter, but he could not stop these memories now. They washed over him, errant, disordered, cruel in their honesty. Training with Haern. Laughing with Delysia after a mission, their table warmed by Tarlak and Brug's presence. That first pregnancy, pacing nervously while Aullienna was born. Aullienna. Her laugh. Her smile. The way even Tessanna had doted over her.

A body, lying face down upon the water.

"I don't deserve this," he whispered as he wept over his grandson. It didn't matter all he had fought. It didn't matter all he had given. A brutal lifetime, killing, so much killing. Traveling across Dezrel, fleeing war demons and hordes of undead. Bleeding and screaming during the Night of Black Wings. It was enough to break him, if he let it. Every hope of peace, met with hatred and war.

It was a question not often wondered by Harruq, but he confronted it now. What legacy would this child inherent by taking a name both cursed and revered in equal measure? A memory of Qurrah's voice echoed within him, not quite his last words, but most certainly his last deed.

But of my life, and my many sins, I know this here and now is the one act which atones for it all.

The child stirred, grumpy whimpers escaping his throat. Harruq felt his little arms shift and press against the bonds of his wrappings. He smiled down at him, letting the joy in his breast wash away the memories of the past. That darkness, it did not belong to the young. Let the future be one free of bloodshed and war, if only in the hopes of his heart.

"Hello there, Qurrah," he said. Something caught in his throat, but he forced out the words, not caring that they released another wave of tears. Harruq felt so old, and yet a child again, side by side upon a wall, watching burning skulls soar across the night sky, a promise of death, and yet magical, strange, and unknown.

"Welcome to Dezrel. There's so much wonder here I cannot wait to show you."

A Second Note from the Author:

It's a strange thing, writing this novel. All the while, it's been hard to shake a very simple question: who is this book for? And it's absurd, if you really do stop to think about it. Not only must you have read the previous eight Half-Orc novels, but to get everything out of it, you'd also need to have read the six Shadowdance novels, too. I'm telling a story you likely need to be fourteen novels dedicated to appreciate. So what does that mean?

Well, for starters, it means if you're reading this note you are unquestionably one of my most dedicated fans. So for that, you already have my thanks. But as for my original question, who is this book for? There was really one answer.

It's for me.

At this point, I'm twenty-two novels deep into the world of Dezrel, but at the same time, I still teased the existence of a long lost child of Haern the Watcher at the end of A Dance of Chaos. In my mind, that was a promise. One day I would tell their story, however long it took. Well. It took a decade. Does anyone still care, all these years later? I don't know. Will Erin be what they hoped for? Again, I don't know. So what *do* I know?

I know that I had to toss all that aside if I were to finish this novel. I tried to not care what it meant to be a Shadowdance or Half-Orc novel. I looked at a decade of baggage and lore, of characters and deaths, and decided I would simply enjoy spending time with Erin, and Harruq, and by god, even Thren Felhorn once more. And so I did. I did what I used to do, before this was my career. I had fun.

Will this mean a better book? I don't know. You will have to be the judge of that.

Speaking of Thren, I suppose I should mention the potentially controversial decision to retcon his death. I've been asked many, many times if there are character deaths I regret. Generally, the answer is no. There's one specific character death in the Keepers Trilogy I regretted, and then in Dezrel, there's Thren. You see, when I first introduced Thren Felhorn, it was in Cost of Betrayal, long before I had ever conceived the idea of the

David Dalglish

Shadowdance series. I'd barely written a handful of chapters with Haern at all, let alone come up with even a fraction of his eventually back story.

What this all means is that Thren's death is...pretty jarring to anyone who started chronologically with the Shadowdance series and then dove into the Half-Orcs. When I wrote A Dance of Chaos, I did my best to kind of rectify this, to write what I thought was the "true" conflict between father and son. When they meet again in Cost of Betrayal, that was but a defeated, hollow husk of the former master of the underworld.

I did my best, but that doesn't mean I still didn't hate how Thren died. So anticlimactic. So clumsily written, being the second book I wrote in what is now a thirty-plus book career. I often debated rewriting portions of Cost of Betrayal to give him a better ending, but then I feared that the newly written parts would stand out compared to the old ones like a fresh brush of paint swiped across an old wall. So I left it alone.

But it irked me.

Zip ahead all these years, and I was pondering what exactly this ninth Half-Orc novel would be. How would I examine Haern's legacy? How would I showcase the potential conflicts and influences that would drive young Erin? And all the while, I kept thinking how there was this gaping hole, the absence of Thren Felhorn. But what could I do? Thren was dead. That was pretty definitive. Wasn't it?

Wasn't it?

I will not pretend here, this was absolutely a retcon. I opened up Cost of Betrayal and examined the chapter with Thren's death with laser focus. How did he die? Where was his body? It seemed pretty clear cut. Sliced throat. A burning building. How could he possibly survive? But then I remembered what I always said, that Thren was a hollowed out, defeated husk. A broken Thren would still contain his pride, and he would loathe suffering under the Watcher's reign, even as he knew he could not win. Yet he would also take a twisted measure of pride at what his son created.

The Spider Guild could not continue with him, but neither would he allow it continue without him. So what if...what if that death was everything he wanted, so he could finally escape the paralyzing Abyss he found himself trapped within?

Legacy of the Watcher

Given the history of Dezrel, necromancy and healing magic are both abundant. And suddenly, I was *excited*. I cannot express how great it felt that fucking *Thren Felhorn* was back in play. To write his scenes. To relive those final moments, now seen from Thren's perspective, and give them a far more interesting dynamic. This final story with Erin went from feeling like a daunting task to something I could no longer predict. And to be able to discuss the legacy of the infamous Watcher, father to granddaughter? Yeah. I don't know how I could have ever finished this book without him.

If you think this was cheap of me, or wrong, or that I should have left him dead, I can only ask for your forgiveness. I sought to rectify what I believed was a mistake, in a manner that did not cheat or directly contradict my prior books. I did it because I thought the character deserved better, and it would lead to a more entertaining story. Even if you disagree with the act, I hope you at least understand and sympathize with the motive.

This all ties to another point I must address. All these books, these interconnected characters and lore; it is exhausting. It is stifling. Even the briefest cameos have me worrying I am remembering a character wrong, or not accurately reflecting their old personalities. Perhaps this new Thren Felhorn does not match the Thren of Shadowdance in your mind, to the point of being unrecognizable. Twenty two novels. Twenty two novels set in this one world, almost all of them covering a scant few years of the second Gods' War.

This is my way of saying: I am done with Dezrel, for now. I will never say never, but at this point, I cannot imagine what more I could write. What more there is to say? How does one continue to up the stakes, after all I have put Harruq and his friends through? The well is dry. The story is told. My promise, to reveal the child of the Watcher, is fulfilled.

The King of the Vile, in many ways, was also meant to be a goodbye to the world of Dezrel, but in a different manner. It was an end to the Gods' War, and all its spiraling threads. An end to Karak and Ashhur, locked in battle. It was brutal, and harsh, and so many characters reached their end, characters I suspect many people never believed could truly die. It was goodbye, but I would hardly call it a "fun" goodbye. It was a bloody separation, me closing many doors and giving one last chance for these characters

David Dalglish

so beloved to me to tear out my heart. It was a sparsely attended funeral. It was a young woman, exhausted in sorrow, lifting a broken bow.

This book? This is the fun goodbye. This is Harruq being a goofball in a tournament. This is Tarlak cracking jokes, and Aurelia threatening once more to polymorph people for their misbehavior. It is a remembrance of the character, Aaron Felhorn turned Haern the Watcher, who launched my entire career. It is a chance to see the potential for good even in those who knew only the worst. A chance to see a new generation rising up, and for that generation to embrace a future that contains hope and promise.

A Qurrah who will grow up a prince, and not an orphan on the streets of a city that hates him.

This is a series that started with the apparent protagonist murdering a child. It shall end with that same protagonist now a grandfather, holding his cherished grandchild. If you wish to see stories beyond this closure, it will likely have to be in your own hearts, minds, imaginations, and fanfiction. Consider yourselves given my blessing in that regard.

As for me, the Godslayer has no gods left to slay. Let Salvation and Condemnation remained sheathed.

I pray you enjoyed the journey. I pray I ended it well, and perhaps with a smile on your face. However many books of mine, be it these nine, the additional thirteen other books on Dezrel, or perhaps if you stumbled here after the Keepers, Seraphim, or Vagrant Gods…I thank you. Fully. Truly. When I started this strange, morbid tale of two half-orc brothers, I thought they would be read by only a few friends as well as my wife, who was the direct inspiration for both Aurelia and Tessanna. Instead, they have become beloved to thousands. It's unreal.

I am stepping away from Dezrel, but I assure you, I will never stop loving it, nor being grateful for the stories that brought us here together, one more time, to rambling a note from the author at the final page.

Thank you.

David Dalglish
October 5th, 2023

Printed in Great Britain
by Amazon